PRINTHOUSE BOOKS PRESENTS

I0585163

Relationships Byte
Inspired by true events

A Romance Novel by
Lorenzo "EL GEE" Gladden

VIP INK Publishing Group; Incorporated
Atlanta, GA.

Lorenzo "El Gee" Gladden

PrintHouse Books, Atlanta, GA.
Published 2-14-2015

www.PrintHouseBooks.com

VIP INK PUBLISHING GROUP; INCORPORATED

Cover Art, designed by SK7.
Editor: Cheryl Hinton

Isbn: 978-0-9861-340-2-9

Library of Congress Cataloging-in-Publication Data

LORENZO 'EL GEE' GLADDEN

Relationships Byte

1. Fiction-African American-Romance
2. Fiction-African American-Urban Life
3. Lorenzo 'El Gee' Gladden

PRINTED IN THE UNITED STATES OF AMERICA

Dedicated to
Tynisha Sanders
Thank you for helping me to create the concept for
this novel.
You have always been a true friend.

In Loving memory of
Luneed "Big Momma" Moore
(1922-2014)

FOREWORD

There once was a time where if you wanted to talk to someone, you picked up your landline and called them. If that person wasn't home, you had to wait until they were. In that same time, if you wanted to meet a man or a woman, you went out to a club or a bar. While at the bar, you would survey the room until you found someone that caught your eye. When that person was identified the next step was to build up the courage to approach that person or wait for an opening. From that initial meeting came different outcomes: rejection or acceptance. If acceptance was the outcome, you exchanged numbers and the courtship began. The courtship included a series of phone conversations — some filled with plenty of awkward breathing. Also in the courtship there was a series of dates and meetings until the two people involved came to a mutual understanding that it was time to move to the next level…the relationship and all that follows.

In this new age, all that has been thrown out of the window. Some still use that route but things have become much more simplified.

With the emergence of the internet, smart phones, and social media websites, in the click of a mouse a person can become connected with millions of people. In the early days of the internet, simple monochrome screened chatrooms evolved into such websites as College Club, Black Planet, and MySpace. With the evolution of today's constanly changing technology, new websites pop up daily. In addition to that, the cell phone technology changes just as fast. As fast as the new I-phone or Galaxy comes out, you better believe that the next generation of those devices are already in the making if not completed.

Entertainment TV once reported that there are over a billion people on Facebook and over 250 million people on Twitter. Those are just two of the most popular social media websites. Under those two powerhouses lie the underlings of the World Wide Web…the dating sites. The ones that most people see are the good, clean, and wholesome ones like eHarmony and Match.com. Since there are so many different types of people in the world looking for different things, there is a website for just about everyone. If you're looking for love and/or a serious long-term relationship, then you might want to spend a few dollars a month to seek that. If you're just looking to hook up, get some good ol' "no strings attached" sex, or looking for someone to tie you up and deficate on your back…there is a site out there for you.

I remember when the chatrooms emerged while in college. I was introduced to it by a good friend. I would sit in the dormitory computer lounge for hours, in the same chatroom, talking to people from all over the world. Back then, there were no pictures on the website. If you met someone you were really interested in you would have to either rely on their personal description of themselves or wait for that person to send you some pictures via snail mail.

Now that the technology has changed, the chatroom sites are extremely advanced. Many of the popular ones, like Web Date are video chat sites where you can actually see the people you're chatting with. Along with these sites came the personal instant messengers. First it was AOL instant messenger, Yahoo IM, and MSN Messenger. Those dinosaurs are still around but, at this writing, have been overpowered by messengers like Skype and Ovoo.

Along with the instant messengers and text message feature that began on the cell phones, arose an entirely new jargon. In the beginning, there was no such thing as unlimited text messages and data. Every message sent meant and extra charge on your phone bill and text messages had limited characters. There had to be a way to cut out some words in order to save money, time and characters. This is where terms like LOL, meaning laughing outloud, IDK, meaning I don't know and LMAO, laughing my ass off, came from. Now there are hundreds of abbreviations. This was all created by the emergence of technology and the need to save money while using this amazing communication tool.

As an author I'm not afraid to admit that I am also a human being. I've spent a lot of time on some of the aforementioned websites. One particular site, that will remain nameless, inspired this novel. I can't remember how I was introduced to the site but it wound up consuming every night of my life for two and a half years. The sight was a video chat site. For the first few days, I bounced around from room to room, trying to find where I fit in. My problem was that I was too green about the goings on of this particular site. When I finally figured it out, I changed my username and assumed an alter-ego named after a popular entertainer.

My intent was to just be a character and to keep myself separated from him. During the day and when offline I was myself but whenever I logged on I became him. Within the chatroom I met a core circle of friends that were constant for those two and a half years. People came and went and some would get into drama, lay low for awhile: and then come back.

The interaction was amazing. We would talk about everything under the sun. In my eyes everybody kept it as real as they could. Problems would rise from time to time and we would talk it out. In a crazy way, we became a family. The only way to become a part of the family was to meet the approval of the members or have a family member vouche for you.

About six months in I lost sight of what was real, and what was fake, and allowed my actual self to become consumed by the character that I'd created. That is what happens when you have a constant interaction between males and females. You meet one particular person that you become interested in and you move outside of the chat room. It happened to me.

This person and I would talk on the phone or chat via an outside messenger while we were still in the chat room interacting with the family. This went on for about six months. When you deal with a person of the opposite sex for a lengthy period, eventually you want that interaction to be in person because of the intimate things that you've talked about. That's where the situation gets sticky because the adventurous side overrules the realistic side. It's that same adventurous side that caused me to get in my truck and drive thirteen hours to the Midwest for a week only to return after two days into my trip. People aren't always who they say they are.

In the battle of what is real and what is fake, it's a constant when you dibble and dabble on these types of websites. It is easier said than done when a person says that I'm too smart or too strong willed to get caught up in this type of nonsense. If you stick your toe in the pool for too long, eventually you're going to want to dive in head first. I speak from experience. I'm grateful that nothing happened to me but some aren't that lucky.

I would be a hypocrite if I said that meeting someone on the internet leads to nothing positive or that you can't find true love on the internet. Even though I haven't found love on the internet, I've met some life long friends and good people. Just because I haven't found that special person, there are people that have. There is no rule in place stating where you are supposed to find love. All I say is be careful. There are people with real and genuine intentions and there are people that only want to hurt. Choose wisely.

Like I stated earlier, this book was inspired by my interactions on a particular website. Those people know who they are and I appreciate all of them. This book is a little different. There are sections in the book that actually read as chatroom text. Each character was inspired by a real person. The names were changed to protect the innocent....LOL! Pay attention to the story within the chatroom as well as the one outside. I think you'll enjoy it.

PrintHouseBooks.com

LORENZO 'EL GEE' GLADDEN

Relationships Byte

VIP INK PUBLISHING GROUP; INCORPORATED

Atlanta, GA.

Table of Contents

\<City Ave Diva\> U CAN NOT BE SERIOUS

\<Got'em Hatin\> I THINK HE IS SERIOUS@DIVA

\<Twinkle Toes Flintstone\> WHERE IN THE BOOK DOES IT SAY THAT YOU CAN'T FIND LOVE ON THE INTERNET????

\<***Mami*Dearest***\> EXACTLY...IF SHE MAKES U HAPPY FUTURE THEN THAT'S ALL THAT MATTERS

\<TEDDY P\> PAY THESE MANLESS INTERNET DIVA'S NO ATTENTION@ FUTURE...THEY'RE JUST JEALOUS CUZ U CHOZE UNIQUE AND NOT THEM

\<Thyk2Def\> I'M HAPPY FOR YOU FUTURE!

\<Futurama\> AT LEAST SOMEBODY IS HAPPY 4 ME!

\<Lady Get Some\> IF U GOT A GOOD ONE...KEEP HER

\<Choco Latte\> ITS NOT THAT WE'RE JEALOUS...WE'RE JUST TRYNA LOOK OUT FOR OUR FRIEND

\<City Ave Diva\> I AGREE WITH CHOCO...WE JUST DON'T WANT YOU TO GET HURT@FUTURE

\<Futurama\> AND I APPRECIATE IT@DIVA AND CHOCO

\<Got'em Hatin\> I DON'T TRUST HER

\<Mr.SexxyB-Baller\> I TOLD FUTURE NOT TO GET CLOSE TO THESE CHICKS IN HERE!

\<Da Ice Cream Man\> he did try to warn u@future

<Futurama> HOW DID THIS WHOLE CONVERSATION TURN INTO BEING ABOUT ME???

<TEDDY P> BECAUSE WE ARE HAVING A FAMILY DISCUSSION

<SlicK> AND THAT'S WHAT FAMILY IS FOR

<TEDDY P> HOW MANY TIMES WE GOTTA TELL YOU SLICK....

<TEDDY P> U

<TEDDY P>R

<TEDDY P>NOT

<TEDDY P>FAMILY....LOL!

<Da Ice Cream Man> lol!

<Lady Get Some> STOP BEING MEAN TEDDY!

<SlicK> GOT TO HELL TEDDY!!!!!!!!!

<***Mami*Dearest***> TEDDY DO YOU WANT A 2 HOUR TIME OUT????

<TEDDY P> OK MAMI...I'LL BE NICE

<Twinkle Toes Flintstone> I THINK YOU SHOULD MAKE HIM APOLOGIZE@MAMI

Optimo Pryme has entered the room

<TEDDY P> THAT IS OUT OF THE QUESTION

<City Ave Diva> LET'S NOT LOSE SIGHT OF THE ISSUE HERE!!! HELLO!!!

<SoopaFly> WHAT WAS WE TALKIN ABOUT?

<Got'em Hatin> FUTURE AND THE FACT THAT HE'S GETTING READY TO LET UNIQUE MOVE IN WITH HIM

<Futurama> THANK U CONNIE CHUNG FOR THE UPDATE@HATIN

<Got'em Hatin> UR WELCOME FUTURE BABY****MUAH!!!****

<City Ave Diva> FUTURE 4 REAL…U'VE KNOWN HER FOR 3 MONTHS

<Thyk2Def> WELL I THINK IT'S ROMANTIC

<Twinkle Toes Flintstone> DIVA'S RIGHT@ FUTURE…MAYBE U NEED A LITTLE MORE TIME TO REALLY GET TO KNOW HER

<Choco Latte> HOW WELL DO U REALLY KNOW HER@ FUTURE

<Optimo Pryme> I'VE SAT BACK AND LISTENED LONG ENOUGH AND I KNOW WHAT THIS IS ALL ABOUT…IF FUTURE WANTS TO BE WITH UNIQUE THEN THAT'S HIS PREROGATIVE…AT ONE POINT AND TIME WE'VE ALL DATED SOMEONE WE'VE MET FROM HERE OR OTHER WEBSITES…BOTTOM LINE IS…FUTURE IS HAPPY WITH UNIQUE AND THAT'S ALL THAT MATTERS. THERE'S NUTHIN U OR ME CAN SAY TO CHANGE THAT

<Twinkle Toes Flintstone> NOW THAT'S HOW U MAKE AN ENTRANCE…LOL!

<Da Ice Cream Man> he said prerogative…lol!

<Futurama> AND THAT'S WHAT I'VE BEEN TRYNA TELL THEM@OPTIMO

<City Ave Diva> BUT MOVIN IN AFTER 3 MONTHS???

\<TEDDY P\> IF THE MAN SAYS HE GOT IT UNDER CONTROL THEN THERE IS NOTHIN ELSE TO BE SAID

\<***Mami*Dearest***\> DAMN!!!THE GUYS STICK TOGETHER MORE THAN THE WOMEN DO...LOL

\<Optimo Pryme\> THAT'S BECAUSE WE DON'T GIVE A SHIT ABOUT HALF THE STUFF THAT Y'ALL WOMEN DO...WE JUST ENJOY MEETING NEW PEOPLE

\<Got'em Hatin\> AND TRYNA SCREW'EM AT THE SAME TIME...LOL!

\<City Ave Diva\> U KNOW WHAT@FUTURE...I'VE SAID MY PEACE AND NOW I'M GONNA LEAVE IT ALONE...JUST KNOW THAT DIVA WILL ALWAYS BE A FRIEND 4 U

\<Futurama\> AND THAT'S EXACTLY WHAT I NEED...A FRIEND

\<TEDDY P\> NOW THAT WE GOT THAT OUT OF THE WAY...WHO'S NAKED ON THEIR WEBCAM????

\<Twinkle Toes Flintstone\> THAT'S WHAT I'M TALKIN BOUT

\<SlicK\> NOBODY'S NAKED...I CHECKED ALREADY

\<TEDDY P\> I TOLD Y'ALL SLICK WAS A PERVERT...LOL! HE PROBABLY LOOKIN AT EVERYBODY AT THE SAME TIME....LOL

\<Optimo Pryme\> THIS NIGGA PROLLY GOT 8 MONITORS HOOKED UP TO HIS COMPUTER...LOL

\<SlicK> Y Y'ALL ALWAYZ GOTTA FUK WIT ME?

\<Twinkle Toes Flintstone> CUZ ITZ FUN

\<TEDDY P> CUZ UR SO FUK-WIT-ABLE....ROFL

\<Choco Latte>LOL

\<Got'em Hatin>LMAO!!!

\<Da Ice Cream Man> that was a good one!

Soopafly has entered the room

Da Wife has entered the room

\<SlicK> HA HA...VERY FUNNY

\<Da Ice Cream Man> is it just me or do Soopa and Wife come in at the same time...all the time?

\<Got'em Hatin> I NOTICED IT TOO@ICE CREAM

\<TEDDY P> ANYWAY...FUTURE...WHAT CAN WE BE EXPECTING NEW FROM FUTURE RECORDS???

\<Choco Latte> YOU FORGOT THE HOTTEST RECORD LABEL IN THE ATL

\<SoopaFly> TRUE DAT!

\<Futurama> I JUST PICKED UP AN INDEPENDENT LABEL OUTTA FLORENCE SOUTH CAROLINA CALLED LUCKY 12 AND A FEMALE R&B ARTIST FROM VA BUT SHE LIVES IN THE ATL NOW

\<Twinkle Toes Flintstone> WHAT'S HER NAME?

\<Futurama> LEGACY

\<Twinkle Toes Flintstone> OUTTA VA BEACH?

\<Futurama> YEAH

<City Ave Diva> DO U KNOW
HER@TWINKLE

<Twinkle Toes Flintstone> I SAW HER
PERFORM AT THIS CLUB ON VA BEACH A
MONTH AGO

<Futurama> CLUB DREAM...SHE OPENED
FOR TYRESE THAT NIGHT

<TEDDY P> THIS NIGGA BE EVERYWHERE

<Twinkle Toes Flintstone> I WAS AT THAT
SHOW WIT MY EX

<Got'em Hatin> WHO BE EVERYWHERE?

<TEDDY P> FUTURE

<Futurama> I GOTTA BE EVERYWHERE...I
NEVER KNOW WHERE I'M GONNA FIND
THE NEXT HOT SHIT

<SoopaFly> I KNOW YOU GOT SOME HEAD
BANGAZ 4 DA FELLAZ

<Futurama> BUDDAH RHATT, FACE AND
LUCKY TWELVE ARE THE HOTTEST THING
TO COME OUTTA DA KILLA KAROLINA'S
SINCE PETEY PABLO

<TEDDY P> I'LL BE DA JUDGE OF
THAT...U KNOW I'M A KAROLINA KID

<Choco Latte> HOW CAN WE FORGET

<Optimo Pryme> I KNOW U NOT GONNA
LET HER CLOWN U LIKE DAT@TED

<TEDDY P> THAT'S JUST HER WAY OF
SAYIN THAT SHE WANT ME

<Got'em Hatin> ROFL

<Choco Latte> NEGRO DON'T FLATTER
YASELF...U KNOW ITS ALL ABOUT DEM
CALI BOYZ

\<Optimo Pryme\> GIRL STOP! U KNOW ITS ALL ABOUT DA SOUF!!!

\<City Ave Diva\> IF I'M NOT MISTAKEN BUT DIDN'T U SAY U WERE FROM NY@OPTIMO

\<Da Ice Cream Man\> that's what he said

\<Optimo Pryme\> ITS NOT WHERE U FROM ITS WHERE U AT AND I'M IN THE M-I-A AND I LOVE IT!!!!!

\<Futurama\> BUT ON THE REAL...BE EXPECTIN SOME HOT SHIT...THE 12 GOT THE STREETZ ON LOCK AND LEGACY IS HOLDIN IT DOWN FOR THE LADIES

\<Da Ice Cream Man\> shameless plugs...damn entertainers...lol!

\<Futurama\> U KNOW IT@ICE CREAM

\<City Ave Diva\> U KNOW WE SUPPORT U@FUTURE

\<Thyk2Def\> THAT'S RIGHT...EVEN THOUGH YOU DON'T HOLLA AT NOBODY WHEN U COME IN TOWN

\<Choco Latte\> SHE DO GOTTA POINT...U CAME TO SAN DIEGO SINCE I'VE KNOWN U AND I HAD TO FIND OUT ABOUT IT FROM THE RADIO

\<City Ave Diva\> DID ME THE SAME WAY WHEN HE CAME TO PHILLY

\<Futurama\> COME ON PEOPLE...BE REAL...WE ALL JUST GOT TIGHT...BEFORE U ALL WERE JUST SOME COOL AND FUNNY PEOPLE I MET ON THE INTERNET...NOW THAT WE'RE ALL FAMILY...I'LL DO BETTER...I PROMISE

<Optimo Pryme> ANYTIME U IN MIAMI JUST HOLLA AT YA BOY…I'M DA MAN AT CLUB ROLEXXX

<Choco Latte> ROLEXXX SOUNDS LIKE A STRIP CLUB

<Twinkle Toes Flintstone> THAT'S BCUZ IT IZ

<TEDDY P> DING! DING! TELL HER WHAT SHE'S WON FRANK

<Da Ice Cream Man> Choco Latte has won a box of rubber bands, a just4kickz.com hoodie and a year supply of NoDoz…for them late nights kickin it….lol

<Got'em Hatin>LOL!

<Twinkle Toes Flintstone> LMAO

<TEDDY P> U A FOOL 4 DAT 1@ ICE CREAM

<Choco Latte> U GOT JOKES@ICE CREAM

<Da Ice Cream Man> teddy made me do it

<Optimo Pryme> DAMN TED…SOLD OUT AGAIN…LOL

<TEDDY P> ICE CREAM SELL ME OUT EVERY CHANCE HE GET JUST TO STAY IN THE GOOD GRACES OF THESE FEMALES

<Da Ice Cream Man> and what man doesn't

<Optimo Pryme> U KNOW WHAT…U RIGHT…LOL

<Got'em Hatin> THAT'S BCUZ HE KNOWS WHO RUNS THE WORLD…DA LADIES!!!!!

<City Ave Diva> HEEEEEEEEEY!!!!

<Thyk2Def> DIVAS UNITE!

<TEDDY P> SEE…ITS GETTING READY TO TURN INTO A WAITING TO EXHALE SISTA TO SISTA MAN HATIN MEETING…LOL

<Twinkle Toes Flintstone> DON\T GET'EM STARTED@ TED

<Choco Latte> AIN'T NOBODY PAYIN TEDDY NO ATTENTION

<TEDDY P>THAT'S YOUR PROBLEM@CHOCO…YOU AIN'T PAYIN A REAL MAN NO ATTENTION

<Optimo Pryme> AWWW SHIT…ITS FINNA GET GOOD!!!!

<Da Ice Cream Man>*****poppin popcorn******

<Choco Latte> SO WHAT YOU SAYIN@ TEDDY…SHOULD I BE PAYIN ATTEENTION TO U?

<TEDDY P> NOT NECESSARILY ME BUT ANYBODY OTHER THAN THAT SCRUB U CALL A MAN

<Optimo Pryme>****MOUTH HITTING THE FLOOR*** HE WENT THERE

<Futurama> COME ON Y'ALL…CHILL OUT

<Choco Latte> WHAT MAKES U THINK MY MAN IS A SCRUB?

<Da Ice Cream Man> yeah teddy…what makes u think her man is a scrub

<***Mami*Dearest***> ICE CREAM….STAY OUT OF IT

<TEDDY P> ITS OBVIOUS HE'S A SCRUB CUZ U SPEND MORE TIME WIT US THAN U SPEND WIT HIM

<City Ave Diva> TEDDY THAT'S ENOUGH

\<Thyk2Def\> DON'T GO THERE@TEDDY

\<TEDDY P\> UR GROWN U DO WHAT U DO BUT I;M JUST SAYIN THAT IF I WAS YA MAN...U WOULDN'T HAVE TIME TO BE JUST KICKIN IT ON JUST4KICKZ

\<Choco Latte\> SO UR THAT KINDA MAN THAT WOULD TELL ME WHAT I CAN AND CANNOT DO

\<TEDDY P\> NAH...I'M THAT MAN THAT WOULD WANT TO SPEND ALL MY TIME WITH THE WOMAN IN MY LIFE AND KEEP HER INTERESTED IN ME INSTEAD OF HAVING TO REACH OUT TO OTHERS

\<Thyk2Def\> I THINK I'M GONNA CRY

\<Da Ice Cream Man\> I wanna be like teddy when I grow up

\<Futurama\> ALRIGHT Y'ALL...ITS BEEN REAL...I'LL BE AWAY FOR AWHILE SO I GUESS I'LL CATCH UP WIT MY FAM WHEN I CAN

\<City Ave Diva\> DON'T STAY AWAY 4EVER

\<Got'em Hatin\> HURRY BACK FUTURE...WE'LL MISS U

\<Optimo Pryme\> AIIIGHT FAM....BRING A PLATINUM PLAQUE HOME

\<TEDDY P\> BE EAZY FUTURE!

\<Futurama\> PEACE OUT Y'ALL!!!!!

2 YEARS LATER

Chapter 1

 The distinct digital tone of someone asking permission to add him to his or her friend list lured Iverson away from his task of looking through sales reports and onto his computer. Iverson Davenport, known as Ivy to everyone in the music industry, is the CEO & Founder of Future Records — one of the hottest record labels in Atlanta, Georgia. He stands a towering 6'4" and has a light brown complexion with hazel eyes. He wears thin dreads that extend to the base of his neck and are very well maintained. Iverson has a slim build and a good head on his shoulders. When it came to the music industry, he had his whole heart and soul into it.

When handling business, he was quite the businessman — tailor-made suits, dress shoes and silk ties. On the social scene, with his entourage, he would dress to fit the occasion. According to the mainstream, that involved throwback football or basketball jerseys, sneakers or boots, jeans and hats. Iverson was a smooth, laid-back guy that kept it real. The only thing that bothered him was a liar.

He double-clicked on the set of lips icon on the far-right end of the toolbar to open his instant messenger to see who it was. The message in the pop-up window read: *XoticMami has requested permission to add you to his/her friend list.* The name drew Iverson's interest and he clicked the "accept & add" button. Once she was added to his list, he double-clicked her name to pull up the message box.

> **Ivy_Dav:** hello?
> **XoticMami:** hi!
> **Ivy_Dav:** how did you get my IM ID?
> **XoticMami:** u have it posted on ur Ebony World page.
> **Ivy_Dav:** oh ok. I guess you read or saw something you liked.
> **XoticMami:** from the looks of ur pic, u got it goin' on.
> **Ivy_Dav:** I'm alright. U got a pic on ur page?
> **XoticMami:** nah. I took'em it down cuz people kept stealin'em. I can
> send u one. what's ur email addy?
> **Ivy_Dav:** ivy_dav@futurerecords.com
> **XoticMami:** ok…hold on. brb

In less than two minutes Iverson received an alert, via another email site, that he had mail at futurerecords.com. He went to the webpage and opened the message that XoticMami sent him. The six pictures revealed a woman in several different poses, standing in front of silver Mercedes Benz. XoticMami was light complexioned with all of her assets in the right places. In the first picture, she stood with her ass towards the camera and her upper body turned to show a little more than just a facial profile. Judging from the height of the car she had to be about 5'10" in heels. The woman in the pictures had long, brownish-black hair and dark, brown eyes. XoticMami was wearing a white bikini top, which only covered her nipples. The white skirt she wore was so short that it allowed the bottoms of her well-rounded cheeks to peek out from under it. He clicked on the messenger box, which was minimized, to return to the conversation.

> **Ivy_Dav:** u there?
> **XoticMami:** yes
> **Ivy_Dav:** that is not you
> **XoticMami:** yes it is. I'm a model.
> **Ivy_Dav:** stop lyin'
> **XoticMami:** for real…that was my XXL eye candy layout from last july
> **Ivy_Dav:** for real?
> **XoticMami:** I take it you like what you saw
> **Ivy_Dav:** I did. I might have to see if I can get u in our next video.
> **XoticMami:** what do you do?
> **Ivy_Dav:** I'm the CEO of Future Records
> **XoticMami:** seriously?

Ivy_Dav: as a matter of fact, we're getting ready to do a video shoot for my newest group

XoticMami: what's the name of the group?

Ivy_Dav: The Southern Sunz

XoticMami: oh ok. I guess I'll holla at u lata, I gotta run. just let

me know about the shoot.

Ivy_Dav: I will…Peace!

XoticMami has logged out

Iverson closed the IM box and pulled her pictures back up. He sat and stared at the picture for a good five minutes before his secretary interrupted his trance.

"Ivy," she called from the door. He looked up from the screen and over the monitor to see a short, Boricua halfway leaned into his office. "Don't forget about your meeting with the Southern Sunz and their manager at 4 o' clock." "What time is it now?" "3:45." "Thank you, Michelle."

On the other side of Atlanta, Natalie Simms was returning home from her afternoon workout with her best friend and teammate, Shanice Foreman. Natalie and Shanice were professional basketball players. They played for the Atlanta Diamonds.

Natalie was an average height woman, that stood five feet, six inches. She displayed a caramel skin tone with a small, oval-shaped face and long micro-braids that she was wearing in a ponytail at that time. Natalie's greatest physical asset was her smile. If the entire city of Atlanta experienced a blackout, her smile could light the city for days. Though she was a female athlete, she was lady-like in every way. The only time she wore anything that pertained to a basketball player was when she had on her uniform or her warm-up.

Shanice, on the other hand was the exact opposite. She was one of those women that you could look at and tell she was an athlete. She was about two inches taller than Natalie and was b-ball crazy. Everything she wore displayed something about basketball. Being that her favorite player of all-times was Dominique Wilkins, it was a dream come true when she joined the Atlanta Diamonds. Shanice was an attractive woman but because of the way she dressed, she often got mistaken for one of the many lesbians that were in Atlanta. Her body would be best described as voluptuous. She was a thick woman but had no stomach. Why she chose to hide the true essence of her chocolate body was unknown.

After a vigorous workout, the ladies decided to unwind in Natalie's new Jacuzzi. They sat in a steaming hot whirlpool of water and planned the next workout. It was imperative that they stayed in shape during the off-season.

"Isn't tomorrow our easy day?" Natalie asked while lifting her head up off of a towel she had rolled up behind her head.

"Yeah," Shanice replied. "We do our five mile run and then we play pick-up games."

"Five miles? You almost as bad as Coach." The two women laughed.

"Are you going with us to the club tomorrow night?"

"What club?"

"Me, Jasmine and Shawna are supposed to be goin' to Club Blaze."

"I was with you until you said Shawna."

"You and Shawna still beefin' over André? That was over a year ago."

There was bad blood between Natalie and Shawna because of an ill incident that happened last year. Natalie met André Marshall at a club after she signed to the Diamonds. They were only friends but Natalie started to develop feelings for him. Those feelings were stifled after André ran into Shawna at a car wash. After their meeting, Shawna came back to Natalie and told her that he tried to talk to her. When she confronted André about the situation, he assured her that after he realized who Shawna was, he left her alone. He didn't want to jeopardize what he and Natalie had. She had a hard time believing him. The situation escalated during a road game in Houston. André agreed to meet Shawna in Houston on the down low but ran into Natalie. Natalie and Dré reconciled their friendship then he confessed the true reason he was in Houston. The night before the game, they returned to his room and found Shawna in the bed. Shawna's jealousy of Natalie came into the open leading them into a brawl. From that night, the only time the two would say anything to each other was in basketball practice and in a game.

"It's not about André," Natalie defended. "It's the fact that she lied and almost caused me to lose a good friend. That bitch is scandalous."

"Girl, you really need to let that go. André is happily married and you are still single. And if I might add, you and Desmond would still be together if you knew how to separate yourself from André."

"Dré and I have been through a lot together. He is my friend. I am not about to turn my back on him because a man doesn't like the fact that we are as close as we are. His wife doesn't have a problem with it."

"If you say so," Shanice mumbled as she covered her head with a towel.

"What's that supposed to mean?" Natalie asked snatching the towel from Shanice's head.

"The only time you and Dré hung out was while you and Desmond were together. How many times have you and him hung out since you and Des broke up?"

"We've hung out a couple of times."

"Exactly! He knows that if you're single, y'all can't chill like you used to. Wifey ain't havin' her man spendin' time with a woman he was involved with."

"Whatever."

"Don't get mad at me cuz you let that good man get away." Natalie looked at Shanice with an evil eye. She realized that Shanice was just joking when she erupted with laughter.

"You play too much," Natalie joked as she splashed water at Shanice.

Ivy sat at a long table in the meeting room waiting for the arrival of his new artists. As he sat, all he could think about were the pictures he saw of XoticMami. Ivy had been back on the Internet dating scene for about six months and was getting ready to call it quits. Seeing XoticMami made him put that idea on hold for a minute. He thought that maybe he might get lucky with this last attempt.

While he sat deep in thought, three guys walked into the room. ATP, short for Attia the Port City Prophet, was a tall, slim guy from Charleston, South Carolina. He was light complexioned, due to his bi-racial background, with a head full of wild hair. It looked like it was recently taken out of cornrows. Just like 99.9% of all Charleston natives, he was *geechie*. Geechie people had a distinct dialect that was like that of a Jamaican with a strong southern draw.

EL GEE was a medium height, light brown skin tone with a razor sharp, temple fade. Having traveled a lot, EL GEE didn't have a southern accent that one could readily identify. Gusto was tall, dark and slim. He was dubbed as the South's hottest upcoming producer. His style of production was so unique — you couldn't compare him to anyone in the industry. With ATP and EL GEE's chemistry, lyrics and pure delivery accompanied by the crisp, distinct sound of Gusto's beats, Ivy knew he had the makings of what Vibe Magazine called the *second-coming of OutKast*.

"Let's get down to business. First of all I'd like to formally welcome you to the Future family. In doing so I'd like to present you with the same thing I give all my new artists."

Ivy handed each of them square, velvet boxes that were about five inches by five inches. Each box contained a long, gold link chain with a medallion of the record label's logo—the word FUTURE in an arc that was laced in diamonds.

"I know all of the artists in the industry are rockin' platinum Jesus-pieces and if you give me a platinum single or album, I'll upgrade ya piece."

"That's gravy," ATP thanked as he took the piece out and placed it around his neck. "Jus' gives us a lil' sumthin' to shoot for. Good lookin' out."

"Now that we got that out of the way, let's talk about the video. We wanna keep it gully but at the same time we have to shoot for the heavy video rotation. If it doesn't fit a certain criteria, point blank, we won't make it to Video Explosion, Rap City or 106 & Park. Feel me?"

"We feel you on that," EL GEE began. "But let it be known that we will not be jumpin' around wit shiny suits on."

"Future Records doesn't get down like that. We focus on raw skills and tight production. That's why I chose you. You fit everything we're trying to do. The first single we're releasing is 'Where You From?' Since there hasn't been a rap artist to come out of the Carolinas since Petey Pablo I want to focus on that. It's time for another Carolina anthem." For an hour, Iverson and the guys discussed the particulars of the video. They decided to play on the differences between the two artists whole incorporating the history of the two states.

"Any questions about the video?" Ivy asked.

"No questions about the video but I would like to know when the first single drops?" Gusto inquired.

"The day we start shootin' the video, about three weeks from now. To prevent internet leaks, we don't release it to the radio stations until the day the single is available on iTunes.

"No doubt," ATP approved.

"Any more questions?" Ivy paused.

"Everything sound good to me," EL GEE answered. "You just don't know how much this mean to us. We been waitin' on this for a minute."

"You earned it. Any group that can push 100,000 units in two states without a deal deserves a shot. Let's get this money."

The meeting adjourned and ATP, EL GEE and Gusto were on their way. Ivy went back to his office to close up shop for the day. On his way to the office, his Sidekick went off with the tone of 'Welcome to Atlanta.' It was his best friend and president of the label, TyQuan Hollister, known to the music industry as T-Bizzy. The message read:

Ivy,

The chickens are definitely cluckin' out here. @ the Dollar with Will and KD. Holla at ya boy. One!

T-Bizzy

In her multi-million dollar estate, Natalie sat alone surfing through television channels. Shanice had gone home for the evening and Natalie was lounging around the house in a pair of red, satin lady boxers and a white top with spaghetti straps. As she curled up on the couch to watch the news, she saw a commercial for a website that caught her eye. The announcement for the commercial said: *"Tired of being alone? Join the thousands of single men and women at one of the hottest web communities in the country, Ebony World. You can connect with endless people looking for friends or maybe more. Log on to www.EbonyWorld.com today. We'll be waiting for you."*

After the commercial went off, she reached over to the end table and picked up the pen and pad that were by the phone. Natalie scribbled the web address down and threw the pad back on the table. She was curious but thought about all the stories she had heard of women meeting crazy guys online. With the passing of that thought, another thought entered her head. She wondered why she was spending all of her evenings alone. Natalie was a beautiful woman with a lot to offer but still she could not find a man that would be into her and not her money. The ring of her telephone broke her train of thought.

"Hello?" Natalie answered.

"Hey girl," the female voice greeted.

"Who is this?"

"It's Alicia."

"André's wife?" Natalie's face wore a look of surprise. She and Alicia had become friends through André but they weren't the type of friends that just called each other to chit chat.

"Yeah. What's up?"

"Nothin' much. I'm just sittin' around watchin' the news."

"Oh, okay. I know you're surprised to hear from me."

"A little. Anyway, what's going on?"

"André took Taylor to a birthday party and I was sittin' here bored. I know this seems odd but we are friends and you are the coolest female I've met since I moved to Atlanta and I just wanted to call and check on you."

"Thanks, girl. You really made my day."

"Hey, I got a crazy idea."

"What is it?"

"Let's go to happy hour at the Silver Dollar."

"When?"

"Now. Won't that be fun?"

"Okay. Let me put some clothes on and I'll meet you there in about thirty minutes."

"Sounds good. See you then. B'bye."

Natalie hung up the phone a little confused. She and Alicia had never hung out unless André was there. From what she knew about Alicia, she was a cool female. She was almost like a female version of her husband. Natalie shrugged her shoulders and ran upstairs to put some clothes on.

At the Silver Dollar, Ivy gathered around the pool table with TyQuan as Will and KD were involved in an intense game. Will was a 5'5", Puerto Rican and had more mouth than a little bit. He wore his clothes two sizes too big and had more hair than the average female. Will held the position as VP of A&R for the label. He had a real eye for talent. KD was Ivy's nephew, by marriage and the white boy of the crew. He was the best engineer Ivy had. When it came to electronics or computers, KD had it locked down. A lot of other labels tried to steal him from Future but he was faithful to his Uncle Ivy.

T-Bizzy is one of the co-founders of Future Records. He was the President of the label and Ivy's right-hand man. T-Bizzy stood as the thick one of the crew. He was around 5'11" and brown-skinned. Though he was a stout guy, he had mad style and flava. Ivy always referred to him as the pretty boy of the crew. T-Bizzy always tried to outdress everybody. He made the perfect President of the label because of his ability to talk. He used to say that he could *talk the panties off of a nun.*

If there were ever two tighter people, it would have to be Ivy and T-Bizzy. The two met in during their freshman year in college. TyQuan had just started out as DJ T-Rock at a local club in DC. He was the DJ for the college night. Their first meeting was actually an altercation. Ivy got mad at T-Bizzy because he was letting MC's freestyle and cut the session off right as he approached for his turn. He tried to explain to Ivy that he had no choice because the club owner told him to cut it because people had stop dancing. The next week he let Ivy be the only one to freestyle. At the end of that night, TyQuan was doing a turntable exhibition when Ivy approached to give him props. He stood in amazement at T-Bizzy's skills on the turntables. When it was all over, they exchanged respect and he told TyQuan: "You was definitely gettin' busy on the ones and twos." A week later, Ivy went back to the club to find that he had changed his name from T-Rock to DJ T-Bizzy. The rest was history. They became friends and five years later founded Future Records.

Ivy and T-Bizzy were laughing as Will and KD argued over the game. Ivy's laughter stopped when he saw Alicia and Natalie walk into the bar. He elbowed TyQuan to get his attention. The two men watched as the ladies walked through the crowd and found a table near the bar.

"I gots to go holla at that light-skinned chick right there," T-Bizzy gestured.

"Which one?" Ivy asked as Will and KD paused from their game to see who they were talking about.

"The one in the black leather jacket with the long hair. That's got to be the future Mrs. T-Bizzy."

"Don't hurt ya'self."

TyQuan started in the direction of Natalie and Alicia. Will and KD disregarded what was going on and continued their game. Ivy's attention was also drawn away from them due to his two-way. TyQuan was on his way to a rude awakening.

"What you drinkin'?" Natalie asked as Alicia sat down.

"You mean to tell me you forgot," she pouted.

"Alicia, we've only been out a couple of times and both times your husband went to get the drinks."

"I'll let you off the hook this time. Let me get a Grey Goose Cosmopolitan." Alicia reached in her purse to get her wallet.

"First round is on me. I'll be right back."

As Natalie walked off, T-Bizzy made his way to where Alicia sat. T-Biz was about twenty feet away from Alicia when he was intercepted by a medium height, Hawaiian girl. She was a dancer from one of their music videos. TyQuan had promised her a spot in the next video — for a small favor.

"Hey T!" she greeted as she hugged him.

"What's up, uh, uh...?" He couldn't remember her name.

"Monica!"

"Yeah, Monica. What's up?"

"It's been almost five months and you haven't called me about another video."

"Trust me. We got one comin' up. I'll call you."

"That's what you said about the last two. You punk ass label execs are all the same..."

As Monica proceeded to cuss T-Bizzy out, he looked past her to Alicia. She was beautiful. She had shoulder-length, black hair that she wore out that night. He watched as her almond-shaped eyes surveyed her surroundings. He knew he had to suppress the situation before Monica blew it for him.

"Listen, there is the CEO," he pointed at Ivy. "Talk to him about it."

"You know what? Screw you."

The dissed dancer gave him the hand and walked away. He continued his mission.

"Excuse me," he lulled as he approached. "I couldn't help but notice you when you walked in. I just wanted to come over and extend a compliment towards the beauty of a woman. My name is TyQuan, President of Future Records. And you are?" He extended his hand.

"Married," Alicia replied extending her left hand to show him her ring.

"No disrespect. I just wanted to tell you how beautiful you were just in case no one has told you today."

"Thank you but my husband did that before he left the house this evening."

"What kind of man would let a woman like you out of his sight?"

"A secure one."

"Respect. You have a nice evening," T-Bizzy bid as he walked away.

"Are you out here tryna cheat on your husband?" Natalie clowned as she approached. "Who was that?"

"Some clown talkin' about he's the president of some record label."

"These guys kill me....always tryin' to use money or a title to impress females. Then when you holla at'em, they wind up being a cook at Mickey-D's." The two women laughed.

Ivy gave T-Bizzy hell for getting rejected. He tried to say that she wasn't his type. You know how guys do when they get shot down. For the rest of the night Ivy kept his eyes on Natalie. It was something about her that he was attracted to. Natalie wasn't the typical woman he was used to seeing. Being in the music industry, he was constantly surrounded by exotic women. Natalie's *around the way girl* look was what he found most alluring about her. Ivy wanted to go over and say something but he couldn't manage to muster up the nerve to do so. Even with his statue, he was still a little shy. He was so used to women throwing themselves at him — he hardly ever had to approach one. The way he saw T-Bizzy get shot down, he just knew it was a no go for him.

Happy hour came to a close and Alicia decided that she better be getting home to her husband. She and Natalie left. An hour after the ladies left, Ivy and T-Bizzy left the bar. Ivy dropped T-Bizzy off at the office to get his car, then headed back to his home on West Paces Ferry — The Beverly Hills of Atlanta. As he rode, he thought about Natalie. Ivy could not figure out what it was about her that attracted him to her the way that it did. When he arrived home, he checked his messages and went upstairs to his in-home office to check his email and see what was up with all of his friends on just4kickz.

Just4Kickz.com was a crazy website. There were all kinds of people that floated through. It wasn't one of those sex sites but on the right night, you could see some pretty freaky stuff — depending on who had what to drink or smoke. Ivy was turned on to the sight by an ex-girlfriend and had been hooked every since. Once he pulled up his internet browser, he clicked on his Favorites. Ivy scrolled down the list until he came to a link that said *Just Kickin' It* and clicked on it. In less than a second, the just4kicks.com homepage loaded and Ivy logged in. On the streets and on other websites, he was known as Ivy or Ivy_Dav. On just4kickz, he was Futurama.

From the homepage, Iverson clicked on the video chat link. Once that page loaded, there was a box in the middle of the screen with a list of names. The list included names of the hosts and moderators for each individual room. To the right of the names were 3 different columns with numbers in them. The columns indicated how many men were in the room, how many women were in the room, and the third number was the total number of people that were in the room. Each room could only have a maximum of 75 people in the room. The moderator had the ability to boot or ban anyone that they wanted out of their room. The popular rooms were usually the hardest to get into but with a little persistence, they could eventually be entered.

Once inside, there was a box at the top left that was the screen that displayed the chatter's webcam images, there was a box in the middle that was larger than the box on the left that would display the picture or webcam images of whoever was being viewed and to the right was a list of all of the people in the room. The guy's names were in blue and the women's names were in pink. Also in that box were 2 icons in front of each person's name — one that looked like a webcam and one that looked like a microphone. When either of the icons were red, that meant that either the person had his webcam on or his mic on — sometimes both.

Futurama has entered the room
<City Ave Diva> LOL...OPTIMO...U R RETARDED!
<Optimo Pryme> I'M SERIOUS!!!!!
<Da Ice Cream Man> I think I just saw a ghost
<Got'em Hatin> FUUUUUUUUUTTTTTUUUUUUURRRRE!!!!
<Thyk2Def> FFFUUUUUUUUUUUUUUTTTTTTTURRRRRRREEEEEE!!!!!
<Optimo Pryme> AWWW SHIT!!! MY MUTHAPHUKIN POTNA IN CRYME!!!

\<City Ave Diva\> HEY FUTURE BABY!!!!
WHERE HAVE U BEEN??? I'VE MISSED YOU
\<Da Wife\> MY BABYDADDY IS HERE!
\<Futurama\> WHAT UP DIVA, OPTIMO,
THYK, BABY MAMA, GOT'EM...
\<Got'em Hatin\> HOW IS IT THAT I WAS
THE FIRST ONE THAT SPOKE TO YOU BUT
THE LAST ONE YOU SPOKE TO...LOL!
\<Futurama\> YOU KNOW I HAD TO SAVE
THE BEST FOR LAST
\<Da Wife\> EXCUSE ME???? I WANT A
DIVORCE...LOL!
\<SlicK\> u wanna go private Choco Latte????
\<Choco Latte\>
FUUUUUUUTTTTTTTTUREEE!!!!
\<*Mami*Dearest***\> WELCOME TO MY
ROOM EVERYBODY BUT YOU KNOW THE
RULES....THIS IS A VIDEO CHAT ROOM
SO YOU NEED TO CAM UP OR BOUNCE!!!**
\<Optimo Pryme\> THAT'S RIGHT
MAMI...PUT THE PRADA'S ON!!!!
\<City Ave Diva\> I SHOULD KICK UR AZZ@
FUTURE...U HAVE BEEN GONE FOR 2
YEARS
\<Futurama\> MY BAD DIVA BUT SHIT HAS
BEEN CRAZY
\<SlicK\> did u get my message choco???
\<Futurama\>LOL! I WAS HOPIN I WOULD
SEE SOME FAMILIAR FACES
Miss Moet has entered the room
\<Miss Moet\> I'm back!!!!

<Futurama> I SEE AIN'T MUCH CHANGED…SLICK STILL TRYNA HOLLA AT EVERYBODY

<Choco Latte> No Slick

<Got'em Hatin> EVERYBODY IS AN UNDERSTATEMENT

<Futurama> YO PRYME…WHERE'S EVERYBODY AT?

<SoopaFly> WHAT UP CUZIN?

<Futurama> SOOPA…WHAT IT DO MY NIG?

<ADAM*ANT> u sure are sexy@thyk2def

<Optimo Pryme> MACK AIN'T GOT OFF WORK YET, LYTE SAID SHE'D BRB, ICE CREAM WENT PRIVATE WIT SOME CHICK, I DON'T KNOW WHAT HAPPENED TO GET SOME, AKBAR ZAMBOOKI WAS HERE EARLIER BUT SAID HE'D BE BACK

Mr.SexxyB-Baller has entered the room

 Teddy Pinned*Her*Ass*Down has entered the room

Da Ice Cream Man has entered the room

MACK Truck has entered the room

<Choco Latte> TEDDDDDDDDDDDYYYYYYYY!!!!!

<Futurama> SPEAK OF THE DAMN DEVILS!!!

<Teddy Pinned*Her*Ass*Down>LOOK WHAT DA DAMN WIND DONE BLEW IN…WHAT UP FUTURE!!!!!

<Futurama>I'M GOOD HOMIE!

<MACK Truck> HOWS DA BIZNESS@FUTURE

<Futurama> THINGS ARE GOOD…I'M BLESSED

<Teddy Pinned*Her*Ass*Down> SO WE SEE…U ALL OVER THE RADIO, BET, MTV, MY MAMA TV AND MY AUNT TEE

<Da Ice Cream Man> lol!

<Futurama>HOW IN THE HELL DID ALL Y'ALL COME IN AT THE SAME TIME. IT TOOK ME DAMN NEAR 8 YEARS TO GET IN THIS BITCH!

<Teddy Pinned*Her*Ass*Down> YOU KNOW I GOT VIP STATUS UP IN THIS BIOTCH! AIN'T THAT RIGHT MAMI DEAREST?

<Choco Latte> Slick…leave me the HELL ALONE!!!!! I DON'T WANT YOUR MESSAGES…I DON'T WANT TO GO PRIVATE AND I DON'T WANT YOUR RAUNCHY ASS!!!!!

<***Mami*Dearest***> YOU KNOW IT TEDDY BABY…NOW PIN MY ASS DOWN!!! LOL!

<SlicK> so it's like that, choco?

<MACK Truck> I SEE THE PEOPLE U SIGNED THE LAST TIME WE TALKED BLEW UP FOR U

<Futurama>EVERYTHING HAS BEEN GOOD. I JUST SIGNED ANOTHER GROUP OUTTA DA CAROLINAS

<Teddy Pinned*Her*Ass*Down> I TOLD U THE KAROLINAS WAS FULL OF TALENT…NOW CAN I GET MY FINDER'S FEE???

<Futurama> THAT'S A NIGGA 4 U...LOL!
<Thyk2Def> FUTURE IS FULL OF SHYT!!!
HE BEEN KICKIN IT WIT US ALL THIS TIME
AND AIN'T PUT NOBODY IN A VIDEO
<City Ave Diva> YEAH FUTURE...WHAT'S
UP WIT DAT?
<Futurama> HOW MANY TIMES DO WE
HAVE TO GO THROUGH THIS...DON'T
NONE OF Y'ALL LIVE IN THE ATL AND
Y'ALL KNOW HOW I FEEL ABOUT MIXIN'
BIZNESS AND PLEASURE.
<Thyk2Def> TO HELL WIT BUSINESS AND
PLEASURE...I'M TRYNA GET PAID...LOL!
<Optimo Pryme> Y'ALL GET UP OFF MY
BOY FUTURE. HE AIN'T GOT TIME TO BE
FOOLIN' WIT Y'ALL GHETTO ASSES
<Choco Latte> YOU JUST SAYIN THAT CUZ
YOU ALREADY BEEN IN TWO OF'EM
<Da Wife> HOW OPTIMO GET TO BE IN A
VIDEO AND YOU AIN'T PUT YA OWN
BABYMAMA IN A VIDEO
<City Ave Diva>PRYME GOT TO BE IN THE
VIDEOS CUZ HE LIVE IN MIAMI
<Optimo Pryme>ITS NOT MY FAULT I JUST
SO HAPPEN TO LIVE IN THE CITY THAT
FUTURE SO HAPPENED TO CHOOSE TO
SHOOT THE VIDEO IN!!!***BRUSHIN
HATERZ OF MY SHOULDERS*** LOL!
<Futurama> FIRST OF ALL, I'VE TOLD
Y'ALL WHEN I HAVE OPEN SHOOTS BUT
Y'ALL NEVER HIT ME UP ABOUT
IT...SECOND OF ALL...I TOLD EVERYBODY
THE AGENCIES I USE TO GET PEOPLE FOR

MY VIDEOS AND HOW MANY HAVE
CALLED....NONE...AND THIRD OF
ALL...BACK UP OFF ME....LOL!
<***Mami*Dearest***> THAT'S OK
FUTURE...YOU DON'T HAVE TO PUT ME
IN A VIDEO...YOU STILL MY BOO BOO
<Futurama> THANK YOU MAMI

As Ivy chatted with his people, he
clicked on different pink names to see who was
in the room. There seemed to be quite a few
new faces in the room. A couple of the new
names that caught his eye were WifeyMaterial
and 2much4u.

Lady Get Some has entered the room
Krystal Lyte has entered the room
Akbar Zambooki Jenkins III has entered the
room
<Optimo Pryme> LOOKS LIKE ALL OF THE
TRIBE IS HERE!!!
<Optimo Pryme>ZULU NATION...
LELELELELELELELE!!!!
<Futurama>LELELELELEL!!!
<Got'em Hatin'>LLELELELELELELELE!!!
<Lady Get Some>LELELELELE!
<Thyk2Def>LELELELELELELELELEL!
<MACK Truck>LELELELELELELE!
<Da Ice Cream Man>LELELE!
**<Mr.SexxyB-
Baller>**LELELELELELELELELELELELELE!
<City Ave Diva>LELELELELELELELELE!!!!!!

<***Mami*Dearest***>LELELELELELELELE!!!!!

<Teddy Pinned*Her*Ass*Down>LELELELELELELELELELELE!!!!

<SoopaFly>LELELELELELELELELELE!!!

<Da Wife>LELELELELELE!!!

<SlicK>LELELELELELELELELELELELELELELELELELELELELELELELELELELELELELELELELELELELELELELELELELELELELELELEEE!!!!!

<Teddy Pinned*Her*Ass*Down> ITS ALWAYS A NIGGA THAT AINT A MEMBER OF THE TRIBE OVER DOIN' SOME SHIT. FOR THE LAST TIME SLICK…YOU ARE NOT IN THE TRIBE!!!!!! LOL!!!!!!

<Da Wife> LEAVE SLICK ALONE TEDDY!

<Futurama>LOL!

 <MACK Truck> GET'EM CUZIN!!!!

<Got'em Hatin'> ROFL!

<Lady Get Some> LMAO!

<Mr.SexxyB-Baller> U STUPID TEDDY

<Thyk2Def> LOL! YEAH SLICK IT TAKES A REAL MAN TO BE A ZULU MAN CUZ A ZULU MAN IS A REAL MAN!!!!

<Da Ice Cream Man> THAT'S NOT NICE TEDDY

<City Ave Diva> SOMEBODY BEEN WATCHIN SKOOL DAZE! LOL!

<***Mami*Dearest***> BE NICE TEDDY!

<SoopaFly>ROFLMAO!!!!!!

<Teddy Pinned*Her*Ass*Down> I'M JUST FUCKIN WIT YOU SLICK...YOU KNOW WE COOL

<SlicK> GO TO HELL TEDDY

<Teddy Pinned*Her*Ass*Down> DON'T ACT LIKE THAT SLICK...HOLD ON...I GOT SOMETHIN FOR YOU...CHOCO... TAKE SLICK PRIVATE AND SHOW HIM YOUR CHEST...LOL

<Futurama> CHOCO IS GONNA KICK UR ASS TEDDY

<Choco Latte> DON'T TELL HIM NOTHIN FUTURE...TEDDY KNOW HE ALREADY IN TROUBLE WIT ME ANYWAY

<Futurama> WHAT U DO NOW TED?

<Teddy Pinned*Her*Ass*Down> BEATS THE SHIT OUTTA ME...I THINK CHOCO JUST TALKIN' SHIT CUZ SHE WANT ME TO COME TO CALI AND HELP HER GET RID OF HER MAN

<Choco Latte> THAT'S ALL TEDDY DO IS TALK SHIT...I BEEN TRYIN TO GET HIM TO CALI FOR HOW LONG NOW? HE KNOW HE CAN'T HANDLE ME

<Da Wife> DAMN TEDDY

<Mr.SexxyB-Baller> CUZIN...I KNOW U NOT LETTIN HER PUNK U LIKE DAT

<Teddy Pinned*Her*Ass*Down> PUNK WHO? CHOCO KNOW SHE DON'T WANT TEDDY TO COME PIN HER CHOCOLATE ASS DOWN...LOL!

<Da Ice Cream Man>LOL!

<Futurama> Y'ALL SILLY...YO OPTIMO!!!!!!

<Optimo Pryme> WZUP FUTURE??????????
<Futurama> I C 2 NEW FACES IN THE ROOM
<Optimo Pryme>****GRABIN HIS BINOCULARS AND LOOKIN AROUND*** WHO DAT FUTURE? POINT'EM OUT!!!!!!
<Futurama> WIFEYMATERIAL AND 2MUCH4U
<MACK Truck> MIGHT BE SOME EBONY WORLD OVERFLOW
<Optimo Pryme>***CLEARING MY THROAT THEN USING BARRY WHITE VOICE*** EXCUSE ME LADIES....
<***Mami*Dearest***>FUTURE, PRYME AND TEDDY...LEAVE THEM GIRLS ALONE
<Teddy Pinned*Her*Ass*Down> DAMN MAMI...I DIDN'T EVEN SAY NOTHIN'
<***Mami*Dearest***> I KNOW YOU...U DON'T HAVE TO SAY NOTHIN
<Futurama>DAMN KID...I THINK THEY JUST STRAIGHT IGGED YOU
The Shizzles has entered the room
<City Ave Diva> IT'S EVERBODY'S FAVORITE COUPLE...THE SHIZZLES!!!!
<Teddy Pinned*Her*Ass*Down> YO FUTURE...I FEEL A PARAGRAPH COMIN ON
<Futurama> I WAS HAVIN THE SAME FEELIN' TED
<***Mami*Dearest***> WELCOME TO MY ROOM EVERYBODY BUT YOU KNOW THE RULES....THIS IS A VIDEO CHAT ROOM SO YOU NEED TO CAM UP OR BOUNCE!!!

\<Optimo Pryme\> THAT'S WHAT'S WRONG WITH THE WORLD TODAY...A BROTHA TRIED TO SPEAK NICELY TO A COUPLE OF YOUNG LADIES (WIFEYMATERIAL AND 2MUCH4U) BUT YOU IGNORE HIM. NOW I'MA TRY THIS AGAIN....EXCUSE ME LADIES!!!!

\<Teddy Pinned*Her*Ass*Down\> TOLD YOU...LOL!

\<WifeyMaterial\> @optimo...FIRST OF ALL YOU DON'T KNOW ME LIKE THAT TO BE PUTTIN ME ON BLAST. IF I DIDN'T WANT TO RESPOND TO YOU, I DIDN'T HAVE TO BUT SINCE YOU KEEP INSISTING...WHAT THE HELL DO YOU WANT?

\<Teddy Pinned*Her*Ass*Down\> AWWWWWWWW SHIT! I KNOW YOU NOT GONNA LET HER TALK TO U LIKE DAT SON!

\<Thyk2Def\> TEDDY STAY OUT OF IT

\<Mr.SexxyB-Baller\>THIS SHIT FINNA GET GOOD ****GRABBIN POPCORN***

\<Optimo Pryme\> HOLD UP MA...U DON'T HAVE TO ACT LIKE THAT....SINCE YOU ARE NEW HERE I JUST WANTED TO SAY HELLO AND WELCOME YOU TO THE ROOM BUT SINCE YOU ACTIN LIKE THAT I COULD GIVE A DAMN

\<Got'em Hatin'\> STOP HOGGIN THE POPCORN@SEXXY

\<Futurama\> WHY I GOTTA MEDIATE EVERY NIGHT...WIFEYMATERIAL...PLEASE

EXCUSE MY POTNA…HE DON'T MEAN NO
HARM…WE ALL KNOW EACH OTHER
AND WE KNOW THAT'S HOW OPTIMO IS
SO WE LOOK PAST HIM. WE JUST NOTICED
THAT WE'VE NOT SEEN YOU BEFORE AND
WERE JUST WONDERING WHO U WERE.
<WifeyMaterial> THEN HE SHOULDA JUST
SAID THAT
<***Mami*Dearest***> NOW OPTIMO I
THINK YOU NEED TO APOLOGIZE
<Choco Latte> YEAH OPTIMO
<Optimo Pryme> APOLOGIZE FOR WHAT?
<WifeyMaterial> I DON'T NEED HIS SORRY
ASS APOLOGIES
<City Ave Diva> I LIKE HER…SHE GOT
SOME SPICE…SHE'LL FIT RIGHT IN
<Futurama> WHERE YOU FROM@WIFEY
Krystal Lyte has entered the room
<WifeyMaterial> I'M FROM VA BUT I LIVE
IN THE ATL
<Futurama> THAT'S WHERE I'M AT
<WifeyMaterial> WHERE U AT IN THE
CITY?
<Teddy Pinned*Her*Ass*Down> MAKE UP
UR MIND@ KRYSTAL…UR GONNA BE IN
OR OUT
<Krystal Lyte>
TEDDY……….SHEEEEEEEDDDUP!!!! LOL!
<Futurama> CLOSE TO BUCKHEAD
<Teddy Pinned*Her*Ass*Down> I LOVE U
TOO LYTE
<WifeyMaterial> ON WHICH SIDE?
<Futurama> THE WEST PACES FERRY SIDE

<Krystal Lyte> YOU KNOW I LOVE YOU
TEDDY
<WifeyMaterial>WEST PACES FERRY...YOU
MUST HAVE A FEW DOLLARS IN YA
POCKETS...LOL!
<Futurama> I DO ALRIGHT....BUT
ANYWAY...I GOTTA GET SOME
SLEEP...I'LL SEE Y'ALL ON THE FLIPSIDE!!!!
<City Ave Diva> NITE FUTURE
<SoopaFly> PEACE OUT CUZIN!
<Thyk2Def>NITE FUTURE
<Got'em Hatin'> NITE NITE...SD
<Optimo Pryme> AIIGHT MY NIG!
<Da Wife> SWEET DREAMS BABY DADDY
<Teddy Pinned*Her*Ass*Down> HOLD IT
DOWN CUZIN
<MACK Truck>LATA CUZIN
<Choco Latte> BYE BABY!

As Ivy signed out of just4kicks,
XoticMami logged in to her messenger. Before
he had the chance to pull up his friend list, a
messenger box popped up.

XoticMami: Hey, sexy! WZUP?
Ivy_Dav: not much... just logged off
just4kickz...what happened to u?
XoticMami: me and my girl just got
finished with a shoot
Ivy_Dav: that's what's up
XoticMami: u been home all nite?
Ivy_Dav: nah, me and my boyz went to
the Silver Dollar earlier for happy

hour. We left around 10 and I'm still a lil
buzzed

XoticMami: buzzed, huh? U want Mami
to come over and

check on you?

Ivy_Dav: stop playin'…lol!

XoticMami: the look on my face does
not say lol

Ivy_Dav: for real, stop it…ur killin me!

XoticMami: I understand if u scared say
u scared

Ivy_Dav: ur serious, aren't you?

XoticMami: I'll show u how serious I
am

> *XoticMami has invited you to view
> his/her webcam*

Ivy accepted her invitation. Once it
connected, XoticMami was sitting in front of
her computer with her C-cups fully exposed.
Ivy could not believe his eyes. He had run into
a true-to-life Internet freak.

XoticMami: now r u takin me seriously?

Ivy_Dav: as a heart attack

With that statement, XoticMami rolled
herself back in her black, leather office chair.
She positioned herself for him to see that she
was totally nude. Ivy sat back in his chair and
folded his arms. XoticMami lifted her legs up
and placed each one over the arms of the chair.
She then took her hands and spread her lower

lips apart and began to fondle her "lil' lady."
As she rubbed her *pleasure zone* with one hand,
she took her other hand and caressed her
breasts and squeezed her nipples. While she
was putting on a show, Ivy felt his nature
begin to get hard and his body temperature
rose. The more intense she got, the more Ivy
wanted her. He wished that he could hear her
moans as she masturbated. The thing that blew
his mind was when XoticMami took her
fingers out of her flesh and placed them in her
mouth and began to suck on them. That was all
that he could take.

> **Ivy_Dav:** OK...THAT'S ENOUGH!!!!
> **XoticMami:** what's wrong? can't take it?
> **Ivy_Dav:** NOPE
> **XoticMami:** All of this can be
> yours...just say the word
> **Ivy_Dav:** not tonite. I have a long day
> tomorrow and I need all
> of my energy and by lookin at you, you
> might wear a nigga out.
> **XoticMami:** Just say when and it's urs
> **Ivy_Dav:** maybe this weekend, I'll let
> you know
> **XoticMami:** ok
> **Ivy_Dav:** what's ur #
> **XoticMami:** 770-555-2469 my cell
> **Ivy_Dav:** and ur name?
> **XoticMami:** that's not important right
> now. Call me
> ***XoticMami had just logged out***

Chapter 2

The next day, Ivy tried to call XoticMami to set up a date for that night. He was tired from all of the day's running around but after what he saw the night before, he knew he could find strength from somewhere. He got up and closed his office door as he dialed her number. Her cell phone rang but she did not answer. Her voicemail picked up. After leaving a message, Ivy folded his cell phone, tossed it on the desk and continued to brainstorm for the Southern Sunz's video shoot. While he scribbled on a legal pad, T-Bizzy knocked on the door. He motioned for him to enter the room.

"What's the deal, Playboy?" T-Bizzy greeted as he sat down in the chair in front of Ivy's desk. "You goin' to Club Blaze tonight?"

"Hadn't planned on it?" he replied as he continued to scribble. "Anything special goin on?"

"Michael Vick and T.J. Duckett are hostin' a party at Club Blaze."

"I thought that was next week."

"Nah, dog. It's tonight. You know we got VIP status. Will hooked it up."

"I'm tryin' to hook up wit this shorty tonight. If that falls through, I might ride out there."

"A shorty? Where you meet her?"

"Online." T-Bizzy busted out with laughter. "What the fuck is so funny?"

"You still fuckin' wit dat shit. I thought you was givin' it up after all that shit that went down wit Candace."

"That was some bullshit. Come check this one out."

T-Bizzy walked around the desk as Ivy pulled up XoticMami's pictures."

"Day-umm! That bitch is blazin'. She got a sister or a homegirl?"

"Why she gotta be a bitch?"

"My bad, dog."

"She saw my page on EbonyWorld.com and hit me up but check this out. After I got home from the Dollar, she hit me up while I was checkin' my email. I told her I was a lil' buzzed and she asked me could she come over. I didn't think she was serious. The next thing I know, she turned on the webcam and was butt-ass naked. She started playin' wit' herself and everything."

"Say word."

"Word. I would have told her to come to the crib but I had an ass of shit to do today."

"Fuck that. I'da had to wax dat ass."

"Believe me. I wanted to but you know how I go, business before pleasure."

"That's ya problem. You handlin' all dis business and ain't getting' enough pleasure. You need to take a vacation or somethin' before you croak."

"Man sit yo' retarded ass down." Ivy closed the picture files as T-Bizzy walked back around the desk. "I don't have time for a vacation, not with The Sunz about to drop."

"You act like I can't handle shit when you're not around. Who ran shit when you went to that conference in New York?"

"I know, man and I appreciate it but this is different. I discovered this one and I want to handle this project. After this one, I might take a vacation."

"To where...the cyber beach?" T-Bizzy laughed. "Maybe Cancun Online." Ivy was not laughing.

"Do me a favor. Get the fuck out."

"Why you gotta act like that?"

"Get out," Ivy commanded as he pointed to the door.

"On the real. If you get a chance, come through the spot. I'm sure you can find some cyber chicks to chill wit." Ivy opened his desk drawer. T-Bizzy knew that's where he kept his gun. He ran out of the office, shut the door behind him, and gave him the middle finger as he passed by his office window. Ivy laughed as T-Bizzy walked away.

At a nearby gym, Natalie and Shanice were finishing up their last pick up game. The two ladies sat on the floor against the wall to rest. As Natalie turned up her water bottle a very familiar face came into sight as she opened her eyes. He was average height with dark brown skin, a slim build, and a low haircut. The tank top he wore exposed his chiseled arms and barely covered his muscular chest. It was Desmond Walker, Natalie's ex-boyfriend.

"How you doin, Nat?" he inquired as he stood over her.

"Hello Desmond," she replied coldly.

"Why it gotta be like that?"

"Because I have nothing to say to you. C'mon, Shanice." Natalie stood up and grabbed her gym bag. Desmond firmly grabbed her arm as she tried to walk past him.

"Will you just listen to me for a minute?"

"Desmond, you have two seconds to let me go." He released her arm. "Thank you. What do you want?"

"Shanice, can you excuse us for a minute?" Shanice looked at Natalie for her approval to leave."

"I'll catch up with you in a minute." Natalie hoisted her tote bag onto her shoulder. "Now, what do you want?"

"Why do we have to be like this? I came over here to apologize and this is how you treat me."

"Seven month's later? It's a little too late for apologies."

"Can't we just talk this out?" Desmond pleaded.

"There's nothing to talk about. You were the one that decided to leave me because you were threatened by my friendship with André. I never gave you a reason to doubt my fidelity. He is a married man and he is my friend. Period. Why couldn't you just accept that?"

"I'm sorry. I was jealous of the relationship that the two of you had. I wanted you to let me in like you let him in."

"You and André are two different people. He and I have been through a lot together. My relationship with you was on another level. If you would have took your head out of your ass for a second you coulda saw that. Instead, you walked away. Here it is seven months later and you want to apologize. Desmond, please."

"So, it's like that?"

"That's how you made it. Goodbye, Des."

Desmond stood and watched as his former Diamond turned to stone before his eyes. Natalie walked away and caught up with Shanice. The two women exited the gym and Natalie headed home. When Natalie walked into her house, she was still thinking about the conversation she had just had with Desmond. She began to question her actions. Was she wrong? She didn't believe that she was. In her eyes, she fell victim to an insecure man. That's all.

A cellular tone broke Ivy's concentration as he sat in the studio while The Southern Sunz and Gusto worked on their album. He motioned for them to continue as he flipped his phone open to see who was calling. It was XoticMami.

"This is Ivy," he answered.

"Hi there," she said in a seductive voice. "Are you busy?"

"Not really. I'm at the studio. What's up?"

"I was calling to take you up on your offer. That's if it still stands."

"Yeah, no doubt," Ivy stood up and walked out of the studio and into the hallway.

"Is it your place or mine?"

"I was thinkin' more along the lines of goin' out?"

"That's good, too. Where?"

"What about Café Intrigue in Buckhead?"

"I've never been there."

"It's a nice lil' spot. What time is good for you?"

"I'm on your time."

"Well, let me finish up here and I'll meet you there around nine."

"Sounds good. I'll be waiting."

"Alright. One." Ivy closed his phone and returned to the studio.

As Gusto, EL GEE and ATP went over songs, Ivy started to watch the time it was only 7:30. He had to stay focused so he could remain productive. Slowly but surely, 8:30 rolled around. Ivy left the studio headed for Café Intrigue. He was fifteen minutes early. Ivy stood at the bar and looked over the room. XoticMami had not arrived. He positioned himself at the far end of the bar so that he was facing the door. About five minutes into his first drink, she walked in.

XoticMami was gorgeous. She was exactly as she was in the picture. The night's cool weather had her in a sleek, form-fitting, black dress that only reached her upper thighs. In the photos, her hair was brownish black. On that night it was black with reddish highlights and was cut to just below her ears. Ivy watched as she looked for him over the room. She spotted him and began to glide towards him. As she neared him, he could smell the sweet scent of the perfume she wore. He stood up to greet her.

"Hello," he greeted as he extended his hand.
"Am I what you were expecting?" she asked placing her hand in his.
"The same two words come to mind as they did the first night I talked to you."
"And what would they be?"

"Just Blaze." The two laughed as they exchanged pleasantries. "Would you like to sit at the bar or would you like to get a table?"

"A table is fine." Ivy led her to a table in a dark corner of the café. He noticed that quite a few guys were staring at them as they passed. As sexy as she was, who wouldn't stare? Little did he know, they were staring for other reasons.

"My lady," Ivy pulled out her chair.

"And you're a gentleman. This is too much."

"That's just me. I'm a brother that believes that chivalry is not dead."

"I see."

"It is a pleasure to finally meet you, Miss…"

"Melissa."

"A pleasure to meet you Melissa. I'm Iverson."

"I know, Mr. Iverson Davenport from Camden, New Jersey, a graduate of Howard University with a BS in Business and a BA in Music. Iverson was also voted by Ebony Magazine as one of America's most eligible bachelors."

"I'm impressed. You really did your homework." The cocktail server approached the table. She was a short, but shapely, white girl with blonde hair and gray eyes that looked to be in her early twenties.

"Good evening. My name is Sarah and I'll be taking care of you this evening."

"What's up, Sarah? Let me get another Hennessy and Coke with a shot of Grand Mariner on the side."

"And for the lady?"

"Belvedere Apple Martini."

"I'll be right back."

"Now, where were we?"

"I was reciting your bio."

"Since you know so much about me, tell me about you."

"I'm a fashion designer and model. I attended Bethune-Cookman in Florida. I'm originally from St. Petersburg but I've been in Atlanta for the past seven years."

"I see. What brought you to the ATL?"

"It's the new Mecca for Blacks. I love being surrounded by my people and my culture."

"No, really. What brought you to Atlanta?"

"The night life." They laughed as the waitress returned with their drinks.

Ivy and Melissa sat and got more acquainted over a couple of drinks. They talked about college life at an HBCU — which is a Historically Black College or University, among other things. As they talked, Ivy picked up on a strong sexual vibe coming from Melissa. Everything that was said, she managed to sneak a sexual gesture or comment in. He really got clued in when she took off her shoe and began to rub her foot up the side of his leg. Before she had a chance to put her foot in his manhood, he grabbed it and then excused himself.

"I'll be right back," he told her as he stood up. "I have to use the restroom."

Ivy released a hard breath when he was out of earshot. He walked into the bathroom and went to the urinal. At the urinal beside him was a brown-skinned male about six feet. There is an underlying rule between men: YOU DO NOT TALK TO ANOTHER MAN WHILE HE IS STANDING AT THE URINAL BESIDE YOU. Once the men finished their business they found themselves at the sink washing their hands.

"What's up, playa?" Ivy greeted as he pumped blue soap into his hand.

"Chillin," he answered as he turned on the water. "Hey bruh, I don't wanna get in yo' business or nuttin but, is that ya ol' lady?"

"Nah, dog. I just met her."

"I ain't tryin to disrespect or cause no trouble but you might wanna let that one go."

"Why you say that?"

"You must not know who that is? That's Melissa a.k.a Missy da Man-Eater."

"Who?"

"She got a rep for fuckin' wit niggaz only cuz they got loot. She done been with

Atlanta Falcons, Atlanta Hawks, rappers, singers..."

"For real?"

"Dawg. I ain't got no reason to lie. She caught a homeboy of mine up. Word on da streets is that she got that thang, dat Fiya, dat Ninja." All terms for the HIV virus.

"You Bullshitin."

"I put that on er'y thang I love, dawg." When a brother says that, you know he's serious.

Ivy was distraught as he exited the bathroom. He didn't know whether to believe it or not. It had to have some truth because brothers just don't come out of the blue and tell you things like that. When he approached the table he couldn't bring himself to look at her. Melissa noticed that his mood had changed.

"Is there something wrong, Ivy?" she inquired. "Are you feeling okay?"

"Not really. I think I should head to the house. I'm sorry."

"Would you like me to come with you?"

"That's ok. I'll be fine. I probably just need some rest."

"Oh, ok. Call me later and let me know how you're doing."

"I will." Ivy knew damn well that he was not going to call her again.

Once at home away from the madness of the outside world, Iverson decided to check in on his other friends. He didn't know what drew him to the site but no matter what, he could always count on just4kickz.com for a good laugh. It was amazing how grown men and women acted towards each other when put in a room together—even it was just a chat room. Once logged on he, he saw that he'd received a message from WifeyMaterial. He decided to check it later and double-clicked on **video chat.** As always, at the top of the list was ***Mami*Dearest***. Iverson clicked on her name and he was in the room.

Futurama has entered the room
<Da Ice Cream Man> hey Teddy...Choco said when u comin to Cali?
<Choco Latte> DO NOT GET TEDDY STARTED@ICE CREAM
<Futurama> WHAT'S GOOD EVERYBODY!!!!!
<Lady Get Some> FUUUUUUUUTTUUUURE!!!!
<SoopaFly> CUZIIIIIIIN!!!
<Teddy Pinned*Her*Ass*Down> I KEEP TELLIN' Y'ALL CHOCO AINT READY FOR ME...SHE STILL GOT THAT PROBLEM...LOL
<Da Ice Cream Man> SUP FUTURE...MANG! LOL!
<*Mami*Dearest***>** HEY FUTURE BABY!
<Choco Latte> FUUUUUUUUTUUUUUUREEEEEE!!!! WHAT PROBLEM@TEDDY

71

\<Thyk2Def\> FUTURE!!!!!!!

\<Optimo Pryme\>LELELELELELELE!!!!!

\<Teddy Pinned*Her*Ass*Down\> THAT LIL BOY YOU GOT IN CALI THAT YOU CALL YA MAN...LOL!

\<Da Ice Cream Man\> that's not right Teddy! LMAO!

\<Choco Latte\> THEN Y DON'T YOU BE A MAN AND COME TO CALI...SINCE YOU THINK MY MAN AINT DOIN HIS JOB

\<SlicK\> when can I come to texas?@THYK

\<Teddy Pinned*Her*Ass*Down\> I KNOW HE AINT DOIN HIS JOB CUZ IF HE WAS YOU WOULDN'T BE IN HERE EVERY NIGHT TRYIN TO GET ME TO COME TO CALI...Y DON'T U COME TO FAYETTEVILLE

\<Futurama\> GET HER, TEDDY!!!!

\<Choco Latte\> THAT'S NOT FAIR...ITS 2 AGAINST 1

\<Thyk2Def\> ON THE 30TH OF NEVERUARY@SLICK

Krystal Lyte has entered the room

\<Optimo Pryme\> MAKE IT 3...CUZ CHOCO YOU HAVE BEEN BULLSHITTIN WIT THE NIGGA TEDDY FOR A MINUTE NOW

\<Teddy Pinned*Her*Ass*Down\> DON'T SWEAT IT FELLAZ...SHE'LL GET TIRED OF OL' BOY SOONER OR LATER AND I DO EMPHASIS THE WORD "BOY"

\<Da Wife\> Y'ALL LEAVE CHOCO ALONE

<Got'em Hatin> THAT'S RIGHT...U KNOW GOOD AND HELL WELL TEDDY CAN'T HANDLE US CALI GIRLS

<Lady Get Some> bout time another white person showed up...I was getting nervous wit all these black people in here....lol!

<Choco Latte> THAT'S RIGHT

<Krystal Lyte> u know I got ya back get some...even if I ain't white

<SoopaFly> u da whitest black girl I ever seen@Krystal

<Teddy Pinned*Her*Ass*Down> WHAT!!! NOT ONLY CAN I HANDLE YOU...I CAN HANDLE YOU TWO AT THE SAME TIME!!!

<City Ave Diva> lol! u silly@soopa

<MACK Truck>TELL'EM CUZ! U KNOW HOW DA TRIBE ROLL!! LELELELELELELE!!!!!

<Got'em Hatin> DON'T THREATEN ME WIT A GOOD TIME..LOL!

<Choco Latte>U WANNA SEE ME FOR REAL@TEDDY

<Teddy Pinned*Her*Ass*Down> DO A BEAR SHIT IN DA WOODS? SEND ME YA IM INFO AND WE'LL TALK

<Got'em Hatin> DON'T DO IT @CHOCO...TEDDY FULL OF SHIT

<Futurama>MIND YA BUSINESS@ GOT'EM

<Choco Latte>YEAH...MIND YA BUSINESS...LOL!

<Got'em Hatin> WOW!!! SEE WHAT HAPPENS WHEN YOU TRY 2 HELP PEOPLE

OUT...THEY TURN ON YOU...BLACK
PEOPLE...LOL!
<City Ave Diva>LOL!
<Optimo Pryme>THAT'S AIGHT MA@
GOT'EM YOU KNOW OPTIMO GOT U!
<Futurama> ANYBODY SEEN
WIFEYMATERIAL?
<Optimo Pryme> WHO?
<City Ave Diva> THE GIRL THAT CUSSED U
OUT LAST NIGHT@PRYME
<SlicK> SHE WAS LOOKIN FOR YOU
EARLIER...SHE SAID SHE'D BE
BACK@FUTURE
<MACK Truck>THAT NIGGA SLICK KNOW
THE LOW DOWN ON EVERYBODY...LOL
<Futurama>GOOD LOOKIN OUT SLICK
<Teddy Pinned*Her*Ass*Down>THAT'S
CUZ SLICK IS A PERVERT. HE BE CHECKIN
OUT ALL THE WOMEN...AT THE SAME
TIME...NIGGA DON'T KNOW WHO TO
JACK OFF TO...LOL
<SoopaFly>LOL!
<SlicK>NO PROB@FUTURE...GO TO
HELL@TEDDY
<***Mami*Dearest***> TEDDY!!!! BE NICE
<Da Ice Cream Man> rofl!
<Teddy Pinned*Her*Ass*Down> MY BAD@
MAMI...AND ICE CREAM FOR THE LAST
TIME...WILL YOU STOP TYPING IN THEM
little ass letters!
<Da Wife> WE STILL GOIN OUT THIS
WEEKEND@SOOPA
<City Ave Diva> LOL!@TEDDY

\<SoopaFly> YEAH...I'LL HIT U LATA SO WE CAN FIGURE OUT WHERE WE GOIN.

\<Teddy Pinned*Her*Ass*Down> WAIT ONE COTTON PICKIN' MINUTE

\<Da Wife> OK@SOOPA

\<Teddy Pinned*Her*Ass*Down> I TURN MY BACK FOR A MINUTE AND NOW MY CUZIN IS GOIN OUT WIT MY BABYMAMA...WHAT IS THE WORLD COMIN TO? LOL

\<SoopaFly> COME ON CUZIN...U CAN'T HAVE ALL DA WOMEN

\<Da Wife> THAT'S RIGHT...YOU CAN'T HAVE ME AND CHOCO ON DA SIDE...SO I HAD TO GET ME A MAN ON DA SIDE

\<Choco Latte> I AIN'T NOBODY'S WOMAN ON DA SIDE

\<Teddy Pinned*Her*Ass*Down> SO U WANT ME TO BE YOUR MAN ON DA SIDE BUT I CAN'T HAVE A WOMAN ON THE SIDE...THAT'S A PRETTY F'ED UP DOUBLE STANDARD

\<City Ave Diva> TEDDY U KNOW THAT ITS ALL ABOUT WHAT THE WOMAN WANTS

\<Futurama> AND TO ME...THAT'S SOME BULL CRAP...LOL

\<Teddy Pinned*Her*Ass*Down> ITS COOL CUZ AS SOON AS SHE MEETS TEDDY, CHOCO GONNA BE TRYNA MOVE TO NORTH CAROLINA

2much4u has entered the room

\<Choco Latte\> OH REALLY??? IT MIGHT BE THE OTHER WAY AROUND…U MIGHT BE TRYNA MOVE TO CALI

\<Optimo Pryme\> DON'T DO IT TEDDY…IT'S A SET UP!

\<Thyk2Def\> LOL

\<Got'em Hatin\> THAT'S OK TEDDY…IF YOU COME OUT HERE AND SHE DON'T WANT YOU…I'M RIGHT UP THE STREET

\<Teddy Pinned*Her*Ass*Down\> CALIFORNIA HERE I COME!

\<Optimo Pryme\> YO FUTURE…AIN'T THAT THE OTHER SHORTY THAT WAS IN HERE LAST NIGHT

\<Futurama\> WHO?****LOOKIN' AROUND***

\<SlicK\> HE'S TALKIN BOUT 2MUCH4U@FUTURE

\<Thyk2Def\> DAMN SLICK!

\<Teddy Pinned*Her*Ass*Down\> I TOLD Y'ALL…SLICK BE ON IT…LOL

\<Futurama\> YUP…THAT'S HER…PIMPS, PLAYERS, KICKERS AND KICKETTES…I'D LIKE FOR EVERYBODY TO GIVE A WARM WELCOME TO 2MUCH4U

\<City Ave Diva\> HEY@2MUCH

\<Optimo Pryme\>WHAT IT DO MAMI@2MUCH

\<Got'em Hatin\> WELCOME!

\<Choco Latte\> HEY@2MUCH

\<SoopaFly\>WHAT'S GOOD, MA@2MUCH

\<Da Ice Cream Man\>GREETINGS!

\<MACK Truck\>SUP MA

<2much4u> what's up everybody…thanx 4 the welcome!

<Optimo Pryme> WHERE U FROM MA?

<2much4u> the ATL

<MACK Truck> DAMN CUZIN@FUTURE…SEEMS LIKE ALL THE WOMEN THAT HAVE BEEN COMIN IN HERE LATELY BEEN FROM YOUR NECK OF THE WOODZ

<Futurama> THAT'S CUZ THE ATL IS DA SHIT!

<City Ave Diva> I THOUGHT U WAS FROM JERSEY@FUTURE

<2much4u> u in Atlanta@future

<Teddy Pinned*Her*Ass*Down> U KNOW ITS ALL ABOUT THE SOUF@DIVA

<Futurama> I AM FROM JERSEY AND I LOVE MY HOME STATE BUT CAMDEN AIN'T GOT NUTTIN ON THE A…THIS IS WHERE I MADE IT…YES@2MUCH…I LIVE IN BUCKHEAD

<City Ave Diva>WHATEVA@TEDDY

<2much4u> I live in Decatur

<Optimo Pryme> FUTURE CAN U TELL YOUR GIRL THAT PEOPLE WHO MATTER IN THIS ROOM DON'T TYPE IN little letters

<*Mami*Dearest***>** OPTIMO….NOT TONIGHT

<2much4u> IS THIS BETTER@OPTIMO

<Optimo Pryme> MUCH BETTER…TY

<2much4u> NP…YW

Natalie sat up in her bed surfing through channels. While flipping, she saw another commercial for EbonyWorld.com. She looked at the commercial and then glanced at her nightstand where she had previously scribbled the web address on the back of her notepad. Curiosity began to churn under her soft locks. The thought of logging on to the website passed through her mind but she dismissed it and continued to flip through the channels. A Lifetime movie caught her eye making her stop. After she was about five minutes into the movie, she tossed the remote aside and got comfortable. Before she got too comfortable, her cell phone interrupted her movie.

The phone's caller ID read "Des."
"What do you want?" she asked in an aggravated tone.
"Damn, girl." Desmond responded. "What is your problem? I just called to say hello."
"No you didn't, Des. At this time of night you called with one thing on your mind. Let me stop you before you get started. Don't think that just because you saw me today and you were trying to be all apologetic, that it is going to change anything. Point blank, you left me high and dry and I don't see or hear from you until seven months later. Negro please."

"See, this is why I left. The woman I'm talking to now is not the woman that I fell in love with."

"Love?" Natalie pulled the phone away from her ear and looked at it as she frowned. "Des you don't love me because if you did, you wouldn't have treated me like you did."

"I was just scared. I'd never felt the way I did about any other woman."

Natalie busted into laughter.

"That was a good one," she said as she regained her composure. "Listen, Des. Do us both a favor and forget you know me. I'm not your woman anymore and I don't want to be your friend. This subject is no longer open for discussion. Goodbye."

"It's like that, huh. Well then to hell with you. I don't need you anyway...CLICK!" Natalie shook her head and laughed as she put her phone back on the nightstand and continued into her movie.

<Teddy Pinned*Her*Ass*Down> I DON'T CARE WHAT YOU SAY...CAP'N CRUNCH IS THE BEST CEREAL EVER MADE!!!!!!!!
<Da Ice Cream Man> WHAT ABOUT FRUIT LOOPS
<Optimo Pryme> LISTEN AT ALL YOU FORTUNATE KIDS...I GREW UP IN DA HOOD...WE COULDN'T AFFORD FRUIT LOOPS...WE HAD FRUIT RINGS...SHIT SO DAMN CHEAP IT CAME IN A BAG INSTEAD OF A BOX
<City Ave Diva> LOL!

<Got'em Hatin> I KEEP IT PIMPIN' WIT FROSTED FLAKES

<SoopaFly> THEEEEEEEEERE GRRRRRRRREAT!!!!

<Choco Latte> IT'S ALL ABOUT THE COCO PUFFS

<2much4u> I KEEPS IT ALL THE WAY TRILL...DON'T FRONT ON FRUITY PEBBLES!!!

<Optimo Pryme> WE HAD FRUITY NUGGETS...WASN'T NO HOODS IN BEDROCK

<Futurama> I'M WIT 2MUCH...I KEEPS IT LIVE WIT FRUITY PEBBLES TOO WIT SOME CINNAMON TOAST CRUCH FOR SPECIAL OCCASIONS

<Teddy Pinned*Her*Ass*Down> @GET SOME...WHAT KINDA CEREALS THEY GOT UP IN CANADA???

<MACK Truck> TEDDY ACT LIKE CANADA IS AROUND THE WORLD...LOL!

<Teddy Pinned*Her*Ass*Down> I'M SERIOUS...I WAS IN THIS OTHER ROOM TALKIN' TO THIS OTHER CHICK FROM CANADA AND SHE WAS TELLIN ME THAT THEY HAVE DIFFERENT CIGARETTES....THE DON'T HAVE NEWPORTS AND MARLBORO

<SoopaFly> THAT'S WHY IT AIN'T THAT MANY NIGGAZ IN CANADA...NO NEWPORTS...LOL

<Da Ice Cream Man> ROFL!

\<Lady Get Some\> YOU'D BE SURPRISED@TEDDY...WE HAVE A LOT OF AMERICAN STUFF BUT JUST LIKE THE US...WE HAVE OUR OWN PRODUCTS AS WELL

\<Choco Latte\> @2MUCH...WHERE DO REGULAR PEOPLE IN ATLANTA PARTY?

\<Futurama\> LOL!

\<2much4u\> R U SERIOUS...YOU MEAN TO TELL ME THAT FUTURE HASN'T TOLD Y'ALL ABOUT ALL THE PARTY SPOTS

\<Choco Latte\> HE TOLD US WHERE HE PARTYS BUT PEOPLE LIKE HIM DON'T PARTY WIT REGULAR PEOPLE.

\<Choco Latte\> THEY PARTY IN PLACES THAT COST A MILLION DOLLARS TO GET IN AND 2 BILLION DOLLARS FOR A DRINK...LOL

\<Teddy Pinned*Her*Ass*Down\> LOL! WHAT SHE'S TRYING TO ASK IS WHERE TO BROKE PEOPLE PARTY BECAUSE ITS OBVIOUS FUTURE CAN'T TELL US THAT

\<2much4u\> I DON'T UNDERSTAND

\<Futurama\> YOU HAVEN'T BEEN HERE LONG ENOUGH TO KNOW WHAT I DO FOR A LIVING...AND NOBODY TELL HER

\<Teddy Pinned*Her*Ass*Down\> DAMN!

\<2much4u\> WHY NOT!

\<Futurama\> ITS G-13 CLASSIFIED...IF I TELL YOU...I'LL HAVE TO KILL YOU...LOL!

\<Thyk2Def\> JUST TELL HER

\<Futurama\>SHE GOTTA FIND OUT ON HER OWN JUST LIKE EVERYBODY ELSE

<2much4u>THAT IS SO NOT FAIR! ***FOLDING MY ARMS AND POUTING***

<Teddy Pinned*Her*Ass*Down> AT LEAST GIVE HER A HINT OR A CLUE

<Futurama> I'LL LET MY FELLOW TRIBAL MEMBER CHIEF OPTIMO PRYME GIVE HER A CLUE....OPTIMO

<Thyk2Def> HERE WE GO...

<***Mami*Dearest***> YOU SHOULDA JUST TOLD HER@FUTURE

<Da Wife> U KNOW HOW OPTIMO IS

<2much4u> SOME HOW ALL OF THIS IS MAKING ME NERVOUS

<Futurama> NO NEED TO BE NERVOUS...ITS JUST THAT MY CUZIN HAS A UNIQUE WAY OF GIVING HINTS...EVERYBODY'S GONE THROUGH IT

<Optimo Pryme> IF UR BLACK AND U ARE ON THIS PLANET, THE IDENITY OF FUTURAMA U'LL HAVE...BUT ONLY IF YOU GO SEARCHING FOR IT ON THE ISLE OF IVY_DAV...GO FORWARD AND PROSPER!

<Futurama> WELL DONE!

<City Ave Diva> C'MON OPTIMO...YOU COULDA DID BETTER THAN THAT...THAT'S TOO EASY!

<Thyk2Def> U THINK IT'S OBVIOUS BECAUSE YOU ALREADY KNOW@DIVA... FUTURE SWITCHED UP...REMEMBER?

<Da Wife> THAT IS RIGHT...THAT'S A GOOD ONE OPTIMO!

<2much4u> I AM SO LOST RIGHT NOW
<Teddy Pinned*Her*Ass*Down> JUST THINK ABOUT IT FOR A MINUTE. THE ANSWER IS RIGHT IN FRONT OF YOU!
<Da Ice Cream Man> LUKE....I AM YOUR FATHER!
<MACK Truck> ????
<Futurama> HUH?@ICE CREAM
<Da Ice Cream Man> ALL THESE RIDDLES AND PLANETS AND LIVE LONG AND PROSPER...A BROTHA FEEL LIKE HE ON AN EPISODE OF STAR TREK
<MACK Truck> LOL
<Futurama> LMAO
<2much4u> I GRADUATED FROM SPELMEN...I SHOULD BE ABLE TO FIGURE IT OUT
<City Ave Diva> HBCU'S IN DA HOUSE!!!! REP YA SKOOL!!!!!
<Optimo Pryme> FAMU....GO RATTLERS!!!!!
<Futurama> ONE TIME FOR...THE MIGHT H-U!!!!! HOWARD UNIVERSITY!!!!
<Choco Latte> SAN DIEGO STATE REPPIN'!!!!
<City Ave Diva> MORGAN STATE!!!!
<Da Ice Cream Man> LET'S GO BIG BLUE!!! UNIVERSITY OF MICHIGAN
<Teddy Pinned*Her*Ass*Down> FRANKLIN MEMORIAL UNIVERSITY!!! PATRIOT PRIDE!!! GO PATS!!!!
<MACK Truck> FLORIDA A&M!!!!
<Choco Latte> WHERE IN DA HELL IS FRANKLIN MEMORIAL!!!@TEDDY

\<SlicK\> LIVINGSTONE COLLEGE

\<2much4u\> ITS IN FLORENCE SC@CHOCO

\<Choco Latte\> O OK

\<Teddy Pinned*Her*Ass*Down\> EVERYBODY DIDN'T GO TO BIG NAME SKOOLS THANK YOU VERY MUCH

\<Teddy Pinned*Her*Ass*Down\> WHAT U KNOW ABOUT FMU@2MUCH

\<MACK Truck\> I ALMOST WENT THERE TO PLAY FOOTBALL@TEDDY

\<Teddy Pinned*Her*Ass*Down\> WE DON'T HAVE A FOOTBALL TEAM

\<Da Ice Cream Man\> THAT'S WHY HE SAID ALMOST…LOL

\<2much4u\> THAT'S WHERE MY BEST FRIEND GOES TO SCHOOL…SHE PLAYS SOCCER

\<Teddy Pinned*Her*Ass*Down\> MUST BE A WHITE CHICK

\<Choco Latte\> SO YOU SAYIN BLACK WOMEN DON'T PLAY SOCCER?

\<Teddy Pinned*Her*Ass*Down\>THAT'S EXACTLY WHAT I'M SAYIN

\<2much4u\> SHE'S WHITE…BUT YOU CAN'T TELL HER SHE'S NOT BLACK

\<SoopaFly\> WOW!

\<Choco Latte\> THERE WENT THE POINT I WAS TRYNA MAKE…LOL

\<Teddy Pinned*Her*Ass*Down\>A BLACK WHITE CHICK…I KNOW THE FELLAZ ARE LOVIN HER RIGHT NOW…I THINK I NEED TO PAY MY SKOOL A VISIT..WHAT'S HER NAME?

\<2much4u\> LOL

\<Futurama\> Y'ALL KNOW TEDDY'S DEAD SERIOUS RIGHT?

\<Teddy Pinned*Her*Ass*Down\> I'M GLAD SOMEBODY KNOW CUZ THE LOOK ON MY FACE RIGHT NOW IS NOT SAYING LOL

\<2much4u\> LOL...IF UR NICE AND IT'S OK WITH HER...I MIGHT TELL YOU

\<Krystal Lyte\> TEDDY U KNOW U DON'T DATE WHITE GIRLZ

\<City Ave Diva\> LET ME AND CHOCO FIND OUT TEDDY BEEN ON THE OTHER SIDE OF THE FENCE

\<MACK Truck\>WE TAKE'EM BLACK WHITE PUERTO RICAN OR ASIAN

\<SoopaFly\> TELL'EM CUZIN...WE DON'T DISCRIMINATE!!!!!

\<Thyk2Def\> NO OFFENSE TO THE WHITE PEOPLE BUT ALL THE BROTHAS KNOW AIN'T NUTTIN LIKE A SISTA...ESPECIALLY ONE THAT'S THYK2DEF!!!!

\<Da Wife\> SOOPA I'VE SEEN SOME OF THE GIRLS U'VE DATED...YOU NEED TO DISCRIMINATE...LOL!

\<Futurama\>ROFL!

\<Optimo Pryme\> FOR THE FIRST TIME IN MY LIFE I'M SPEECHLESS!

\<Futurama\> WOW!

\<Teddy Pinned*Her*Ass*Down\> YO CUZIN...SHE STRAIGHT PLAYED YOU!

\<Da Ice Cream Man\> FUNNY THING IS...SHE'S RIGHT. WE ALL WENT TO HIGH SKOOL TOGETHER...LOL

\<Futurama\> DAMN CUZIN...I HATE TO DO THIS BUT I THINK THE TRIBE NEEDS TO BRING YOU UP ON CHARGES!!!!

\<Optimo Pryme\> CUZIN SOOPAFLY...YOU ARE BEING BROUGHT UP ON CHARGES FOR 8 COUNTS OF DATIN' UGLY CHICKS...HOW DO YOU PLEAD?

\<Da Wife\> 12 COUNTS!

\<SoopaFly\> NOT GUILTY!

\<Da Ice Cream Man\> HE'S LYING YOUR HONOR!

\<Choco Latte\> GIVE HIM THE CHAIR!

\<Thyk2Def\> SEND HIM TO TEXAS...WE'LL HANG HIS ASS!!!!

\<Optimo Pryme\> ORDER! ORDER IN THE COURTROOM!!!

\<Da Ice Cream Man\> I'LL HAVE A HAM AND CHEESE ON RYE...LOL!

\<Futurama\> ANY LAST WORDS BEFORE WE PAST JUDGEMENT?

\<SoopaFly\> ITS NOT ALWAYS ABOUT WHAT'S ON THE INSIDE, ITS ABOUT HOW PHAT DA ASS IS!

\<Optimo Pryme\> CUZIN SOOPAFLY WE SENTENCE YOU TO 5 DAYS AND FIVE NIGHTS WITH MISS MOET!

\<Thyk2Def\> WOW!

\<Da Ice Cream Man\> ANYTHING BUT THAT!

\<SoopaFly\> I'D RATHER HAVE THE CHAIR!!!!!

\<Futurama\> SINCE YOU PLEAD TEMPORARY INSANITY DUE TO A PHAT

ASS WE ARE GOING TO GIVE YOU TIME
SERVED!!!!! CASE DISMISSED!
<Da Wife> BOOOOOOOOOOOOOO!!!!!!!
<Thyk2Def> BOOOOOOOO!!! KILL THE
JUDGE!!!
<2much4u> U GUYS ARE TOO FUNNY! I'VE
REALLY BEEN ENJOYIN MYSELF
<Teddy Pinned*Her*Ass*Down> THAT'S
WHAT WE DO MA@2MUCH... WE JUST
LIKE TO HAVE FUN AND TALK SHYT!!!
<Da Ice Cream Man> SOME PEOPLE TALK
MORE SHIT THAN OTHERS
<Futurama> THIS IS TRUE!
<Teddy Pinned*Her*Ass*Down> SO WHAT
Y'ALL TRYNA SAY?
<Choco Latte> LOOKS LIKE THE GUILTY
WILL TELL ON HISELF EVERY TIME
<City Ave Diva> LOL!
<Futurama> AIIGHT Y'ALL....U KNOW THE
ROUTINE...I GOT SHIT TO DO IN DA
MORNIN'....I'LL SEE YOU IN DA FUTURE!
PEACE!
<Optimo Pryme>PEACE OUT CUZIN!
<2much4u> NITE NITE...SD@FUTURE
<MACK Truck> AIIGHT CUZIN
<City Ave Diva> BYE FUTURE BABY!
<Da Wife> BYE BABYDADDY!!!

Ivy laughed as he bid his cyber family
good night. No matter how his day went, he
could always count on them for a good laugh
because that's what just4kickz.com was, pure
comedy. It was amazing how a group of

people spread and scattered about like they were could be so close. It wasn't always good times because every now and again people forget that its not just the internet and real life situations get drug into the room — especially when people start meeting each other outside of the chat room.

Chapter 3

That next morning Iverson sat at his desk going over the final ideas for the video when an instant messenger box popped up. As he saw it popping up, he prayed that it wasn't XoticMami.

2much4u: Hello there, Ivy

Ivy_Dav: I c u found me…lol!

2much4u: it was hard but I'm a persistent person when I see something I like

Ivy_Dav: oh really?

2much4u: indeed…I like those guys in the room…they're pretty cool

Ivy_Dav: yeah…they're a good group of people when they wanna be

2much4u: after reading your profile I c y u just don't come out and tell people who u are

Ivy_Dav: I think its fun when people find out who I am…were u surprised?

2much4u: surprised is an understatement…I'm a huge fan of your label

Ivy_Dav: who's ur favorite artist?

2much4u: i would have to say Legacy…I'm really feelin' her sound

Ivy_Dav: I noticed on ur profile you didn't have a pic…do u have one u can send

2much4u: hold on a sec
2much4u is sending u a file!
Accept (Alt+A) or **Decline** (Alt+D)

Ivy clicked "Accept" and waited for the file to download. Upon completion of the download and opening of the file, he was amazed once again. The woman in the photo was another knock-out. It wasn't a full body shot but it was enough. 2much4u was a brown-skinned woman with her hair cut into a bob. She had coffee-brown eyes and a full, wide smile that displayed a beautiful set of white teeth. The top that she wore in the photo was low cut and revealed a nice set of full D-cups and a small but noticeable birthmark on the right side of her neck.

2much4u: did u get the pic?
Ivy_Dav: yeah I got it
2much4u: so what do you think? Am I sexy enuff to talk to a big time record label CEO?
Ivy_Dav: without a doubt...how old are u?
2much4u: how old do I look?
Ivy_Dav: let's not play that game
2much4u: I'm 23 and u?
Ivy_Dav: 29...where r u from
2much4u: I'm originally from VA but I moved here from St. Louis after I transferred to Spelmen from Mizzou

Ivy_Dav: so ur from Nellyville...no
doubt....listen, I have some business I
have
to take care of...hopefully, I can catch u
online later.
2much4u: ok...ttyl
Ivy_Dav: peace

Iverson closed his IM box and logged of.
For a split second, reality started to bite at him
causing him to assess the situation. The last
two encounters he had via the internet ended
in disaster. What would make this go around
any different from the other two? Though Ivy
was a bit skeptical, he still had that
adventurous streak in him and was willing to
give it another try. After those thoughts passed
through his head, he proceeded to continue
with his day's agenda.

Shanice pulled into Natalie's driveway
as she was coming out of the house. The two
Atlanta Diamonds were on their way to Phipps
Plaza for a day of shopping. When Natalie
went out, she was always dressed. Her
philosophy about that was that she never knew
whom she might run into. The day was
unusually warm for a December day. Natalie
wore cream colored skirt that was
complimented by a pair of light brown colored,
calf-length boots. On top of the skirt hung a
chocolate brown, angora top that hugged the
contour of her upper body. Her freshly done

micro-braids hung to her shoulders and her make-up was flawless. Shanice poked fun at Natalie as she entered the vehicle.

"Damn, Girl," she joshed. "We're goin' shoppin', not clubbin'."

"If anybody should know me by now, it should be you. You know I don't half-step when I'm in public."

"I know. You're the only woman that I know that has to put on make-up to check the mail." The two women laughed.

"You need to start dressin' a little better when we go out."

"And what's that supposed to mean?"

"It was brought to my attention that people have been asking whether we're a couple or not."

"Are you serious?"

"Yes I am and now I see why. Everywhere we go you always have on something that relates to basketball. We know you play ball. Besides, you are a beautiful girl and you have a nice body. You should let me give you a makeover."

"You tryin' to make a pass at me?" Natalie stopped and looked at Shanice with a confused look on her face.

Shanice tried to keep her composure but she couldn't. She had to laugh.

"This is how I've always been and no one has ever questioned my sexuality. I'm just the tomboy type."

"I know that but we're in Atlanta now. People see us together and I'm dressed like this and you're dressed like that, they automatically assume that we are apart of the *Rainbow Coalition.*"

"If that bothers you then maybe we shouldn't hangout."

"It's not like that. You're my girl and besides, I don't care what people think."

"It's obvious that you do because if you didn't, we wouldn't be having this conversation right now." Shanice's entire expression changed. She seemed to be offended by Natalie's remarks.

"You know what? I don't feel like going shopping anymore. I think I'm just going to go back home."

"Don't act like that. Listen, I'm sorry if I offended you."

"I'm cool. I just don't feel like going out right now."

"Okay," Natalie sighed. "Are we still workin' out tomorrow?"

"I'll call you."

Natalie exited Shanice's car and watched her distraught teammate drove off. She didn't mean any harm; she was only trying to be helpful. When it came to the questioning of someone's sexuality, it was a serious matter. Natalie walked back into her house and sat on the couch and laid her head back. An array of thoughts ran through her head as she watched the ceiling fan slowly spin around and around.

Natalie sat on the couch for about 30 minutes before dragging herself upstairs. She could not believe that she offended her best friend the way she did. Though she was only trying to help, her words got taken the wrong way. After she got upstairs she went into her library to choose a book to read. Her collection was so large that it took her about fifteen minutes to decide on something to read. "Good Peoples by Marcus Major," she said to herself. "I haven't read this one in a minute."

The Atlanta Diamond stretched out on the over-stuffed, cream couch that was in her library. About twenty minutes into her reading, she looked over the top of the book and saw her computer. As she stared at the screensaver, the only thing she could hear was the commercial for EbonyWorld.com. She placed her bookmark at her stopping point and tossed the book at her feet onto the couch. Natalie lifted herself off of the couch and repositioned in front of the computer. With a touch of the mouse, the screensaver went away exposing her desktop icons. She double-clicked on the Internet Explorer icon and waited for the web browser to emerge.

In the address bar she typed: *ebonyworld.com*. When the page opened, their

homepage was a real eye catcher. The
background looked like outer space with stars
everywhere. There was a place for members to
log in and there was a place for potential
members to take a virtual tour. Natalie clicked
on the tour. After about ten minutes of
browsing, Natalie decided to create her profile.
Being that she was a professional athlete, she
wanted to be discreet as possible. She began to
fill in the necessary fields.

First Name:	Natalia
Last Name:	Simone
Age:	26
Sex:	Female
City:	Atlanta
State:	GA
Occupation:	H.S. Teacher
Salary:	25,000-30,000
DOB:	June 9, 1978
Marital Status:	Single
Sexual Orientation:	Heterosexual
Children:	Someday
Education:	College Grad/BA
School:	Univ. of Tennessee
Race:	African American
Religion:	Holiness Church
Hobbies:	Physical Fitness, Shopping, Clubs
Interests:	Entertainment, Sports, Cultural Events, Fine Arts,

Performing Arts,
Education and
Politics

After all of the fields had been filled in she was taken to another page.

Screen ID: Dymond4eva
Password: ********
Confirm Password: ********

Natalie chose the screen ID "dymond4eva" because no matter how untruthful she was in the cyber world, she would always be Natalie Simms, Atlanta Diamond. From that screen, she was lead to the next page. This was the page where she had to write a few words about herself. She sat and stared blankly into the screen. She was never good at that type of thing. Nat ticked away at the keyboard until she came up with her profile essay. It read:

WHAT'S UP EBONY WORLD? THIS IS YA GIRL, **DYMOND4EVA**. LIKE MANY WOMEN, I'M FED UP WITH THE DATING GAME. I'M NOT LOOKING FOR A "BED BUDDY" OR A "CUTFRIEND." I'M LOOKING TO MEET INTERESTING MEN BETWEEN THE AGES OF 25 & 35. HE MUST HAVE HIS LIFE TOGETHER. NO PLAYERS, WANNABE PIMPS AND NO BABY MAMA DRAMA. NOT TRYING TO SOUND

SHALLOW BUT YOU HAVE TO BE
ATTRACTIVE. I'M JUST KEEPING IT REAL. I
LIKE MY MEN TO BE SIX FEET AND ABOVE
WITH AN ATHLETIC BUILD. HE MUST BE
WELL GROOMED AND CLEAN-CUT (IF
YOU HAVE BRAIDS OR DREADS THEY
BETTER BE WELL MAINTAINED) WITH A
KEEN FASHION SENSE. SO IF YOU THINK
YOU FIT THE DESCRIPTION OR YOU
THINK YOU'RE A GUY THAT I MIGHT LIKE
AND WANT TO GET TO KNOW ME, HIT ME
UP. ONE LOVE!

P.S. PHOTO AVAILABLE UPON REQUEST

Once her profile was completed and she
decided against posting a photo of herself,
Natalie began to browse around to see what
kind of men hung out on Ebony World. The
first profiles she came across weren't the best
of profiles — not with screen names like
9inchzopleasure, HotlantaPimpin, or
Lickemlow. She wanted to stop but she was
actually becoming humored by some of the
things she saw.

After passing by countless zeros, she
landed on a page that caught her eye. The male
in the picture was a light brown complexioned
brother with shoulder-length dreadlocks
sitting in a leather office chair behind a desk.
The screen ID read: Ivy_Dav. It was Iverson.
Because his screen ID was normal and the fact

that she found him to be attractive, she took time and read his page. On Ivy's page, he did state that he owned his own record label but he didn't over glorify it. His sincerity was the thing that held her attention. The thing that grabbed her was the part of his profile that said that he was looking for *an around the way girl* — someone that was down to earth, a lady at all times but wasn't afraid to let her hair down and kick it like one of the fellas.

Natalie saw his contact information at the bottom of his profile but was hesitant. Instead of contacting him, she saved him to her hot list and wrote down his IM information. For about an hour she surfed through the website but kept returning to Iverson's page.

Chapter 4

Three hours had passed and Natalie was still on the computer. The phone rang and broke her trance. It was Shanice.

"Hello?" Natalie answered as she logged off of Ebony World.

"Hey girl. What you up to?"

"Just messin' around on this computer." She got up from the computer and walked into her bedroom. "What you doin'?"

"I was thinking about goin' out but I don't know."

"Listen, Shanice. About earlier today…"

"Forget about it," she replied cutting Natalie off. "I know you were just looking out for me. I never told you this but I believe the way I carry myself is the reason why I'm single. I look like the rest of the kit-kat girls runnin' around the ATL. That's probably why guys don't approach me. It was different in high school and college. The guys knew I played ball. Down here, if they've never been to a game or saw me on TV, they wouldn't know."

"Like I tried to tell you today, you are a beautiful girl and every now and then you need to let these men know that." There was a brief pause. "You down for a girl's night at my house?"

"What you got in mind?"

"You call Jasmine and I'll call Alicia and we can chill out at my house."

"Alicia?"

"Yeah, Dré s wife."

"Since when y'all start hangin' out?"

"We went to the Silver Dollar the other night."

"The Silver Dollar. Why didn't you call me?

"My bad, girl. It was kinda a last minute thing."

"Oh," Natalie sensed a hint of jealousy in Shanice's voice.

"Anyway, call Jasmine and I'll see y'all in a lil' while."

"Okay."

Natalie hung up the phone and went down stairs to put the wine on ice and prepare some stuff for their *Gyrlz Night*. As she was slicing cheese for the crackers, she picked up the phone to call Alicia. After about three rings, a male voice answered.

"Smooth Dré!" Natalie greeted as she pulled the champagne bucket from under the counter. "Is Alicia around?"

"May I ask who's calling?"

"That's a damn shame. I get into a fight in Houston in front of you and…"

"What's up, Nat?" he said with surprise.

"Nothin'. Me and a couple of the girls are having a girls night and I wanted to invite Alicia."

"One of them niggaz ain't shit, Waiting to Exhale parties, huh?"

"André Marshall! Stop that and put your wife on the phone."

"Alright but don't y'all be tryin' to corrupt my wife."

"If you haven't already corrupted her, she's fair game."

"Hold on," he laughed and pulled the phone away from his mouth. "Alicia! Bernadine, I mean Natalie is on the phone."

"You got jokes." Natalie laughed. "How's Taylor?"

"Bad as hell."

"Just like her Daddy."

"I got it, boo. Hang up. Hey girl. What's up?"

"I wanted to…"

"Hold on, Natalie. André Marcellus Marshall."

"Huh?" he answered.

"Hang up the phone."

"My bad…<click>"

"What were you sayin'?"

"Me and a couple of my teammates are getting ready to have a girls night at my house and I wanted you to come. I'm getting ready to give my best friend a complete overhaul and I need all the help I can get. You down?"

"Let me ask my husband. You know how he can be sometimes."

"I know. He won't let Taylor be the only baby in the house." They laughed.

"Hold on a minute."

Alicia put the phone down and called for André. He came into the bedroom and she asked him if he would be okay with her to step out for a couple of hours.

"Natalie? Everything is good. I'll see you in a minute. Do I need to bring anything?"

"Ice Cream…Butter Pecan and Chocolate Chip Cookie Dough."

"Ben & Jerry's?"

"Did you have to ask?"

"See you in a bit."

After the meeting with the Sunz and Shakeem was over, Iverson returned to his office to see if he could catch **2much4u** online. He logged on to his instant messenger but she was not there. Seeing that there was no one that he really wanted to talk to online at the time, he minimized his instant messenger and proceeded to do a little work. He tried to concentrate but could not help but think about someone in particular. Her name was Candace — known to the cyber world as **Unique_Pleazures**.

Iverson met Candace online about two years ago. The two of them were new to Internet dating. Candace and Ivy would talk for hours at a time about any and everything. After about three months of friendly conversations, via the Internet and over the phone, they decided to meet. Ivy paid for her to fly from Miami to Atlanta. When Iverson saw Candace for the first time, it was something about her that he could not explain. Candace wasn't a drop-dead, gorgeous woman but she wasn't unattractive. She reminded him of a toned down version of Aaliyah. The thing that he liked the most about her was the fact that she was an ordinary girl. Being submerged in the music industry, Ivy came across all types of exotic women trying to do everything they could to get a little piece of fame.

From that first meeting, Candace and Iverson found that there was something between them that drew them closer. Before long, Iverson was ready to move her from Miami to Atlanta and in with him. When she got there, they seemed to be the perfect couple. Iverson took care of her as she chased her modeling dreams. Any given day or night, Candace would pop up at the studio just to see how her man was doing. Things were great in the beginning. Somewhere along the way, things changed. There was a lot of hoopla that came out of their relationship. The media soon got involved and ultimately caused the demise of the union between Ivy_Dav and Unique_Pleazures.

Because of the nature of the music industry, Candace became very insecure. It was hard for her to stomach seeing Iverson in videos with all types of women surrounding him. The relationship's closing point came when Future Records signed Latino lyricist and R&B vocalist, Mysterio. It wasn't a big deal until Mysterio started his tour of Latin America. Once Ivy left town, the media was all over the tour. Mysterio's success caught the attention of MTV, BET and a couple of Spanish networks — Telemundo and Univision.

Every time anything was mentioned about Mysterio and they would show footage from a performance or a club appearance, there was always a host of women intertwined with the entourage. Though Ivy was 100% faithful to Candace, it was hard for her to cope with seeing him with other women — even if it was for promotional purposes. Things would not have been so bad if Iverson would have continued his nightly calls.

Once the tour got into it's eighth stop, Iverson stopped calling. When she tried to call him, she kept getting his voicemail or he didn't have time to talk. The final breaking point came the night she was flipping through channels and passed by one of the Spanish channels and saw Mysterio. Univision was doing an interview with the Latino artist at a hotel in the Dominican Republic. When they went into a full shot of the entire crew, there he was. Iverson Davenport was lying on his stomach in a bed with a barely dressed, Hispanic woman sitting on his back massaging his shoulders. That's all she could take.

At the time, Candace and Ivy were living together. In a fit of rage Candace turned on all of the water in the house and plugged all of the drains and left his College Park condominium to flood. Two days later Ivy received a call from the complex. They called to inform him that his place had been flooded. Iverson caught the first plane back to Atlanta to find his condo ruined and Candace gone— without a word, "Dear John Letter," or a clue. After Candace he left the Internet alone for awhile.

"Yo, Ivy!" T-Bizzy called from the door. Ivy snapped out of his trance. "You aight?"

"Yeah, I'm straight. I was just thinkin' about a few things."

"You was thinkin' about Candace again. Weren't you?"

"Nah. What makes you think that?"

"The only time you ever zoned out was when you thought about her. What's the deal?" T-Bizzy walked in and sat on the couch in Ivy's office.

"I don't know, man. It's been a couple of years since she left and it's still a hard pill to swallow."

"How so?"

"The way she left. What would make a woman fuck a nigga's shit up and just bounce? I gave that girl everything and she repays me like that."

"I don't know what to tell you, bruh. Sounds like some Twilight Zone type shit."

"If I could just find out why, maybe then I could be at ease."

"Be careful what you wish for." Iverson looked at Ty with a very puzzled look on his face. "Anyway, forget about it. Me, Will and KD are about to go to Dave and Buster's. You down?"

"Maybe later. Let me get my head straight."

"Come on man. You been stressing over Candace for too long now. It's over and done. Look at you. Sittin' there lookin' like a sad ass puppy. That's not how a CEO should be."

"True," Iverson took a long pause. "But I'm still a human being."

"I feel you but before I let you bring my mood down, I'ma be out. I'll be at Dave and Buster's. I'll holla." TyQuan shot Ivy the deuces and left.

Iverson swiveled around in his chair and blankly stared at his computer screen as the Future Records logo bounced around on the screen. Once again, the tone of someone trying to summon him through the instant messenger broke his train of thought.

> **2much4u**: Ivy....u there
> **Ivy_Dav**: WZUP?
> **2much4u**: nothing much...just got back home. U?
> **Ivy_Dav**: about to leave the office...might go to D&B's wit da fellaz
> **2much4u**: me and my girlz were thinking about goin out there tonite
> **Ivy_Dav**: if you go I'll go
> **2much4u**: maybe....anyway...I just wanted to holla at you for a minute. I'm about to chill out for a while.
> **Ivy_Dav**: iight....holla at ya boy!

Iverson logged off and left the office. As he pulled out of the parking lot he received a message on his 2-way. It was T-Bizzy. The message read:

> IVY,
>
> THE CHICKENS ARE
> DEFINITLEY CLUCKIN' OUT HERE!
>
> T-BIZZY

He tossed the idea around in his head for about fifteen minutes but decided against it and went home.

"Ladies," Natalie held her wine glass in the air. "I would like to propose a toast." The other three women held their glasses in the air. "To the independent women in this room..."

"That don't need a man for shit...," Jasmine added.

Jasmine was back up point guard behind Natalie. She was around five feet, four inches with a slim build. All the guys said that she reminded them of a brown-skinned version of Dawn Staley. During the season, Jasmine wore cornrows but since it was the off-season, she let her shoulder length, black hair hang long and straight. She had the biggest and brightest round eyes and pair of full lips. Jasmine was a lot like Natalie in the personality department especially when it came to having a good time.

"I can toast to the independence," Alicia started. "But I have a good man."

"Yeah, we all know about Super Dré," Shanice mumbled.

"Excuse me?" Alicia moved her hair from over her ear. There was an ill vibe in the air coming from Shanice towards Alicia. Natalie picked up on it and did her best to divert the situation.

"To the Ladies..." They all clanged their glasses together.

"Now, its time to get down to the reason we came here tonight...Project Shanice. I gotta tell you, this is not going to be an easy task so ladies, if you're weak at heart, you might want to leave now." After that being said, Natalie pulled Shanice's scarf from around her hair and exposed a head full of thick, untamed hair.

"Damn, girl," Jasmine laughed. "I just saw a flock of birds fly out the back that nest." The ladies laughed.

"Not everybody can put chemicals in their hair or wear a weave." In saying that, Shanice looked directly at Alicia.

Feeling that the comment was aimed at her, Alicia replied. "I'm sorry. I wouldn't know any thing about that. This is all me."

"Okay," Natalie said trying to deflate the situation. "First thing we gotta do is relax this monster."

After the relaxer was applied and time had passed, the four women went into the kitchen to wash Shanice's hair. Alicia didn't know Jasmine and Shanice before that night. She was kind of off to the side. Alicia pulled herself up onto the counter by the sink and sipped her wine. From under the water, Shanice kept throwing little comments towards Alicia.

"So Alicia," echoed out of the sink from Shanice. "How's Dré treatin' you these days."

"Everything is absolutely wonderful."

"If my man was a big time executive at a TV network, I'd have to apply for a job just to keep my eyes on him." Jasmine instigated.

"I trust my husband."

"So naïve," Shanice exclaimed. "A man is a man and you can't trust'em as far as you can see'em."

Natalie knew where Shanice was getting ready to take the conversation so she pulled her hair as she washed to get her to stop.

"What do you mean naïve?" she inquired.

"Can we change the subject please?" Natalie asked.

"Its cool, Nat. I want to know what Shanice means by saying I'm naïve."

"How soon we forget about your man's escapades before you got to Atlanta. Do the names Estacia Morgan or Karen Union ring a bell?" Alicia paused for a minute then slid down off of the counter and walked back into the living room.

"What the hell is wrong with you?" Natalie asked Shanice as she stopped washing her hair. "Alicia hasn't done anything to you. Why you have to bring her man in to this? She knows André's past. Its bad enough everything happened how it did. Alicia's been through a lot and still she loves her man. Don't hate on her because you don't have one." Natalie stormed out of the kitchen into the living room where Alicia was sitting on the couch gathering her things to leave.

"Alicia wait," Natalie pleaded.

"I didn't come over here for this. She's your girl but she don't know me like that to be broadcasting my business."

"I know and I'm sorry. It's my fault. I told her about everything. I should have never said anything."

"I don't blame you. I'm a woman and I know how we are with our best friends."

"Shanice has been through a lot and she's still a little upset that things between André and I turned out like they did. That's all."

"That's one of the reasons I came over here tonight. You and I met through Dré and you and Dré are good friends. I don't have problem with that. I used to but I'm okay now. I just figured that you and I could be friends as well."

"I feel the same way but with Shanice it's different." As that statement came out of Natalie's mouth, Shanice walked into the room, unnoticed.

"Outside of her teammates, I'm the only true friend that she has and sometimes I don't know why I'm her friend considering some of the things she's put me through."

"I don't know either," Shanice replied as she threw the towel that was around her hair onto the couch.

"I was there for you when shit went foul with Dré and I was there for you when Des left you. After hearing that bullshit you just said, I see why Desmond left. You don't know how to appreciate having someone in your life that cares about your well-being. You let Dré come between you and Des and now you're letting this bitch come between us." Shanice snatched her scarf from the back of the couch and left.

"What just happened?" Jasmine asked as she walked into the room.

"To tell you the truth," Natalie began with a look of confusion on her face. "I couldn't tell you."

"I think I'm going to call it a night," Alicia sighed as she put her jacket on. "This has been one hellavah night."

"Come on, Alicia. We still got wine and we still got Ben and Jerry." Natalie turned to the doorway where Jasmine was standing. "You still down?"

Jasmine walked over to the couch, grabbed her glass and filled it up again. After a brief pause and a little more convincing, Alicia took her coat off and joined the other two women on the couch. The three began to laugh and talk about a whole lot of everything.

Futurama has entered the room

<Krystal Lyte> I don't give a shit who u r and where ur from. Bring dat shit to VA!

<Da Ice Cream Man> teddy I told u not to start...lol!

<Teddy Pinned*Her*Ass*Down> LMAO!

<City Ave Diva> TEDDY YOU KNOW U WRONG

<Da Wife> BITCH PLEASE! I WOULDN'T WASTE MY TIME COMING TO VA TO WHOOP YO TRICK ASS!

<Futurama> WTF? WHAT IN THE HELL IS GOIN ON IN HERE???

<Got'em Hatin> ITS TEDDY'S FAULT

<Thyk2Def> SOMEBODY SAID THAT SOOPAFLY AND KRYSTAL BEEN MESSIN AROUND

<Krystal Lyte> FUKKIN WHORE!!!!!

<Futurama> SO????

<Got'em Hatin> U KNOW WIFE AND SOOPA SUPPOSED TO BE KICKIN IT

<Futurama> SINCE WHEN??

<Choco Latte> SINCE LAST NIGHT AFTER U LEFT...LOL!

<Da Ice Cream Man> lol!

<Da Wife> I KNOW THIS BITCH DID NOT JUST CALL ME A WHORE

<Futurama> R U SERIOUS?

<Teddy Pinned*Her*Ass*Down> CUZIN...THIS IS WHAT HAPPENED...LAST NIGHT I TOLD ALL THE FELLAZ TO CLAIM THEM A WIFEY AND SETTLE DOWN AND YES WIFE SHE CALLED U A WHORE

<City Ave Diva> TEDDY ALWAYS STARTIN SHIT SO HE CAN HAVE SOMETHIN TO CLOWN ABOUT

<***Mami*Dearest***> THAT'S HOW TEDDY IS...EVERYBODY SHOULD KNOW THAT BY NOW...LEAVE MY BABY ALONE!

<Teddy Pinned*Her*Ass*Down> MACK TOOK DIVA, OPTIMO TOOK THYK, ICE CREAM TOOK MOET(LOL), I CHOSE CHOCO AND NOW THE ONLY TWO TRIBAL MEMBERS WITHOUT A WIFEY IS U AND B-BALLER

<Da Ice Cream Man> screw u teddy...mang...lol!

<Futurama> IS TEDDY SERIOUS@ANYBODY

<City Ave Diva> THAT'S WHAT HAPPENED@FUTURE

<Futurama>SO HOW DID IT GET TO THIS POINT?

<Thyk2Def>TEDDY OPENED HIS BIG MOUTH!

<Choco Latte> STOP BLAMIN THIS ON MY BABY! TEDDY DID NOTHIN' WRONG!

<Teddy Pinned*Her*Ass*Down> U TELL'EM BOO! SOME CHICK THAT WAS IN HERE EARLIER SAID THAT SOOPA AND KRYSTAL WENT INTO A PRIVATE ROOM

<Da Ice Cream Man> in teddy's defense...this is a public chat room...so if u don't want ur business in here don't bring it in here

<Teddy Pinned*Her*Ass*Down> THANK U@ICE CREAM...I JUST REPEATED WHAT WAS SAID

<Choco Latte> SO WHO U GONNA MAKE UR WIFEY@FUTURE

<Futurama> LOOKS LIKE ALL THE GOOD ONES R GONE...LOL

<MACK Truck> U KNO WE HAD TO GETT'EM B4 U CUZIN...US MERE PEASANTS AIN'T GOT CHIPS LIKE U...LOL

<Teddy Pinned*Her*Ass*Down> I GOT ONE 4 U FUTURE...2MUCH4U

<City Ave Diva> YEAH FUTURE...SHE SEEMS COOL..AND SHE'S IN THE ATL

<Futurama> SPEAKING OF WHICH...HAS ANYBODY SEEN HER TONITE?

<MACK Truck>NOT YET CUZIN BUT IT IS STILL EARLY

<Thyk2Def> HAS SHE FOUND OUT WHO U R YET@FUTURE

<Futurama> YEAH...SHE FIGURED IT OUT LAST NIGHT

<Teddy Pinned*Her*Ass*Down> THEN ITS ALL GRAVY BABY... SHE'LL BE UP IN YO ASS LIKE A CHEAP THONG...LOL!

<Da Ice Cream Man> lol!

Optimo Pryme has entered the room

Lady Get Some has entered the room

Mr.SexxyB-Baller has entered the room

<Optimo Pryme> ****TAKING A DEEP BREATH*** LELELELELELELELELE!!!!

<Futurama> LELELELELELELE!!!!!!!!!!!!!!!!!!!!!!!!!!11

<Choco Latte> LELELELELELELELELELE!

<Got'em Hatin> LELELELELELEL!!!!!

\<City Ave Diva\>
LELELELELELELELELLELE!!!111!!!
\<Mr.SexxyB-Baller\>LELELELE!!!!
\<Thyk2Def\> LELELELELELELELE!!!!
\<Da Wife\> LELELELELE!
\<Optimo Pryme\> WHAT IT DO
E'RYBODY!!!!!!
\<Thyk2Def\> HEY HUSBAND!!!!
\<City Ave Diva\> HEY OPTIMO BABY
\<Optimo Pryme\> WHAT'S UP WIFEY@THYK
\<Optimo Pryme\>WHAT'S GOOD MA@DIVA
\<***Mami*Dearest***\> OPTIMO!!!!!
\<Mr.SexxyB-Baller\> WHAT'S ALL THIS
HUSBAND AND WIFE TALK?
\<City Ave Diva\>LOG INTO UR EW IM AND
I'LL TELL U ABOUT IT@SEXXY
SlicK has entered the room
\<Futurama\> OH YEAH B4 I FORGET...MY
BOY IS HAVING A BIRTHDAY PARTY
TOMORROW NIGHT IN ATLANTA@ CLUB
BLAZE IN BUCKHEAD
\<Choco Latte\> WHO'S YA BOY?
\<Futurama\> CHRIS
\<Teddy Pinned*Her*Ass*Down\> BRB
\<Choco Latte\> HB
\<Thyk2Def\> WHO IS CHRIS??
\<Futurama\> OH YEAH THAT IS
RIGHT...Y'ALL CALL HIM
LUDACRIS...LOL!
\<Got'em Hatin\> HOW U WAIT UNTIL THE
DAY B4 TO TELL SOMEBODY ABOUT A
PARTY IN ATLANTA...U ACK LIKE WE

GOT MONEY TO JUST BE HOPPIN ON A
PLANE AND COMIN TO ATLANTA
<Futurama> I WAS JUST TELLIN Y'ALL
SINCE Y'ALL SAY I DON'T TELL Y'ALL
WHAT DA GOINZ ONZ IS IN ATLANTAZ
<MACK Truck> CUZIN...I'M PULLIN A
LOAD THROUGH THERE TOMORROW...I
MIGHT JUST BE ABLE TO STOP THROUGH
<Futurama> IF U COME THROUGH JUST
HIT ME...I'LL SEND U THE CELL#
<Choco Latte> CAN I GET THE CELL#
TOO???
<Da Ice Cream Man> teddy gon get u
<Choco Latte> MIND YA BUSINESS@ICE
CREAM
<Futurama> U KNOW DA
DRILL@CHOCO...ONLY IF UR COMIN TO
ATLANTA
<Da Ice Cream Man> I'm telling...lol!
<Futurama> R U COMING TO ATLANTA?
NO UR NOT...LOL!
<Choco Latte> U DON'T KNOW THAT...I
MIGHT
<Futurama> LOL!
<Choco Latte> SHEEEDUP!@ICE CREAM
<Teddy Pinned*Her*Ass*Down> I'M
BACK...WHAT I MISS?
<Futurama> OK SINCE YOU SAY I DON'T
GIVE YOU ANY NOTICE IN
ADVANCE...I'M HAVING THE OFFICIAL
ALBUM RELEASE FOR MY NEW GROUP
THE SOUTHERN SUNZ IN JANUARY...THE
EXACT DATE IS TBA

<Choco Latte> U DIDN'T MISS NOTHIN BUT I MISSED U BABY!

<Thyk2Def> **********VOMIT********

<Choco Latte> STOP HATIN@THYK...LOL!

<Da Ice Cream Man>u missed ur wife hittin on ur cuzin

<Teddy Pinned*Her*Ass*Down> WHAT!!!!! WHICH CUZIN??? YO OPTIMO ITS POPPIN!

<Optimo Pryme>****LOOKIN AROUND**** WHO DAT IZ CUZIN!!!!

<Choco Latte> STOP STARTIN TROUBLE ICE CREAM

<Da Ice Cream Man> I was just jokin teddy

<Optimo Pryme> ***PUTTIN THE CHOPPA BACK ON SAFETY*** I THOUGHT I HAD TO PUT A FEW HOLES IN A NIGGA

<City Ave Diva> TEDDY DON'T NOBODY WANT YOU BUT CHOCO...LOL!

<Thyk2Def> FUTURE WAS TELLIN US ABOUT LUDACRIS'S PARTY IN ATLANTA TOMORROW NIGHT

<Teddy Pinned*Her*Ass*Down> HOW IN DA HELL YOU WAIT TIL THE NIGHT BEFORE TO TELL SOMEBODY ABOUT A PARTY

<City Ave Diva> SAME THING WE SAID

<Futurama> ANYWAY...I GOTTA BE OUT...Y'ALL BE EASY AND I'LL HOLLA ON THE FLIPSIDE...PEACE

<Optimo Pryme> PEACE OUT HOMIE!

<City Ave Diva> NITE FUTURE BABY

<Thyk2Def> NITE NITE...SD

<Da Ice Cream Man> lata future

<Got'em Hatin> BYE FUTURE

Chapter 5

It was a Saturday night and the ATL was in full swing. Iverson was at his house getting prepared for the night's events. He stood in one of his huge walk-in closets trying to decide what he wanted to wear for the evening. After about twenty-five minutes of pulling outfit after outfit, he decided. Ivy selected a black, Sean John velour suit with the matching black and white Timberland boots to match. Atop his dreads, that he had pulled under a stocking cap, sat a black Atlanta Braves baseball cap. He was ready to hit Club Blaze for a party hosted by Ludacris and the rest of Disturbing the Peace.

As he walked past his study/office, he heard the familiar chime of someone summoning him through the instant messenger. He tried to walk past it but his curiosity wouldn't let him. Ivy walked to the computer and shook the mouse to make the screen saver go away. It was **2much4u** trying to get his attention.

Ivy_Dav: What's the deal? I missed u last nite
2much4u: I had to work late…what's up wit u?
Ivy_Dav: I was on my way out

2much4u: where to?
Ivy_Dav: Club Blaze to Luda's party
2much4u: fo real?
Ivy_Dav: yup…y don't you and a couple of ya girls come out and chill?
2much4u: I might just do that
Ivy_Dav: no doubt….by the way…what's ya name?
2much4u: Shayla
Ivy_Dav: last name?
2much4u: why?
Ivy_Dav: If you and ya girls comin' I gotta put u on the list. So what's ya last name and how many girls you bringin?
2much4u: Stallings and I'll have 3 other girls with me…if I come
Ivy_Dav: iight….see you later.

Iverson minimized his instant messenger and left for the club. When he arrived at Club Blaze there was a line around the building. He pulled his midnight blue, Chrysler 300C, with cream leather interior that was sitting on 22" chrome spinners to the front of the club for valet parking. As he stepped onto the curb he saw T-Bizzy, Will and KD talking to three females that were standing in line.

"What's the deal?" Ivy called to his boys.

"There he go! It's da man right chea'!" T-Bizzy shouted and pointed. "The man behind Future."

"What up, son?" he greeted as he dapped up his crew.

"Why y'all still out here?"

"I was just tellin' these young ladies about the upcoming video and I think they got what it take to be down wit Future."

"You must be Ivy," said a short, brown-skinned girl wearing a black mini-skirt, red tube top and a pair of six-inch stilettos. "T-Bizzy was tellin' us that you were the man to talk to about the video."

"You gotta talk to Chyna over at Too Hot. All the females in the video come through her. Now if you excuse us, we got some bottles to pop. See you inside."

The four men walked towards the entrance.

"T, you gotta stop tellin' girls I can put'em in videos."

"But you can."

"I know that and you know that but they don't need to know that."

Ivy, T-Bizzy, Will and KD stepped through the velvet rope and into club. Club Blaze was where all of the A-town stars hosted parties or just went to kick it. When you walk past the girl in the booth and past the coat check girl, you had to walk down a long hall and through another door. To the left was a bar surrounded by men and women. Directly in front of the door about 100 feet into the club was the main, hardwood dance floor that you had to walk down about seven steps to get to. In the middle of the dance floor was a platform that was reserved for only the sexiest women to dance — no ducks and no dudes. On the far back wall was the DJ booth that over-looked the dance floor. Further back on the left was a smaller bar and to the right of the dance floor was another dance area. Behind that dance floor were large booths that were enclosed by black sheer drapes. Those were the VIP booths that were usually occupied by the celebrities. In front of each booth was about 10 feet of space and there was a post for the bouncer and more velvet ropes.

The crew of Future Records took their place in their VIP booth and posted. They had the bouncer to pull the curtain back so they could see out into the club. As soon as the women found out who they were, they began to act like groupies starving to touch status. Will, KD and T-Bizzy wanted all the women they could fit into the VIP but Ivy told them to chill.

"Ivy," T-Bizzy began. "This is gay. Four dudes sittin' on couches and the only bitch we got is Cristal."

"Yeah," KD cosigned. "This is gay."

"Beavis and Buckhead, do me a favor. Sit back, relax, chill and stop callin' women bitches. I'm waitin' on somebody."

"Somebody for you. What about us?" Will asked.

"I met this girl named Shayla and she supposed to be comin' through with some friends."

"Hold up," T interrupted. "Where did you meet her?"

"Online." Will, KD and T-Bizzy busted out with laughter. "What the fuck is so funny?"

"The Internet?" T-Bizzy laughed "Come on, man."

"Just chill."

Natalie sat alone again on a Saturday night. After their girl's night, Shanice and Natalie were not speaking to each other. She tried to call Jasmine but she had already left for Club Blaze. Natalie was about to go crazy but she didn't want to go out by herself. A notion led her to give Alicia a call.

"Hey girl," Natalie greeted.

"What's up with you tonight?"

"Sittin' in this house bored as hell."

"Where's Dré?"

"Him, Zack, Troy and Smoke went out."

"They probably went to J-Rock's nasty lil' booty house."

"Nah. They went to Classics."

"So you got Taylor."

"Nope. She's with her Godmother Vanessa. What about you?"

"Debatin' whether or not I'm going to Ludacris's party at Club Blaze."

"You wanna go?"

"Why not. Who's driving me or you?"

"You plannin' to drink?"

"Yeah. Why?"

"I'll drive. I know you Miss Grand Mariner and Hennessy. I'll be there in about an hour."

"See you in a minute."

Natalie hung up the phone and jumped in the shower. While in the shower, she decided that she was going to cleanse herself of the foolishness between her and Shanice. She felt that if she wanted to act like a high school girl because she and Alicia were becoming good friends then it was her loss. Life was too short to dwell on bullshit.

After her shower, the Atlanta Diamond slid into a black, satin and lace thong and bra set by Victoria's Secret. In nothing but her undergarments she stood in her closet sifting through dresses, skirts and blouses. Natalie chose a hip hugging, black and white, floral print skirt. The skirt was high on the left side extending to her mid thigh while the rest of the skirt hung down just below her knee on the right side. Because the bra to the set was lace, she chose a sheer, black top that also clung to the contour of her upper body. Once the outfit was to her satisfaction, she walked into an adjoining closet. In that closet was nothing but shoes for miles sorted by style and color. The ensemble Nat was wearing screamed for a pair of heels. She looked and looked until she found the perfect pair. After about ten minutes of searching she found the perfect pair. Ironically, they were the same shoes that she wore the first time she and André went out to dinner.

Just as Natalie was finishing her make-up, she heard the horn of André's Escalade. Alicia was outside waiting for her. She put the final touches on her make-up and grabbed her short, black leather jacket. The two women exchanged pleasantries and were off to blaze the night away at Atlanta's hottest nightspot.

When the two divas arrived at Club Blaze the wolves began to swarm. They heard everything from "Aye, Shawty" to "What's up, Ma?" Natalie used her Atlanta Diamond pull to get them into the club without having to stand in line. The first stop was the bar for Hennessy and Coke for Natalie and a Grey Goose Cosmopolitan for Alicia. After the women acquired their drinks they worked their way around the club to find a table. As they walked, they passed by the VIP section where Ivy and his crew were.

"Yo," Ivy nudged TyQuan. "Ain't that ol' girl that from the Dollar?"

"Where?" T-Bizzy looked up and spotted Alicia and Natalie.

"Yeah that's her." T-Bizzy got up and walked out of the VIP and walked to the velvet rope.

"Excuse me ladies." Natalie and Alicia kept walking as the fellas laughed once again at T-Bizzy. "I'ma holla at you later then."

"Damn, T. Give up." Ivy laughed as Ty walked back in the booth and picked his glass up. "That's twice."

"I got this."

"Yeah right." Will gestured.

While the four sat and laughed, they notice four women step up to the rope — three stallions and one not so stallion. One of the women was a Latina with long brown hair highlighted with blonde streaks. She was around 5'0" with a body like J to the L-O. She even had the small mole on her right cheek. Another one of the women was what is described as *sexy, dark chocolate*. She had a smooth, dark complexion with large brown eyes. Her hair was in spiral curls that came down to her shoulders. Lady number three was a plain Jane. There was nothing spectacular about her looks but she wasn't an unattractive girl. She was light-skinned with grey eyes and had a body that would make a wino stop drinking and get his life together.

Her hair was short and flipped in the back. The fourth member of the quartet was the one that would be best fit to be the *bodyguard* of the crew. She was the Sista Big Boned of the crew. She had a pretty face and she was dressed nice but she was just slightly overweight. With chinky, brown eyes and a cute, button nose she wore her weight well. Her hair was in braids that were pulled back into a ponytail.

"Do you know them?" Ivy asked T-Bizzy

"I was about to ask you the same thing."

"They know somebody because dude's let'em in."Ivy looked at Will and KD but neither of them confirmed their identities.

"What's up, ladies?"

"We're looking for Ivy," explained the Latina with a thick Spanish accent.

"I'm Ivy," he introduced as the *bodyguard* stepped forward.

"I'm Shayla," she responded as she extended her hand. "Nice to finally meet you."

"Likewise." Ivy shook her hand in disbelief. This was not the female in the picture.

"This is Sonja," she introduced the Latina. "That's Alexis (the plain Jane) and this is Kawanna."

"Excuse us for a minute," T-Bizzy stood up and turned to Ivy. "Can I talk to you for a minute at the bar."

"Yeah. Ladies, make yourselves comfortable and we'll be right back." T and Ivy walked out of the VIP towards the bar.

"Don't say shit."

"Dog!" T-Bizzy laughed as soon as they were far enough away. "You fuckin' wit big broads now?"

"That can't be her. The picture she sent...."

"Ivy, it's the internet. Not everybody tells the truth. When you gonna give all that cyber shit a rest and step back into reality."

"Aight, I deserve that but I gotta do somethin'. Tell them I had to go."

"No siree. You gotta face this one like a man, pimpin'. Them yo people. But as far as Me, Will and KD are concerned, we appreciate it."

"I can't go out like that. I have a reputation."

"Payback is a muthafucka cuz now you gotta take one for da team. Besides, she ain't ugly."

"I know but dog, that's not my style."

"Just sit there, smile and be cordial while I make a move on lil' J. Lo."

"Only cuz we fam."

"Good. Now let's get a couple more bottles of Cris and some wings for your girl."

"Go to Hell." T-Bizzy clowned Ivy all the way to the bar and all the way back to the VIP. Once they returned, T found that he had slipped and KD had already made a move on

Lil' J. Lo. Will had sexual chocolate on lock.
The only one left for T-Bizzy was plain Jane. It
looked like they were both assed out. The eight
partygoers sat in the VIP and popped bottle
after bottle of Cristal and vibed to the music
that was playing.

After they were into the third bottle of
champagne, Ivy excused himself and walked
towards the restroom. On his way there he saw
Natalie. Once again she captivated him. Before
he got too close, he stopped and leaned against
a rail and watched as two guys were standing
at the table where she and Alicia sat.
Everything about her was beautiful to him. She
had a girlish innocence about her. He didn't
know whether it was just him or the
champagne but her every move seemed to be
in slow motion. From the way she smiled to
the way her hair brushed the tops of her
shoulders when she turned her head—every
motion had him stuck. Five minutes of
watching Natalie passed and he gathered
himself and continued to the bathroom.

Just as he was about to pass the table the
two rejected men that were once standing there
talking to the women walked off. As Ivy
walked passed someone bumped him causing
him to lose his balance. The only way he could
keep from falling was to grab the chair and use
their table to catch himself. His sudden motion
startled the two ladies.

"Excuse me," Ivy apologized.

"Are you okay?" Natalie asked. Ivy locked eyes with Natalie and for a brief moment, time stood still. The smell of the fragrance she wore danced in his nostrils as he gazed at her like she had seen him somewhere before. It was only about 30 seconds but to Iverson, the moment seemed like lifetime. He gathered up, apologized once more and continued to his destination. Once inside the men's room he wanted to kick himself in the ass for not stepping to Natalie but at that moment, he just couldn't. While in the restroom, Iverson tried to think of a million excuses to get him out of club but kept coming up empty. He eventually gave up and decided to return to the VIP and make the most out of the evening. When Ivy exited the men's room, Shayla was standing in the corridor waiting for him. He stood face to face with a woman that had misrepresented herself.

"Listen," Shayla sighed. "I'm sorry I lied. I just thought that you wouldn't want to talk to me if you knew who I really was. I don't exactly fit the description of a girl who usually hangs out with record execs."

"Its not about how you look, it's about the fact that you lied. Everything on my page is me. I'm the type of guy that looks at the inside before I judge. Having a face to put with the personality is only a plus. I would have been more than happy to talk to you if you would have kept it real with me."

"So what are you saying?"

"I have this thing about dishonest people…we don't mix."

Ivy left Shayla standing in the corridor and returned to the crew. Once inside, he said his goodbyes and left the club. The ladies sat in surprise considering they came out for Shayla to meet him. That mood was stifled for a quick second but quickly returned to how it was before.

Natalie and Alicia continued to have good time until a couple of familiar faces popped up. Natalie's mood went from pleasant to pissed off in 3.6 seconds. From off of the dance floor ascended the faces of Desmond and Shanice — hand in hand.

"What's wrong?" Alicia asked as she noticed Natalie's facial expression change.

"I don't believe this bitch." Alicia began to look around to see what had pissed Natalie off. "Look coming off the dance floor."

"You talking about Shanice and that dude?"

"That's my ex, Desmond."

"Wooow! Are you serious? You wanna leave?"

"And let her have the satisfaction, Uh…no."

Before Alicia could stop her Natalie got up and was headed for the couple. Desmond saw Natalie before Shanice did and his eyes widened tremendously.

"What the hell is this?"
"Natalie, don't start," Desmond pleaded.
"So now I guess Diamonds are a guy's best friend," Natalie remarked.

Looking Natalie up and down Shanice replied, "If that's what you want to call it. I guess me and Alicia have something in common after all."Natalie did everything she could do to restrain herself because that New Jersey girl inside of her was getting ready to unleash. Before she could say any thing else, Alicia grabbed her by the wrist and led her away from the confrontation.

"It's not worth it," Alicia remarked as she walked Natalie towards the exit.
"I'm not ready to leave."
"If you stay here, there's gonna be trouble."

Stopping in her tracks Natalie turned to Alicia, "I'm cool. Trust me. Neither Desmond nor Shanice is worth it. I got this."
"You sure?"
"As long as she keeps her distance, I'm good."

"If you say so. We'll stay a little while longer."Alicia and Natalie returned into the club and positioned themselves on the opposite side beside the VIP booths. Natalie summoned the cocktail waitress as she walked by and ordered another round of drinks. She sat in disgust as she watched Shanice throw herself at Desmond — out of spite. After about thirty minutes and a couple of more drinks, Natalie forgot about Des and Shanice and continued to enjoy her night. Two handsome gentlemen approached the ladies and were able to coax them onto the dance floor. Just as they hit the last of seven steps on their way to the floor, the DJ dropped a little Old School hip-hop and it was on. The four danced to Slick Rick, Rob Base and a little E.U. — "Doin' da Butt." After about thirty minutes of dancing, Nat and Alicia left the dance floor out of breath and thirsty. The two ladies were able to reclaim the table they left.

"Whew!" Natalie began as she let out a deep breath. "I haven't danced like that since college."

"You mean to tell me that you and André never went dancin'." Alicia inquired.

"Not really. When me and Dré used to hangout it was more like goin' out with a brother. We went to places like pool halls, sports bars and concerts. You know?"

"That's really surprising considering how much he loved to dance when we were in college." A tall, light complexioned male with neatly designed cornrows and the subtle scent of Cool Water cologne interrupted the conversation.

"Excuse me," he began as he locked eyes on Natalie.

"My name is Ellis and I couldn't help but notice you as you were walking off the dance floor. Can I buy you ladies a drink?"

Natalie answered, "Thanks, but we're okay."

"Are you sure?" Natalie nodded. "You ladies enjoy the rest of your night."

Ellis walked off into the crowd.

"What was wrong with him?" Alicia asked.

"Not my style."

"Why because his hair was braided?"

"The braids I don't mind but his outfit was all wrong. The button-up shirt with the jeans and sneakers, that's a little too Usher for me."

"So you're tellin' me...if that was Usher, you would have turned him down."

"I'm not sayin' all that...but still."

"O-Kay," they said simultaneously as they laughed and gave a friendly hi-five.

It was about one o' clock in the morning. Iverson sat ticking away at his keyboard preparing the itinerary for the video shoot in Charleston. While working, an instant messenger box popped up.

WifeyMaterial: Iverson?

Ivy ignored it and continued with his task. Five minutes later the box popped up again.

WifeyMaterial: Are you there?
Ivy_Dav: who is this
WifeyMaterial: we met a few days ago on just4kickz and then I saw your page on Ebony World and decided to hit you up. Is that okay with you?
Ivy_Dav: Its all good
WifeyMaterial: What r u doin up so late?
Ivy_Dav: late…in my line of work, 1 am is early
WifeyMaterial: true
Ivy_Dav: how old r u?
WifeyMaterial: 27 and u?
Ivy_Dav: 29…any kids?
WifeyMaterial: a little girl. She's 3
Ivy_Dav: oh ok…do you have a pic?
WifeyMaterial: there are pics on my ebony world profile. Listen, I gotta run check'em out and if u like what u see, hit me tomorrow. I should be on after 9
Ivy_Dav: no doubt…One

Ivy closed the box and continued with his work. As time passed, the urge to check out WifeyMaterial's page was starting to eat at

him. He tried to shake it but it kept growing.
After about ten minutes passed, Ivy logged on
to ebonyworld.com. He typed her name in the
box that was labeled "member search." After
her page loaded, Iverson was impressed. Her
page was a work of art. The background was a
tropical island surrounded by crystal, blue
water and the sun setting in the distance. There
was no picture at the top of the page, so Ivy
scrolled down. While scrolling he read her
profile and some of her poetry. Out of the three
poems that were on her page, one stood out. It
was entitled "I Do." It read:

I DO

I promised to love you for eternity,
or until time comes to an end.
My heaven sent companion,
that started as just a friend.
The calmer of my fears,
the drier of my tears
My only reason for maintaining life,
through all these years.
If ever there were a person that embodies the
things that I do,
I realize that if I were not me,
I would be you.

Because of the barrage of poetry found
on every other page on ebonyworld.com, Ivy
paid it no mind and continued on to her
pictures. When he reached them he sat and
stared. WifeyMaterial was a gorgeous woman.

Her hair was long and silky and her eyes were a dark shade of "innocent" brown. WifeyMaterial had full, pouty lips and high cheekbones. She had the face of an angel. Ivy scrolled on hoping that he would find a full body shot but his search ended empty. Ivy tried not to get himself too worked up about it—considering his recent experiences. "She's a very beautiful girl," he thought to himself. He read more of her page in order to get a feel for her. The words on her page seemed to sing to him as he read.

Thirty minutes passed and Ivy closed up shop for the night. He thought about everything he had read and the pictures he saw as he prepared for bed. Iverson stared at the ceiling, thinking about WifeyMaterial, and then drifted off to sleep.

"Girl," Natalie began as the two ladies walked to the car. "I had a ball tonight."
"We definitely have to do this again."
"Whenever you're ready, just let me know."
"You know what Nat?" Alicia paused. "I had doubts about this because of your relationship with my husband but after what happened the other night at your house and tonight, I realized something."
"What's that?" Natalie asked as she started her Navigator. "You're a cool ass chick." "You ain't too bad yourself."

Chapter 6

The next morning Natalie woke up around eleven. While lying in bed, she reached for her Sidekick to check her agenda for the day. Her day was empty. Natalie pulled herself out of bed and into the bathroom. Once in her plush sanctuary, she turned on the shower. She looked at her reflection in the mirror as she peeled off her nightclothes. While waiting for the water to get just right, she examined her body. After a couple of minutes, she stepped into a steaming, hot shower. As piercing streams of hot water flooded her caramel body, she began to cry. She could not figure out why her love life was in shambles — first André, now Desmond. Even though she was beautiful and successful, Natalie could not understand why she could not find a good man that would love her for her. Natalie tried to gather herself as she finished her shower.

Sniffles filled the silent bathroom. Natalie wrapped a towel around her hair and body and walked back into her bedroom. Once she slipped into her basketball shorts and a sports bra, she went into her study to check her email. While sifting through the spam and other bullshit, to her left Natalie spied the notepad that she wrote Ivy's IM ID. In her web browser's address bar she typed: www.ebonyworld.com. When the site loaded, she logged on and found that she had about 50 new messages — of pure bullshit. Natalie deleted all of the messages and went to her hot list. The only profile there was Ivy's. Natalie looked at Iverson's picture. As she looked closer, she realized that he was the guy from the club. To her, he was the sexiest man she had seen in a while. She added him to her IM buddy list.

Ivy was sitting at his desk when a small box popped up that read: ***dymond4eva*** *has requested permission to add you to his/her friend list.* He clicked on the *Accept & Add* box. After doing so, he double-clicked on the icon and pulled up his friend list. Then he double-clicked on **dymond4eva** bringing up an IM box.

Ivy_Dav: who is this?

When Ivy's message popped up, it startled Natalie. She didn't know whether to respond or ignore him. She responded.

Dymond4eva: I saw you on ebonyworld…u seemed like a nice guy
Ivy_Dav: oh really?
Dymond4eva: yeah. I liked your profile. looks like success hasn't gone to ur head.
Ivy_Dav: I'm just a cool, laid-back kinda guy
Dymond4eva: how old r u?

Ivy_Dav: 29 u?

Dymond4eva: I'll be 27 in June

Ivy_Dav: what day?

Dymond4eva: the 9th

Ivy_Dav: quit lyin'. Mine is on the 11th

Dymond4eva: GEMINIS IN DA HOUSE...LOL

Ivy_Dav: LOL maybe we can celebrate together this year

Dymond4eva: maybe

Ivy_Dav: so what do you do for a livin'?

Dymond4eva: I am a high school teacher and a coach

Ivy_Dav: a coach? What sport...volleyball, track, tennis?

Dymond4eva: B-ball

Ivy_Dav: this is too much

Dymond4eva: what do u mean?

Ivy_Dav: ur a Gemini and u can ball...one more thing

Dymond4eva: what?

Ivy_Dav: u into music?

Dymond4eva: that's my second love...next to b-ball

Ivy_Dav: I'm in love   LOL

Dymond4eva: ur sillie

Ivy_Dav: old skool or new skool

Dymond4eva: old skool...of course

Ivy_Dav: MARRY ME....LOL

Dymond4eva: boy stop!

Ivy_Dav: j/k but for real, I gotta run. maybe I can catch you later

Dymond4eva: maybe

Ivy_Dav: my name is Iverson but
everybody calls me Ivy and u r?
Dymond4eva: I'll tell u later
Ivy_Dav: ok…I'll take that. Guess I'll
talk to u later
Dymond4eva: maybe
  Dymond4eva has logged out***

Natalie logged off of her messenger
with a huge smile on her face. "His words
seemed to be so genuine," she thought to
herself.

A week had passed and Ivy and the rest
of the crew touched down in Charleston, South
Carolina. When they arrived at the hotel, they
found swarms of people—all there to welcome
ATP, EL GEE and Gusto back to Chucktown.

"Okay," Ivy began. "Who leaked?"
"My bad, dog," ATP confessed. "I told
Momma and a couple of other people. I guess
they told a few people."
"This ain't necessarily a bad thing. This
just shows you how much ya people love you."

Hotel security guards led the entourage
through the hoard of screaming Southern Sunz
fans into the hotel. Once checked in, they all
met in one of the conference rooms for a brief
meeting. Ivy went over the week's itinerary
and a couple of other things. While he spoke,
he stressed the timetable that they were

working with — with specific emphasis towards TyQuan, Will and KD.

"We got this, Chief," T-Bizzy stated.

"Good. We have to be at 93.3 at 6:30 for a promo for the video shoot. Y'all got about three hours to chill and then it's business as usual."Ivy adjourned the meeting.

"Ivy," ATP approached. "Can I holla at you for a minute"

They walked towards the elevator.

"What's good?"

"Me, EL and Gus gettin' ready to hit the neighborhood for a minute. We wanna go holla at Momma."

"That's cool. You comin' back here or you meetin' us at the station?"

"We'll be back around 5."

"Cool. I gotta run over and meet with the modeling agency to check out the girls for the shoot. Anything particular you looking for?"

"I told you. We wit' you. I seen ya videos."

"No doubt. Y'all be safe and please don't be late."

"No doubt."

ATP bypassed the elevator, met Gusto and EL GEE and left for his old neighborhood. Iverson went up to his room and set up his laptop. Iverson logged into his Ebony World IM account and his buddy list popped up.

WifeyMaterial and Dymond4eva were both online but a small stop sign icon beside Dymond4eva's name indicated that she was away from the computer. He double-clicked on WifeyMaterial.

> **Ivy_Dav:** u there?
> **WifeyMaterial:** hey there…what u up too?
> **Ivy_Dav:** I just got to Charleston
> **WifeyMaterial:** what u doin in Chucktown?
> **Ivy_Dav:** what you know about da Chuck?
> **WifeyMaterial:** One of my girls from college was from there. I've been a couple of times during holidays.
> **Ivy_Dav:** Tru…anyway…we're here for a video shoot
> **WifeyMaterial:** really?
> **Ivy_Dav:** yeah…one of my new artists iz from here and I thought it would be a good idea to shoot part of their first video in their home states
> **WifeyMaterial:** sounds like fun…wish I was there to join in all the fun
> **Ivy_Dav:** maybe u can come back with me for the Album release after the New Year
> **WifeyMaterial:** that depends…
> **Ivy_Dav:** on what?
> **WifeyMaterial:** first of all, I don't know you like that to be goin out of town with

you…u might me a lunatic…lol
Ivy_Dav: lol…I respect that. Maybe you can get to know me a little better when I get back home next week.
WifeyMaterial: that's a possibility…we'll see.
Ivy_Dav: well, I gotta run. I got some things to do before we go to the radio station
WifeyMaterial: well, if I don't hear from u, I know ur busy. Hit me when u get home
Ivy_Dav: Will do
Ivy_Dav has logged out

Back in the ATL, Natalie and Alicia were out shopping at the Cumberland Mall. The two ladies tore in and out of stores — taking no prisoners. After they had been in about six stores, they took a smoothie break in the Food Court.

"Alicia," Natalie called pausing from her smoothie. "You ever dated anybody you met on the Internet?"

"Yes and no. I didn't meet him on the Internet. I met him in college. He went to New York for the summer and we kept in touch through the net."

"Oh, ok."

"Now, ya boy, Dré! He used to mess around wit girls he met online. I remember this one girl he met that went to Grambling State.

He went all the way to Louisiana for the Bayou Classic to meet this girl. I don't think it went too well because when he got back, he didn't have much to say about it. Why do you ask?"

"No reason," Nat replied as she continued to sip her drink.

"You met somebody on the Internet, didn't you?"

"Not entirely. There is this guy. We've seen him before but he doesn't know that I'm the girl he met. Remember the guy that stumbled by our table at Club Blaze?"

"You mean the light skinned guy with the dreads?"

"He's the CEO of Future Records."

"Have you talked to him?"

"We spoke for a minute on the IM but I haven't talked to him since."

"You know how those music industry guys are."

"I know but he seems so different. In the brief moment that we talked, he seemed so genuine. Plus, he loves music and basketball."

"Does he know you play for the Diamonds?"

"I told him I was a teacher and a basketball coach. Was I wrong for that?"

"Girl, it's the internet. Anything goes. All I can tell you is to feel him out. If it feels right, follow your heart. Just be careful."

"I knew I could talk to you about this. My other friends probably would have clowned me."

"That's what true friends are for."

The ladies sat for a while longer and shot the breeze and continued on their mission. As they walked into Lady Foot Locker, Natalie saw a familiar but unfriendly face leaving the register. It was Shawna McKenzie — the teammate she had got into a brawl with in Houston. Shawna stood a towering 6'5". She was brown skinned with her hair cut to just below her neck. Shawna was a lot like Natalie when it came to dressing off of the court. That day she wore a pair of dark denim Apple Bottom Jeans, a white blouse with the bell sleeves and wheat colored boots.

"What's up, teammate?" Shawna greeted as if she and Natalie were on speaking terms.
"Shawna," Natalie replied.
"Doin a little shoppin', I see."
"Yeah."
"You have to excuse Natalie," she aimed the comment towards Alicia. "She can be rude at times. I'm Shawna." She extended her hand.
"I'm Alicia. Nice to meet you."
"We'll I gotta run. Don't spend too much money, Nat."
"Uh huh." Natalie disregarded. Shawna walked out of the store.
"Was that the same Shawna that Dré knows?"Natalie nodded her head. "What did

my husband see in her? She's not even his type."

"I asked myself the same question," Natalie laughed. Natalie and Alicia walked around the mall for about two more hours and then left. About halfway to Alicia's house, Alicia asked Natalie a couple of edgy questions.

"How long had André been in Atlanta when the two of you met?" Alicia inquired.

"I believe he had been here for a couple weeks. We met at Club Blaze the night I signed with the Diamonds."

"Oh, ok. When did he tell you about me?"

"The first time we went to the Silver Dollar to shoot pool. After he told me about you, Dré and I became more like best friends. He used to tell me a lot of different things that he felt he couldn't tell anyone else."

"Like what?"

"Things like," Natalie paused. "His relationship with you. Let me tell you. Dré was a mess. You meant the world to him but his feelings had to smack him in the face. He was scared as hell because he thought that somebody else was going to ease their way into your life while he was in here and you were still in school."

"Really?"

"Even when him and Karen started working on the show. You were still his main focus. At first it was strictly business between them. When Karen started catchin' feelings, things got sticky. He used to tell me that everything Karen did for him, reminded him of you. It was like he had two of you. Feel me?"

"So, you're saying that because his feelings for me on the level of a relationship were unclear to him, it was hard for him to keep from falling for Karen."

"Exactly. When he went back to South Carolina and broke things off between you and him, it was one of the hardest decisions he ever had to make. He valued your friendship so much that he didn't want to loose that. He felt that before he cheated on you, he was willing to let you go."

"I never knew it was that serious. Damn."

"It was deep."

"One last question and you don't have to answer if you don't want to."

"Me and Dré never slept together. We slept in the same bed together the night me and Shawna got into it in Houston but all we did was sleep. Fully clothed and on top of the covers."

"How'd you know that's what I was going to ask?"

"I'm a woman and if my man was close to a woman like me and Dré are, I'd wanna know to."

"After finding all of this out, I'm surprised that he chose Karen over you. You're more his type."

"I guess everything happens for a reason. Had he chose me, he probably wouldn't have Taylor and the two of you probably would have never came back together."

"This is true. Thanks for looking after my boo."

"Not a problem."

"And thanks for being a true friend…to me and him."

"Ok, ok, ok," Natalie laughed. "Enough with the Oprah moment." Natalie pulled into Alicia's driveway just as André was pulling into the garage. André got out of his truck and walked up on Natalie's side of the Navigator.

"What's up, Mr. Man?" Natalie greeted as she rolled down the window.

"I'm good," he replied."How's life treatin' ya?"

"Can't complain. Just livin' it one day at a time."

"Girl stop," Dré laughed. "You sound like an old ass woman talkin' like that."

"But for real, I'm doin' pretty good. Just tryin' to stay in shape. You should come down to the gym and ball with us sometimes."

"I barely have time to do anything. Between Taylor and that big baby right there, my life is hectic." They all laughed. "Oh yeah, before I forget, the network is havin' a

Christmas party on the 22nd. You're more than welcome to come as one of my guests."

"I know where this is headed André Marcellus Marshall."

"Why she gotta call my whole name?"

"I might come if you promise me one thing."

"What's that?"

"No matchmaking."

"Who me?" Alicia and Natalie gave him the same scowl. "Ok, I see what this is. This is a two on one, sista to sista thing. Alright, no match making but if somebody asks about you, I'm tellin'."

"Ok, girl," Alicia began as she got out of the SUV. "I gotta go in here and get dinner started. Vanessa should be bringing Taylor home in a little while. Call me tomorrow."

"Will do. Bye Dré."

"Be safe, Sis."

"Sis?"

"Yeah, you're like a sister to me now."

"I'll accept that. Be good."

Natalie pulled off with all smiles. She was happy that she could maintain her friendship with André and build a stronger friendship between her and Alicia. When it really came down to it, those were the only two that she could call on if she needed a favor or just someone to talk to. Good friends were hard to find but Natalie had two good ones.

Chapter 7

A week had passed and business was finished in Charleston. Ivy and the rest of the Future Records crew were back in Atlanta getting prepared for the next part of the video shoot. While in South Carolina, Ivy had a chance to sit back and reflect on his most recent internet experiences in order to figure out whether the two women he had just met were worth the time and effort. From a normal man's stand point it wasn't worth it but because Ivy had that serious adventurous streak in him, the thoughts of WifeyMaterial and Dymond4Eva still danced in his head.

"Ivy," TyQuan called from the door. "Ivy!"

"I heard you the first time, damn," Ivy answered as he slowly spun around in his office chair. "What's up?"

"You alright?"

"Yeah. What's up?"

"Ever since we got back, you been real quiet."

"Just got some shit in my mind. That's all."

"Still thinking about Candace?" T-Bizzy asked as he sat down on the couch and picked up a basketball.

"Not really. Just random thoughts." Ivy paused for about two minutes. "You ever think it's the industry that keeps us single?"

"Never really thought about it."

"Look at us. We're successful, black businessmen living in a city that has more women in it than a little bit. The only women we ever meet are chickenheads, gold diggers, and women willing to do any and everything they can do to touch a little bit of status."

"What's wrong with the last one?"

"Seriously, man. I'm 29 years old and haven't had a steady woman in my life since we started Future. Why? They think that the facades that we portray are our real lives. The industry makes people think it's all about bitches and Bentleys. If you didn't have a wife or a girlfriend coming in to this business, its hell tryin' to find one after the money starts rollin' in. The majority of the married men in this business had women by their sides before they got big or either their woman is in the industry too. Look at all the leaders of the business. Russell got Kimora, Babyface got Tracy, Jermaine Dupri got Janet, Jay-Z got Beyonce but who do I have?"

"Don't tell me you thinkin' 'bout leavin the industry."

"I'm not sayin' that but at least once, I'd like to meet a real sista that doesn't feel like she has to lie to kick it or be something that she's not."

"She's out there. Just let her find you. You're my boy and I know for a fact that you're one of the good ones. When she comes along, you'll know it. Me, myself, personally...I'm just enjoyin' the ride. When it's time to settle down, I'll settle down."

"I feel you but this business is a beast. It's hard to go home to an empty house every night." In the middle of their conversation messenger box popped up. "Hold on a minute, T."

WifeyMaterial: Ivy....u there?
Ivy_Dav: I'm in the middle of a meeting. Can I hit you back?
WifeyMaterial: yeah. I'll be on for a minute
Ivy_Dav: true...in a minute

Ivy minimized the Instant Messenger box and continued his conversation.

"Please don't tell me you still fuckin' wit dat shit."

"Nah. That was Big Tyme from Low Life Entertainment in Jersey. After ol' girl from Luda's party, the net is no place for me."

"I was just checkin'," T-Bizzy stood up. "I hate to cut this short but me and Will 'bout to head to the ESPNZone. You rollin?"

"Not tonight. I got a few things I need to do here and then I'm headed to the house."

"Aight but go straight home," T-Bizzy laughed as he got up to leave.

154

"No stops at bigbootyhoes.com. If you change ya mind, you know where I'm at. Holla." T-Bizzy walked out closing the door behind him.

Ivy_Dav: u still there?
WifeyMaterial: I'm here
Ivy_Dav: what's good?
WifeyMaterial: me
Ivy_Dav: oh really...
WifeyMaterial: yup...anyway, how was the Charleston?
Ivy_Dav: Chucktown was good. We had a lot of fun and gotta whole lot of work done
WifeyMaterial: and probably gotta whole lotta booty in the process
Ivy_Dav: that's not my style
WifeyMaterial: stop lyin'. All u music guys are the same. A bunch of horny dogs runnin around messin wit women's heads talking about you can put'em in ya next video.
Ivy_Dav: if that's what you think then y u hit me up? u tryin to be in a video?
WifeyMaterial: NOT...I have better things to do...honestly, I think your different
Ivy_Dav: how so?
WifeyMaterial: when I read ur page on ebony world, it was something different you did state that you owned Future Records but it was like that was

something minor to you. You didn't over glorify it like most men would. You actually talked about your hobbies and things you like to do.

Ivy_Dav: not every man in the industry is a bad one

WifeyMaterial: how do I know that?

Ivy_Dav: you have to get to know one to find out that answer

WifeyMaterial: and how do I do that?

Ivy_Dav: How bout we start with dinner?

WifeyMaterial: name the time, place and date

Ivy_Dav: Let me check my schedule and I'll get back to you

WifeyMaterial: y don't we exchange numbers

Ivy_Dav: y don't you just give me urs and I'll call you

WifeyMaterial: 404-555-1920

Ivy_Dav: I'll be in touch

Ivy_Dav has logged out

Iverson closed the office for the night and headed home. On his way home he stopped off at a convenience store to get a case of beer. As he pulled into the parking lot he saw a medium height, caramel complexioned woman hop into a black Navigator. After he acquired his spirits for the evening he continued home.

Minutes later, Natalie arrived at the Silver Dollar Sports Bar & Grill. Everyone hailed her as she walked in. As she walked into the billiard room, she saw a couple of familiar faces.

"Do you ever stay home André Marshall?" Natalie joked as she sat her drink on the table behind the pool table.

"What's up, Nat Dog?" Dré greeted as the two hugged.

"You remember Smoke, don't you?"

"Yeah, I remember crazy ass Smoke."

"What's crackin', Miss MVP?" Smoke clowned as he hugged Natalie. "You here to work on ya bank shots?"

"Sista was bored sittin in that big ass house by myself. I had to get out and if I knew you two were here, I woulda went some place else."

"She got jokes, Dré. Get ya girl."

"Guess who me and Alicia ran into in the mall last week?"

"Who?" Dré asked as he set up for his next shot.

"Shawna."

"For real? What she say?"

"You shoulda seen how fake she acted in front of Alicia. Like we cool like that or somethin'."

"That's ya girl."

"I wasn't the one that flew all the way to Houston for a booty call wit Miss Thang."

"She got you on that one," Smoke instigated.

"Can you please mind ya business?" Dré insisted.

"I can tell when I'm not wanted. I'll be at the bar if you need me." Smoke walked off.

"Bring back two Henny and Cokes," Dré called to Smoke.

"Who I look like? Benson?" he laughed.

Natalie racked the balls as André chalked his stick.

"You gotta a good one," Nat replied as she leaned against the table. "You better hold onto her."

"Alicia and Taylor are my only reasons to live. If it hadn't been for them, I might've went crazy after Karen died."

"But you knew Alicia was the one for you in the first place."

"To be honest with you…I didn't. I knew that I held her closer to my heart than anyone else but out of all of the years we've known each other, I never saw us as a couple. I always felt that if we got into a relationship and it didn't work, it would have affected our friendship."

"I can understand that. She's cool people. Even over the past couple weeks that we've been hangin' tight, she's already become like a sister to me. I never thought we'd be this close. I think the reason we're cool is because she reminds me so much of you."

"That's what everybody says. Alicia's the type of person that if she's down for you, she's down for you. There might be a couple of minor bumps along the way but she doesn't hold grudges and she'll fight for you and beside you until the end."

"I used to say the same thing about Shanice but she changed my mind about that."

"Have you talked to her?"

"I try to call but she doesn't accept my calls and doesn't return them. I'm not gonna chase her to be her friend. I did my part. Now she has to meet me halfway."

"I'm sure she'll come to her senses." As that conversation came to a close, Smoke returned and joined Natalie and André in a few friendly games of pool. The trio laughed and enjoyed each other's company until the time came for André to be heading back to his wife and child. Natalie hugged the fellas then headed for home.

Iverson sat at his computer looking over record sales and other business related things. He was pleased at his success and was looking forward to the success of his newest artist. Just as he was about to finish up, he heard a familiar tone and a small box in the bottom right hand corner of the monitor read: *dymond4eva has just logged in.* Before he had a chance to pull up his contact list, an IM box popped up.

> **Dymond4eva:** u there?
> **Ivy_Dav:** Hey! what's good?
> **Dymond4eva:** nothing much, just got in from chillin wit some friends...
> what u up to?
> **Ivy_Dav:** I was looking over some numbers...u know business
> **Dymond4eva:** kewl...how u been?
> **Ivy_Dav:** I'm good, just a little worn out from the video shoot we did in SC
> **Dymond4eva:** how did that go?
> **Ivy_Dav:** it went pretty good...I got a real headbanga about to drop
> **Dymond4eva:** fo sho. What's his name
> **Ivy_Dav:** the group is called the Southern Sunz...ATP aka Attia the Port City
> Prophet str8 outta Charleston SC and EL GEE from Fayetteville NC

Ivy and Natalie continued with their idle chat for about thirty minutes. They found that the two of them had more in common than they thought or expected. They are both from New Jersey and they both played basketball in high school and college. Natalie was surprised when the conversation never went sexual. In a matter of moments, she realized that he wasn't like the cyber riff raff she had heard stories about.

Dymond4eva: so what r u looking for in a woman

Ivy_Dav: being in the music and entertainment business, I run across a lot of fake people, especially women. The majority of the women that approach me r the exotic types tryin to get into the videos or tryin to get a deal. I just want an around the way girl

Dymond4eva: around the way girl?

Ivy_Dav: I want a girl with extensions in her hair...bamboo earrings at least two pair

Dymond4eva: lol! ok LL

Ivy_Dav: lmao... but on the real...the type of girl I can chill wit like I chill wit my boyz but at the same time be 100% woman.

Dymond4eva: I feel you...but...can a girl like that handle a man in the industry?

Ivy_Dav: that's a good question...I would say that she could as long as I stay tru
2 her and always be truthful.

Dymond4eva: sounds like you know what u want. I'm sure she's out there

Ivy_Dav: I know she's out there...findin' her is the hard part

Dymond4eva: let her find you

Ivy_Dav: listen, I gotta long day tomorrow. R u gonna be on tomorrow night?

Dymond4eva: maybe...

Ivy_Dav: well, Miss Maybe, if I catch u, I catch u. if I don't I guess u didn't wanna be caught...

Dymond4eva: and what is that supposed 2 mean?

Ivy_Dav: think about it...holla
Ivy_Dav has just logged out

Natalie sat in shock for about five minutes. No man has ever left her hanging in suspense. She was the one that was supposed to leave him wondering. After she gathered her senses, Natalie laughed it off and readied herself for bed. In her mind she thought about Ivy. Where had he come from and who was the real man behind those words? As she lay engulfed in her king-sized bed, she saw Ivy's face every time she closed her eyes until she finally fell asleep.

Curiosity can be a serious issue sometimes. It was funny how Natalie and Iverson found themselves thinking about one another during their daily activities that next day. The situation seemed a little more far-fetched for Natalie to grasp because she had never really talked to anyone she met over the Internet. Iverson was going with the flow because he had dated women he met online

before. Just from the few conversations that
he's had with dymond4eva, he knew it was
something different about her. But what about
WifeyMaterial?

Happy hour rolled around in the city of
Atlanta. Businesses were closing for the day
and rush hour was on the brink of madness.
All the local bars downtown began to fill with
people that were trying to ease the pains of
their day with spirits and good conversation.
Natalie and Alicia sat at the bar in Justin's, one
of Atlanta's premier establishments. As the
ladies sat, the wolves began to circle. For a half
hour Natalie and Alicia shot down almost
twenty men. It wasn't because they were being
stuck up or rude; sometimes it's girl time.

"Why did you turn him down?" Alicia
asked as she sipped her Cosmopolitan. "He
was cute."
"I wasn't really feeling him. Besides I
got a lot on my mind right now."
"Like what?"
"Remember that guy I was telling you
about that I met online?"
"Yeah, what about him?"
"I think I want to meet him."
"Are you serious?"
"We've been talking a lot for the past
couple of days and he's really got me curious. I
want to see what he's about."

"All I can say is be cool about it. Don't let on to him that you want to see him. Wait until he initiates the first meeting then you say no."

"No? Why no?"

"That's how you feel him out. If he accepts that and continues to talk to you then you know he's not just tryin' to one-night stand you. If he questions you a lot, asking you why you don't want to meet him, he's full of it."

"What makes you so sure? If I hesitate to long, he might lose interest."

"Trust me. If he's real wit his, he'll wait."

"I hope your right cuz that brother is fine."

"He is kinda cute."

"Kinda my ass."

"I mean he's alright but he's no André Marshall."

"Boooooo!" The ladies continued to laugh and have idle girl talk as the evening progressed.

Back at Future Records, Iverson was closing his meeting with Lil Jon about the remix of the Southern Sunz's first single. Lil Jon loved the idea and was ready to record the remix immediately. Iverson sat in his chair at the end of the long meeting table and watched as everyone emptied the room. Lil Jon was talking to ATP, EL GEE and Gusto in the hallway, as Will, KD and T-Bizzy left for the ESPNZone.

As he reflected on his success at Future Records, he became slightly downtrodden. With all of his success, he had no one to share it with. As that thought passed through his head, so did the thought of Dymond4eva and WifeyMaterial. He had met two women, one in which he had seen and one that he had seen but doesn't know he's seen her. Dymond4eva still remained a mystery to him. Ivy pulled himself out of his chair and slowly walked to his office and logged on to his Instant Messenger service to retrieve WifeyMaterial's phone number.

"Hello?" answered a sweet voice.
"This is Ivy."
"Well hello there. I've been waiting for your call."
"Really?"
"What's up?"
"I know this is short notice but I was wondering if you would like to go out tonight."
"Sure. Just tell me when and where."
"How about Copeland's on Cobb Parkway at nine?"
"Sounds delicious. I'll see you then."
"Ok...see you then."

Ivy's feelings of melancholy wisped away at the close of that conversation. New life had been breathed into his body. He rushed home to get prepared for his dinner date. After he showered and shaved, he chose his ensemble for the evening. Being that it was December in Georgia; the nights were cold but not as cold as the winter nights in New Jersey. Iverson selected a pair of navy blue slacks, a navy blue sweater with highlighted patterns of light blue swirled around in it and a pair of black, casual boots. He was dressed for success and on his way to meet WifeyMaterial.

Iverson sat at the bar just as he did the night he met XoticMami. Because of that meeting, he felt a slight queasy feeling in his stomach. He tried to put it out of his mind so he could concentrate on WifeyMaterial. Nine o'clock came and went. At 9:30, she walked through the door. WifeyMaterial was wearing a three quarter length leather coat that only revealed a pair of dark brown thighs and a pair of black pumps with about a four-inch heel. Iverson stood up as she approached.

"Iverson Davenport, I presume," she said as she stopped one foot from him.
"That would be me and you are?"
"Shelby Cortez."
"It's a pleasure to finally meet you." The two embraced as the hostess approached.
"Mr. Davenport, your table is ready."

"Thank you. After you."

Iverson watched Shelby walk as the hostess led them to their table. When they arrived the moment that he had been waiting on since he first saw her picture was getting ready to come to past—the grand unveiling. Shelby untied the belt of her coat that was holding it closed.

"Let me help you with that," Iverson suggested.

Shelby turned her back to Iverson and began to remove her coat. Ivy grabbed it by the lapels and slowly peeled it from her body. Shelby stood in front of him wearing a form fitting red skirt that extended to midway her thighs and hugged her assets ever so gently. She turned around just as he took his eyes off of her bottom half. Now that she faced him his eyes followed a familiar path from her stomach, hidden by the tight black blouse, past her perfect D-cups to her eyes.

"I take it you like what you see," Shelby smiled.
"Indeed I do." The two sat down in their booth. "I'm glad you could make it on such short notice."
"I wasn't doing anything anyway. I was just sitting around the house."

"Just waitin' for something to get into?" Shelby gave Iverson a devilish grin.

"Something like that."

Their conversation was paused by the approach of their server. She took the drink order and left. Shelby and Iverson continued with the awkward *getting acquainted* conversation until the server returned to take their entrée order.

"So tell me," Ivy began as he sipped his drink.

"How did you come up with your screen name?"

"It's simple because I am just that. I'm a career woman, I feel that I have a great personality and I'm old-fashioned."

"Old-fashioned meaning?"

"I know how to please and cater to my man."

"That definitely classifies you as wife material."

"Yeah, but it's hard trying to find someone that knows how to appreciate the type of woman that I am."

"I can feel you on that one. I feel that I'm a good man but it's hard to find someone that's true because of the industry that I'm in. When most women see me and know who I am, that's when the madness begins."

"What do you mean?"

"They look right past me and see the label and all the benefits and perks of the label instead of taking the time to get to know me."

"I bet that can be rough sometimes."

"Sometimes is an understatement."

"With me, material things don't matter because anything a man can buy me, or do for me, I can do for myself. I wish that just once, a man would stop trying to buy me and start trying to love me."

That statement struck a nerve in Iverson. For the first time since Candace, he was out with a woman that didn't care about what he had. It seemed too good to be true. Iverson and Shelby continued to have a great evening. Before long, time had slipped away.

"Oh my gosh!" Shelby exclaimed as she looked at her watch.

"It's almost eleven."

"What's wrong?"

"I have to go. I told my babysitter that I would be home by eleven. She's in high school and she has to get home."

Shelby gathered her coat and purse as Iverson paid the bill and escorted her to her car. He gave her a hug and she rushed off. As she drove away, Iverson noticed something about her car that puzzled him. Around her license plate was a tag border. The border read: Omega Psi Phi. That car belonged to a man.

Maybe it was a friend's car she borrowed for the evening. Anything was possible. Iverson paid it no mind and headed for home.

Chapter 8

A thousand thoughts raced through Iverson's mind as he pulled into his garage. Thoughts of Shelby danced around. She seemed to be the perfect woman but it can take one fouled piece of evidence to cause one to second guess her perfection. The way she spoke, the way she carried herself — even her thoughts of a relationship — made Shelby definite wife material. Iverson tried to stay focused but the night's end had him rattled.

As the Ivy's night came to an end, he entered into the last part of his day like clockwork. He positioned himself in front of his computer to check his messages, emails and numbers. Before he got to the first message, dymond4eva must have sensed his presence.

Dymond4eva: U there?
Ivy_Dav: what's up?
Dymond4eva: it's about time u showed up, I was getting' ready to call it a night
Ivy_Dav: I'm sorry. It's been a long day
Dymond4eva: is everything ok?
Ivy_Dav: things are cool
Dymond4eva: it doesn't seem like it
Ivy_Dav: I went on a date tonite
Dymond4eva: that doesn't seem too bad
Ivy_Dav: everything was perfect until the end

Dymond4eva: how so?

Ivy_Dav: I'm sorry...I really shouldn't be boring you with this

Dymond4eva: it's cool, sometimes u need someone 2 talk 2

Ivy_Dav: r u sure?

Dymond4eva: positive

Ivy_Dav: well, I met this girl and she seems to be what I'm looking for but there's just something about her. It's almost like she's too perfect

Dymond4eva: what do u mean?

Ivy_Dav: we share similar interests, she doesn't care about what I do, she just wants to get to know me for who I am.

Dymond4eva: and what's wrong with that?

Ivy_Dav: there's nothing wrong with that or at least it wasn't until the end of the night.

Dymond4eva: what happened?

Ivy_Dav: at about 11 she got kinda frantic and had to rush off. She said she had to get home because she had to let her hi skool babysitter go home.

Dymond4eva: that sounds legit

Ivy_Dav: here's the twisted part...as she drove away, there was something strange about her car. There was a greek tag liner around her license plate.

Dymond4eva: what's so strange about that? A lot of Greeks have tag liners

Ivy_Dav: true… but I don't know too many female members of Omega Psi Phi
Dymond4eva: really?
Ivy_Dav: yup
Dymond4eva: before you jump to any conclusions, ask her about it. It coulda just belonged to a friend.
Ivy_Dav: maybe ur right and I'm just buggin…
Dymond4eva: listen, I understand you might be a little skeptical but if you think
she's worth getting to know, check her out…what goes on in the dark will eventually come into the light
Ivy_Dav: that is true. You know what, dymond?
Dymond4eva: what?
Ivy_Dav: you're a good person to talk to…thanks for listening
Dymond4eva: everybody needs someone in their life that they can talk to…if you
ever need me again, I'm here…but for now, I gotta run. ttyl
Dymond4eva has logged out*

What just happened? Natalie just had a conversation about another woman with the man that she wanted to get to know. She could not believe it—it was like André Marshall all over again. "I'm just buggin," Natalie thought to herself as she walked into her bedroom. For thirty minutes, Natalie sat up in her bed looking off into the silence of her empty house trying to find justification for what had transpired. She kept coming up empty. After an hour of searching, Natalie boarded the 1 o'clock express to dreamland.

Iverson didn't really do much that day so he wasn't tired. He had no desire to watch television so he did what he always did to pass the time. Futurama decided to drop in and pay his friends on just4kickz.com a visit. He hadn't been on since he got back from the Carolinas.

Futurama has just entered the room
Choco Latte has just entered the room
<Teddy Pinned*Her*Ass*Down> YALL JUST DON'T UNDERSTAND ME...I'M TOO COMPLEX
<Got'em Hatin> COMPLEX MY ASS...U JUST FULL OF SHIT...LOL
<Choco Latte> GET OFF MY BABY GOT'EM...LOL
<Da Ice Cream Man>I'm not the one to start trouble but did anybody else besides me notice that Choco and Future came in at the same time...lol!
<Futurama>C'MON ICE CREAM...YOU KNOW HOW JEALOUS TEDDY IZ
<Teddy Pinned*Her*Ass*Down> I KNOW MY CUZIN WOULDN'T DO ME LIKE THAT ICE CREAM
<Choco Latte> THAT'S RIGHT BOO

<Got'em Hatin> IT AINT YA CUZIN U GOTTA WORRY ABOUT...DON'T FORGET CHOCO IS FROM CALI...LOL!

<Da Ice Cream Man>what's that supposed to mean?@Got'em

<Choco Latte> YEAH...WHAT IS THAT SUPPOSED TO MEAN

<Got'em Hatin> WE SEE SOMETHIN WE WANT AND WE GO GET IT

<Teddy Pinned*Her*Ass*Down> SHE ALREADY GOT WHAT SHE WANT

<Choco Latte> THAT'S RIGHT BABY

<Got'em Hatin> TEDDY BE 4 REAL...DO YOU HONESTLY THINK CHOCO WOULD CHOOSE YOU OVER FUTURE?

<Da Ice Cream Man> she would be living a glamorous life

<Teddy Pinned*Her*Ass*Down> ITS NOT ALWAYS ABOUT WHAT SOMEBODY HAS...ITS ABOUT HOW THAT SOMEBODY TREATS HER

<City Ave Diva> PREACH TEDDY!

<MACK Truck> THAT'S RIGHT CUZIN...STAND UP FOR US BROKE NIGGAZ...LOL

<Futurama> TEDDY DOES HAVE A POINT...I WANT A WOMAN THAT'S IN TO ME FOR ME NOT BECAUSE OF WHAT I CAN GIVE OER OR THE LIFE SHE'LL LIVE

<Thyk2Def> SOME WOMEN DON'T UNDERSTAND THAT@FUTURE

<City Ave Diva> MOST MEN DON'T UNDERSTAND THAT EITHER

\<Futurama\> I CAN'T DENY WHAT I HAVE BUT ANY REAL WOMAN KNOWS THAT IN ORDER TO REAP THOSE BENEFITS SHE HAS TO BE FOUND WORTHY
\<Got'em Hatin\>\<\<\<\<\<\<\<\<\<\<\<TAKIN NOTES
\<Da Ice Cream Man\>lol!
\<Teddy Pinned*Her*Ass*Down\> THAT'S MY POINT EXACTLY@FUTURE
\<Choco Latte\> ITS NOT ALWAYS ABOUT MONEY BUT HAVING A MAN THAT IS FINANCIAL SECURE 4 A CHANGE IS A BREATH OF FRESH AIR SOMETIMES
\<City Ave Diva\> THAT IS SO TRU@CHOCO...YOU MEN WOULD BE SURPRISED AT A LOT OF THE SHIT WE PUT UP WITH TRYIN TO GIVE A MAN A CHANCE
\<Futurama\> I FEEL THAT@DIVA BUT SOME OF THE THINGS WOMEN PUT THEMSELVES THROUGH IS SOMETIMES YOUR OWN FAULT
\<Teddy Pinned*Her*Ass*Down\> U HAVE TO REALIZE WHEN ENOUGH IS ENOUGH@CHOCO
\<Choco Latte\> TEDDY DON'T GO THERE
\<Teddy Pinned*Her*Ass*Down\> I AM GOING THERE...WHAT UR GOIN THROUGH AIN'T NO SECRET...EVERYBODY KNOWS
\<Thyk2Def\> U MY GIRL CHOCO BUT TEDDY DOES HAVE A POINT

<Teddy Pinned*Her*Ass*Down>
COUNTLESS TIMES YOU'VE COME IN
HERE PISSED OFF TELL'N US ABOUT YA
MAN'S SHORT COMINGS AND YET U STILL
STAY
<Futurama> TEDDY THAT'S SOMETHING
THAT YOU SHOULD TALK TO HER ABOUT
IN PRIVATE
<Choco Latte>IT'S COOL…WE ALL
FAMILY…I KNOW TEDDY LIKES TO SPEAK
HIS MIND…THAT'S WHAT I LIKE
ABOUT'EM
<Teddy Pinned*Her*Ass*Down> I'M NOT
TRYNA SINGLE YOU OUT CHOCO I JUST
WANNA SAY WHAT'S ON MY MIND
<Choco Latte> SPEAK YA MIND THEN
<Got'em Hatin>****GRABBIN POPCORN
AND TISSUSE****
<Teddy Pinned*Her*Ass*Down> I'M NOT A
BALLER LIKE FUTURE BUT I DO PRETTY
GOOD FOR MYSELF
<City Ave Diva> NOBODY IS A BALLER
LIKE FUTURE…LOL
<Da Ice Cream Man> Future do be ballin
<Teddy Pinned*Her*Ass*Down> I AM A
COLLEGE GRAD, A FRATERNIY MAN AND
I OWN MY OWN BUSINESS…ON TOP OF
ALL OF THAT…I KNOW HOW TO TREAT A
WOMAN
<Choco Latte> THEN Y R U SINGLE
<Thyk2Def> YEAH TEDDY…Y R U SINGLE
<City Ave Diva> TEDDY I DIN'T KNOW U
HAD IT GOIN ON LIKE THAT

<Teddy Pinned*Her*Ass*Down> I'M LIKE MY CUZIN FUTURE...I DON'T HAVE TO BROADCAST WHAT I HAVE...GET TO KNOW ME AND ANYTHING YOU WANT TO KNOW...I'LL TELL YOU AOUT ME

<Teddy Pinned*Her*Ass*Down> AOUT=ABOUT

<Choco Latte> OUTTA ALL THE PEOPLE YOU'VE MET ON HERE...Y R U TELLING ME THIS

<Teddy Pinned*Her*Ass*Down> CUZ OUTTA ALL THE PEOPLE I'VE MET, UR THE ONE I'M FEELIN'

<Got'em Hatin>****WIPING AWAY TEARS***

<Thyk2Def> AWWWWWWWWWW!!!! THAT IS SO SWEET

<Teddy Pinned*Her*Ass*Down>SERIOUSLY CHOCO...IT AIN'T NOTHIN TO ME...ALL THE TIMES YOU'VE JOKED ABOUT ME COMIN TO CALI ...IF YOU WERE SERIOUS...I WOULDA HOPPED A FLIGHT THE NEXT DAY

<Choco Latte> R U SERIOUS?

<Teddy Pinned*Her*Ass*Down> AS A HEART ATTACK

<Choco Latte> FOR THE FIRST TIME IN MY LIFE I'M SPEECHLESS

<City Ave Diva> I THINK I'M GONNA CRY

<Got'em Hatin>TEDDY GOT PEOPLE ALL TEARY EYED SHIT

<Teddy Pinned*Her*Ass*Down> I DIDN'T MEAN TO PUT U ON THE SPOT CHOCO BUT I'M THE TYPE OF PERSON THAT HAS

TO GET THINGS OFF MY CHEST AS THEY
COME

<Choco Latte>ITS COOL...TO BE
HONEST...I'M GLAD YOU TOLD ME

<MACK Truck>THAT'S MY
MUTHAPHUCKIN CUZIN!!!!!
LELELELELE!!!!

<Teddy Pinned*Her*Ass*Down> SO ABOUT
ME COMIN TO CALI...WHENEVER UR
READY...I'M READY

<Choco Latte>WE'LL TALK MORE ABOUT
THAT BUT FIRST I GOT A PROBLEM I HAVE
TO GET RID OF

<MACK Truck> AIGHT CUZIN...THAT'S
ENUFF...CHILL OUT FOR YOU HAVE ME
CRYIN UP IN DIS BIOTCH...LOL!

<Teddy Pinned*Her*Ass*Down> MY BAD
CUZIN BUT YOU KNOW HOW I FEEL
ABOUT THAT SEXY CHOCOLATE THANG
OUT IN CALI

<Got'em Hatin> IF HE DIDN' B4...HE KNOW
NOW...LOL!

<Da Ice Cream Man> I thought this was a chat
room not the young and the restless

<City Ave Diva> GREEN IS NOT UR
COLOR@ ICE CREAM

<Thyk2Def>THAT'S RIGHT...TEDDY JUST
DID WHAT MOST NIGGAZ R AFRAID TO
DO...EXPRESS HOW THEY FEEL

<Da Ice Cream Man> I still say teddy is full of
shyt!

\<Thyk2Def\> JUST BCUZ I SAID HE WAS A REAL MAN DOESN'T MEAN THAT I DON'T THINK HE'S STILL FULL-O-SHYT…LOL!

\<Futurama\> Y'ALL R 2 MUCH

\<Teddy Pinned*Her*Ass*Down\> SPEAKING OF 2MUCH…HAS ANYBODY SEEN HER?

\<MACK Truck\> SHE AIN'T BEEN IN SINCE RIGHT B4 FUTURE LEFT TO GO TO DA KAROLINAS

\<Futurama\> I DOUBT THAT WE'LL BE SEEING HER ANYMORE

\<Got'em Hatin\> WHAT U DO 2 DAT GIRL@FUTURE

\<Futurama\> NOT WHAT I DID…ITS WHAT SHE DID…SHE LIED TO ME

\<City Ave Diva\> WHAT HAPPENED?

\<Futurama\> SINCE SHE'S HERE IN THE ATL, I INVITED HER TO BE MY GUEST AT LUDACRIS'S PARTY

\<Thyk2Def\> HOW'D SHE LIE IS WHAT I WANNA KNOW

\<Got'em Hatin\> YEAH…THAT'S WHAT I WANNA KNOW

\<Futurama\> SHE SENT ME PICTURES OF HER THAT WEREN'T HER.

\<City Ave Diva\> STEALING PICS SHOULD BE A FELONY…LOL!

\<Futurama\> SHE SENT ME PICS OF THIS PRETTY SLIM GIRL AND A LIL CHUNKY CHICK SHOWED UP AT THE PARTY

\<Thyk2Def\> U GOT SOMETHIN AGAINST THICK CHICKS?

<Futurama> BY NO MEANS...I HAVE SOMETHING AGAINST LIARS

<MACK Truck> DAMN CUZIN...WHAT DID U DO?

<Futurama> I WANTED TO LEAVE BUT SHE HAD A FEW GIRLS WIT HER THAT MY CREW WAS DIGGIN SO I CHILLED LONG ENOUGH FOR THEM TO DO THEM

<Teddy Pinned*Her*Ass*Down> THAT'S WHAT I CALL TAKIN 1 4 DA TEAM...I KNEW FUTURE WAS A REAL ASS NIGGA

<City Ave Diva> DAMN...THAT WAS SHITTY...I THOUGHT SHE WAS COOL

<Futurama> SHE PROBABLY IS A COOL CHICK BUT SHE DIDN'T HAVE TO LIE TO KICK IT

<City Ave Diva> TRU

MRZ.SOOPAFLY has entered the room

<MRZ.SOOPAFLY> WHAT'S UP EVERYBODY!!!

<Teddy Pinned*Her*Ass*Down> EXCUSE US MA'AM BUT DO WE KNOW U?

<MRZ.SOOPAFLY> STOP PLAYIN TEDDY...ITS ME...DA WIFE

<Thyk2Def> GIRL WE ALMOST CUSSED YOU OUT...LOL!

<Got'em Hatin> I KNOW I WAS...I THOUGHT SOME CHICK THAT SOOPAFLY DONE MESSED WIT HAD COME IN HERE AND LOST HER MIND...LOL

<MRZ.SOOPAFLY> LOL! ANYBODY SEEN MY BOO?

\<Thyk2Def\> HE LEFT WHEN YOU LEFT AND HASN'T BEEN BACK SINCE
\<MRZ.SOOPAFLY\> THAT'S FUNNY...HIS PROFILE SAYS THAT HE'S ONLINE
\<City Ave Diva\> MAYBE HE LEFT THE ROOM BUT DIDN'T LOG OUT
\<Got'em Hatin\> MAYBE HE'S IN ANOTHER ROOM
\<MRZ.SOOPAFLY\>HE BETTER NOT BE!
\<Teddy Pinned*Her*Ass*Down\> U KNOW U CANT SAY SHIT LIKE THAT@GOT'EM
\<***Mami*Dearest***\> I'M BACK! WHAT I MISS?
\<Futurama\>I'VE BEEN NOTICING SOMETHING...IS IT JUST ME BUT HERE LATELY THE ROOM HAS BEEN FULL BUT THE ONLY PEOPLE TALKIN IS THE FAM
\<Thyk2Def\> NOT A DAMN THING@MAMI
\<Da Ice Cream Man\> that's cuz teddy got people scared to say anything...lol!
\<Teddy Pinned*Her*Ass*Down\> U NOT PUTTIN THAT ON ME@ICE CREAM
\<***Mami*Dearest***\> WELCOME TO MY ROOM EVERYBODY BUT YOU KNOW THE RULES....THIS IS A VIDEO CHAT ROOM SO YOU NEED TO CAM UP OR BOUNCE!!!
\<Got'em Hatin\> ITS ON NOW...MAMI GETTING READY TO START CLEANIN HOUSE
Optimo Pryme has entered the room
\<Thyk2Def\> MY BABY IS HERE...YAY!
Krystal Lyte has entered the room
Mr.SexxyB-Baller has entered the room

\<Optimo Pryme\> WHAT IT DO MA?@THYK … WHAT'S UP FAM!!!

Lady Get Some has entered the room

SoopaFly has entered the room

\<Teddy Pinned*Her*Ass*Down\> AWWWW SHIT!!! THE FAM IS ALL 2GETHER…ITS TIME TO ACK A ASS!!!!

\<MRZ.SOOPAFLY\>WHERE U BEEN@SOOPAFLY

\<City Ave Diva\> U OK@CHOCO…U BEEN KINDA QUIET

\<SoopaFly\> I TRIED TO COME BACK IN EARLIER BUT COULDN'T SO I WAS ROOM HOPPIN

\<Choco Latte\> I'M COOL@DIVA…TEDDY JUST GOT ME THINKIN

\<Teddy Pinned*Her*Ass*Down\> YO CUZIN…U AIN'T GOTTA EXPLAIN URSELF 2 NO BODY…UR A GROWN AZZ MAN!

\<Futurama\> DON'T LET TEDDY GET U IN TROUBLE@SOOPA

\<SoopaFly\> I'M GOOD FUTURE…I AIN'T GOT NUTHIN TO HIDE

\<City Ave Diva\> THAT'S RIGHT@SOOPA PAY TEDDY NO MIND

\<Teddy Pinned*Her*Ass*Down\> DAMN CUZ…DON'T TELL ME U SPRUNG ALREADY…LOL

\<Da Ice Cream Man\> r u sitting there naked@thyk

\<Optimo Pryme\> SHE BETTER NOT BE!!!!

\<Thyk2Def\> NO ICE CREAM…I HAVE ON A HALTER TOP

\<Da Ice Cream Man> just checkin

\<Futurama> I DON'T KNOW WHO'S
WORSE...ICE CREAM OR SLICK...LOL

\<Got'em Hatin> SLICK GOT ICE CREAM
BEAT HANDS DOWN

\<City Ave Diva> SLICK IZ JUST DOWN
RIGHT NASTY

\<Lady Get Some> ABOUT 3 NITES AGO I
WAS CAM BROWSIN AND I GOT TO
SLICK'S CAM AND HE WAS SITTIN THERE
WIT HIS DICK OUT FOR NO REASON

\<Got'em Hatin> HOW BIG WAS IT?

\<City Ave Diva> THAT AIN'T THE FIRST
TIME@GET SOME

\<Lady Get Some> LET'S JUST SAY HE HAS A
MAJOR SHORT COMING...LOL!

\<MRZ.SOOPAFLY> LOL!

\<Futurama> WOW! I KNEW THAT DUDE
WAS STRANGE

\<Teddy Pinned*Her*Ass*Down> WAIT TIL
HE COMES BACK IN HERE...I'MA STR8
ROAST HIS NASTY ASS

\<Futurama> LOL! AIGHT Y'ALL...I'M FIXIN'
TO BE OUT AS DA SOUTHERNERS WOULD
SAY

\<Thyk2Def> DON'T BE HATIN ON DA
SOUF JUST CUZ U FROM NEW
JERSEY@FUTURE LOL!

\<Da Ice Cream Man> lata Future

\<Teddy Pinned*Her*Ass*Down> PEACE
OUT CUZIN!

\<Futurama> B 4 I FORGET...IF ANYBODY IS
TRYNA COME TO THE ATL FOR THE

SOUTHERN SUNZ ALBUM RELEASE PARTY
I NEED TO KNOW BY NEXT SUNDAY
<Thyk2Def> FUTURE ACT LIKE WE GOT
MONEY LIKE DAT
<Futurama> TO MAKE IT EVEN
BETTER...WHOEVER COMES, I'LL PUT YOU
UP IN A HOTEL FOR THE WEEKEND AND
WE'LL HAVE A PARTY AT MY
HOUSE...JUST4KICKZ STYLE
<Optimo Pryme> FO' SHO CUZIN....PUT ME
ON THE LIST NOW
<Teddy Pinned*Her*Ass*Down> CHOCO IF
YOU WANNA GO TO THE PARTY WIT ME,
I'LL PAY FOR YA FLIGHT
<City Ave Diva> YOU PAYIN FOR THYK IF
SHE WANNA GO TOO@OPTIMO
<Mr.SexxyB-Baller> COUNT ME IN CUZIN
<Optimo Pryme> I TELL YOU
BOY...FUTURE AND TEDDY BE TRYNA
MAKE A NIGGA LOOK BAD
<Futurama> ASSUMING ALL MY FAM HAS
MY EMAIL ADDY...JUST RSVP BY NEXT
SUNDAY SO I CAN GET SHYT
TOGETHER...I'M OUT!

The next morning, Natalie's slumber
was interrupted by the ring of her cell phone.
She tried to ignore it but whoever was on the
other end was persistent.

"Hello?" she answered with sleep in her
voice.

"Girl, I know you ain't still in the bed." Alicia inquired.

"Why should I get up? The same thing is going to happen today that happened yesterday...absolutely nothing."

"I know you're sleepy but that's not the Natalie I know talkin' like that. I'm on my way over."

"Alicia, wait..."

Alicia hung up the phone and was half way out the door. Natalie pulled herself out of bed and into the shower. By the time she finished her shower and slipped on a black sports bra and a pair of basketball shorts, Alicia was ringing her doorbell.

"I'm comin, I'm comin," Natalie called as she came down the stairs. She opened the door to find Alicia and Taylor on the other side. As soon as she saw Taylor, Natalie perked up.

"I knew she'd help brighten up your day."

"Wait, wait, wait. It's 10:30 on a Wednesday, What are you doing off work."

"I took some time off. After that campaign we just did for Coca-Cola, I needed a break."

"Come on in. You have to excuse the house."

"Girl, please. Try living with a toddler in your house then I'll excuse the mess." Alicia laughed as she sat Taylor on the couch. "So, what's the problem?"

"There is no problem."

"Natalie stop it. I've never heard you talk like I heard you this morning. Somethin's wrong. I can see right through you."

"Okay, I'll tell you. Hold on a minute."Natalie walked into the kitchen and returned with a pitcher of orange juice and two glasses. "Remember the guy I was telling you about?"

"The record label guy."

"Yeah. He's seeing someone."

"How do you know?"

"We talked about her last night. I take that back. They're not together. Last night was the first time they went out."

"Okay. So he dates."

"But you should have heard the way he talked about her. He talked about her as if she was 'The One'. He also said that the evening was perfect until the end of the night when she rushed off like Cinderella."

"What does that mean?"

"He said that around 10:30 she got frantic and said she had to rush home to let her babysitter leave. Then he said that the car she was driving might have belonged to a guy because it had an Omega Psi Phi tag liner around it like the Sigma one Dré has on his truck."

"Something doesn't sound right about that. It seems like she's double-dealing or hiding something. Where did he say he met her?"

"He didn't say."

"I'll betcha he met her online. Has he asked to meet you yet?"

"Nope. That's what puzzled me."

"If Iverson is the good man that you think he is and she's hiding something, it'll come out eventually."

"What do I do in the mean time?"

"Be his friend."

"Honestly Alicia, I've been through that before and didn't wind up with the man. Remember?"

"I got a feeling about this one. Just trust me. Now for you Miss Thing, put some clothes on."

"For what?"

"What do women do when we have a problem?"

"Sit around the house all day and sulk."

"No, Girl. We're goin' shoppin'!"

No woman can resist a shopping trip — especially Natalie Simms. Natalie went upstairs and threw on jeans, T-shirt and sneakers and the three left the house. Twenty minutes later they arrived at Lennox Mall. They browsed around looking in store after store until Natalie saw a familiar face coming out of a store.

"Don't look now," Natalie whispered. "That's Iverson coming out of that store across the way."

"Where?" Alicia blurted. "I don't see him."

"Thank you for being so discreet. You see the tall guy with the black leather jacket on and the chain around his neck. That's him." As Iverson walked away from the store he noticed Natalie and Alicia looking at him. He recognized them from the club. Instead of going over, he gave a casual wave and kept walking.

"Why didn't you go over and speak?" Alicia scolded.

"Because. He doesn't know who I am and I'm not ready for him to meet me."

"Yes you are. You said it the other day."

"You're right but I wasn't nervous when I said it the first time."

"You play in front of thousands of people but when it comes to meeting a fine man like that, you're nervous."

"So?"

"Whatever. Let him slip away if you want to."

"I got it under control. I just need it to be a little more structured."

"Okay structure."

Later on that night, Ivy found himself at TyQuan's place involved in a heated game of Spades. It was Ivy and T-Bizzy verses Will and

KD. If one had walked into the house you could tell who was winning and who was losing. Will sat slumped in his chair complaining about his partner's playing and KD continued to talk cash shit, despite the fact that the score was 90-260.

"You just a glutton for pain," T-Bizzy remarked as he cut KD's Ace of Hearts with a Jack of Spades. "Keep pissin' and I'ma learns ya."

"It's obvious he ain't learned from the first 4 hands," Will complained.

"Who side you on?" KD asked his partner.

"The man is stating a fact," Ivy defended.

"GAME TIME!" T-Bizzy shouted.

"Good cuz I quit," Will stated as he got up from the table and went sat on the couch.

"Come on man," Ivy consoled. "You can't be a quitter all your life." Will gave Ivy the middle finger as the remaining three gathered on the sofa, the love seat and the recliner.

"Now tell me why you didn't come out to the Zone?" TyQuan asked Ivy.

"I had a prior engagement."

"Prior engagement my ass. You was probably at the Cyber Café sippin' mocha lattes with some girl you just met." Iverson tried to motion to T-Bizzy to stop.

"What!" Will interrupted. "You still fuckin' wit bitches online?"

"First and foremost, all you motherfuckas need to mind ya business. Second of all, I went out with this girl I met at Jermaine Dupri's birthday party."

"But that was month's ago," KD interjected.

"She's a model...hard to catch up wit."

"Okay, model. Yeah right." TyQuan walked to the refrigerator in his game room and got another round of beer.

"Seriously. After Candace I left it alone for a while but when I met ol' girl at the club, I decided that it wasn't for me."

"What girl from the club?" KD asked.

"That big ass Star Jones lookin' broad," TyQuan laughed.

"You talking about the girl that came to Blaze? Please tell me you're lyin'."

"So from that experience, I'm out of the Internet datin' game."

"I would be too if Shamu came all the way from Sea World to see me." The foursome continued with idle chatter, as the night grew old. Eventually KD and Will left leaving TyQuan and Iverson behind.

"Be straight with me Ivy, Who'd you go out with last night."

"Shelby Cortez."

"Where did you meet her?"

"JD's party." TyQuan gave him that *yeah-right* look. "Okay, I met her online. You happy?"

"I'm ya boy. You ain't gotta lie to me."

"True but I knew if you knew I was still internet datin', you'd give me hell."

"You're a grown ass man. I give you hell anyway. You do what you want to do. You know I got ya back no matter what. If that's how you feel comfortable meeting women, hey, do you."

"I just feel that it's easier for them to get to know the man behind Future instead of seeing me on the scene. Feel me?"

"I feel you but it's just that whole truth thing. 95% of the people you meet either lie, have hidden lives or aren't who they portray themselves to be. I'm not saying that everybody online is like that but the percentage of dishonesty is kinda high. Just watch ya'self."

"I got it under control."

"If you got it then I ain't got nothin' else to say about it."

"Cool. Well, dog. I'm 'bout to be out. We got a lot of shit to do tomorrow. We only got 4 more days before Christmas and I'm tryin' to wrap up this Atlanta shoot tomorrow so we can get back to the Carolinas for the 4 college stops we gotta make."

"I thought we were gonna chill and pick it up after the New Year and what college stops?"

"You didn't get the memo about the itinerary change?"

"Ivy, my office is right down the hall from yours. You know I don't check memos."

"Then I suggest you start."

"Then I suggest you spring for me a secretary."

"The last secretary I hired you fucked off. If you want a secretary then you hire her."

"Anyway...This ain't about me. What college stops?"

"ATP is from Charleston and EL GEE is from Fayetteville. He went to A&T. he has the whole college boy image. Now we're going back to the Carolinas to do scenes at A&T, Johnson C. Smith, Fayetteville State and South Carolina State and we got seven days to do it."

"Are you serious? That's 4 cities in seven days."

"You act like we haven't done multi-city tours before. This is a good start before the summer hits. Get it together and let's do this."

"You know I gotta complain about it first," TyQuan laughed.

"Shakeem said it was going better than he expected. If we grind out 12-15 hours tomorrow, we can wrap it up and have the rest of the time to chill before the holidays."

"Then let's grind it out."

T-Bizzy walked Iverson to the door and they exchanged one love. Iverson headed for home. When he arrived and went upstairs to check his messages and to see who was online, he found a message from WifeyMaterial. It read:

> **WifeyMaterial:** sorry I had to rush off last night just as the evening was going well. I had to get home to my baby. I hope that we can get together again so I can make it up to you. I promise you won't be disappointed.

Iverson let out a soft chuckle as he closed the box and continued on with his messages. After about six more, he found one from Dymond4eva that read:

> **Dymond4eva:** hoped to catch you tonite but I know ur a busy man. Just hit me up when you get a minute. ttyl

Natalie had Ivy intrigued because he had never seen her face. He tried to picture her but his mental images were still cloudy. That night as Iverson sat in his bed thinking about Wifey and Dymond, Natalie was on the other side of town thinking about him. As thoughts passed, Ivy logged into his other world to see what was poppin on just4kickz.

***

Futurama has entered the room
<Teddy Pinned*Her*Ass*Down> C'MON DIVA...U KNOW THAT WAS FOUL

\<Choco Latte\> WE ALL KNOW THAT
TEDDY BUT U DON'T HAVE TO TREAT HER
LIKE THAT...PEOPLE MAKE MISTAKES
\<City Ave Diva\> THAT'S RIGHT TEDDY...IF
FUTURE WAS HERE YOU KNOW HE
WOULD SAY THE SAME THING
\<Futurama\>AND FUTURE IS HERE....SO
WHAT THE HELL IS GOIN ON
\<Choco Latte\> TEDDY'S GOIN OFF ON
2MUCH BCUZ OF WHAT SHE DID
\<Futurama\> EASE UP CUZIN...ITS ALL
GOOD...IT HAPPENS...I AIN'T MAD
\<Teddy Pinned*Her*Ass*Down\> STILL YET
FUTURE...HOW SHE DO YOU LIKE THAT
AND COME UP IN HERE LIKE
EVERYTHING IS COOL
\<City Ave Diva\> SHE PROBABLY DIDN'T
KNOW WE WERE AS TIGHT AS WE ARE
\<Futurama\> CHILL OUT CUZIN...SHE STILL
COOL
\<2much4u\> IF I WOULDA KNOWN IT WAS
LIKE THAT IN HERE I WOULDA NEVER
LET IT HAPPEN@FUTURE
\<Teddy Pinned*Her*Ass*Down\> LIKE
WHAT??? REAL???
\<Futurama\> LIKE I SAID MA...AIN'T NO
HARD FEELIN'S...TEDDY IS MY BOY AND
HE'S JUST TRYNA LOOK OUT FOR HIS
PEOPLE
\<City Ave Diva\> WE ALL BEEN KICKIN IT
FOR A LONG TIME@2MUCH...WE'RE LIKE
A FAMILY. WHEN SOMETHING HAPPENS
TO ONE, IT AFFECTS US ALL

<2much4u> I C THAT
<Choco Latte> NOW TEDDY YOU
APOLOGIZE
<Teddy Pinned*Her*Ass*Down>FOR
WHAT???
<City Ave Diva> YOU KNOW FOR
WHAT@TEDDY
<2much4u> ITS COOL...TEDDY DOESN'T
HAVE TO APOLOGIZE...HE WAS JUST
TRYNA LOOK OUT FOR HIS PEOPLE...IDA
DONE THE SAME THING
<Da Ice Cream Man> if teddy has to
apologize...a couple of outher people should
be apologizin' 2
<Teddy Pinned*Her*Ass*Down> THAT'S
RIGHT...THYK AND GOT'EM HATIN
<Thyk2Def> BUT THIS AIN'T ABOUT ME
<Got'em Hatin> ME NEITHER
<2much4u> SINCE FUTURE IS YOUR BOY
AND I MET HIM HERE I WOULD LIKE TO
APOLOGIZE TO HIM FOR WHAT I DID
AND HOPE THERE IS NO HARD FEELINGS
AND WE CAN STILL BE COOL
<Da Ice Cream Man> now there's something u
don't c everyday
<Futurama> APOLOGY ACCEPTED AND I
SPEAK FOR EVERYONE WHEN I SAY THAT
U ARE ALWAYS WELCOME...NO HARD
FEELINGS
<Da Ice Cream Man> I didn't get a chance to
tell you@Future   me, soopafly and da wife are
comin to the Atlanta for the album release

\<Futurama\> THAT'S WHAT'S UP BUT MAKE SURE U RSVP...THAT'S WHAT I'M GOIN BY TO MAKE THE NECESSARY ACCOMODATIONS

\<Da Ice Cream Man\>no doubt

\<City Ave Diva\> YOU AND CHOCO STILL GOIN@TEDDY

\<Teddy Pinned*Her*Ass*Down\> CHOCO HASN'T MADE UP HER MIND YET BUT YA BOY IS AS GOOD AS THERE

\<Choco Latte\> I STILL HAVEN'T FIGURED OUT WHAT I'M GONNA TELL MY MAN

\<Teddy Pinned*Her*Ass*Down\> BE REAL...TELL HIM YOU GOIN TO A PARTY IN THE ATL WIT YA MAN

\<Got'em Hatin\> JUST TELL HIM YOU GOIN TO ATLANTA WIT ME

\<City Ave Diva\> THAT SHOULD WORK

\<Choco Latte\> I DIDN'T THINK ABOUT THAT

\<Got'em Hatin\> YOU KNOW I'M THE QUEEN OF DOIN DIRT...LOL!

\<Futurama\> I ALMOST FORGOT TO TELL YOU@TEDDY...I'LL BE IN THE VILLE AFTER THE NEW YEAR

\<Teddy Pinned*Her*Ass*Down\> THAT'S WHAT'S UP...I'LL SEND YOU DA CELL AND U CAN HIT ME WHEN YOU TOUCH DOWN

\<Thyk2Def\> WHY CAN'T YOU EVER COME TO HOUSTON@FUTURE

\<Futurama\> ONE OF THE ARTISTS IN MY NEW GROUP IS FROM DA VILLE AND HE'S REPPIN DA KOLLEGE SCENE

\<Teddy Pinned*Her*Ass*Down\> YOU DOIN A VIDEO SHOOT HERE OR SUMTHIN?@FUTURE

\<Futurama\> WE'RE FINISHING UP THEIR 1ST VIDEO SHOOT BY DOING SCENES AT FAYETTEVILLE STATE, NC A&T, JCSU AND SC STATE

\<Thyk2Def\> ITS COLLEGES IN HOUSTON…COME HERE…LOL!

\<Futurama\> DON'T WORRY@THYK…WHEN THE TOUR STARTS, I'LL MAKE SURE THAT HOUSTON IS ON THE LIST

\<City Ave Diva\> I KNOW U COMIN TO PHILLY@FUTURE

\<Got'em Hatin\> DON'T FORGET ABOUT THE 619 EITHER

\<Choco Latte\> IF YOU COME TO DA 619 DON'T FORGET TO BRING MY BABY WIT U FUTURE

\<Teddy Pinned*Her*Ass*Down\> AWWWW…THAT'S SO SWEET

\<Choco Latte\> I WAS TALKIN ABOUT MY OTHER BABY…FACE

\<Futurama\> DAMN CUZIN…SHE PLAYED U…LOL

\<Got'em Hatin\> I DIDN'T KNOW U KNEW BABYFACE@FUTURE

\<Futurama\> SHE'S TALKIN ABOUT FACE…ONE OF MY OTHER ARTISTS…LOL

\<Choco Latte\> LOL!

\<City Ave Diva\> I THOUGHT SHE WAS
TALKIN ABOUT BABYFACE TOO...LOL

\<Da Ice Cream Man\> I think everybody
thought she was talking about babyface...he is
in Atlanta

\<Futurama\> UNLESS AN ARTIST IS ON HIS
OWN TOUR, THE WHOLE FUTURE CAMP
GOES ON TOUR TOGETHER TO SUPPORT
EACH OTHER

\<Choco Latte\> IS FACE ON TOUR OR IS HE
GOING TO BE THERE?

\<Teddy Pinned*Her*Ass*Down\> THE ONLY
FACE THAT U NEED TO BE CONCERNED
WITH IS MINE

\<City Ave Diva\> SOUNDS LIKE
SOMEBODY'S JEALOUS...LOL!

\<Choco Latte\> TEDDY U KNO U MY
BABY...I JUST WANNA MEET FACE

\<Futurama\> IF WE COME TO SAN DIEGO, U
CAN MEET FACE@CHOCO

\<Got'em Hatin\> WHAT U MEAN IF?

\<Futurama\> THE PROMOTERS SET UP THE
TOURS...I KNOW 4 SURE THAT LA IS ON
THE LIST, PHILLY, MEW YORK, HOUSTON,
DALLAS, CHARLESTON AND
FAYETTEVILLE

\<Da Ice Cream Man\> I don't wanna sound
dumb or anything but where in da hell is MEW
YORK...lol!

\<Teddy Pinned*Her*Ass*Down\> LOL

\<City Ave Diva\> LMAO!

\<Futurama\> U KNOW WHAT DA HELL I
MEANT...SMART ASS...LOL

\<Teddy Pinned*Her*Ass*Down\> U HAVE TO EXCUSE FUTURE...HE WENT TO HOWARD AND ALL THEY TEACH UP THERE IS HOW TO BE GREEK...LOL!
\<City Ave Diva\> R U GREEK@FUTURE
\<Futurama\> PHI BETA SIGMA UNTIL I DIE
\<Teddy Pinned*Her*Ass*Down\> BLUUUUUUUUUUE PHHHIIIII!!! DAMN FUTURE...I DIDN'T KNOW U WAS FRAT. G.O.M.A.B.
\<Teddy Pinned*Her*Ass*Down\> WHEN U CROSS?
\<City Ave Diva\> ZZZZZZZZZZZZZZ-PHI!
\<Futurama\> SPRING 97... #7...LINE NAME "CROSSOVER"
\<Choco Latte\>OOOOOOOOOOOOOOO-OOOOOOP! SPRING Y2K "CHOCOLATE GIRL WONDER" DELTA SIGMA THETA IN DA HOUSE!
\<Teddy Pinned*Her*Ass*Down\> FALL 97 #2 "RZAREKSHUN"
\<Da Ice Cream Man\> YO! YO!
\<Teddy Pinned*Her*Ass*Down\> U WOULD USE CAPS FOR DAT BULLSHIT...LOL!
\<City Ave Diva\> Z_PHI! SPRING 98...#1...BIG SISTER "1ST CLASS"
\<Got'em Hatin\> ME PHI ME...UNIQUE DESIGNS SCHOOL OF COSMETOLOGY
\<Thyk2Def\> A SISTA NEED AN APPOINTMENT@ GOT'EM
\<Futurama\> AIGHT Y'ALL...I JUST STOPPED IN FOR A MINUTE...I GOTTA LAY MY AZZ DOWN...CYA WHEN I CYA...ONE!

\<Got'em Hatin\> NITE NITE…SD
\<Thyk2Def\> NITE FUTURE
\<Teddy Pinned*Her*Ass*Down\> G.O.M.A.B.@FUTURE
\<City Ave Diva\> NITE FRAT! ZZZZZZ-PHI!!!!!!!
SlicK has entered the room
MRZ.SOOPAFLY has entered the room

Chapter 9

That next night, Natalie, André and Alicia arrived at the Ritz-Carlton Buckhead for Black Reign's annual Christmas party. The trio was dressed to kill. Natalie wore her red, Donna Karen evening gown that hugged the full contour of her body. Her braids were fresh and hung to her shoulders. The rhinestones in the straps of her shoes sparkled as she walked through the lobby. Alicia had on an all black Versace gown. The upper part of the gown, over the breast area, was sheer and came to her neck. It was the perfect ensemble to wear the diamond choker that André bought her for her birthday that summer. As always, André Marshall was dressed to impress in his custom fit black, Sean John tuxedo.

André was the man of the hour because he arrived to the gala with two beautiful women on his arm — his wife and his Diamond. As they walked to their table, the three exchanged pleasantries with everyone. Everybody knew André but surprisingly, there were a lot of Atlanta Diamond fans in attendance. After the three took their seats at the head table, Joseph and Jonathan Conrad, the owners of Black Reign, stepped on stage on welcomed every one. Following their welcome, the live band kicked it into gear with some oldies but goodies.

"Come on, baby," André stood up and grabbed Alicia's hand. "Let's dance."

"You gon' be alright?" Alicia asked Natalie.

"Alicia, this is not a high school dance. I'm a big girl." They laughed as André escorted Alicia to the dance floor. A familiar person walked up behind Natalie.

"Excuse me," Smoke disguised his voice. "Would you like to dance?"

"That's okay," Natalie began as she turned to face the stranger. She busted into laughter when she saw that it was Smoke. "You are so silly."

"What's up, Nat?" Smoke greeted as he hugged Natalie. "So, how about it?" Smoke extended his hand.

"Only cuz it's you." Natalie took Smoke's hand as he led her to the dance floor beside Dré and Alicia. "And you better not be tryna grab my booty."

They laughed as they found their spot on the dance floor. The four danced through two songs and returned to their seats. Natalie noticed that every guy that passed by her table checked her out. Though she saw some handsome men she was reluctant to inquire about any of them. In the middle of conversation, a gentleman approached the table. He was around 6' 1" with curly hair, a light complexion and green eyes.

"André," he greeted as he approached. "Good to see you again."

"Calvin," André obliged as he stood to shake his hand. "You remember my wife, Alicia and this is my sister Natalie."

"Ladies. André, I know we're supposed to be enjoying the evening and not talking business but I think I have some information that you might find interesting. Can I talk to you for a minute?"

"Sure. Excuse me for a minute ladies." The two men walked out of the ballroom and into the lobby.

"Who was that?" Natalie inquired.

"That's Calvin Isley. His father used to own the Isley firm. He died a few months ago and left it to Calvin."

"You talkin' about the same Isley firm in Atlanta?"

"Yup. His sister is André's secretary."

"How old is he?"

"I think Calvin and André are the same age. Why? You interested? "

"Not. I was just curious."

"Come on, Nat, the brotha's young, handsome and doin' something with his life. At least check him out."

"I will if he approaches me and not because you or Dré set me up."

"Okay."

"I mean it. Tell your husband, No match making." Five minutes later Calvin and Dré returned to the table.

"Alicia, it was good seeing you again. Natalie, it was a pleasure to meet you."

"Likewise." Natalie smiled.

"Gimme a call in the morning, André. We can set everything up."

"Will do."

"You all enjoy the rest of the evening. I have to get back to my wife." Calvin walked off.

"Baby, when did Calvin get married?"

"About four months ago. I thought I told you."

"Who did he marry?"

"Shelby...the same girl he's been with.

"But I thought they broke up right after we got married?"

"They did but they got back together after we had that cookout for my birthday. They eloped and had a private ceremony in Jamaica."

"Oh okay."

"Another good man off the market," Natalie thought to herself.

The threesome enjoyed the rest of the evening. Before long, twelve o'clock came and they left. Alicia and André dropped Natalie off and headed to Vanessa's to pick up Taylor. Natalie drug herself into the house and upstairs to her bedroom. She stood and looked at herself in the mirror and questioned herself: Why was she still single and was there a good man out there for her?

"That's a wrap!" Shakeem shouted. Everyone in the room exploded with applause.

"Before you leave," Ivy interrupted as he stepped up on a chair. "I have something to say. First I wanna thank everyone for their hard work on this video shoot. Big ups to Shakeem and his crew, all the ladies from Too Hot and the entire Future Records crew." Everyone cheered and applauded again. "For those who don't know, 'Where You From?' has been number one on both countdowns, V-103 and Hot 107.9. After the New Year, we go back in the studio to record the remix with Lil Jon and it's going to feature Ludacris and Ciara. Have a Merry Christmas and a safe New Year."

The entire crew gave The Southern Sunz a warm ovation and cleared out of the studio leaving T-Bizzy, Ivy, ATP, EL GEE and Gusto. After some heavy convincing of ATP and Gusto, the five went to the Silver Dollar to kick it. Inside the Silver Dollar, Ivy and his crew toasted to the success of the Southern Sunz. They laughed and had a great time for a couple of hours. As the evening grew old, most of the members of the Future Records camp left.

Ivy stayed at the Silver Dollar and had one more drink. As he sat he thought about a couple of things. Through his mind ran thoughts of Candace, XoticMami and

2much4u — all failed Internet experiences. Because of those three failures he wondered what was going to be so different about WifeyMaterial. She seemed to be a perfect match for him but there was something about her that he just couldn't put his finger on. He continued to dwell on WifeyMaterial until a thought of Dymond4eva crossed his mind. She reminded him a lot of a girl that he dated while in college. Just like Dymond4eva, Tina played basketball. He was on the men's team and she played for the women.

Iverson met Tina during their freshman year at Howard — right after he had just broke up with his high school sweetheart, Annette. He and his ex-girlfriend were together for six years. She was a cheerleader and he was a baller. They went their separate ways because he chose to play ball at Howard instead of going to Morgan State with her. Ivy and Tina hit it off from the beginning but he wasn't ready to jump into another relationship. Tina was cool with the two of them just being friends. They spent almost everyday of their first semester together and by the time the season started, they had become a couple. Everything was fine until the end of their senior year.

Right before graduation, Tina got offered a job in Los Angeles. She wanted Iverson to go with her but he didn't want to leave the East Coast. After college Iverson hooked up with an agent and entered the draft. He didn't get drafted but did manage to get signed as a free agent to the Los Angeles Clippers for one year for 750 thousand dollars. It was music to Tina's ears when Ivy called and told her the good news. He moved to LA and he and Tina got a place together.

Once the season started, the relationship began to fall apart. There was a big difference between dating a college ball player and a NBA player. In college, you go on the road, play one game and come right back. In the NBA, a player was gone for weeks at a time. Being a pro ball player was never a dream for Ivy but because he loved Tina, he gave it a shot. By the middle of the season, Ivy moved into a starting position and became a star over night despite the Clippers losing season. He went from playing 5 minutes and averaging 5 points and 3 assists a game to playing almost the entire game averaging 25 points, 7 assists and 3 steals per game.

Even though things were good for him, he was not happy. His relationship with Tina began to spiral downwards. All Iverson wanted to do was go back to New Jersey. If he was able to go back as a ball player it would have been cool. If he didn't, that was cool too. Because of his success, the Clippers offered him a five-year deal worth 17 million dollars.

Iverson turned the offer down, terminated his already broken relationship with Tina and returned to Camden, New Jersey to run a club for his uncle.

Iverson was back in Jersey for two weeks when he got a call from T-Bizzy telling him that he was moving to Atlanta and wanted to see if he wanted to go with him. After much contemplating, Iverson moved to Atlanta with a dream of owning his own club in the home of the *Dirty South* nightlife. Iverson took all the money he had left from the NBA and opened a club with T-Bizzy. Before long, promoters started approaching him left and right. He started hosting concerts and open mic nights at his club. During the open mic nights he met an MC that was hot but nobody would give him a shot because he didn't have the "down south" sound that was starting to get hot. Iverson took him under his wing and began to promote him in his own club with T-Bizzy as his DJ. He had his first artist.

From that artist he picked up a female R&B artist and then a male R&B artist. In one year he managed to create a little family that was going to be his future. When his artists began to gain popularity outside of Atlanta, Ivy realized he had something special on his hands. It was time to go all in. Iverson took everything he had and invested it into what is now, Future Records. It started off rough but after he got a distribution deal with Universal, he was on his way. After two years passed, Iverson was making so much noise with Future Records; he sold the club and bought his current office space with the studio in it. He made T-Bizzy his President and the rest is history. By the close of the year, he got his first platinum single which was followed by four more platinum albums. Future Records was on the rise with tremendous success but no one for him to share it with.

Time flew by as Iverson sat thinking about his rise to the top. Before he knew it, it was three o'clock and the Dollar was getting ready to close. Ivy pulled himself off of his bar stool and into his car. As he drove through Buckhead he gazed at the lights and all of the clubs and bars. His face gave a wide smile when he passed one particular club. It was the one that he opened years ago. Iverson would have never thought in a million years that giving up 17 million dollars would have brought him more in less time — doing something that he always enjoyed. As he pulled into his garage and into his empty house he paused in his living room for a second and continued upstairs. Because it was so late, he decided to go straight to bed and check his messages and numbers the next day. Ivy continued to think about his rise to fame and the women that had passed through his life as he lay in his bed. The thing he couldn't figure out was: Why was he sleeping alone every night?

The next morning Iverson awoke to the sound of his cell phone. With his eyes still closed, he rolled over and reached towards the nightstand. In the process of searching for his phone, he knocked it off of the nightstand and on to the floor. After hitting the floor it rolled under the bed. "If it's important, they'll call back," he thought as he repositioned himself. Five minutes later it rang again. Iverson pulled all of the strength that he had and hung his upper body over the side of the bed and reached for the phone.

"Yeah," Iverson grumbled.
"Well good morning to you, too," the voice answered.
"Who dis?"
"It's Shelby."
As he woke up immediately, "Hey, What's up?"
"You were asleep, weren't you?"
"Nah, I was just screening my calls."
"Uh huh."
"Anyway, what's good?"
"I was calling to see if you had some free time today."
"I might be able to pencil you in," Ivy chuckled.
"Pencil me in? Shelby Cortez doesn't get penciled in. She is priority."

"And what makes Shelby Cortez priority?"

"You have to wait and find out."

"How long do I have to wait to find out?"

"That depends on you. How about you meet me in Centennial Park at noon."

"What time is it now?"

"8:45."

"I guess I can do that since you took time out of your busy schedule to fit me in," Ivy laughed.

"You do music and you're a comedian. How nice."

"I try."

"Okay, I try. I'll see you at noon."

"It's a date." Iverson hung up the phone, placed it back on the nightstand and went back to sleep.

On the other side of Atlanta, Natalie was in the middle of a serious cardio-vascular workout. Every step she took on the treadmill, she wished that were taking her away from the things she had been through. Her thoughts began to overpower the music that played in her headphones and the television that once played Sports Center began to get fuzzy. In the blink of an eye, the screen went blank and a familiar scene appeared. Before her eyes was the day that she was selected as the number one draft choice to the Atlanta Diamonds. That was one of the happiest days of her life. All of her hard work and determination, since she was six years old, had paid off.

From that scene it changed to the night that she met André Marshall at Club Blaze. There they sat in *The Network* – a room on the top floor of the club. She could see the desire in her eyes that she had for him on that first night. From there she saw a night that she tried to put out of her mind. It was the night that she sat and cried on Shanice's shoulder after she was lied to by her teammate, Shawna. In an attempt to steal André from her, Shawna lied and told her that André was all up on her at the car wash when it was merely a conversation.

Mixed emotions ran through Natalie's body as she watched replays of her life. The next thing that came on the screen was the night she and Shawna got into a fight in Houston after she and André reconciled their friendship after the truth came out. "We're there any happy points in my life?" she thought. As that thought passed she watched as she lead the Atlanta Diamonds to their first WNBA Championship and was named Most Valuable Player. She began to smile. Shortly there after, came Desmond and the hardships of their relationship that started out so wonderful. From there passed the falling out of her and her best friend, Shanice.

In the middle of her workout, Natalie hung her head down as tears began to fall from her soft, brown eyes. Since she had been in Atlanta she had more bad times than good. In an instant she thought about running away from Atlanta but that was short lived due to the new contract that she signed with the Diamonds for six more years — looks like she had to make the best of it. Just as she was pulling herself back together she looked to the television that was beside the one that was positioned in front of her. The station was tuned to BET as they were playing a video with a familiar face in it. Natalie watched as Iverson sat in the driver's seat of a convertible Bentley with one of his artists beside him. She thought she was still seeing things but it was real — just like the curiosity that dwelled within her about him. In her eyes, Iverson was one of the sexiest men that had it going on she had come across in awhile. What he was really about remained a mystery.

Natalie's train of thought was interrupted by the beep of her treadmill as it notified her that her workout was complete. She draped her towel over her head as she stepped off the treadmill and walked towards the basketball court. Just when seeing Iverson had brightened up her day, it went sour once again. When she opened the door to the basketball court she saw a sight that made her sick to her stomach. There they stood engaged in a deep and passionate kiss, Desmond and Shanice. The sudden open of the door interrupted their kiss and they both looked towards the door and saw Natalie standing there. In an instant her feelings went from hurt to rage as she stormed out of the room towards the locker room.

"Natalie, wait!" Desmond shouted from across the fitness center as he ran toward her. She didn't look back and she never broke her stride. Desmond caught her just before she walked into the locker room.

"Desmond, go to hell!" Natalie roared.
"Baby, I'm sorry."
"Yes you are."
"Okay. I deserved that."
"What you really deserve is illegal in all 50 states."
"What happened to the Natalie I once loved?"
"You walked out on her, remember? Then you started fuckin' her best friend!" With that statement everyone in the gym paused and looked towards the conflict. "You know what Desmond? I'm through. You can screw who you wanna screw. I don't care anymore. I'm over it. As of now you're dead to me but remember this. Karma is real and it's a bitch. The way you hurt me, is going to have no comparison to what's gonna happen to you."

"Who you supposed to be now? Miss Ciely from The Color Purple?"

"You're an asshole." Natalie turned her back and walked into the locker room. She took two steps after she passed through the door and stopped.

"Bitch," Desmond mumbled. Natalie turned around and walked back into the hall. SMACK! Natalie tried to knock Desmond's head off. He stood holding his face in shock and disbelief as Natalie walked back into the locker room. In a frenzy, she threw her things in her gym bag and rushed out of the building. When she got in her SUV she put both of her hands at twelve o'clock on the steering wheel, put her head on her hands and cried. She had to let it out before she tried to drive off. "What did I do to deserve this?" she whined and sobbed. Through all of her success, she had to endure one let down after another. Something had to give because Natalie didn't think she could take much more before she broke down beyond repair.

It was noon and the day was cold. Iverson sat on a bench in Centennial Park in a black, New York Yankees baseball cap, a black, signature Sean John leather jacket, a pair of dark blue jeans and black Timberland boots. He was fiddling with his Sidekick when Shelby walked up behind him.

"You been waiting long?" she asked as Iverson turned around when he heard her voice. The days weather had Shelby dressed in a pair of tight, light blue Baby Phat jeans, a dark brown, short leather jacket and a pair of dark brown leather boots to match. Her hair was curly and down to her shoulders with a pair of brown, tinted Chanel shades covering her eyes.

"Actually, I just got here." He replied as she sat on the bench beside him.

"Feel like walking?"

"Sure." Iverson stood up and grabbed Shelby by the hand.

"I'm sorry about the other night."

"It's all good. You had a baby to get home to."

"I was having such a good time with you, I lost track of time."

"That's understandable. I thought you were gonna be tied up until after the holidays."

"Sometimes you have to make time for certain things," Shelby smiled.

Iverson and Shelby walked out of the park and around downtown Atlanta. Times like that were the times that Iverson enjoyed most. Being the busy man that he was, he forgot how much there was to do downtown that didn't pertain to music. Before long Iverson and Shelby were on Peachtree Street. They stopped by a vendor and got two hot dogs and a couple of sodas. After they finished their lunch, they ran into a man sitting on a bench with an easel and some pencils. He was an artist that drew portraits of people as they sat. Iverson and Shelby stopped and let the man draw the two of them. As just a passerby, one would have thought that Iverson and Shelby had been together for a long time by the way they laughed and interacted with each other. After the man finished their portrait they walked back towards the park hand in hand.

"I haven't done this in a long time," Shelby began as she let Ivy's hand go and put her arm around his waist.

"The life I live is a monster. This is definitely a change for me."

"I bet it is," Shelby laughed. "Too many hoochies, clubs and bottles of Cristal can be tiring."

"Sometimes I feel like giving it all up just to have a normal life with a wife and a family but then I think about how much I love music."

"It's possible to have both. You just gotta find the right one."

"That's easier said than done."

"It's all in God's plan for you. When he feels that you're ready, he'll bless you with the woman your heart desires."

"What if you're the one my heart desires?" Iverson asked as he stopped.

"If I'm the one then time will tell." The two continued to walk until they were in the parking lot across the street from the park. When they got to Shelby's car Iverson noticed that the car she drove off in that first night wasn't the car she was driving that day.

"Did you get a new car?"

"Huh," Shelby paused. "Oh! This is my car. I was having it serviced the night we went out. I was driving my brother's car."

"So that explains it."

"Explains what?"

"Never mind. Anyway, we have to do this again sometimes."

"Definitely."Shelby hugged Ivy, gave him a kiss on the lips then began to get into the car. As Shelby got into her car, Iverson tossed the picture they had drawn into the back seat, unnoticed. "I'll give you a call later or catch you online sometime tonight."

"That's a bet. Peace."

Iverson closed her car door and began to walk across the parking lot to his car. Shelby honked her horn as she drove off. Since he was already downtown, he decided to stop by the studio and check on things. When he arrived T-Bizzy was sitting on Michelle's desk having a conversation with her.

"Do you sit on the furniture at your Mom's house?" he asked as he paused in the doorway to his office.

"Yes."

"That's why she put yo' ass out,"
Iverson laughed.

"Lemme holla at you for a minute." Ivy
walked into his office and took his place
behind his desk.

"What's good?" T-Bizzy inquired as he
sat on the couch.

"I think I finally found the one."

"Here we go again."

"I'm serious. I just spent the afternoon
wit' Shelby."

"Who is Shelby?"

"The girl I met online."

"You know what? I'm callin' ya mom."
T-Bizzy picked up the phone.

"Put the phone down."

"Hello, Mrs. Davenport. Ya son is down
here in Atlanta trippin'. He's datin' make
believe women again."

"See, that's why I don't tell ya dumb ass
nothin'."

"My bad," T-Bizzy apologized as he
hung up the phone. "Seriously Ivy, take your
time. I know you're ready for Miss Right and
all but just be easy."

"I got the situation under control. Trust
me."

"No disrespect but we've had this
conversation before."

"I know but this time is different. I think
Shelby's really the one."

"How do you know?"

"Because the whole time we were together, she didn't say one thing about a video, the music industry or money. She's diggin' me for me."

"Hold up," T-Bizzy picks up the phone again. "I need to call Oprah. Hello Ofra. I have an idea for your next show. The show's called Grown Ass Men that Meet Women on the Internet and Fall in Love." T-Bizzy laughed.

"You know what. Forget it."

"Ivy, think about what you're sayin'. Where you gonna tell people y'all met?"

"I'm not worried about what other people think."

"At least think about your image. If this gets out you'll be the laughing stock of the industry."

"Didn't I just tell you that I don't care what other people think?"

"Ok. If you got it under control then I got ya back MC Cataract."

"Thank you. You shoulda said that in the beginning and bypassed the other bullshit." T-Bizzy got up to leave. "Where you goin?"

"Down to the studio. I got this honey down there I think might be good for the label."

"An artist."

"Nah. I'm interviewing for a secretary."

"I already got one startin' next week."

"I know that and you know that but...she don't need to know that. Peace."

Ivy shook his head as T-Bizzy walked out of his office. As he laughed at his friend he wiggled his mouse so that the screensaver would go away. Once he was set, he pulled up his instant messenger box. He scanned the bold-faced names — bold-faced signified that they were online — to see who was there. He saw that Dymond4eva was online but her status was set to Away from her desk. He decided to leave her a message.

> **Ivy_Dav:** Hey Dymond! I was just hittin you up to say hello. I guess your out and about. Maybe I'll catch you later.

Once the message was sent, Iverson pulled up his sales records and began to go over his artist's numbers. He sat for about five minutes looking over sales when an IM box popped up.

> **Dymond4eva:** hey, Ivy.
> **Ivy_Dav:** dymond, what's up? I thought you weren't online.
> **Dymond4eya:** Yeah, I'm here. I was in the middle of ordering a couple of books
> when I got your message.
> **Ivy_Dav:** oh ok…what books did you order?
> **Dymond4eva:** When Love Comes Back and Waiting to Exhale

Ivy_Dav: I got both of those. You coulda borrowed mine…wait a minute… what's wrong?

Dymond4eva: nothing's wrong…y do you ask?

Ivy_Dav: I may not have known you for that long but I know that women don't read books like that unless they're goin' through some tough times… what's his name?

Dymond4eva: Desmond…he's my ex-boyfriend.

Ivy_Dav: if he's your ex, then y u stressin'?

Dymond4eva: I really don't wanna talk about this

Ivy_Dav: c'mon D…I talked about my problem with you.

Dymond4eva: well…me and him broke up about 8 months ago and I found out that he's seeing my best friend.

Ivy_Dav: now that's cold-blooded.

Dymond4eva: tell me about it…but the thing is I don't know if he's doing it 2 get back at me or if she's doing it to be spiteful.

Ivy_Dav: how so?

Dymond4eva: about a month ago I saw Des for the first time after we broke up & I told him that I didn't wanna have anything else to do with him…a few days later me and my best friend had a fallin out because she got jealous because I have a new homegirl.

Ivy_Dav: Don't even sweat that…they're both just being childish…when you do dirt…you get dirt and you'll come out on top…trust me.

Dymond4eva: but why does it hurt so bad?

Ivy_Dav: ur best friend and ur ex….did you love him?

Dymond4eva: more than anything in this world…

Ivy_Dav: that's why it hurts. Y did u break up?

Dymond4eva: he was jealous of my best male friend Dré but he shouldn't have been b/c Dre's married.

Ivy_Dav: sounds like you had two people in ur life that wanted u all to themselves…I've been through that and trust me when I say, ur better off without'em

Dymond4eva: Thanks Ivy, I feel better already.

Ivy_Dav: you know what? Maybe we should get together tomorrow and play ball or somethin'. It'll help take ya mind off of things…

Dymond4eva: thanks but me and my girl, Alicia are going to the spa 2morrow.

Ivy_Dav: ok…well, when you get some free time, hit me up   404-555-2308.
Dymond4eva: ok. I got the number…I'll give you a call…well, I gotta run…I need to lay down for a lil while…I have a headache.
Ivy_Dav: ok but don't stress ya self too much over it….
Dymond4eva: I'll try not 2. ttyl
Dymond4eva had logged out

After Natalie logged off she sat at her computer for a while longer. She could not understand why her love life was in shambles. "Any man would be lucky to have me in his life," she thought. Natalie was a beautiful woman with a great personality and a good head on her shoulders. She didn't have to ask anybody for anything. Natalie let out a huge sigh as she shut her computer down and went to her room to lie down. Silence filled the air as she knelt beside her king-sized bed.

"Dear Lord," she began. "I want to take this time to thank you for everything that you have done for me. Thank you for your many blessings and for the people that you have put in my life to help me through my rough times. Thank you for André and Alicia. Please continue to bless them and keep their family safe and strong. God, I'm not asking you to send me a man. I'm just asking that when you feel that I am ready; bless me with the king that you have chosen for me." Tears slowly rolled from Natalie's eyes. "You can do all things but fail so I know that everything is in your hands. I ask you to forgive Desmond and Shanice for the things that they are doing. All of these things I ask in Jesus name, Amen."

Natalie pulled herself off of her knees and crawled into bed. She wiped the tears from her eyes as she slid under the comforter and wrapped her arms around her favorite teddy bear since childhood. After fifteen minutes of sniffling, Natalie fell asleep.

Chapter 10

The holidays passed and the New Year had arrived. The Southern Sunz's album dropped and was number one on the charts. It had been a month since Natalie talked to Iverson due to the promo tour. Shelby and Iverson were spending a lot of time with each other when he wasn't on the road. It looked like Iverson's streak of bad luck with Internet women had finally come to an end. To be honest, Ivy never thought that the two of them would have lasted that long. Because of his previous experiences, the odds were not in his favor. It was a cold February day at Future Records. Iverson and T-Bizzy were sitting in his office shooting the breeze when Ivy got a visitor.

"Ivy," Michelle called via the intercom. "There's someone here to see you."

"Send'em in." Shelby walked into to Iverson's office. "Hey boo, what are you doing here?" Iverson asked as he got up to greet her with a hug and a kiss.

"You told me to stop by anytime I was in the area."

"That I did. T-Bizzy, this is Shelby. Shelby, this is my right hand man and co-founder of Future Records, TyQuan a.k.a DJ T-Bizzy."

"Nice to meet you," Shelby replied as she extended her hand.

"So this is the woman that got my boy smilin' a lot these days," T-Bizzy greeted as Shelby blushed. "Well, if you two will excuse me, I have a meeting to get to. Shelby, it was a pleasure. Ivy, see you tonight."

"Alright, dog." T-Bizzy walked out of the office.

"I didn't catch you at a bad time, did I?" Shelby asked as she sat on the couch.

"You know I always have time for you. What you up to today?"

"Nothing really. Me and my girlfriend just had lunch for her birthday. Other than that I just wanted to stop in and see what you were up to."

"We were just doing some last minute things for The Southern Sunz platinum party this weekend. You still comin', right?"

"This weekend?"

"Yeah. I told you about it last week."

"Baby, I'm so sorry. I got my days mixed up. I thought it was next week. I have to go out of town this weekend."

"Are you serious? I really wanted you to be there."

"I'm sorry, Boo," she apologized as she got up and walked around Iverson's desk and gave him a kiss. "I'll make it up to you, I promise."

"You know I'm gonna hold you to that, right."

"I know you will. Well baby, I gotta run. I have to pick my daughter up in a little while. I'll call you later."

Iverson leaned back in his chair and smiled as the woman he had been waiting for switched out of his office. It had been a long time coming. He hadn't felt the way that he felt about a woman since Candace. It had only been a little over a month since Ivy met Shelby but things were going good — almost too good. The chime of someone sending him an instant message broke Iverson's train of thought.

> **Dymond4eva:** Ivy? U there?
> **Ivy_Dav:** Hey D!
> **Dymond4eva:** wzup, stranger?
> **Ivy_Dav:** man, it's been crazy…we're on a short break from the tour I told u about with my new artists. The album just went platinum.
> **Dymond4eva:** sounds like your new year is comin in wit a bang
> **Ivy_Dav:** it's truly a blessing… what's up wit you?
> **Dymond4eva:** not a lot, just sittin around.
> **Ivy_Dav:** you don't have class right now?
> **Dymond4eva:** class?

For a split-second Natalie forgot that she told Iverson that she was a teacher.

Ivy_Dav: yeah...it is the middle of the day on a Thursday

Dymond4eva: this is my planning period. U have to forgive me...I have a lot

on my mind.

Ivy_Dav: big game comin up?

Dymond4eva: yeah...our rival

Ivy_Dav: you'll do fine....oh yeah I just thought about something. All this time we've been chattin' online, I don't know you're name...

Dymond4eva: Natalia

Ivy_Dav: that's a pretty name

Dymond4eva: thank you.

Ivy_Dav: before I forget...we're having a platinum party for my new artist this Saturday at Club Blaze. You should come out.

Dymond4eva: maybe...

Ivy_Dav: I'll put you on the VIP list just in case. What's your last name?

Dymond4eva: Simone

Ivy_Dav: Miss Natalia Simone...if you come will you be bringin' anybody with you? friend, boyfriend, a date?

Dymond4eva: If I do come and I stress **IF**, more than likely it will be with my friend Alicia and maybe Jasmine.

Ivy_Dav: I'll put you down for 3 guests just to be on the safe side.

Dymond4eva: thanks…well…I gotta run. I guess I'll ttyl
Ivy_Dav: ok…be good and good luck!
Dymond4eva: good luck?
Ivy_Dav: for your game
Dymond4eva: oh yeah…thanx
Ivy_Dav: peace @}-;--

Dymond4eva has logged out

Natalie sat at her computer sifting through different websites and doing a whole lot of nothing. Her days had become boring. The only time she left the house was when Alicia got tired of her sitting around all day. After thirty minutes had passed, her cell phone rang.

"Hey girl," Alicia greeted. "What you up to?"

"Sittin' here lookin' over my stats from last year."

"Oh, okay. I was calling to invite you to a dinner party that André and I are hosting tomorrow night."

"What's the occasion?"

"There's not really an occasion. We just wanted to do it since it's been a while since the last one."

"I did have a good time at the last one but I need to ask you a question."

"I'm listening."

"Is it going to be mostly couples like it was last time?

"We're pretty much having the same people over."

"Thanks but I think I'll pass this time."

"And do what? Sit in the house and do nothing all night?"

"I don't want to impose."

"Impose? What makes you think you'd be imposing?"

"I'll probably be the only single person there. It just wouldn't feel right."

"Come on, Nat. It'll be fun."

"Nah, I think I'm gonna just sit here with Ben and his brother Jerry and watch a movie."

"Natalie Nicole Simms! You're coming to this dinner party if I have to come to your house and drag you here kicking and screaming."

"Alright, Alright. I'll come but on two conditions."

"And those are?"

"If there are any single men there, no matchmaking and you have to go some where with me on Saturday night."

"Where?"

"To The Southern Sunz platinum party."

"Who are the Southern Sunz?"

"Iverson's new artists. The CD went platinum and Ivy invited me to the platinum party at Club Blaze."

"Oh, Ivy invited you to the party," Alicia laughed. "Since when did he become Ivy?"

"Since never mind. Are you going or not?"

"Okay, it's a deal. No matchmaking and we go out together Saturday."

"He put me on the VIP list for up to three guests. Tell your big-headed husband he's invited too."

"Will do. Listen girl, I gotta get back to work. I'll give you a call later."

"Ok, talk to you later."

The next night, Natalie arrived to André and Alicia's house dressed to kill. There were about eight cars parked in the driveway and along the street in front of the house. After ringing the doorbell, she was greeted with a hug from André.

"Thanks for coming. Let me take your coat."

"Thanks for the invite if that's what you wanna call it," Natalie replied as she turned her back to Dré for him to help her with her coat.

"You know how Alicia is," he laughed. "Damn, girl!"

Upon the removal of her coat, André was amazed at her evening's ensemble. Her ensemble consisted of a hip-hugging, black skirt that flared out about midway her thighs with splits on both sides that extended to mid-thigh. Her blouse was white with long-sleeves that belled at the wrists. The V in her top was complimented by her perky D-cups that sat perfectly in place.

"You tryin' to get somebody's husband in trouble tonight?"

"Boy, shut up," she laughed as she playfully pushed Dré.

"If anybody should know how I dress, it should be you."

"I'm just sayin. You lucky I didn't see you in this before I got married. You might be Mrs. André Marshall." The two laughed as they walked into the living room where the other guests were. "Ladies and Gentlemen, the WNBA's MVP has arrived."

"Hello everyone."

All the men in attendance paused when they saw Natalie. A couple of them received sharp elbows to the rib cage from their spouses. Natalie exchanged pleasantries with everyone and proceeded to have a glass of champagne. Alicia walked over to her and gave her a sisterly hug and thanked her for coming. She sat and shot the breeze with André, Alicia, Smoke and his fiancé until the doorbell rang again. André excused himself and went to answer the door. Two minutes

later he returned and introduced Calvin and
Shelby Isley.

Once the Isley's arrived they all
gathered in the dining room to eat. To keep
any possible confusion down, Natalie sat in
between André and Alicia. The same guys that
received elbows from their wives when Natalie
first entered the room got kicks under the table
for staring at her. It seemed like she became the
center of attention when the conversation
started.

"So Natalie," one of the male guests
began, "What does this year's season hold for
us?"

"Well, we just picked up Shannon
Johnson from Orlando. We also have a couple
of rookies that are going to help us shake
things up a bit this season."

"Really?" another guest inquired. "What
schools did they come from?"

"One played for my Alma Mater, which
is Tennessee, and one played for Alicia and
André's university, Franklin Memorial."

"Who?" André asked as he sipped his
drink.

"Precious Anderson."

"She's not a rookie. She's been playing
overseas for the past five years."

"She's a rookie to the WNBA but she
looks good."

"Is she going to keep her position?"

"Actually, she might be replacing Shawna at power forward." André gave Alicia a devilish grin due to the history between him, Natalie and Shawna. "I'm not one to sit and talk about my teammates but according to the coaches and the people that make all the decisions, Shawna stopped producing what the team needed so they had to bring someone in."

"I wonder why that is," Alicia laughed.

"Who knows?"

"If you don't mind me asking," Calvin spoke. "Who does your investing?"

"At this moment, I don't have any money invested in anything but I've hired Baxter and Associates to handle my financial advisory."

"Baxter and Associates is a reputable company and I mean no disrespect, but their company is not equipped to efficiently handle assets as large as yours." With that statement Shelby gave Calvin a very evil look. André and Alicia had to hold back their laughter because they knew where Natalie was going with the conversation.

"And who is better equipped to handle my large assets, you?" Natalie asked playing devil's advocate after she noticed the look he received from his wife.

"But of course. As you probably know, I took over as owner and CEO of the Isley Firm. With us, you get more for your money. We offer investment services as well as financial advisory." Calvin reached in his coat pocket and handed Natalie a business card. "If you need proof of my firm's expertise, talk it over with André then give me a call. I'll be happy to set up a meeting with you."

"If I do decide to give the Isley Firm my business, would you be handling my assets, personally?"

"We like to accommodate all of our client's requests and if you'd like for me to personally handle you and your account..." Before Calvin could finish his statement, Shelby got up and stormed out of the dining room. "Consider it done. Now if you all will excuse me, I have to attend to this situation before I have to sleep on the couch tonight." Everyone laughed and continued on with their meals as Calvin walked out of the dining room and into the living room.

"You are too much," André laughed as he leaned over to Natalie.

"What?" Natalie asked with surprise. "He started it. I was just talking business with the man."

"Okay business. You tryna get that man shot." Calvin managed to get Shelby to join the party again. As she sat and ate, she kept giving Natalie nasty looks. After the meal was over, everyone retired to the living room for after dinner drinks and friendly conversation. Once again, Natalie became the target of everyone's questions.

"From a woman's point of view," one of the female guests began. "Why do you think that the WNBA players don't get all the hype, publicity and money that the NBA players get?"

"Well as far as hype, that's not what our league is about. Women are more low-key and low profile then men, in my opinion. We try to conduct ourselves as ladies at all times to maintain the reputation of our league as a whole. We've fought long and hard for this league. We're proud and privileged to be a part of it and we don't want to do anything to jeopardize that."

"I can understand that," interjected another female guest. "But what about the money? Why don't the women get the large multi-million dollar contracts that the men get?"

"The WNBA is still fairly new. It's still growing and with growth comes improvement. We still lack the sponsors that the NBA has as well as the fan base. The NBA didn't start off giving multi-million dollar contracts. It had to build to that point."

"But you just signed a six year contract extension worth 22.5 million dollars," Shelby interrupted. "So how can you sit there and say that?"

"First of all, it's not about the money. I play for the love of the game because that's what every ball player should do. Secondly, I'm what they call a franchise player. I was the first to sign with the Diamonds and the team was built around me and that's all fine and good. Compared to Allen Iverson, Shaquille O'Neil and Kobe Bryant, players in the NBA that are considered to be franchise players, my deal is small change."

"So you're saying you're underpaid."

"I'm not saying that. I feel that I'm compensated fairly for what I produce."

"And exactly what do you produce for 22.5 million dollars." Natalie could tell that the conversation that she had with Calvin over dinner had was having an effect on the current discussion.

"Being that you almost knew what my contract was for, I thought you would have been up on your WNBA knowledge but I guess not. Last season was my rookie season and I set the standard for our franchise meaning that my stats are considered records. I averaged 30 plus points a game, which is a WNBA record, 11 assists and 5 steals per game. I scored 57 points in game 5 of the WNBA finals shattering the previous record held by Sheryl Swoops, which lead to Atlanta's first WNBA Championship. I feel that those are major accomplishments alone but I can tell by the look on your face that you still aren't impressed. In addition to that I was selected as MVP of the finals and the WNBA as a whole and to top it all off, Rookie of the year. I made WNBA history for the simple fact that no one player has ever accomplished all three in a single season and that ma'am is what I produce for 25.5 million dollars." The entire room erupted with applause and cheers for Natalie. Even Calvin applauded for Natalie.

"If you ask me," Calvin began. "I think you're under paid. There are players in the NBA that don't produce stats and feats like that."

"My sister's definitely a star," André said looking at Natalie. "But you didn't tell me you signed for 25 million." He paused. "Lemme hold somethin'."

"You silly," Natalie giggled. "Well everyone, I've enjoyed myself but I must retire for the evening. I have to be in the gym in the morning."

"Training camp started already?" Calvin asked.

"Not yet but you don't win games and put up good numbers sittin' around the house eating ice cream and Bon Bon's all day. It was good to see you all again and I hope to see you all in the stands when the season starts."Everyone bid Natalie a healthy good night as the Marshalls walked her outside and to her car.

"You didn't have to do her like that," André joked as he opened her door for her.

"Yes she did," Alicia defended. "Shelby was asking for it. All up in her business like that. You shoulda gave the bitch a dollar and told her to go get her own business."

"She felt a need to try to get back at me because I held her husband's attention more than she did but it's all good. Thank you two for another lovely evening."

"It's always a pleasure, Sis," André exclaimed as the three exchanged hugs. "Be safe."

"I will. Alicia, I'll call you tomorrow so we can grab a bite to eat before the party."

"What party? I didn't give her permission to go out tomorrow."

"André stop actin' like that. You know good and well you and your friends are goin' to J-Rock's House of Hoe's tomorrow."

"SHHH!" André put his finger of his lips and whispered. "Not so loud. I don't want my wife to find out." They all laughed as Natalie said her final goodbyes and drove away. Alicia paused before they walked back in the house.

"I was watching Shelby tonight," Alicia began. "There's something about her that's not sittin' well with me."

"What do you mean?"

"It's like she was distant from Calvin tonight. Any other time she would have been cool, not to mention being all over him. Tonight was different. Something's not right."

"Baby, they're married."

"And so are we but you and I are still like newlyweds and we've been married longer then they have."

"That's because you got some good stuff," André replied as he playfully grabbed

Alicia around her waist from behind and
kissed her on her neck.

"Now let's get rid of everybody and
practice makin' Taylor a baby brother."

"You are so nasty."

"Nasty just the way you like it."

The two laughed as they walked back
into the house to wrap up the evening's event.

Saturday Night came and Club Blaze
was bananas. It was around 10:30 and the club
was filling up fast. Alicia and Natalie were
about a block away from the club when Natalie
realized that she had to make sure Alicia was
up to speed so that her cover wasn't blown by
mistake. She began to fill in all of the gaps that
Alicia didn't know about.

"Ok," Natalie began. "Let's go over this
one more time. What is my name and what do
I do for a living."

"Your name is Natalie Simms and you
play for the Atlanta Diamonds."

"Arrrgh!"

"I'm just kidding," Alicia joshed. "You
are Natalia Simone and you're a high school
basketball coach."

"Thank you."

"Natalie relax. Everything's going to be
ok. Besides, with all the people that are going
to be in the club, you'll be lucky if you see him
for more than five minutes. Is this really how

you wanted your first meeting with him to be?"

"Not really but over the past couple of months, Ivy and I have become pretty good friends. I just wanted to come out and support a friend."

"Ok, friend."

Natalie and Alicia pulled up in front of Club Blaze for valet parking. They could see people stop and stare to see who was going to get out of the Navigator. Even though Natalie was all woman, she still had a slight mannish streak in her when it came to cars. Every car she's ever owned was tricked out with at least rims and a booming stereo system. Since the rise of the tricked out cars of the New Millennium, *Natalie's Navi* fit the bill. Her Lincoln Navigator was all black with twenty-two inch, chrome spinners, with her initials N.S. etched into the center cap of each rim, with a twelve speaker BOSE sound system. She could have stopped there but she couldn't resist putting 6 TV's in it—one in each headrest, one that flipped up from the CD player and a flip-down 13" screen in the ceiling. It was hard for men to believe that that was her SUV for the simple fact that most women didn't put that much money into a vehicle.

Dressed to kill, the two women stepped out of the SUV. Natalie was wearing light blue denim, Baby Phat jean outfit with the matching denim Manolo boots. For the evening she took her braids out and wore her hair down and bone straight. Her brownish black locks extended to her shoulders allowing the two carats that she wore in each ear to peek out when her hair swayed. Over her eyes was a pair of Dolce & Gabana shades with a blue tint and silver frames that accented the Tiffany's choker around her neck.

Alicia was no slouch either. She was draped in Donna Karen from head to toe. Her top was a black, tight and sheer with a black, lace Victoria's Secret bra under it — of course she had on the thongs to match. Her skirt was solid black and form-fitting as well. It was made in the essence of the dress that Morticia Addams used to wear — form-fitting until it got to the legs and it flared just enough for her to walk normally. On her feet was a pair of black, Donna Karen pumps with a thin, four inch heel. It was unusual for Alicia but for the night, she had her hair in a ponytail that started high off of the back of her head and extended to the base of her neck. To top it all off, the night was cold enough for her to put on her black, waist-length mink jacket.

They walked towards the door like the party was going on was for them. Every man in view of the two women was focused on their every move. It was like Remy Ma and Trina were on their way into the party. When they got to the door, they were greeted by security.

"What's up, ladies?" he greeted. "I know y'all fine and e'rything but the line starts back their."He pointed to the line that was down the side of the building and started to wrap around.

"Excuse me?" Natalie remarked as she pulled of her shades. "I'm on Ivy's guest list."

"You and every other female out here. Back of the line."

"What!"

"Calm down," Alicia tried to keep Natalie from going off on the bouncer.

"You didn't even ask me my name or check the list."

"I don't have to check the list. I know who Ivy's expecting." Just as Natalie and the bouncer started to get into a heated argument, Ivy walked outside.

"Whoa, whoa, whoa!" Ivy shouted as he stepped between security and Natalie. "What's the problem?"

"Foxy Brown and Lil' Kim said they're on the list and I know for a fact they ain't."

"He didn't even ask me what my name was."

"I apologize for the inconvenience. What's ya name, Ma?"

"It's me, Natalia."

"Natalia?" Ivy paused.

"Dymond."

"Oh shit! What's up girl?" a surprised Iverson greeted as he embraced her. "She's cool. She's with me. I'm so sorry for the mix-up"

"It's ok. It's just too cold out here to be goin' through it with Top Flight Security of the World."

"I know, Boo. I'm sorry," Ivy apologized as he placed a VIP tag around each of their necks. "Thank you so much for comin' out tonight. Listen, my VIP section is upstairs. They'll let you in with these. No questions asked. Get you some Cris', relax and as soon as ATP and EL GEE get here, I'll be right there."

Alicia and Natalie gave the bouncer the nastiest look as they passed him on the way into corridor that led to the inside of the club. The music was pumpin' and it got louder as they neared the final entrance. When they walked through the final entrance into the main area, people were everywhere. As they passed through the club on their way to the stairs that led to the VIP area they turned heads. They even managed to catch the eyes of a few celebrities that were in attendance. Just as they neared the stairs, T-Bizzy spied Alicia and stepped in front of the stairs.

"Ladies," he greeted.

"What's the deal? Thanks for comin' out to support my mans ATP and EL GEE. I see that you are on the guest list so go on up and enjoy ya'selves."

"Thank you," Natalie replied as he walked past him.

"What's up wit you, Red?" T-Bizzy gently grabbed Alicia's hand as she tried to walk past him. "You still married?"

"You just don't quit, do you?" Alicia asked.

"I'm persistent."

"That's a good quality to have and I like that in a man."

"Oh really?"

"Uh huh. That's why I married him. Holla!" Alicia threw up the peace sign and continued upstairs with Natalie.

When they finally arrived to Ivy's VIP section, all of ATL's celebs were in attendance to help The Southern Sunz celebrate their first platinum plaque. Lil Jon was sitting on a couch on the far right wall holding his signature pimp cup with the words *Crunk Juice* displayed in diamonds. Along with Lil Jon were T.I., Ludacris, André 3000, Big Boi and Jazze Pha. Everyone spoke to the ladies as they approached the bar. Natalie and Alicia got two glasses of Cristal and took a seat on a couch between André 3000 and Big Boi. The two ATLiens struck up a conversation with the ladies. About ten minutes into the conversation, Ivy walked into the VIP section with ATP, EL GEE and Gusto. Everyone in the

VIP gave them a warm ovation of cheers, applause and whistles. After Iverson said a few words to the partygoers he made his way to Natalie. Natalie greeted Iverson with another hug and introduced him to Alicia.

"Ivy," Natalie began. "This my best friend, Alicia Marshall. Alicia, this is Iverson Davenport, CEO of Future Records."

"It's a pleasure to meet you, Iverson."

"Please, call me Ivy. I'm glad you could make it."

"You got a really nice turnout," Natalie commented.

"That's the thing I love about the ATL. Regardless of what label you're on, it's all family and its all love, like the industry is supposed to be. But anyway, enough about the industry, let's have a good time."

At the end of that statement the DJ Gregg Street kicked it into high gear with a classic reggae cut, *Murder She Wrote*. Iverson noticed Natalie's reaction to the song.

"Would you like to dance?"

"I would love to but I don't want to leave my girl up here by herself."

"Natalie," Alicia began. "I am a grown woman, if you want to go dance, go dance. I'll be alright."

"No sweat. I can handle this. Give me one second." Iverson walked away from the ladies.

"What are you doing?" Alicia asked. "The man asked you to dance and you're worried about me."

"I know, girl. He caught me off guard and I got a little nervous." In less than a minute, Ivy returned with a good friend.

"Ladies, I'd like you to meet a very good friend of mine." Alicia turned around and looked into the face of the CEO of Disturbing the Peace Records, Ludacris.

"My man told me that there was a young lady over here that needed a partner."

"Luda, I'd like to introduce you to Alicia Marshall."

"Nice to meet you," he replied as he shook Alicia's hand. She was too star-struck to speak so she replied with a smile. "Shall we?" Luda extended his hand to Alicia and the four headed for the dance floor.

The foursome hit the dance floor as the song was ending but the DJ kept the Caribbean vibe rolling. Iverson was amazed at how beautiful Natalie was and how the music controlled her body. It was as if she was a puppet to the rhythm. In the midst of all the freak nasty women grinding and throwing themselves at the men they were dancing with, Natalie kept it very lady-like—even though that's how she liked to dance from time to time. She didn't want to give off the wrong vibe because regardless of the fact that she was with him and his girl wasn't. He still had someone in his life. After five of six songs, they left the dance floor and returned to the VIP.

"Alicia," Luda began. "It was a pleasure but I have to get back to my people. Enjoy the rest of the night."

"You do the same. Thank you." Alicia stood motionless as she watched one of her favorite hip-hop stars walk away.

"Stop coveting that man before I call your husband," Natalie laughed.

"Girl, if I was still single..."

"Alicia!"

"I'm just sayin'."

"Natalie, do you mind if we go somewhere quiet and talk for a minute?" Iverson asked.

"Sure. Give me a minute." Natalie walked with Alicia over to the bar. "Are you going to be ok?"

"Natalie, This is not 8th grade. I'll be fine."

"Okay. I won't be long."

"Just go." Natalie started to walk away but she stopped and turned back towards Alicia. "Go!"

Natalie walked back to Ivy and they walked out of the VIP area. The path that they were traveling was leading them to a very familiar place. On the third floor of the club there was a room called *The Network*. That was the place that she had her first conversation with Alicia's husband, André. The room was dimly lit and the music that was playing on the main floor played quietly in the background. When you first walk in there was a bar to the right and the wall was lined with large, leather couches. In the middle of the floor were a few love seats and bar tables. Iverson led Natalie to the back of the room and sat down.

"You just don't know how happy I am to have you here."

"I'm happy to be here."

"I didn't think you were going to come."

"Why not?"

"Just a feeling I had." As Iverson gazed at Natalie he noticed what she was wearing. Being that he was in the industry, he was up on his fashion and what Natalie was wearing was a little too expensive for the average teacher to be wearing.

"You look nice tonight."

"Thank you. I like to dress to impress when I go out."

"I see and I'm impressed."

"How'd the game go?"

"The game?" Natalie had to remember that Ivy thought that she was a basketball coach. "Oh, it went well. We won."

"That's good. What's your record?"

"As of now we're undefeated, 8-0."

"You must have a bomb squad."

"You can say that but enough about me. What's up with you? Has your girl got here yet?"

"Nah, she couldn't make it tonight. She's out of town for the weekend."

"I'm sorry."

"It's cool though. At least I have my Dymond here to support me."

"I told you," Natalie smiled. "I got ya back. So what's the luck lady's name?"

"Shelby Cortez." Iverson reached into his wallet and pulled out a picture. Natalie's heart dropped when she saw the picture but she kept her composure. It was Shelby Isley, wife of Calvin Isley — the same Shelby that she got into it with the night before.

"She's beautiful. Where'd you meet her?"

"Promise me you won't laugh when I tell you."

"I promise."

"Same place I met you."

"Online?" Iverson nodded his head. "Really?"

"She saw my page on Ebony World and hit me up. We talked for a couple of weeks, went out a couple of times and next thing I know, I'm spending all my time with her."

"That's amazing," Natalie replied as she looked at her watch. "Oh my!"

"What's wrong?"

"I didn't realize it was so late. I have something I have to do in the morning. I wish I could stay longer."

"You're not going to stay for the performance?"

"I wish I could but I have a big day tomorrow. You know how it is."

"It's cool. Maybe we can do dinner sometime."

"I'd like that. I'll give you a call." Ivy gave Natalie a hug and the two walked back to the VIP area. When they arrived Alicia was sitting at the surrounded by a crowd of guys. "What are you doin'?"

"I'm entertaining."

"Ok, entertaining. It's time for us to go. We have things to do in the morning."

"Well gentlemen, it was fun but I must leave you now."

"Come on, shorty," one of the guys interrupted. "If you need a ride I can take you home if you wanna stay."

"Thanks but no thanks. I don't think my husband would like me accepting rides from strange men. Ta ta!"

Ivy escorted Natalie and Alicia outside to the valet to get Nat's car. Ivy stood in surprise as the valet pulled the tricked out Navigator to the front. Being the gentleman that he was, Iverson opened the door for Alicia then walked around and opened Natalie's.

"You sure you just a school teacher?" Ivy asked as he laughed.

"I'm good at what I do."

"I see."

"Do me a favor. Hit me up so I'll know you got home safe. If I don't answer that means I'm still inside the club."

"I'll just send you a text message."

"Cool. Y'all drive safe and it was nice meeting you, Alicia."

"Same here."

"Talk to you later." Ivy kissed Natalie on the cheek and drove away.

"Okay, what happened?" Alicia asked.

"Nothin' happened."

"You don't just leave at one o'clock in the middle of a good party. What happened?" Alicia paused. "Did Iverson come on to you?"

"No! Iverson is a gentleman."

"Then why did you run off in the middle of the night like Cinderella tryin to get home before her wicked step-mother?"

"If I tell you, you have to promise to keep this between me and you. You can't even tell Dré."

"I promise."

"When we got upstairs, we started a little small talk. When I asked him about the girl he was seeing, he showed me a picture. She's married."

"He told you she was married?"

"No, I recognized her face."

"Who is she?"

"Shelby."

"Shelby?" Alicia paused for a moment. "It's not ringing a bell."

"Shelby that was at your house last night, Calvin's wife."

"Are you serious?" Natalie nodded her head. "I told Dré there was something funny about her."

"When I saw that picture I almost fainted."

"So are you going to tell Ivy?"

"I can't do that."

"Why not? You are his friend, aren't you?"

"Yeah but how can I tell a man that I'm attracted to that the woman he is head over heels about is married? I don't want him to think that I'm trying to break him and Shelby up."

"Just tell him."

"I can't. He has to find out on his own. The sad thing about it is that he is really into this girl."

"How long have they been seeing each other?"

"A little over a month."

"I see what's going on now."

"What?"

"About two months before they got married, they broke up because Calvin cheated on her with one of the brokers in his father's firm. After his father died and Shelby found out he took over the company, she went back which leads me to believe it was because of the money. She doesn't love Calvin she loves his money. So if she's planning to leave him, she has to find someone with just as much money as he has if not more."

"I knew that bitch was scandalous."

"You gotta tell him."

"I can't."

"If you don't, and he finds out you knew, he's not going to be too happy about that because he considers you to be a friend."

"How'd I get caught up in a catch twenty-two like this?"

"I don't know. All I can say that what happens in the dark will eventually come into the light. For Iverson's sake, I hope he finds out before it's too late."

"Me too." Before long, Natalie was at Alicia's place.

"Everything will work out. Just be prepared to be there for him when he finds out."

"Ok, girl. Call me tomorrow."

"I will."

After Alicia was in the house Natalie drove off. Twenty minutes later she was pulling into her garage. Before she got out of her car she sent Iverson a message.

IVY,
I MADE IT HOME. SORRY I HAD TO LEAVE SO SOON BUT I HAD A GREAT TIME. HOPE

WE CAN DO IT AGAIN SOMETIMES. I'LL
GIVE YOU A CALL. TTYL
DYMOND

Natalie sent the message and went into
the house. After she took off her clothes and
showered, she sat up in her bed and thought
about the situation. For thirty minutes she
tossed it around in her head until she was
exhausted and fell asleep.

It was 1:30a.m. and while Natalie drifted
to sleep, on the other side of town, Club Blaze
was still on fire. Ivy stood on stage as ATP
rocked the crowed. Atlanta was very
supportive of the Southern Sunz though they
weren't Atlanta natives. At the close of their
final song, ATP and EL GEE exited the stage to
a roaring applause. Ivy and T-Bizzy walked
outside to cool off. Though it was getting late,
the line was still wrapped around the club.

"What happened to ya girl?" T-Bizzy
asked as he pulled a piece of gum out of his
pocket.
"Who?"
"Shelby."
"She had to go out of town this
weekend."
"True. Did ya other girl and her friend
leave?"
"Yeah. They left right before we went on
stage."

"When'd you meet her?"

"Around the same time I met Shelby."

"What's up wit' y'all?"

"We're are just friends."

"I like her. I think she's better for you."

"You don't even know her."

"I know but she gives a certain vibe that I didn't get with Shelby."

"What's that supposed to mean?"

"Don't get mad when I tell you this but..." T-Bizzy paused for a minute. "Never mind."

"What?"

"It's nothin'. Just forget it."

"Fuck it. I'm goin back in the club." Iverson started to walk away.

"Alright," T gave in as Iverson turned around. "Look. I know you and Shelby only been kickin' it for about a month but somethin's just not right with her."

"What makes you say that?"

"I get the same vibe from her that I got when I first met Candace."

"That's it. I'm goin back inside."

"Dog, I'm serious. Think about it. How well do you really know her?"

"I'm still getting to know her."

"Let me ask you something. Since you've been goin' out with her, how many times have you been to her house?"

"I haven't."

"Have you met her daughter?"

"No."

"Do you even know what she does for a living?"

"Now that you mention it, I don't."

"She's a desperate housewife."

"Now you trippin'," Ivy laughed.

"I'm serious. She got a husband."

"How much you had to drink?"

"Ivy, look at it. You met her online. The only time you see her is when it's convenient for her. Y'all don't spend much time together at night. Her daughter is old enough to know a man that's not her daddy and could possibly slip up and mention your name around him. To top it all off, you don't know where she works or if she works. Maybe I might be a little off as far as the husband but I think she's hiding something. If she's not married, she lives with another man."

"I can't listen to this anymore. I'm goin' back inside."

"Just check her out a little more. Ask her a few questions and check out how she responds and don't ask her on the computer. Wait until the two of you are together." Iverson turned to walk back in the club. "Ivy, I'm serious. Somethin's not right about her. I'm ya man and I know everything you've been through. I'm not tryin' to come between y'all; I'm just tryin' to look out for my boy." Iverson turned back and faced T-Bizzy.

"You know what? You're right. Maybe I do need to find out a little more about her cuz now that you brought it up; I don't know that much about her. All I know is that I like spending time with her and we have a good time together. You opened up my eyes to a couple things. Good lookin' out." Ivy and T exchanged one love.

"I'm ya right-hand man. That's my job."

"And I pay you well."

"Now that you mention it, counseling and mediation wasn't in my job description. I think I need a raise."

"A raise? You betta raise yo ass back in the club and get a chickenhead to give you a raise."

"I think I need that type of raise, too." They laughed and walked back inside.

Chapter 11

The next day, Natalie woke up around noon. As she sat up in her bed and gathered her senses, the first thought that ran through her mind was Iverson's situation. She considered Ivy to be a friend but how could she tell him the woman that he is involved with was married. "How could someone lie like that?" she thought but who was she to pass judgment considering the fact that Iverson believes that she's a school teacher. In Natalie's mind she felt that her dishonesty about her profession wasn't as bad Shelby being untruthful about her marital status—was it?

The doorbell rang as Natalie trotted down her spiral staircase. It was Alicia. Natalie invited her into the kitchen for a midday glass of White Zinfandel. The two women conversed about the previous night's event when Alicia began to question her next move concerning Ivy.

"So," Alicia began as she sipped her wine. "What are you gonna do about Iverson?"

"To tell you the truth, I don't know."

"Have you talked to him?"

"Not yet. I'm supposed to call him later."

"You have to tell him."

"I can't do that."

"Why not?"

"I don't want to get involved. Ivy really seems to be into her and I don't want him to feel as if I'm trying to come in between the two of them. You know how guys are."

"True, but if he considers you a friend, you should tell him. I think if the shoe were in the other foot, he'd tell you."

"Arrrrgh!" Natalie grumbled. "Why does life have to be so complicated?"

"You're making this harder than it really is."

Alicia sat for the next hour trying to convince Natalie that telling Iverson that Shelby was married was the right thing to do. After awhile Alicia grew tired of saying the same thing over and over again, she dropped the subject and convinced Natalie to ride with her downtown.

Iverson sat in his office, at home, scrolling through emails that he had neglected because of the weekends events. He laughed as he deleted messages from XoticMami and 2much4u. About ten minutes into it, a messenger box popped up.

WifeyMaterial: Hey SEXY!
Ivy_Dav: What's up, boo
WifeyMaterial: thinkin bout u
Ivy_Dav: stop lyin...lol!

WifeyMaterial: I'm serious. I got back in town last night around 12. I started to come to the club but I was too tired.
Ivy_Dav: you shoulda came out…the party was bananas
WifeyMaterial: I bet it was but I wouldn't have been good company
Ivy_Dav: I feel u. it's all good
WifeyMaterial: but I'm well rested now. What u up to today?
Ivy_Dav: I'm just chillin 2day…Y? what's up?
WifeyMaterial: I wanna see you today.
Ivy_Dav: I think I can work that out. What time u talkin'?
WifeyMaterial: how about now?
Ivy_Dav: how about in an hour?
WifeyMaterial: how about **NOW**?
Ivy_Dav: ok, ok…where u wanna meet at?
WifeyMaterial: my place
Ivy_Dav: r u serious?
WifeyMaterial: yes…my daughter is with my Mom and I don't have to pick her up until later on tonite
Ivy_Dav: what's ur address?
WifeyMaterial: 1976 Ridgecrest Drive, Norcross
Ivy_Dav: got it….c u in a few

WifeyMaterial had logged out

Iverson did a quick MapQuest and jumped in the shower. Twenty minutes later he was on his way to see Shelby. As he was getting off of I-85 Shelby sent him a text message.

IVY,

WHEN YOU GET HERE JUST COME ON IN.

SHELBY

When Iverson arrived he walked in he called for Shelby but got no answer. He called to her again.

"Sheeellby," he called.
"I'm upstairs," she answered. "Come on up." Iverson paused for a moment and proceeded up the stairs. He walked down the hall towards the sound of soft music. When he got to the master bedroom the door was slightly closed. He pushed the door open and walked in.
"Shelby," he called again.
"I'll be out in a minute," she answered through a closed bathroom door. "You can have a seat on the bed."

Five minutes after sitting down on the bed, Shelby came out of the bathroom and damn near blew Ivy's mind. Shelby stepped into the bedroom wearing a maraschino cherry red lace bra with the matching boy shorts. Draped over her body, but hanging off of her left shoulder, was a sheer, white robe that was wide open.

"Do you like what you see?" she asked as she turned slowly.

"Like would definitely be an understatement," he replied as he stood up and walked towards her.

"When you said..."

Shelby placed her index and middle fingers to Ivy's lips as he tried to speak again. She replaced her fingers with her lips. Ivy and Shelby stood in her bedroom engaged in a deep and passionate kiss. This was the moment that the couple had been waiting on.

Shelby began to undress Iverson as the track on the CD switched. Ruben Studdard's *After the Candles Burn* floated out of the speakers intensifying the sexual mood. After Shelby stripped Ivy down to his boxers, she pushed him back onto the bed and straddled his lap. She let out a soft moan as she pressed her little lady down on the bulge that poked through. Shelby took her hands and placed them at the top of his chest and gently raked her fingernails across the ripples of his chest and abs while he reached behind her and unleashed her round, soft breasts. Ivy's body shivered as a chill of passion shot through his body. He sat up and grabbed Shelby by her waist, stood up, and laid her on her back.

Iverson began to kiss her neck and suck on her breasts. Every movement of Iverson's tongue on Shelby's body drove her crazy. It had been a while since she had been touched in that way. As he laid between her legs he pressed his manhood against her little lady causing Shelby to release a stuttered breath and wrap her legs around his waist in order to pull him closer to her.

"Take me now," she whispered. As Iverson pulled back to reach for his pants on the floor, they heard a car pull up and a car door slam. Panic shot across Shelby's face as she pushed Iverson off of her and ran to the window.

"Oh Shit!" she exclaimed as she rushed to grab her robe that was on the floor.
"What's wrong?"
"He's home."
"He who?"
"Calvin!" she answered as she grabbed Iverson's clothes and shoved into his chest.
"Who the fuck is Calvin?"
"My husband."
"Husband!"
"Hurry up, get in the closet."
"What the fuck? Who I look like, R Kelly?"

"Iverson please," Shelby pleaded.

"I'm not gettin in no fuckin' closet," he barked as he put his jeans back on. "I don't believe this shit."

"Shelby!" Calvin called from downstairs.

"I came in through the front door and I'm leavin' out the front door."

"Ivy you don't understand..."Just as Shelby got the word understand out of her mouth, Calvin kicked the bedroom door open. Shelby noticed that he had something rolled up in his left hand.

"I don't believe this shit!" Calvin roared as he saw his wife stripped down to her bottoms in their bedroom standing with another man. "You're the motherfucka from the picture."

"Picture?" Iverson inquired. Calvin unrolled the picture that Iverson and Shelby had drawn of the two of them on their second meeting.

"Calvin please! Calm down."

"Calm down? Somebody's gonna have to calm my foot outta somebody's ass in a minute. Who the fuck is this?"

"First of all, bruh," Ivy began. "Watch ya tone."

"Nigga, you in my house, in my bedroom, with my wife talkin' 'bout watch my tone. Fuck you!"

"You know what," Ivy paused to calm himself. "I'm out. This shit's between y'all."

Iverson put his coat on and tried to walk out of the bedroom but Calvin would not move from in front of the door. "Pardon me."

Calvin wouldn't budge. After asking politely three times Iverson pushed Calvin into the hallway and onto the floor. Shelby screamed as Calvin jumped up and lunged into Iverson pushing him into the wall. With a lift of a knee into the stomach, Calvin let Iverson go to clutch his stomach. Iverson didn't want to fight. He just wanted to get out of the house. As Calvin gasped for breath, Iverson pushed him aside and started down the hallway towards the stairs. Right before he got to the steps, he heard footsteps approaching him. He spun around to find Calvin rushing towards him dragging Shelby behind him as she tried to stop him.

"Don't do it to yaself," Iverson commanded.

"Calvin please," Shelby cried as he stopped in his tracks. "It's not his fault. He didn't know I was married."

"What?"

"I didn't tell him I was married," she sniffled.

"What the fuck is wrong with you? I give you everything in this world that you could possibly want and this is how you do me."

"Calvin stop. The only reason why you do the things you do for me is because I took you back after you screwed that tramp at the firm."

"That's what this is about. That happened almost two years ago. I thought you forgave me for that."

"It's obvious that y'all got some issues y'all need to work out. I'm out."

"I'm sorry, Ivy."

Iverson turned and walked down the stairs and out of the house. He was furious as he drove away.

"Why do I keep fallin' for this shit?" he asked himself.

Because he was not all together, his instincts lead him downtown to his office. As he exited his car and walked out of the parking garage and onto Peachtree Street, he bumped into a couple of familiar faces.

"Iverson," Natalie greeted with surprise.

"Natalie, Alicia. What's up?"

"What are you doin' down here?"

"On my way to my office."

"What's wrong?" Natalie asked after she noticed his mood and the expression on his face.

"If you only knew. You got a minute to talk?"

"Do you mind?" Natalie asked Alicia.

"Not at all. I'm gonna run across the street and check out that shoe store."

"When you finish, we'll be in my office. Just come in, take the stairs to the left and then come to the end of the hall."

"Okay." Natalie waited until Alicia had crossed the street and was inside of the store before they walked into the building. Iverson didn't say anything as he led Natalie to his office.

"Please, have a seat," he offered as pointing to the couch. When he sat down, Iverson put his elbows on his knees, his face in his hands and began to rock back and forth.

"Iverson, what's wrong?"

"To tell you the truth Dymond, I don't really know. All I know is that I was lied to by the woman that I cared about."

"What do you mean?"

"I found out Shelby was married."

"How'd you find out?"

"She hit me up a couple of hours ago and asked me to come see her at her house. I get there and things start getting heated and right before we got ready to do the deed, her husband busts in the house while we were in the bedroom."

"What?"

"Yeah. He came in screamin'. I tried to walk away but he would let me so we got into a tussle and the next thing I know, I'm here." Iverson's emotions started to get the best of him. He fought the oncoming tears as hard as he could until he couldn't hold them any longer. "Why does shit like this have to happen to me?"

"It's okay," she consoled. Natalie put her arms around him and pulled him close to her.

"After all that I've been through, I thought I had finally found the right woman. She's the first woman that I've cared about in a long time."Iverson stood up and walked towards his desk. "I try to be the best man that I can be but I still wind up gettin' fucked over. Why do all the women I meet have to hide behind a bunch of lies? What's so hard about being honest?" He sat on his desk. Natalie was silent for about two minutes and then she stood up and walked over to Iverson.

"Ivy I have a confession..."

"Aww shit. Not you too. What's your secret?"

"I knew Shelby was married."

"You knew?"

"I met Shelby and her husband Friday night at a dinner party at Alicia's house. When you showed me her picture last night I almost died. That's why I rushed off like I did. I didn't know what to do. I've been beating myself up since last night trying to decide whether or not I was going to tell you and if I did tell you, how would I tell you. I was scared of your reaction and I didn't want to lose you as a friend. I'm sorry and I'll understand if you don't want to have anything to do with me anymore." Iverson paused and then opened his arms to Natalie.

"Come here," Natalie walked into his arms. "It's all good. I know your heart was in the right place. Honestly, I probably wouldn't have believed you if you hadda told me. She really had me twisted. I can't believe I fell for her that fast."

"It be like that sometimes."

"Am I interrupting something?" Alicia asked as she peeked into Ivy's office.

"Hey girl," Natalie laughed.

"Come on in and have a seat. Do you know that your girl is the best?"

"Who? Her?" Alicia joshed.

"I just went through some shit and she managed to help brighten up my day."

"She's good people."

"Well, Ivy. I have to go. I'll call you tonight."

"If you wanna stay I'm sure Ivy will take you home."

"Yeah, it's no problem."

"I would but I have a couple more errands to run."

"You sure?" He asked.

"Maybe next time."

"I'ma hold you to that. Alicia it was nice to see you again and Ludacris told me to tell you hello if I saw you again."

"For real? Well tell him that I said thank you for a fun night."

"Talk to you later Dymond."

"Bye, Ivy." Alicia and Natalie walked out of Ivy's office and out onto Peachtree. "Girl what is wrong with you?"

"What?"

"I'm sure Ivy will take you home. What high school teacher do you know that lives in a house like mine?"

"Whoops...my bad. I got beside myself when I saw how cute the two of you looked together."

"Okay cupid," Natalie laughed.

Five minutes after Natalie and Alicia left Shelby walked into Iverson's office wearing a pair of large-framed sunglasses. Iverson was sitting in his chair with his back to the door with his head leaned back and his eyes closed.

"Iverson," Shelby called in a hoarse tone.

"Shelby," he replied with surprise. "What are you doing here?"

"I called your house but you didn't answer. I thought I might be able to find you here. Iverson, I am so sorry. I never meant to hurt you."

"Somehow I find that hard to believe."

"I know what I did was wrong but please don't act like that."

"How the fuck am I supposed to act?" he asked as he stood up and walked from behind his desk. Shelby's previous encounter with her husband caused her body to tense at

Iverson's reaction. "Shelby I cared about you more than you will ever know and…" Iverson paused and took a close look at Shelby's face.

"What?"

"Take your glasses off for a minute."

"That's ok. I'm fine with them on."

"He hit you, didn't he?" Ivy walked up to Shelby and slid her shades off of her face to reveal a severely blackened eye and some other bruises on her face.

"I deserved it," she explained as she put her head down.

"Regardless of what you did, no woman deserves to be hit by any man."

"I never thought it would go this far. I thought you were going to be just somebody I talked to online from time to time."

"Listen, what's done is done and we can't change that."

"I wish there was something I could do to right this terrible wrong."

"You can."

"Please tell me. I'll do anything."

"Get out."

"Excuse me?"

"I want you to leave."

"But I don't have anywhere else to go."

"I really don't feel like that's my problem nor is it my concern."

"You son-of-a-bitch! Because of you I've probably lost my husband."

"And that's my fault? You shoulda thought about that while you were on the

Internet frontin' like you were a single woman."

Just as Natalie and Alicia arrived to Alicia's car, Alicia came up with an idea.

"I have an idea," Alicia began. "If you want to chill with Iverson, you can have him bring you to my house and I'll take you back home."

Natalie paused and thought about it, "that sounds like a good idea but I don't know. Maybe he wants to be alone right now."

"It would help him out a lot right now especially the way he's feeling. He needs a friend right now."

"I think you're right. I'll call you when I'm on my way."

"Okay, girl," Alicia replied as she unlocked the door. "And don't be tryin to take advantage of that man. He's vulnerable right now."

"That's why I don't like you or ya husband," Natalie laughed. "I'll see you later. After what had just happened between Shelby and Iverson, she was still trying to convince Ivy that it was his fault in some way.

"I'm tired of talking about this," Iverson stated in a stern tone. "For the last time, will you please leave?"

"Iverson, please don't do me like this. I know I was wrong but I do have feelings for you." Shelby walked towards Iverson, whom was sitting on his desk, and tried to put her arms around him. "Iverson, please! Just hold me." She started to cry uncontrollably.

"Shelby, stop it!" Iverson commanded as he grabbed her arms and pushed them away from him. "I have nothing else to say to you." Shelby's sorrow turned to rage as she took a swing at Iverson. Iverson dodged her fist and grabbed her by both of her arms and put them down by her sides. "Calm the fuck down!" He shook her. Just as that came out of his mouth, Natalie walked into Ivy's office. The picture was confusing to the eye. Iverson had a scowl on his face, he was holding Shelby by the arms, she was crying and she had a black eye.

"Iverson!" she called. Ivy let Shelby go. In an instant, Shelby tried to turn the situation in her favor to make Natalie think that Iverson had hit her.

"How could you do this to me?" Shelby cried. "I loved you but this is how you treat me."

"What? You know damn well I didn't put my hands on you."

"Liar!"

"Now you buggin'." Frustration and embarrassment caused Shelby to storm out of the office almost knocking Natalie down.

"Natalie…"

"I know you didn't hit her," she cut him off. "I don't think you're that kinda guy." Natalie walked over to the couch and sat down.

"This shit is really gettin' out of hand."

"Everything's gonna be alright. She just needs time to calm down. Once her emotions settle, she'll realize her wrong."

"I hope so. I don't need no scandals right now." Ivy walked over and sat down on the couch beside Natalie. "What made you come back?"

"I thought you could use a friend right now."

"Thanks."

"You feel like goin' to get something to eat? My treat."

"I have built up an appetite dealin' wit this bullshit."

"How about Justin's?"

"Cool. Let me shut my computer down and we can ride out."

Natalie and Ivy left his office and headed for the parking garage. Ten minutes later they were at Justin's. Once inside they sat at the bar as they waited for their table. Natalie had her signature Hennessey and Coke with Grand Marnier on the side while Ivy sipped on Belvedere and cranberry.

"I don't know too many women that drink Hen or Grand Marnier."

"My homeboys in college turned me on to it. Absolut used to be my drink but when you in college and somebody else is buyin' you drink what you can."

"You strike me as the type that didn't hang with a lot of females in college."

"At Tennessee, most of the athletes hung together. I loved my teammates but I was more comfortable with the guys. I started hangin' wit the fellas freshmen year and hung wit'em for the rest of my years. It was just like being home in Jersey. It also helped my game a lot. Playin' with guys that didn't take it easy on you just because you're a girl helped me step up my game."

"Ever thought about playin pro ball?"

"I thought about it but never really thought I was good enough. Look at Dawn Staley. She was my idol and she didn't make it to the league until recently. I didn't feel I was as good as her and if she didn't make it when the WNBA was founded, I knew I wasn't gonna make it."

"I think you're being modest about your game." With that statement the hostess approached.

"Mr. Davenport, your table is ready. If you would, follow me, please."

The hostess led Ivy and Natalie to a quaint table in a far corner of the restaurant.

"Your server will be right with you. Enjoy your meal." Soon the server came and Iverson and Natalie ordered their meals. As they waited for their entrees they continued to chat over salads.

"Let me ask you something," Ivy paused as he sipped his drink. "How do you

know when you've found the right
relationship?" The question stunned Natalie
and had her silent for a couple of minutes
before she answered.

"That's a tough one," Natalie began.
"It's a complex question that requires a
complex answer."

"And your answer is...."

"A very close friend of mine had the
best answer I've ever heard. Let me see if I can
break it down like him."

"Let it be broke," Ivy laughed.

"Everyone searches and hopes to find
that special someone. Finding that special
someone and building a relationship is like
building a house. Nobody wants a house that
has had a lot of occupants so the best way to
begin is to build from the ground up. Finding
the right person is like finding that perfect
piece of property to build on — some like land
in the country and some like that city land.
After you've found the land, you have to clear
it and get it ready for construction. That's the
dating part. Clearing the land is like clearing
the air between two people. It's the building up
of the safe or comfort zone. Over a period of
time you begin to find out that person's likes,
dislikes, favorites, turn-ons and turn-offs — you
know...things like that. After the land is
cleared the foundation can be dug. That
consists of the time spent around each other.
The best way to find out about a person is to be
around them and that doesn't necessarily

consist of anything physical. That's the "becoming friends" part. Now that the foundation is dug the concrete can be poured and left to dry to ensure strength and stability. You don't want to build on a foundation that's not completely solid because it could lead to problems down the road. Once a friendship has been established it has to be solid and strong. While the foundation is still drying, you can pull out your tools to begin construction of the framework for your relationship. You can build a house with any tools but if you want it to last, you have to use the right ones."

"And what tools are the right tools to use?"

"You need the tools of communication, loyalty, respect, admiration, spontaneity, compromise and the most important tools of them all, honesty and trust. With these tools you can construct something more beautiful than you can ever imagine. If you've done the right thing you can look at the framework alone and see its beauty and potential. When covering the frame work, you should always use bricks—never vinyl siding."

"Isn't siding more cost efficient?"

"For someone trying to build love on a budget. True, vinyl siding is pleasing to the eye, as well as economical; in this case, it represents something that is temporary. Over time it wears and you get tired of it and one day, it has to be replaced. Bricks represent something that will hold strong and last for an eternity. A good house also has to have large windows."

"Why large windows as opposed to smaller or average sized ones?"

"Large windows represent the openness of the relationship and small windows represent secrets and the unwillingness to open up."

"I see."

"Once the exterior is complete the interior has to be completed and filled. After a house is built no one, even if they have the money, furnishes it all at once. It takes time to add things like special moments and memories to hang on the wall, soft hugs to comfort, a security system of trust and respect to protect the entire construction."

"Where does love fit into this?"

"Love is the final thing that is added. Love is like the perfectly landscaped yard that intensifies the entire beauty of the structure. It represents the growth of the relationship because as everyone knows, nothing grows overnight. After everything is said and done, just like the house, the two inhabitants have to work together on the maintenance and upkeep and just like a house; the value of the relationship will appreciate and mean more to you years down the road." Iverson sat in amazement as Natalie broke down the answer to a question that he had been searching for a long time. After Natalie finished, Ivy was speechless.

"Wow," Ivy took a swallow of his drink. "That is unbelievable. I've never heard something put so eloquently."

"It is beautiful but I can't take the credit for that. That is the same answer my best friend gave me when I asked him the same question you just asked me."

"How did he come up with that?"

"He lived it."

"And what was his outcome?"

"He married his soul mate, has a beautiful baby girl, a lucrative career and all the love a man could ever need in his life."

"Now that's what I'm talkin' about."

"Everybody can have that; they just have to be willing to work toward it. The question is: are you willing?"

"Ready and able," Ivy smiled.

"I hear you talkin'," Natalie remarked as she finished her last piece of cheesecake.

The rest of night was spent laughing and talking about life's experiences. They shared basketball stories, college experiences and other moments of their lives. Before they realized it timed had slipped away and 7 o'clock was approaching.

"Damn," Ivy exclaimed as he looked at his watch.

"We've been sitting here for almost six hours."

"Are you serious? I know our server is pissed off with us. I know I would be. I used to hate people like us when I waited tables."

"You were a server, too?"

"I started off as a hostess for Applebee's when I was in high school on weekends and in the summertime. I started serving after I went off to college and came back during the summers. Where'd you work at?"

"I started out as a busser at Red Lobster and started serving after I turned eighteen. I had to quit when I started playin' college ball. You know how it is being a student athlete."

"Please don't remind me. I'll have to make it worth her while."

"Me too, whatever you leave, I'll match that."

"Are you sure? I'm not the average tipper."

"Since you ballin' like that, I'll double it."

"Ok big baller."

Natalie picked up the binder and looked at the credit card receipt. She couldn't write a tip in because if he were to look at the receipt he would see that her name wasn't Natalia Simone. After she signed the slip she reached into her purse, pulled out a Louis Vuttion wallet and pulled out a one hundred dollar bill. She placed it on the closed check presenter.

"Like that? Talkin 'bout me big ballin'." Iverson reached into his pocket and pulled out a very large wad of money and peeled off two more one hundred dollar bills and placed them on top of Natalie's.

"You were serious."

"I'm a man of my word."

"That's good to know." With that statement, their server approached the table.

"Can I get you two anything else?" she asked.

"Everything was wonderful," Natalie replied. "I hope we didn't inconvenience you by holding up your table all day. Here you go." Natalie handed her the check presenter.

"And this is for you," Iverson added as he handed her the three one hundred dollar bills.

"Oh my gosh! I don't know what to say. Thank you guys so much."

"And what was your name again?" Ivy asked.

"Jessica."

"Ok, Jessica. Thanks again for everything. The next time we come in we'll ask for you."

"Thank you so much. You have a blessed night." Ivy and Natalie watched as she walked over to another server and began to talk. They could tell by her mannerisms and facial expression of the other server that she was telling her how much she had just made off of the table. Ivy and Natalie laughed.

"I remember those days," Natalie chuckled as she sipped her last bit of Grand Mariner. "Looks like it's time for me to be getting over to my girl's place."

"I need to be getting home my damn self. I have some things to set up for tomorrow. We need to do this more often."

"Indeed we do."

"Of course with out all of the drama that preceded."

"Sometimes drama can be a good thing. It brought us here today, didn't it?"

"I can feel that. You ready."

"Whenever you are." Ivy stood up and held his hand out for Natalie. She grabbed it and the two of them walked hand in hand out of the restaurant. Fifteen minutes later Ivy arrived at Alicia's house.

"This is a nice crib," Ivy marveled. "What does ya girl do?"

"She's an Advertising Executive for a huge firm in Atlanta and her husband is an Executive Producer at Black Reign. You ever heard of the show 'Matters of the Heart?'"

"You talking bout' the one that comes on Friday nights at nine?"

"Yeah."

"That's my show!"

"Her husband created that show."

"You serious?"

"You know it was a spin-off of 'Tryin' Tymes'."

"Yeah. I watch that one, too."

"He started out as a writer for that show."

"Money doin' his thing. Well, Miss Lady. I'm not gonna hold you up any longer. Get at me later or hit me when you get a chance."

"I will," Natalie leaned in and kissed Iverson on his right cheek. "Talk to you later."She began to exit the car.

"Dymond," he called. Natalie turned back and leaned her head back into the car. "Thanks for everything."

"That's what friends do for each other. Remember that." Ivy watched as Natalie walked away and to the door. As Alicia opened the door she stepped out and waved goodbye to Iverson. They stood in the doorway until he drove away.

"Alright girl," Alicia bubbled with excitement like a high school girl waiting on her best friend to return from her first date. "I wanna here all about it and don't leave nothin' out."

"I'll tell you about it on the way to my house."

"Okay. Let me get my keys and let André know I'm steppin' out." André walked around the corner.

"Steppin out where?" he asked.

"I'm getting ready to take Nat home."

"Don't have my wife out all times of the night. She might get in trouble. I need my wife home at night."

"And why is that Mr. Man?" Natalie asked.

"You didn't know? The freaks come out at night."

"André!" Alicia punched Dré in is arm as he laughed. "Not in front of company."

"Company? Who, Natalie? She a freak, too."

"And how would you know?" Natalie asked as she put her hands on her hips.

"True freaks recognize their own kind and you know me and my baby get our freak on. On top of all that, y'all are best friends."

"What does that have to do with anything?"

"Don't ask him things like that? You know he ain't stable."

"Because freaks of a feather flock together."

"I hate you," Natalie laughed.

"You ready, girl?"

"Yeah. I'll be back in a lil' while." Alicia kissed Dré on his lips.

"Love you , baby."

"Love you, too," André responded.

"Bye, Dymond." Natalie stopped in her tracks then turned around with stretched eyes and her mouth wide open. Then she looked at Alicia.

"Dré!" Alicia playfully shouted.

"My bad."

"I knew you couldn't keep it to yourself. You can't hold water."

"You know me and Dré talk about everything. It was bound to come up."

"So does Dré know you were at the club lustin' over Ludacris?"

"What?" Dré exclaimed. Alicia rushed Natalie towards the door.

"Okay, Baby. Love you. Bye! Kiss, Kiss! Muah!" André laughed as the two hurried out the door.

"I got ya kiss, kiss!" Dré shouted through the door. "Wait 'til you get home!"

Chapter 12

It is believed to be true that there is someone for everyone — for every man there is a woman. If this were not true then when God created Adam, he would have stop there and there would be no life as we live it today. Countless nights men and women find themselves knee-bowed and body-bent asking for that special one. The question is: What do you do to keep this person? In a bitter sea of predators that prey on innocent victims, young lovers find themselves clinging to each other desperately trying to maintain a union that yet has the strength to survive on its own.

> **Dymond4eva:** you are so silly!
> **Ivy_Dav:** I'm serious…mayonnaise will increase the size of your breasts
> **Dymond4eva:** and where did you hear such a retarded thing?
> **Ivy_Dav:** my cousin told me that. She said that in one summer her chest went from B's to double D's
> **Dymond4eva:** LOL! How old was your cuzin at the time…..
> **Ivy_Dav:** probably around 14
> **Dymond4eva:** sweetie…you honestly don't believe that…tell me u r jokin'
> **Ivy_Dav:** Y would my cousin lie to me?

Dymond4eva: because she is a female and you are a male...u believe every thing we tell u.

Ivy_Dav: whatever...Anyway...you still goin' with me to the Grammy's

Dymond4eva: I wouldn't miss it for the world...how often does a person have the chance to go to support a friend at one of the most prestigious music awards
ceremonies

Ivy_Dav: no, seriously...why r u going again?

Dymond4eva: 4 the free trip to LA...LOL

Ivy_Dav: LOL...that's what I thought. Well, Mami...I have to get off this thing and actually do some work.

Dymnond4eva: work...like what? auditioning girls wit big booty girls 4 ur next video?

Ivy_Dav: if you must know...Future Records is planning it's 3rd Annual Athletes vs. Entertainers Celebrity basketball game to help raise money for my homegirl's group home...Humphrey House

Dymond4eva: Awwww! How sweet...and here I was thinkin' that all you Music industry guys did was buy cars, hold ya crotch and pour 400 dollar bottles of champagne on women

Ivy_Dav: you just full of jokes today...

Dymond4eva: you know I'm just messin wit you, baby!
Ivy_Dav: baby? since when did I become ur baby?
Dymond4eva: u don't have a choice cuz don't nobody else want u LOL
Ivy_Dav: LOL...anyway...I'll talk to you 2nite...Peace!
Dymond4eva: ttyl

Ivy_Dav has logged out

Fate can be a real bitch sometimes. One minute you can be the happiest person in the world, the next minute the rug is being pulled out from under you, leaving your world in shambles. Fortunately for Iverson, he had Natalie's support during his time of need. Most people that believe in God, or a higher being, feel that the Creator put people in your life for specific reasons and it is left to that particular person to figure out what they are there for. Sometimes you figure it out but most of the time people slide in and out of your life and it is never said why they were there.

In the heart of Buckhead, Ivy and T-Bizzy sat in TyQuan's office discussing plans for the basketball game. They had been at it for hours and decided that they needed a breather. As they were ordering lunch, a familiar name popped into the conversation.

"Alright," Ivy began. "Michelle is ordering lunch. What's next?"

"What's up with you and ol' girl?"

"Who?"

"Baby girl from the party."

"You talking 'bout Dymond? We're cool."

"I think that's the one for you."

"She's a good girl but after what I been through, I'm mentally exhausted and takin' a break for a minute."

"Now you tired. You finally meet somebody that I approve of and now you tired. Just like a nigga."

"She's cool and I've been feelin' her for a minute but I just have to take this one slow."

"You are the most backwards ass Negro that I have ever met."

"Why you say that?"

"The women that are no good for you, you rush in blind. The women that are good for you, you take too much time and wind up loosing."

"What makes you say something like that?"

"Does the name Marva Bailey ring a bell? USDA Prime cut beef. She had it all. Marva was hella sexy, she had money, a successful career and an ass of girlfriends just like her."

"Marva was cool but she had issues."

"What kind of issues?"

"She was too independent. She had that 'I don't need a man for shit' attitude. She was too serious all of the time and to top it all off, she couldn't cook."

"Damn. I didn't know all of that."

"So as you can see, all that glitters is not gold."

"Then Shelby and Candace must have been sterling silver tryin to pass as platinum," T-Bizzy burst into laughter.

"That's not funny,"

"I don't care who you are, that's funny." He managed to get Ivy to laugh. "But seriously, be open-minded with her. She seems like a good person. Let it happen."

"But when is the right time to tell him?" Natalie asked as she followed Alicia into her kitchen.

"I don't think it's that big of a deal," Alicia answered. "Ivy strikes me as the type of person that will understand your reasoning behind it."

"I don't know girl," Natalie paused putting her plate in the dishwasher. "Since we've been talking, I've found that he has this thing about dishonesty."

"Natalie, we all lie in the beginning of a relationship. It is what we do. Besides, it's not like you're being dishonest for personal gain or to be devious. You we're just trying to protect yourself."

"So you're tellin' me that you and Dré lied to each other in the beginning of your relationship."

"I don't think we count considering we've known each other since we were kids but to be honest there were a couple of lies in the beginning."

"Like what?"

"After we parted ways, right before he found out Karen was pregnant, I started dating again. When we came back together, he asked me how many people I had slept with after he left South Carolina. I told him that I only slept with one guy."

"And how many did you sleep with?"

"Four."

"You're such a slut," Natalie laughed. "Have you told him since then?"

"Hell no! André thinks I'm his innocent lil' angel and I'm not going to do anything to taint my husbands image of me."

"Then why do I have to tell Iverson?"

"Because your situation is different. If you want to have anything in the future with Ivy, you have to tell him what you do for a living. He'll understand. The only way he won't is if he finds out through someone else. Just tell him."

"I will. I will."

"When?"

"When the time is right."

"And when is that?"

"On our honeymoon." Natalie laughed. "But seriously I'm going to tell him."

As children on into adolescence and adulthood, especially those who were brought up in the church, people have been taught that "honesty is the best policy" and for the churchgoers, "the truth shall set you free." Since society has changed so much over the years, people now believe that honesty is not always the best policy. It is that same mentality that causes lovers, both young and old, to get caught up in tangled webs of deception and unfortunate events. Natalie's situation is a unique one because of who she is. If she paraded around on the Internet boasting to be a professional basketball player, she would attract every low-life from the ATL to Baghdad. But what about Iverson? He is who he says he is. For Ivy, it's acceptable because he is a male and the Internet is a good place to find talent and make connections. Not to say that he wouldn't come across gold diggin' skeezers because he has and will as long as he is Iverson Davenport, CEO of Future Records.

Every Thursday night at Club Blaze was open mic night. Every poet, singer, MC and comedian in Atlanta flocked to the club to get a piece of the mic. On occasion, record label execs, A&Rs, talent scouts and other influential people stopped through the club looking for the next hot act. Because of this, Thursday's at

Blaze drew more than just artists. It attracted a variety of other people — men seeking women, women seeking men, gold diggers seeking a come up and the bad seeking the good.

It was around seven o'clock that Thursday evening. Ivy, T-Bizzy and the rest of the Future Records camp were still at the office getting ready to adjourn their weekly meeting. A phone call drew T-Bizzy away from the meeting and out into the hallway. After about ten minutes Ivy closed the meeting as T walked back into the room.

"Dog," he began with excitement in his voice. "Its on and poppin' at Club Blaze tonight."

"What's up?"

"I just got off the phone with Black from Entouch Management and he just told me that Purrfection didn't sign with Capitol Records because the deal wasn't what they wanted. They're performing at Club Blaze tonight."

"Who is Purrfection and what does that have to do with me?"

"Who is Purrfection? Only the hottest female trio to come out of the ATL since TLC. I've been watching them for the past eight months and they are hot."

Ivy laughed, "Scouting? You?"

"I'm serious. They're the real deal. They already have a large fan base and their CD has sold almost 75,000 units without a major promotion or distribution. They would be the perfect group to follow the Southern Sunz. "

"Alright, give me the vitals."

"Two Black, One Latina. All three girls are in their early twenties. They range between the heights of 5'2" and 5'5". All three are hella sexy with versatile voices. It's like a collaboration of Amerie, a Jennifer Lopez that can sing and LeToya."

"LeToya?"

"LeToya Luckett. You know…the one from the original Destiny's Child that I like."

"No doubt."

"All of them dance and one of them is an MC. The marketability is through the roof. As hot as The Southern Sunz are right now, you can put them on their first single over a Gusto Jones track and you know what all that equals? Mo' Money, Mo' Platinum and Mo' plaques."

"I don't know."

"What you mean you don't know. Have I ever let you down?"

"Do I really have to answer that question?"

"Look. I know I do some off-the-wall shit sometimes but I've put a lot of time and effort into getting them interested in Future."

"Then why is this the first time I'm hearing about this?"

"Because Capitol already had their offer on the table when I met them and we were tied up with getting the Sunz out."

"Well, if you feel they're hot, go out there, check'em out and set up a meeting."

"I can't go out there by myself tonight."

"You scared?"

"The only reason they are performing tonight is because I told Black that you were going to be out there and he doesn't want to deal with anybody but you."

"What makes him so special? That's why I have you and Will."

"Dog, do this solid for me. Please."

"Alright, but only cuz you my man."

"I promise you it's a good move."

"It better be."

Ivy left the meeting room and returned to his office to work on a few things. As he sat down at his desk to pull up the information for the basketball game, he found that he had just missed Dymond.

Dymond4eva: Ivy…u there?

Dymond4eva: I was just hittin' u up 2 c how ur day waz goin…hit me later☺

Ivy looked at the time of the message then looked at his watch. The message was only 5 minutes old.

Ivy_Dav: Dymond??????

After about two minutes passed, she responded.

Dymond4eva: Hey there!
Ivy_Dav: What u up 2?
Dymond4eva: nuttin much…just got back from the gym
Ivy_Dav: true…what u doin' 2nite?
Dymond4eva: I have a date
Ivy_Dav: a date? With who?
Dymond4eva: Ben, Jerry and Jamie Foxx…lol
Ivy_Dav: lol
Dymond4eva: I'm just relaxin 2nite. I'll probably watch a movie and go 2 bed
Ivy_Dav: change of plans…I'm goin' to check out this girl group @ Club Blaze 2nite…ride wit me
Dymond4eva: on a skool nite?
Ivy_Dav: I know but it'll be fun
Dymond4eva: I don't know
Ivy_Dav: C'mon…live a little…pleeease!!!
Dymond4eva: OK Keith Sweat…stop beggin'…lol…I'll go but I'm driving.
Ivy_Dav: Cool. I'll meet you out front around 10.
Dymond4eva: ok babe
Ivy_Dav has logged out

A quarter past ten arrived and Ivy stood in front of Club Blaze. His anticipation of Natalie's arrival was beginning to escalate. As he waited, he was hailed by everybody that passed him. Because Ivy was known for being open to new artists, he would have been standing with a hand full of demos if he had not told the artists that he was not there on business. He just believed that there are proper steps that should be taken.

Knowing that women like to be fashionably late, he didn't get too agitated by the fact that Natalie was thirty minutes late. Five minutes prior to her arrival, a familiar face approached Ivy. It was Melissa a.k.a. XoticMami.

"Hello there, stranger," Melissa greeted.
"Melissa," Ivy hesitated. "What's up?"
"Not a whole lot. I just got back from Paris doing a photo shoot. I'm only in town for a couple of days and then I'm off to New York for a Baby Phat fashion show."
"That's what's up."
"So, how have you been?"
"I'm good. My latest artists have gone platinum, the CD is sellin' out of the stores and as of right now, I'm in the process of planning my 3rd annual celebrity basketball game."
"Busy man."
"You know how this industry is."
"Believe me, I know. Well, it was good seeing you again. Maybe we can have a drink inside."
"If I'm not too tied up."

"I guess I'll see you later," Melissa walked past Iverson and after about for or five steps, she stopped and turned around. "Ivy?"

"Yes," he answered.

"Why did you cut me off like that?"

Seeing Natalie approaching from behind Melissa, "I really don't have time to get into that right now. Maybe some other time."

"Are you serious?" Natalie walked past Melissa and greeted Ivy with a hug and a kiss on the cheek."

"Never mind," Melissa replied. "I think I just got my answer." She rolled her eyes and walked off.

"I'm sorry," Natalie apologized. "Did I interrupt something?"

"Not really. That was just an old acquaintance. Let's go inside."

Ivy and Natalie walked into the club and straight to the bar. Natalie was impressed when she found that Ivy remembered what she liked to drink. After a couple of humorous compliments, they headed for his table. The couple was engaged in small talk as a tall, slim man with an extremely dark complexion approached the table. It was Black, Purrfection's manager. Black wore a silk, paisley print shirt, half-way open displaying the hairs on his chest—which looked like taco meat—a pair of shiny black slacks and red loafers. The thing that stood out the most about Black was the fact that he was black as night but his teeth were snow white and big as hell. He looked like he had a mouth full of Chiclets.

"Ivy!" he greeted.

"What's good, Black?" Ivy stood up and dapped him up.

"It's your world. Look. I got the girls backstage getting ready to blow the roof off this place."

"No doubt. My man, T-Bizzy told me they're the real deal."

"The next big thing to come out the A since TLC. But anyway, I see you chillin' wit ya lady…"

"My bad, man. Dymond this is Black from Entouch Management. Black this is Dymond."

"Nice to meet you, Dymond," he greeted as he extended his hand.

"A pleasure," she smiled.

"Ivy thanks for comin' out to check out the girls. I'll talk to you after the show. Enjoy yaselves." Black trotted off and disappeared backstage.

"He seems nice," Natalie replied.

"About as nice as a snake in heat."

"IVY!" Natalie laughed as she playfully shoved him.

"I'm serious," he began. "This industry is a beast. It's hard to trust anybody because everybody is out for self."

"Well what about your camp?"

"I guess we're an exception to the rule. Me and T built Future on something my Dad told me when I was a kid."

"And what was that?"

"He told me that good business was the only way to do business. You can't prosper through dishonesty but even with that, I find it hard to trust people. T-Bizzy, Will, and KD are like family to me. We've been through some rough times but through it all we've always had each other's back."

"What about me? Do you trust me?"

"Maybe I will one day."

"Good answer."

Time marched on as the population of the club continued to grow. When you were in good with the promoters you got primetime slots. If you weren't in good either you were opening or closing the show — either way, no one was paying you any attention. Around twelve o'clock, Purrfection was set to hit the stage. The MC walked onto the stage and began to hype up the crowd.

"Ladies and Gentlemen, Pimps and Pimpettes…the time has finally arrived. These next three sexy ladies are representin' the Eastside of the ATL." Before he could go any further the crowd erupted. Everybody in attendance that was representing the Eastside began to scream, clap and make hellafied noise. The ovation lasted for about two to three minutes before the MC gained control again. "Damn! I guess its safe to say that the Eastside is in the house. I want everybody to show your love for...PURRFECTION!"

Synthetic smoke swallowed the stage as the curtains opened. The group stood on stage with their back to the crowd; each in their own spotlight. Two of the ladies were dressed in electric blue catsuits and the other wore silver that glistened in the light. Just as the music began for them to start their opening dance number, one of the bouncers approached Iverson.

As he leaned towards his ear, "Ivy, we got a problem outside."
"Damn it! I can't chill without something poppin' off." Leaning over to Dymond, "I'll be right back. Check the group out and tell me what you think. I'll be right back."

Ivy excused himself from the table and walked out of the club. Natalie sat and observed the group as if she worked for Future Records. She really looked official when she reached into her purse and pulled out her notepad. Paying close attention to detail, she jotted down several notes concerning the group's performance and overall look. Ten minutes passed and Purrfection's performance was over. Iverson still hadn't returned to the table. Natalie waited patiently but she began to get worried. She decided to give him five more minutes. As she continued to wait, Black walked up to the table.

"Where's Ivy?" Black inquired as he sat down. "Did he see the show?"

"He had to check something out but he left me to check the group out."

"Exactly what is your position with the label?" Black leaned closed to Natalie and propped his arm on the back of Natalie's chair.

"First of all, what I do at Future is not your concern. Second of all, back up off me."

"Damn, Miss Lady, you kinda feisty. I like that." Black removed his arm from the chair and leaned back in his. "So what'd you think?"

"I am not at liberty to discuss this matter with you without Iverson's presence or consent." Black sat looking dumbfounded. "In other words, we'll call you."

Natalie stood up and worked her way through the crowd towards the club's exit. When she got outside she saw three police and a group of officers surrounding Iverson. She walked swiftly toward him. As she approached she noticed a female sitting in the back of a police car with a scowl on her face. Right before she got to where Iverson and the police were, one of the officers blocked her path.

"I'm sorry ma'am but you can't go beyond this point."

"Ivy!" she called. Iverson looked and saw that the officer wouldn't let Natalie past him.

"Its okay officer," Ivy assured. "She's with me."

The officer moved aside to let her on her way. Once she made it passed the officers, she found out what all the commotion was about. Iverson's baby, his Chrysler 300, had been vandalized. The windshield looked as if someone had done a little batting practice, all of the lights were busted out, the tires were flat and the car had been keyed to hell.

"Ivy, what happened?"

"That crazy chick right there is what happened," Ivy barked as he pointed to the female in the backseat of the police car.

"Who is she?"

"I'll tell you about it later."

"Ok sir," the investigating officer approached with a pad in his hand. "According to the witness, we have everything we need to prosecute. The only thing you have to do is come down to the station tomorrow and file the necessary paperwork."

"What about her?" Ivy asked.

"She's going to be spending the night in the DeKalb County Inn tonight. Take her away, Officer Perez."

"So what about my car?"

"Unfortunately, there is nothing else we can do. You are responsible for getting it to where it needs to go. Word to the wise, make sure you take pictures of the damage for the insurance company. Here's my card. Call before you come down to the station and I'll tell you exactly what you need to do. Have a good night."

"How the hell am I supposed to have a good night!"

"Ivy calm down," Natalie tried to comfort. "Let's just go."

"You know what, you're right." The crowd disbursed as the police drove away. Natalie put her arm around Iverson's waist as they walked to her truck. Once inside the SUV, Iverson put both of his hands over his face and wiped it down as he let out a heavy breathe.

"Are you ok?" Natalie asked in a concerned tone.

"I'm cool."

"Where do you need me to take you?"

"To the house if it's not too much trouble."

"Not at all." Just as Natalie put the truck in gear to pull off, Black jumped in front of the Navigator causing Natalie to slam on brakes.

As he let down the window, "Yo, man! What is wrong with you?" Black walked over to the passenger side.

"What about the group?"

"Not right now, Black. I'll call you in a couple of days."

"A couple of days?"

"Yeah a couple of days."

"I turned down a deal from Capitol just so I could keep Purrfection in Atlanta for you. I can have them signed in a couple of days."

"Then do what you gotta do, pimp. It's plenty of talent in Atlanta. Let's go, Dymond." Natalie began to pull off.

"Alright, man! Just call me!" Iverson raised the window as they drove off. Black noticed the girls were standing in front of the club watching him. "I'ma get at you tomorrow!" Iverson sat in silence for the first ten minutes of the ride. Natalie wanted to say something but she decided to give him his space. She felt that when he was ready, he'd talk about it. The only words he spoke were the ones that led Natalie to his home.

"This is nice," Natalie marveled looking at Iverson's house. "Are you sure all you do is music?" Iverson managed to let out a laugh. "There's that smile I like to see."

"Thanks Dymond. I needed that. Well, I guess I'm out for the night. Is it okay if I call you so we can talk about the show?"

"Sure. Just hit me up tomorrow evening."

"Cool." Ivy leaned over and kissed Natalie on her cheek. "You just don't know how much I appreciate you."

"That's what real friends do for each other. You've had a long day now go in the house and go right to bed. No late night creepin'." The two laughed as Iverson got out of the car.

"Talk to you tomorrow, babe."

Iverson closed the door and walked towards his house. Natalie waited until he was in the house before she drove off. Once she saw that Ivy was safely inside Natalie backed out of the driveway and headed towards home. You could see the girlish glow on Natalie's face as she cruised down I-75. Before long she was safe inside her own home — alone — but this time, she didn't feel empty.

The night's events had Iverson livid, distraught and frustrated — all at the same time. In all the years that men roam this earth, they will never know the answer to the age old question: What causes a woman to fuck a man's shit up just because she is not happy with him at that time? For an hour he tossed and turned in his bed. Knowing that it was no way he could sleep feeling the way that he did, he decided to see what was going on the internet. You know…just4kickz.

Futurama has entered the room
<Thyk2Def> THAT'S IT OPTIMO…I WANT A DIVORCE! I'M TIRED OF U CHEATING ON ME!

\<Teddy Pinned*Her*Ass*Down> SAY IT
AIN'T SO CUZIN!
\<Choco Latte>
FUUUUUUUTURRRRRRRRRREEEEEEE!!!!!!
!!!!!!
\<City Ave Diva> LOOK WHAT THE DAMN
KAT DONE DRUG IN...LOL
\<MACK Truck>CUZIN!!!!!!!
\<Teddy Pinned*Her*Ass*Down> LADIES
AND GENTELMAN...RUSSELL DUPRI
PHARELL DIDDY GOTTI HOVA SIMMONS
CARTER HAS ENTERED DA
BUILDIN!!!!!!!!!!!!!!!!!!!
\<Futurama> WHAT'S UP E'RYBODY!!!!
WHAT'S GOOD!!!!
\<City Ave Diva>WE THOUGHT U HAD GOT
TOO BIG FOR US COMMON FOLK
\<Got'em Hatin>LIKE WE AIN'T GOOD
ENUFF 4 U TO HANG OUT WIT NO MORE
\<Futurama>C'MON NOW, YOU KNOW I
ALWAYS COME BACK TO DA FAM NO
MATTER HOW LONG I STAY AWAY
\<Optimo Pryme>WELCOME BACK
HOMIE...CONGRATS ON THE PLATINUM
PLAQUE!!!!
\<Futurama> THANKS OPTIMO!
\<Choco Latte> SO HOW WAS THE ALBUM
RELEASE? WAS FACE THERE?
\<Krystal Lyte> WHAT ALBUM RELEASE?
\<Teddy Pinned*Her*Ass*Down> HERE WE
GO WIT THAT FACE SHIT AGAIN
\<Futurama> LOL! I'M NOT TELLIN NOBODY
ABOUT THE PARTY CUZ ALL OF U

MUTHAPHUCKAS WERE INVITED AND
NOBODY SHOWED UP

<Da Ice Cream Man> even after he said that he
would put u up 4 the weekend

<Got'em Hatin> STOP INSTIGATIN'@ICE
CREAM   THAT'S MY JOB!

<Futurama> ONLY PERSON THAT CAME TO
SHOW A BROTHA SOME LOVE WAS MY
ACE!

<City Ave Diva> WHO?

<Got'em Hatin> WHO IN HERE WENT TO
THE PARTY AND SISN'T TELL NOBODY
ABOUT IT

<Teddy Pinned*Her*Ass*Down> YEAH
WHO'S THE LOW LIFE THAT KEPT INFO
LIKE DAT FROM THE FAMILY?

<Futurama> IF U WOULDA BEEN THERE U
WOULD KNOWWHO THIS PERSON IS BUT
THEY ASKED ME NOT TO SAY ANYTHING
TO ANYBODY ABOUT IT

<Thyk2Def> THAT IS SO NOT FAIR!

<***Mami*Dearest***> I KNOW WHO IT WAS
AND I'M TELLIN'!

<Futurama> DON'T SPOIL IT MAMI...LET'EM
FIGURE IT OUT...

<***Mami*Dearest***> CAN I GIVE A BROAD
CLUE?

<Got'em Hatin> JUST SPILL IT GIRL!

<***Mami*Dearest***> THINK BACK TO
THAT WEEKEND...EVERYBODY WAS IN
THE ROOM THAT WEEKEND EXCEPT ONE
PERSON BESIDES FUTURE

<City Ave Diva> I THOUGHT EVERYBODY
WAS HERE

<Da Ice Cream Man> damm@MAMI that was a
little too broad

<***Mami*Dearest***> NOT REALLY@ICE
CREAM...U EVEN COMMENTED ABOUT
THIS PERSON NOT BEING IN THE ROOM

<Choco Latte>
TTTTTEEEEEEDDDDDDDDDYYYYYYYYYY!!!!!
!!!!! I'M GOING TO KILL YOU!!!!!!!!!!!!!!!!!!!!!!!!!

<Futurama> RUN CUZIN!!!! THE JIG'S UP!!!!!
SHE'S ON TO YOU!!!! LOL!!!!

<Teddy Pinned*Her*Ass*Down>
ROFLMAO!!!!

<Da Ice Cream Man> wow teddy!

<Optimo Pryme> DAMN CUZIN...I
THOUGHT WE WAS FAMILY...YOU DIDN'T
EVEN TELL YA BOY! I'M HURT!

<Teddy Pinned*Her*Ass*Down> BECAUSE I
KNOW U...U WOULDA TOLD THYK AND
THYK WOULDA TOLD DA WORLD!

<City Ave Diva> SO TEDDY...WHAT WAS IT
LIKE PARTYIN' LIKE A ROCK STAR

<Choco Latte> I AM SO MAD AT YOU RIGHT
NOW TEDDY!!!!

<Futurama> U CAN'T BE MAD @ TEDDY @
CHOCO....U SAID U COULDN'T MAKE IT

<Da Ice Cream Man> u did say u couldn't
go@choco

<Choco Latte> ICE CREAM AGAIN I TELL
YOU....SHEEEEEED UP!!!

<Teddy Pinned*Her*Ass*Down> IT WAS
BANANAS!!! MR. DAVENPORT IS FIRST

CLASS ALL THE WAY!!! I'M TALKIN BOUT CRISTAL, LIMOS, SUPERSTARS AND THE THING I LOVE THE MOST....GROUPIES!!!!

<Choco Latte> EXCUSE ME??? GROUPIES???

<Futurama>************PLEADING THE FIF***********

<Da Ice Cream Man> u better think of something quick@teddy

<Teddy Pinned*Her*Ass*Down> DID I SAY GROUPIES...I MEANT TO SAY GROUP OF WOMEN THAT HAD ALL THEIR CLOTHES ON HAVING SPLENDID CONVERSATION...U KNOW ITS ALL ABOUT YOU MY CHOCOLATE GOODNESS...LOL

<***Mami*Dearest***> WHAT STARS DID U MEET?@TEDDY

<City Ave Diva> WAS LUDACRIS THERE@TEDDY

<Choco Latte> TEDDY IF U WOULD KINDLY DIRECT URSELF TO MY CAM U WILL SEE THAT THE EXPRESSION ON MY FACE DOES NOT SAY LOL

<Da Ice Cream Man> that face definitely does not say lol...lol!

<Teddy Pinned*Her*Ass*Down> WHO WASN'T THERE...I MET LIL JON, JD, OUTKAST, LUDACRIS, JAZZE PHA, BIG GIPP

<Got'em Hatin> NOW THAT'S MY BABY...I LOVE ME SOME JAZZE PHA! HE LOOK LIKE A BIG OL TEDDY BEAR

<Da Ice Cream Man> I didn't know Big Gipp was still alive...lol!

<MACK Truck> ALL DEM FELLAZ IZ COOL AND ALL CUZIN BUT WHAT FEMALES WAS IN DA HOUSE

<Teddy Pinned*Her*Ass*Down>OMG!!!!!!

<Futurama> UH OH!!! HERE IT COMES!

<Teddy Pinned*Her*Ass*Down> GUESS WHO WAS ALL UP ON YA BOY?!?!?!?!

<Optimo Pryme> WHO CUZIN!!!

<Teddy Pinned*Her*Ass*Down> GUESS?

<***Mami*Dearest***> CHILI FROM TLC?

<City Ave Diva> SOME STRIPPER FROM MAGIC CITY?

<Teddy Pinned*Her*Ass*Down> THAT WAS LATER ON THAT NIGHT@DIVA LOL!

<Got'em Hatin> TEDDY JUST TELL US!

<Choco Latte> YEAH TEDDY....JUST TELL US...

<Da Ice Cream Man> was it Gladys Knight?

<Thyk2Def> Gladys Knight?

<Da Ice Cream Man> u never know...she do have a chicken and waffles spot in Atlanta

<Thyk2Def> THAT'S ROSCOE'S

<Futurama> ACTUALLY SHE DOES HAVE A CHICKEN AND WAFFLES SPOT HERE IN ATLANTA@THYK

<Teddy Pinned*Her*Ass*Down> I WILL REVEAL THE MYSTERY LADY'S NAME ONLY UNDER THE CONDITIONS THAT CHOCO DOES NOT GET MAD

<Choco Latte> WHAT? I AM NOT GOING TO GET MAD

\<Teddy Pinned*Her*Ass*Down\> PROMISE?

\<MACK Truck\> CUZIN JUST SPIT IT OUT!

\<Choco Latte\> I PROMISE, BOO!****BATTING MY EYE LASHES****

\<Da Ice Cream Man\> like u always tell everybody else@teddy....don't do it, it's a set up..lol!

\<Teddy Pinned*Her*Ass*Down\> I CAN'T DO IT...U TELL'EM@FUTURE THAT'S THE ONLY WAY THEY'LL BELIEVE IT HAPPENED!

\<City Ave Diva\> WILL SOMEBODY PLEASE TELL US!!!

\<Futurama\> IT WAS CIARA

\<Optimo Pryme\> FO REAL? CUZZZINNNN!!!!!

\<MACK Truck\> THAT'S MY BOY!!!!

\<Choco Latte\> AIN'T SHE LIKE 17

\<Da Ice Cream Man\> green is not your color@Choco

\<City Ave Diva\> DID U HAVE ANYTHING TO DO WITH IT@FUTURE

\<Futurama\> TEDDY TOLD ME HE WANTED TO MEET HER AND I INTRODUCED THEM...HE DID THE REST

\<Got'em Hatin\> THAT DAMN TEDDY P!!!!! DO DA DAMN THING!

\<Teddy Pinned*Her*Ass*Down\> U STILL MY BOO?@CHOCO

\<Choco Latte\> WE COOL@TEDDY

\<MACK Truck\> THAT DIDN'T SOUND LIKE A GOOD "WE COOL"@CUZIN

\<Choco Latte> U CAN GO TO ATLANTA AND PARTY WIT FUTURE AND BE ALL UP ON ANOTHER BROAD BUT CAN'T COME TO CALI TO SEE ME

\<Teddy Pinned*Her*Ass*Down> R U SERIOUS? CUZ WE CAN GO THERE IF YOU WANT TO...

\<Optimo Pryme> TEDDY...LET IT GO

\<Futurama> YEAH CUZIN...COOL OUT

\<Choco Latte> HE CAN SPEAK HIS MIND IF HE WANTS TO...HE ALWAYS DOES

\<Da Ice Cream Man> ouch!

\<Teddy Pinned*Her*Ass*Down> FIRST OF ALL I WAS INVITED TO ATLANTA JUST LIKE EVERYBODY ELSE WAS...I HAVEN'T RECEIVED A SERIOUS INVITE TO COME TO CALI YET...WHICH MEANS WHEN I AM INVITED SOMEWHERE...I JUST MIGHT GO

\<Thyk2Def> Y DID Y'ALL GET HIM STARTED...WE WAS HAVIN A GOOD NIGHT

\<Teddy Pinned*Her*Ass*Down>THANK U AGAIN FUTURE FOR LETTING ME CRASH AT THE MANSION

\<City Ave Diva> U DIDN'T TELL US U WENT TO THE MANSION@TEDDY

\<Futurama> ANYTIME CUZIN...Y PAY 4 A HOTEL FOR ONE PERSON AND I GOT 9 OTHER BEDROOMS NOT BEIN USED

\<City Ave Diva> TRUE

\<Teddy Pinned*Her*Ass*Down>2ND OF ALL U CANT GET MAD CUZ I PARTIED WIT CIARA OR ANYBODY ELSE THAT I

PARTIED WIT...Y...BECAUSE U WEREN'T
THERE AND HAD THE OPPORTUNITY TO
COME
<***Mami*Dearest***> OK TEDDY...U MADE
UR POINT
<Got'em Hatin> HE'S NOT FINISHED...I BET
YOU
<Optimo Pryme> EASE UP CUZIN!
<Teddy Pinned*Her*Ass*Down> SO U MEAN
TO TELL ME THAT HAD IT BEEN THE
OTHER WAY AROUND AND U WENT TO
ATLANTA AND MET FACE YOU
WOULDN'T HAVE KICKED IT WIT'EM
BCUZ OF A NIGGA U STRINGIN ALONG
ON THE NET...GET SERIOUS!
<***Mami*Dearest***> TEDDY THAT'S
ENOUGH!!!!!!
<Thyk2Def> WOW!
<MACK Truck><<<<<<<<<IS
SPEECHLESS>>>>>>>>>>
<Choco Latte> I GUESS I DESERVED THAT
<Futurama>AIGHT TED...LIGHTEN UP
<Teddy Pinned*Her*Ass*Down> I'M SORRY
CHOCO...I GOT A LITTLE CARRIED AWAY
<Choco Latte> BUT UR ABSOLUTLY
RIGHT...MAYBE I HAVE BEEN STRINGIN
YOU ALONG BECAUSE I'M SCARED TO LET
GO OF WHAT STANDS IN BETWEEN US
<City Ave Diva> HERE COMES THE OPRAH
MOMENT
<Choco Latte> I'M GOING TO SAY THIS IN
FRONT OF EVERYBODY BCUZ I HAVE

NOTHING TO HIDE CONCERNING U
TEDDY

\<Da Ice Cream Man\> maybe u 2 should talk
this out in private

\<City Ave Diva\> SHHHHHH!@ICE CREAM

\<Choco Latte\> ME AND TEDDY HAVE BEEN
TALKING ON THE PHONE EVERY NIGHT
FOR THE PAST 3 MONTHS AND I FOUND
OUT SOMETHING VERY INTERESTING

\<City Ave Diva\> UH OH!

\<Got'em Hatin\> I KNEW SHE WAN'T
GONNA LET THAT NIGGA BLAST HER
LIKE DAT AND NOT SAY NOTHIN

\<Choco Latte\> TEDDY IS THE MOST
WONDERFUL PERSON THAT I'VE EVER
MET

\<Da Ice Cream Man\> what????

\<Thyk2Def\> SHE MUST BE TALKIN ABOUT
A DIFFERENT TEDDY

\<Got'em Hatin\> SHE HAS TO BE TALKIN
ABOUT SOMEBODY ELSE

\<Choco Latte\> TEDDY MAY TALK A LOT OF
SHIT AND PUT PEOPLE ON FRONT STREET
BUT THAT'S JUST THE TEDDY Y'ALL
KNOW

\<Got'em Hatin\> SOUNDS LIKE THE TEDDY I
KNOW

\<Thyk2Def\> SHE HIT THE NAIL ON THE
HEAD

\<Choco Latte\> BUT THE TEDDY THAT I GOT
TO KNOW OVER THESE PAST COUPLE OF
MONTHS IS TRULY THE MAN THAT EVERY

WOMAN DREAMS OF HAVING IN HER LIFE

<Da Ice Cream Man> I think there's something wrong wit my screen

<MACK Truck> I CANT BE READIN THIS CORRECTLY

<Futurama> LADIES PAY CLOSE ATTENTION

<Choco Latte> HE IS THE FIRST PERSON THAT I HAVE MET THAT CARES ABOUT MY WELL BEING...EVERY TIME WE TALK...HE ASKS ME ABOUT MY DAY...IF I'M DOWN HE MAKES ME LAUGH...HE SENDS SILLY TEXT MESSAGES JUST TO MAKE ME SMILE AND TO LET ME KNOW HE'S THINKIN ABOUT ME

<Optimo Pryme> TEDDY SOUNDS A LIL SOFT TO ME...LOL!

<Teddy Pinned*Her*Ass*Down> WATCH YA MOUF!

<Choco Latte> I GUESS WHAT I'M TRYNA SAY TO YOU TEDDY IS THAT I KNOW I WOULD BE HAPPY WITH YOU BUT WE ARE ON TWO DIFFERENT SIDES OF THE COUNTRY...I WANT TO TAKE IT TO THE NEXT LEVEL BUT PART OF ME IS SCARED BECAUSE OF WHAT I HAVE HERE AND THE THOUGHT OF ME UPROOTING MY LIFE HERE, COMING THERE AND IT NOT WORK

<Teddy Pinned*Her*Ass*Down> IF YOU DON'T MIND ME SAYING...U JUST CONTRADICTED UR SELF

MRZ.SOOPAFLY has entered the room

<Da Ice Cream Man> I thought I was the only one that saw that

<Choco Latte> I KNOW I DID....AND THAT'S THE SAD PART...THE THING THAT GETS ME IS THE FACT THAT THIS IS THE INTERNET AND I DON'T KNOW TOO MANY PEOPLE THAT HAVE ACTUALLY FOUND TRUE LOVE IN A CHAT ROOM

<Teddy Pinned*Her*Ass*Down> IN WHAT BOOK DOES IT SAY WHERE TRUE LOVE IS SUPPOSED TO BE FOUND?

<MACK Truck> ****WRITING THAT ONE DOWN**** THAT WAS A GOOD ONE@CUZIN

<Teddy Pinned*Her*Ass*Down> I'M THE TYPE OF PERSON THAT DOESN'T LIKE TO WONDER THROUGH LIFE WONDERING "WHAT IF"...IF IT DOESN'T HAPPEN...IT DOESN'T HAPPEN

<Optimo Pryme> WHO IS THIS DUDE AND CAN WE PLEASE GET TEDDY BACK

<Futurama>Y'ALL SHOULD PAY ATTENTION...U COULD LEARN A THING OR TWO FROM TED

<Teddy Pinned*Her*Ass*Down> LIKE I TOLD YOU...MY LIFE IS HERE IN FAYETTEVILLE, NC...AND I LIVE A DAMN GOOD ONE...I TOLD YOU BEFORE AND I'LL TELL U AGAIN INFRONT OF EVERYBODY...THERE IS ROOM IN MY LIFE FOR YOU...YOU JUST HAVE TO WANT TO BE APART OF IT

<City Ave Diva> GIRL...U BETTA GET THAT
GOOD MAN FOR SOMEBODY ELSE GET'EM

<MACK Truck> YOU GON FUCK AROUND
AND SEE TEDDY IN THE NEXT CIARA
VIDEO...LOL!

<MRZ.SOOPAFLY> WHAT IN THE HELL
HAVE I MISSED

<Da Ice Cream Man> I'll fill u in later@da wife

<Choco Latte> ALL U HAVE TO DO IS
PROMISE ME THAT YOU WILL NOT HURT
ME

<Teddy Pinned*Her*Ass*Down> I CANT
PROMISE U THAT...NO MAN CAN

<Krystal Lyte> IS IT JUST ME OR WAS THIS
ON AN EPISODE OF THE YOUNG AND THE
RESTLESS

<Teddy Pinned*Her*Ass*Down> BUT I CAN
PROMISE YOU THIS...IF YOU GIVE ME A
FAIR CHANCE...I PROMISE YOU WON'T
REGRET IT

<City Ave Diva> I THINK I'M GONNA CRY

<Choco Latte> CAN U CALL ME IN ABOUT
10 MINS@TEDDY

<Da Ice Cream Man> they about to have make
up phone sex...lol!

<Thyk2Def> TEDDY WAS RIGHT ABOUT
U@ ICE CREAM...U R A PERVERT...LOL!

<Teddy Pinned*Her*Ass*Down> TALK 2 U
IN 10

<Futurama> I GOTTA TELL Y'ALL AS MY
FAMILY...I WAS HAVIN A REAL SHITTY
NIGHT BUT JUST COMING IN HERE WIT
MY FAM REALLY CHEERED ME UP.

\<City Ave Diva\> THAT'S WHAT FAMILY'S 4@FUTURE
\<Thyk2Def\> JUST WHEN YOU THINK THAT U AIN'T GOT NOBODY…U ALWAYS GOT US!
\<Futurama\> AND THAT'S ALL ANYBODY CAN ASK FOR

Chapter 13

The next morning, Natalie awoke to a sun-drenched bedroom. The rays hugged the contour of her body as she lay half-awake in her humongous bed still thinking about Iverson. It may seem strange due to the fact that the evening was ruined but somehow, Natalie overlooked that part—just being in Iverson's presence was enough for her. After about ten minutes of lying there, she reached for her remote and turned on the stereo. Once the music began to blare through the speakers, Natalie sprang from the bed and danced into the bathroom. To the average on-looker, she looked like a schoolgirl on the morning after her first date. Natalie seemed to be floating on air as Janet Jackson filled the house. After her shower, she made her way to her computer to check her email and messages. Once logged on a box that said: *drewifey has requested permission to add you to his/her friend list.* Natalie chuckled as she added Alicia to her friend list then double-clicked on her name.

> **Dymond4eva:** what's up girl?
> **Drewifey:** bored as hell…what u up 2?
> **Dymond4eva:** nuttin…just woke up…prolly go to the gym later
> **Drewifey:** kewl
> **Dymond4eva:** shouldn't u b workin

Drewifey: shhhhh! Somebody might hear u… lol! but seriously not 2 much goin on today... I think I'm leavin early
Dymond4eva: guess who I was wit last nite
Drewifey: Mr. Dildo? lol
Dymond4eva: ALICIA MARSHALL!
Drewifey: j/k…who where u with?
Dymond4eva: just 4 that I'm not tellin<folds her arms and pouts>
Drewifey: awwwww! C'mon don't act like dat…lmao!
Dymond4eva: I was wit Ivy
Drewifey: you r such a slut! Lol
Dymond4eva: NOT LIKE THAT! We went to open mic nite at Blaze so he could
check out a new group.
Drewifey: hold on a sec…brb
Dymond4eva: ok

Natalie continued to check her messages while she waited for Alicia to come back to the messenger.

Drewifey: Nat????
Dymond4eva: wzup?
Drewifey: listen I gotta run, my boss needs to see me
Dymond4eva: uh oh…little ms vp gotta go to the principal's office…lol
Drewifey: lol…what u doin 4 lunch so u can tell me bout last nite?

Dymond4eva: nuttin...where u wanna go?
Drewifey: how about copeland's on cobb pkwy@ 1
Dymond4eva: see u there...lata
Drewifey: tootles!

Down on Peachtree Street Iverson was finishing up a call with his insurance company when T-Bizzy walked into his office. Ivy motioned for him to hold on a minute as T sat down on the couch.

"Thank you so much." Ivy hung up the phone. "What's up, pimp?"

"So what'd you think about Purrfection?"

"I didn't see the show."

"WHAT!" T-Bizzy stood up. "Come on, man. I thought you went to the show."

"Calm down. I went to the show but some shit popped off right before they hit the stage."

"What happened?" T-Bizzy inquired as he sat back down.

"Melissa vandalized my 300."

"Who?"

"Melissa. The model chick I met on the net. She broke ya boy down to his brake pads."

"You bullshitin'."

"I wish I was. She busted all the lights, smashed the windshield and flattened all the tires."

"What'd you do to her?"

"That's just it. I didn't do anything. We went out; some dude told me that she was Missy the Man-eater…"

"I knew that chick looked familiar. She done ran through the whole industry, the NFL, the NBA and the Major League." He paused. "Tell me you didn't hit that."

"Hell no!"

"Whew! Word on the streets is she got Da Ninja."

"That's the same thing dude said."

"So what are we gonna do about the group?"

"Dymond saw them perform. I'm supposed to be hooking up with her tonight to see how it was."

"Dymond? You really diggin' this chick, ain't you?"

"I am but after my last experiences, I'm a lil shook."

"Dude, don't sweat it. Just go with the flow. To tell you the truth, I'm feelin' this one."

"Well thank you Mother Love," Ivy laughed "But for real, I think I'm gonna take my time with this one."

"Do what you do, pimpin'. In the meantime, I'll be down in the studio."

"Please tell me you're not using the studio as a hoe house."

"Not this time. I promised a couple of cats some studio time. They did some work for me."

"No doubt," Ivy gave T a pound as he left for the studio.

"You still playin' ball at 2?"

"Yeah. I'll meet y'all out there."

The one o' clock hour found Natalie and Alicia sitting in Copeland's. They sat engaged in small talk as short, brown complexioned male wearing all black, approached the table. They soon found out he was very, Very, VERY queenish.

"Good afternoon ladiesth," he greeted as Natalie and Alicia looked at each other and snickered.

"My name isth Stheven and I will be stherving you today." Natalie tried to suppress her laughter as he ran down the specials. "Stho ladiesth. What can I get you to drink? Costhmosths? Pina Colodaths?

"That sounds good," Alicia began. "Let me get a Grey Goose Cosmo."

"You are such an alcoholic," Natalie laughed. "But I do know your husband you better make it a double."

"And what would you like?"

"Hennesthey and Coke." Alicia busted out laughing as Natalie mocked the server.

Rolling his eyes, "I'll be right back."

"No sweet thing didn't roll his eyes at you."

"He'sth justh jealousth," Natalie laughed.

"So, tell me about last night."

"Last night was crazy. Me and Ivy went to Blaze to check out a group he might sign. Right before they went on, Ivy got called outside. I sat and watched the show but he still didn't come back. So I went outside. When I got outside there were cops and a mob of people."

"What happened?"

"Apparently some crazy chick messed up his car."

"Not the 300."

"The 300 girl. I almost cried for him."

"Did he say who she was?"

"It was kinda hectic and he was upset so I didn't stress him about it. He said that he would tell me about it tonight."

"Tonight?"

"Hold on. Here comes Stheven." The server returned with drinks and took their order. "Before he left he asked me to check out the group and let him know how they performed. The night went foul so we're going over it tonight."

"You're really feelin' Iverson aren't you?"

"Alicia he is like a dream come true. He's handsome, sexy, and successful."

"And he's black."

"What does that have to do with anything?"

"I know how you ball players are."

"Hello…I'm in the WNBA not the NBA." They laughed. "But seriously, I really like him but I don't want to seem eager or come on to strong."

"Just relax. I think he really likes you, too. Just ride it out."

"How can I ride it out? He thinks I'm a school teacher for Christ's sake."

"That's so minor. Just tell him."

"That's easier said than done."

"How?"

"He stresses the fact that he has a problem with dishonesty."

"We all tell little white lies every now and then. I'm sure if you talk to him he'll understand. Its not like you are out to get him, you're just trying to protect yourself."

"You think?"

"Just talk to him."

"Maybe you're right but I still need a little more time."

Soon the meal came and the ladies feasted on some Cajun cooking. They continued to chat over lunch. After the meal the ladies parted ways. Alicia went back to the office and Natalie headed for the gym.

"Ain't that ya girl?" T asked.

"Dymond!" Ivy called across the gym. A smile crossed Natalie's face when she saw Iverson and began to walk toward him.

"Daaaayum!" Will and KD ogled simultaneously.

"Beavis and Buckhead...pick ya tongues up off the floor and act like you got manners."

"Hey Ivy!" Natalie greeted as she hugged him. "I didn't know you came here."

"We usually go to Run-n-Shoot but we didn't feel like it today. What are you doin' here? Aren't you supposed to be in school?"

"I overslept this morning so I decided to take a three day weekend. Can I get next?"

"You can get my spot," Will offered.

"You sure?" Natalie confirmed.

"I'm sorry Dymond. This is my crew from the label. That's my engineer and nephew, KD. This foreigner right here is my VP of A&R, Will and you already met T-Bizzy, my right hand man.

"Nice to meet you guys." They all exchanged pleasantries. "Who's team am I on?"

"Why don't you team with Ivy," T suggested.

"Let me guess, you don't want a girl on your team." Natalie folded her arms with attitude.

"Nah it's not that. I was just... Well since you and..."

"Its cool," Natalie laughed. "I was just joking."

"Come on, Dymond. Let's do these clowns."

"Do who?" T asked?

"You...clown."

"Put ya money where ya mouth is."

"I'll bet you a c-note that you and Lil' Kim don't make it to five." Natalie and Iverson looked at each other and smiled.

"I'll take that bet," Natalie replied.

"I can't take money from a young lady."

"From what I hear, it never stopped you before."

"Ivy, get ya girl."

"Is it a bet or what?" Natalie taunted. "Unless you're scared. If that's the case let me know. I'll understand."

"It's a bet. Shoot for ball."

"Make it, take it?"

"You know it. Oh yeah, all we have is a man ball. Can you work with that?"

Natalie walked to the top of the key — behind the three point line directly in front of the basket — and shot the ball. SWISH!

"I'll manage," Natalie assured. "Check ball."

"I got Dawn Staley. You get Ivy. Ball in." T got into his best defensive stance. Natalie gave him a head fake, took one step back and launched the ball. SWISH!

"That's one."

"That's luck."

Natalie passed the ball to Iverson, faked right and spun left leaving T-Bizzy standing still. Iverson passed her the ball on her cut to the basket and she laid it up.

"That's two," Ivy poked. "You wanna quit now?"

"Just play ball."

Natalie faked the pass to Ivy and dribbled it between T-Bizzy's legs. He turned to catch up to her but she had already let the ball go. SWISH!

"3-0."

"You wanna switch up?" KD asked.

"Mind ya business. I got this." T-Bizzy really started to get irritated when Natalie began talking trash to him as she dribbled.

"You ready? I'll tell you which way I'm goin this time. I'm going to my right." Natalie faked right and T went left. She backed up and continued to dribble. "What are you doin'? I told you I was goin' to the right."

"Just play ball!" Natalie stared T in his eyes but saw Iverson cutting to the basket out of her peripheral. Once she saw that he had KD beat she tossed it up. Alley-Oop…BOOM! Iverson threw Natalie's perfect pass down with authority.

"That's…"

"I know! I know!" T barked as he cut her off. "Play ball." Natalie began to dribble and talk trash again.

"This is the money shot, Ivy. You wanna take it or you want me to take it."

"You take it," Ivy insisted.

"I think you should take it. Okay, I'll take it." Natalie tried to go past T but he stuck his hip out and tried to come around her and swat the ball out of her right hand. As she collided with T's hip she began to lose her balance and she was on her way to the floor. In the process, she tossed the ball towards the basket and crashed to the floor. The ball hit high of the glass, then hit the front of the rim and rolled twice around the rim. It stopped as it got to the back of the rim and paused for about 5 seconds then rolled in the basket.

"That's five," Natalie taunted from the floor. Iverson walked over and helped her up.

"We can keep playin' but I need my money now. Oh yeah, I forgot to tell you, I played a lil' basketball back in college." Natalie and Ivy laughed as T-Bizzy reached into his pocket and handed Natalie a hundred dollar bill.

"How does it feel to be givin' a girl money without her taking her clothes off?"

"A comedian, too," T laughed and turned to Ivy. "Get ya girl."

The foursome gathered up and finished their game. Iverson looked in amazement as Natalie moved around the court hitting shot after shot. When it came to basketball, Natalie was poetry in motion. When the game was retired, KD and T-Bizzy went into the weight room. Natalie and Iverson took their places on two stationary bikes that sat side by side.

"We still on for tonight?" Iverson asked.

"Yes indeed. Where you wanna go?"

"I don't know. What you in the mood for?"

"Well since we will be discussing business, we should go somewhere nice."

"How does the Sun Dial sound?"

"The Sun Dial? I've never been there?"

"You haven't. You'll love it. Hold on a minute." Iverson picked up his cell phone and called the office. "Hey, Michelle. I need you to make a reservation for two at the Sun Dial for 8 o'clock. Thank you." Ivy closed the phone and placed it back on the console of the stationary bike.

"Reservations are being made. What time should I pick you up?"

"Is it okay if I just come to your place? I've had a couple of bad experiences in the past so I'm just a little cautious about who comes to my place. Not that you are a bad person but I just need to get to know you a little better."

"I respect that. Why don't you just come through around seven and we can have a drink before dinner."

"Sounds good to me. It's a date." As Natalie and Iverson were talking, T-Bizzy walked up.

"What did you think about Purrfection?" T asked.

"I'll tell you like I told Black. I am not at liberty to discuss that matter without the consent of Iverson." T looked at Iverson as he shrugged his shoulders.

"Y'all on some bullshit." T-Bizzy walked off as Ivy and Natalie laughed. Once they cooled down they said their goodbyes and walked into their perspective locker rooms to shower and finish up the days events.

It was a cold, late February night. The evening was clear and you could tell it was Friday. All major interstates where flooded with people getting ready to unleash the woes of the work week at their chosen spots of relief. Natalie blazed up I-75, northbound, headed to Iverson's. After exiting off of 75, Natalie smiled as she thought of Iverson. She also thought about the fact that she had never seen Iverson in anything other than jeans and sneakers. What would he be wearing? Natalie's chosen ensemble was nothing less than stunning. She wore a form-fitting emerald green dress that extended to just above her knees. The v-neck of the dress, which extended down her chest to show a lovely amount of cleavage, was laced in gold studs that matched the six inch heels that she wore. Her hair hung long and brushed her shoulders and her make-up was flawless. When she arrived in front of the cast iron gate displaying Iverson's initials she pressed the button for him to open the gate.

Iverson opened the gate from the house and Natalie drove in. Due to the previous night's events, Natalie did not get a chance to drive in the gate. She just dropped Ivy off and he went inside. As the driveway curved around to the front door, Natalie was impressed by the beauty of Iverson's estate. She parked her car, walked up the stairs and stood in front of two huge doors with brass music notes in the middle of each one. With a closer looker she also saw that Iverson had his initials, I&D, etched into his door knobs. "Now that's hot," Natalie thought to herself.

Standing in the middle of the foyer was like stepping into a Cathedral. It looked very old-fashioned. The ceiling was domed with a beautiful mural of a sky pained on it. In front of her was a U-shaped staircase that went up on one side and came down on the other giving you two ways to get to the second floor. Beneath her feet was a beautiful menagerie of natural colors — browns, tans and beiges. The colors swirled together and matched all of the woodwork, crown molding and the extras that were in the foyer. To Natalie's left and right was a door on either side. There was also a door in the middle of the U of the staircase. After about a minute, the doors began to open and she heard Iverson's voice via an intercom.

"Come on in. I'll be right down."

Natalie continued to admire what she'd seen so far. Just as she was noticing a couple of platinum plaques Iverson had displayed on the walls, the door that was in front of her slid open and out stepped Iverson. Iverson was wearing a pair of olive green slacks with cuffs that were about an inch and a quarter. The top of the outfit was a multicolored sweater containing the colors of olive green and a dark tan.

"Wow," Natalie marveled as he approached. "You clean up very well."

"You're not too bad ya damn self," Iverson complimented as he hugged Natalie and grabbed her hand to spin her around. "Very sexy."

"Is this what I missed last night by dropping you off at the gate?"

"It's a little somethin' somethin' I picked up," He replied. "It's not much but it'll do for now. Would you like a tour?"

"Do we have time?" Natalie laughed. Iverson grabbed Natalie's hand and began to lead her towards the door to the left.

"This is sort of like a relaxation room. When I get stressed or have had a stressful day, I come in here to unwind." This room had a huge sectional that was also U-shaped in the middle of the room. The wall to the left was one huge bookcase full of books.

"Now that's a lot of books. I didn't know you could read." They laughed.

"I can't. I just look at the pictures." They left that room and walked across the foyer to the other door. "This is a guest bathroom or for when you can't make it to the second floor."

This bathroom was bigger than some people's master bedroom. Iverson kept the color scheme going through out the previous room and the bathroom. After leaving the bathroom, they headed towards the door that Iverson entered from. As they stood in front of the door, which had no knob or handle, Iverson reached over and pressed one of the two buttons that were on the wall beside the door.

"You do not have an elevator in your house."

"I have to. My grandmother is up in age and she likes to come visit me from time to time."

"Awwww! That is so sweet. It's hard to find someone that thinks of others and not just themselves all of the time."

The door opened and Natalie noticed that there was a door on the other side as well as a table on the right of them that held a bottle of wine in a silver wine bucket. Iverson pulled the frosty bottle out of the ice and poured Natalie a glass of white wine. Natalie accepted the glass and took a sip.

"This is amazing. What kind of wine is this?"

"It's from my private vineyard in Napa Valley. This is our Riesling."

"Wooow! You own a vineyard? That is impressive. I thought all you music people bought were Cars, jewelry, expensive champagne and cognac."

"That's what most people think. I think I'm a rare breed in the industry."

"Indeed you are," Natalie mumbled as she sipped her wine.

"What was that?"

"I was saying I wonder what's on the other side of that door."

"I bet. That's how I get to the garage. You'll see that on the way out."

"Are we just going to stand in the elevator or are you going to show me the rest of the house?"

"T was right," Iverson chuckled. "You are a comedian." Iverson pressed another one of the three buttons on the panel and they went up to the next level. When the door opened Ivy motioned for Natalie to step out. "After you, Madame."

"I don't care what anybody says, chivalry is not dead."

"Contrary to popular belief it isn't. There are a few of us left out there that were raised the right way."

"Tell Mr. and Mrs. Davenport they did a very good job."

"I can't tell them but I can tell Mr. and Mrs. McDonald. I was adopted."

"What happened to your parents, if you don't mind me asking?"

"Not at all. My father left my mother before I was born and it was too much for my mother to handle. The state took me from her because of drugs when I was three. I stayed in an orphanage for two years and the McDonalds took me home when I was five."

"I couldn't imagine what that was like," Natalie replied with a look of sympathy on her face.

"Me neither cuz I was just joking." Iverson busted out in laughter.

"Iverson!"

"I'm sorry. I had to get you back for that one earlier. You looked so concerned wit it, too." Iverson mocked how Natalie was looking at him as he told her his story.

"But honestly, the Smiths are my grandparents. My mom and dad were young when they had me so you know how that goes." Natalie had this *yeah right* look on her face.

"Seriously?"

"That's the truth. I can call my grandma right now. Hold on." Iverson reached in his pocket and pulled out his house phone.

"Okay, okay. I believe you." Iverson proceeded to dial the number. "Iverson do not call your grandmother." Natalie tried to get the phone away from him but he turned his back to her and used his arm to hold Natalie back.

"Hey Grandma, how you doin? That's good. Listen Grandma. Somebody wants to talk to you." Iverson handed Natalie the phone. She refused it but he put it up to her ear. "Say hello."

"Hello?"

"What's up, Dymond?" the male voice greeted.

"Who is this?"

"That's a damn shame. Give a girl a hundred dollars and she forgets all about you."

"TyQuan?" Natalie laughed. "I can't stand you or your big-head friend." Natalie handed Iverson the phone back as he laughed at her.

"Aye, Dog, I'ma hit you later."

"You got me," Natalie replied shaking her head.

From the foyer to the second level was like stepping into another house. It was like stepping out of an early 1800's, southern style home into the house of the future. The walls were a beautiful shade of gray with contemporary artwork and movie posters on display. The floors were made of the same hardwood that most basketball courts were made of.

"This floor looks familiar," Natalie commented.

"This is the same hardwood that is the Hawks and the Diamonds play on. The same people did it for me."

"That's why it looked familiar," she thought to herself.

Out of the elevator they made a right. Iverson showed her the bedrooms that were on the east wing of the house. The rooms were very contemporary and each room had its own personal touch and color scheme. After she saw the rooms they headed to the kitchen. The kitchen was decked with marble counter tops that looked just like the floors in the foyer only they displayed the colors of dark grey, light grey and black. All of the appliances were stainless steel and the stove was on an island in the middle of the floor. Above the stove were racks that held stainless steel sauté pans and an assortment of pots.

"You remember when you dropped me off over my people's house?" Natalie asked.

"Yeah I remember."

"This looks just like their kitchen."

"Damn. Now I gotta have it remodeled." Natalie laughed but noticed Iverson wasn't laughing.

"Are you serious?"

"No, I'm just playin'," Iverson joshed.

"I was gettin' ready to say."

"So where's the studio and the man room?"

"Man room?"

"You know. The room with the big screen, the bar, the pool table and video games."

"That's downstairs under the Garage. You wanna go down there?"

"I'll see it some other time but what I do wanna see the master bedroom."

"You can't see that just yet."

"I don't care if the bed's not made or you got clothes all over the place. I just want to see it."

"You know how you are about guys coming to your house?"

"Yeah."

"That's how I feel about my bedroom." Iverson walked over to Natalie and stood directly in front of her and looked down at her. "It takes a very special person to see the inside of the palace."

"What makes it so special?"

"That is my sanctuary. Only a woman that is fit to be a queen can stand within those four walls."

"Am I not fit to be a queen?"

"From what I'm seeing you have queen-like qualities but I still don't know who you are. Indeed you are gorgeous and down to earth but what can a man really find out about a woman in the time that we've known each other."

Natalie's body became warm all over. The feeling was a mixture of Iverson's words and his presence — the other part was the secret about herself that she was hiding.

"And as you respected me and my house, I respect your sanctuary."

Iverson leaned in to kiss Natalie. As his lips approached hers, Natalie closed her eyes. Iverson kissed her on her nose and walked off. With lips still puckered, she opened her eyes. Iverson laughed when he saw the expression on Natalie's face.

"You ready to go?"

"Are you serious?"

"On a serious note, I would really love to kiss you but I don't want you to think that I'm tryin' to make a move on you just because I have you in my home. I feel when the time is right, it'll happen."

"Just now felt pretty damn right to me," Natalie exhaled. "You know what Iverson? Either your runnin' hellah game or you're too good to be true."

"What would make you say that I'm too good to be true?"

"It's almost like you're two people in one. Ivy is the person that I can hang out with chill and have fun with. Iverson is a perfect gentleman, he's respectful and he knows how to treat a lady."

"A lot of women don't take the time to get to know Iverson because of the stereotypes and facades of the music industry so I don't present Iverson. I present Ivy. Ivy is a people person because he has to be. Iverson is very personal. Not too many people know him."

"How many women outside of your family know Iverson?"

"Three."

"Wow. That's impressive."

"But the thing about them was that they didn't know how do deal with Ivy. They wanted me all to themselves."

"With the type of business that you do, there is no room for insecurities. A real woman should know that as long as you respect her and give her no reason to doubt you, she should not have a problem."

"There goes another one of those queen-like qualities shinin' through." Iverson looked at his watch. "It's 7:30. We should be making our way downtown."

"I'm ready whenever you are."

"Let me put my phones in the room and we can be out."

"You're not taking your phones?"

"I do take one but I leave it in the car. Iverson doesn't like to be interrupted when he's out with someone special."

"You never cease to amaze me."

Iverson walked down the hall to relieve himself of his Sidekick and his personal phone and grabbed his Metro phone. Once he returned to Natalie, he led her back to the elevator and down into the garage. Natalie's mouth dropped when he saw Iverson's collection of cars. Among the cars was a royal blue 1964 Chevy Impala Super Sport, a silver Lexus LX470, a black S500 Mercedes Benz, a pearl white Rolls Royce Phantom and two motorcycles. Natalie noticed that one of the bikes was pink and white.

"What does one man need with this many cars?"

"I drive a different car according to my mood, where I'm going and who I'm going with."

"I don't mean to pry but where do you go on the pink bike, Midtown?" Natalie laughed. Midtown is an area in Atlanta that is known for its gay population.

"That's not funny. That belonged to my ex. She wanted a bike so I bought her one. I just haven't gotten around to selling it."

"How are you feeling tonight?" Iverson walked over to a grey case that was bolted to the wall and placed his right thumb on the sensor. The case opened and he pulled out a set of keys.

"I'm feeling like a king tonight," Ivy answered as he walked back to Natalie. He grabbed her hand and led her to the Rolls Royce. He opened the door for her.

"Your chariot awaits you my queen."

"Thank you, kind sir," Natalie obliged as she stepped into the car.

Though Natalie had the money to buy a Phantom if she wanted to, she had never ridden in one. A feeling of royalty came over her as the couple cruised through downtown Atlanta. Despite the other cars that were on the streets, all eyes were on Iverson and Natalie. They arrived at the Westin on Peachtree with ten minutes to spare.

"Iverson," Natalie began. "Why are we at a hotel?"

"Because I'm trying to get you in bed," Ivy laughed.

"If that was the case we coulda stayed at your place."

"The restaurant is at the top," he pointed towards the sky.

"I knew that."

"I know you did. Shall we?"

Iverson extended his arm after giving the valet his keys. He looked at Natalie's facial expressions as they walked through the hotel lobby on the way to the elevator leading to the Sun Dial. Natalie and Iverson were greeted by the lobby hostess as they approached. She informed them that their table was ready and they could go up. The outer wall of the elevator was made of glass so that you could look out over the city as you ascend to the top. Once on the top floor, they were greeted by another hostess that led them to their table by the window.

"Wow," Natalie gasped as she marveled over the beauty of the city of Atlanta.

"I've been in this city for two years now and I never realized it was this beautiful."

"That's the same thing I said the first time I came here."

"So how many women have you brought here?"

"The first girl I dated when I moved to Atlanta."

"Is this your first time back since then?"

"Nah…We usually have dinner parties and our annual New Year's Eve party. This was the first year that we didn't have it. We got tied up with the video shoot."

"Oh yeah…I saw it the other day. They're still number one on 106&Park."

"They're havin' a good run. The album is still selling well…"

"Wow! You're old."

"Where did that come from?"

"You said album," Natalie giggled.

"You are so silly. Speaking of albums and artists, let's go ahead and get business out of the way."

Just as Iverson got those words out of his mouth, the server approached with a bottle of wine and poured two glasses.

"This tastes familiar," Natalie commented as she sipped her wine.

"It should. You just had some at my place."

"They carry your wines here?"

"Select fine dining establishments in select cities carry Château Davenport."

"Impressive."

Over a simple conversation about wine, the spark between Iverson and Natalie was obvious. Their eyes were locked on each other's every movement. Looking at the entire situation and what each one had been through, they deserved each other. Iverson was a successful business man with no queen to share his castle and Natalie was a basketball star that deserved to be treated like royalty. The two seemed to be made for each other. There was a brief pause in the conversation as the server began to serve the appetizers. As she placed the items on the table Iverson and Natalie were locked in a heated moment of mental flirting.

"Did I tell you how beautiful you are tonight?" Iverson lulled.

A smile spread across Natalie's face as she replied," Thank you. You are looking very handsome tonight yourself."

"Gracias, Mami."

"De Nada, Papi."

"Before we get side tracked again, let's get this business out of the way. What did you think about Purrfection?"

"They were amazing. They had the look, the attitude and the sound."

"How did the crowd react to them?"

"From the moment they hit the stage they had the audience captivated."

"Did the group have a leader and how could you tell?"

"Two of the girls were wearing the same color outfit and the lead vocalist wore a different color in the same style. They worked the stage like professionals. The group looks like a combination of Jennifer Lopez, Amerie and Aaliyah with flavor of TLC.

"Aaliyah? T said there was a girl in the grouped that looked like LeToya Luckett."

"Maybe they pulled a Destiny's Child. You know how groups do."

"True. Looks like I have to call Black and set up a meeting."

"Looks like you got the next big thing on ya hands."

"If it wasn't for you, I woulda missed them for the simple fact that I don't deal with Black. You have a real eye for talent. Ever thought about the music business?"

"Judging by your crew, the music industry might be too much for me."

"What is wrong with my crew?"

"Where do I start? I'll start with ya boy, T-Bizzy. Every time he sees my girl, he tryna holla at her."

"What's wrong with that?"

"She's married and he knows that."

"Ok, you got that one."

"I'm just joking. You got a good crew. They're down for you and that's what matters."

"I'm blessed. That's the only way I can put it. I am also thankful for the newest blessing that He has given me in you."

"Awww!" Natalie blushed. "You are too sweet."

The rest of the evening was full of electricity between Natalie and Iverson. The way they carried on the average onlooker would have thought that they had known each other for years and had been together just as long. Ivy treated Natalie like a true lady. For the first time in a long while Natalie was at ease in the presence of a man. For the moment she forgot about all of her former deception and enjoyed the evening but knew that soon, she would have to come clean if she wanted to pursue this relationship with Iverson.

Dinner drew to a close and the cozy couple found their way back downstairs to claim their chariot once again. Valet pulled the car around and Natalie and Iverson were off once again. Cruising down Peachtree, once again, reality began to set back in for Natalie. She tried to suppress it but it kept nagging at her. Though she'd only known Iverson for a couple months, she felt that he was so right for her. If she didn't come clean and come clean soon, she was going to lose him.

"The night's still young," Iverson began. "What would you like to do?"

"I don't know. If I tell you something you promise not to laugh at me?"

"I promise."

Mumbling under her breath," This the first date I've been on in six months."

"What was that?" Iverson inquired holding his hand up to his ear like Hulk Hogan.

"You are the first man that I have been out with in six months. There I said it. Are you happy now?"

"Happy? I'm flattered that you would choose me for such an event in your life?"

"Come on now," Natalie laughed. "You make it sound like it's my first date ever."

"After everything I've been through with women, I am thankful that you chose me. You're like a breath of fresh air that has given me new life." Any other time a compliment like that would have made a woman feel like she was on top of the world but not for Natalie. That was the one that did it. It was time for Natalie to come clean.

"Can we just go back to your place? I don't feel like being out on the town tonight."

"Are you sure?" Iverson asked.

"Yes." Minutes later the twosome was back at Iverson's house. Iverson led Natalie into his Game Room beneath the garage.

"Would you like more wine?" Iverson offered as he walked behind the bar.

"If it's not too much trouble, I'd like something a little stronger."

Ivy turned around to survey the numerous bottles that were lined on the glass shelves.

"Look what I found. How does some Hennessy V.S.O.P. sound?"

"Throw in a little Grand Mariner, make it a French Connection and that sounds great."

Iverson mixed the drinks and returned to where Natalie was seated on one of the leather couches near the pool table.

"Here you go my lady," Iverson presented as he noticed Natalie's facial expression.

"Are you okay?" Natalie didn't answer. Instead she sat and looked deep into Iverson's hazel eyes. The sincerity and concern that she found in his eyes brought on tears.

"What's wrong?"

"Iverson I am so sorry," Natalie sniffled. "I don't deserve to be here right now."

"What are you talking about?"

"I'm not who you think I am." Iverson's facial expression changed as well. He felt as if he was getting ready to get blindsided. "Before you say anything, just hear me all the way out. The person that you enjoy hanging out with and talking to is really me but the life you think I live is not true."

"Here it comes."

"I am not Natalia Simone, high school basketball coach. I am Natalie Simms WNBA point guard for the Atlanta Diamonds."

"What!"

"I didn't do it because I was trying to take advantage of you or get anything out of you. I was only trying to protect myself. You know how some guys can be on the internet. I never thought that it would go this far."

"I don't believe you. I was completely honest with you from the beginning and this is what I get!"

"Iverson please don't be angry? I'm so, so sorry! I never meant to hurt you. Iverson wait..."

Iverson stormed out of the bar area and walked through a door leading him into another room. Natalie was devastated. She sunk her head down into her arms and sobbed heavily. After about five minutes Iverson returned to the room undetected carrying two wall hangings that were facing him.

"Natalie," He called.

Natalie pulled her head out of her arms and looked up at Iverson. He turned the wall hangings around. One of them was an autographed poster of Natalie doing a lay-up in her Tennessee uniform. The second was an autographed Natalie Simms game jersey with a picture of her beside it.

"You knew?"

"The entire time. I'm a Diamonds season ticket holder and an even bigger Tennessee fan. My cousin played for Tennessee."

"Who is your cousin?"

"Shaniqua Holdsclaw."

"If you knew, why didn't you say something?"

"I figured that you had your reasons. It is easier for a man because we handle things a little different. I wouldn't expect a wealthy and attractive woman to be parading her riches around on the internet. To tell you the truth, I thought it was fun."

"You know I really can't stand you right now."

"Come here."

Natalie stood up and wiped her eyes and face. Ivy held out his hands and Natalie put her hands in his. He pulled her into his body and placed her arms around his neck as he bent over.

"I'm sorry, too. I should have told you I knew but I didn't want to ruin my chances with you. To be honest, I thought it was a little cute."

"Iverson, you don't know how hard it was for me to walk around knowing that I was deceiving you, even if you did know. This is like a release for me. I know you've been through a lot with women in general…"

"Especially internet women."

"I don't feel that there is anything wrong with how we met. Let's just make a promise to each other on this night. No more dishonesty and no more internet."

"I have no need for the internet. I believe I've found my computer love."

Chapter 14

Drugs are addictive. Cigarettes are addictive. Alcohol is addictive but the biggest addiction of them all sits under the radar and never goes detected — the World Wide Web, also known as, The Internet. People spend hours at a time on the internet not realizing that they are being sucked in by the web of high-speed intrigue. With the stroke of a few keys, a person can download their favorite music, purchase a car, pay bills and meet the man or woman of their dreams — all without leaving the comfort of their own home. With the emergence of dating sites, people can play Russian roulette with their own and other people's love lives. It is a real gamble. You sift through profile after profile hoping to find someone that is right for you. When a person does get a bite, the person that they think they are talking to or communicating with is not always who they portray themselves to be. Then there is the situation where a person finds what they are looking for and leaves the dating sites alone to fulfill life with the one that they found. It is a beautiful thing until the drug begins to call again. The internet is a useful tool but, even as a hammer is also a useful tool, it can also be a deadly weapon.

Covered in warm mud, Alicia and Natalie relaxed at one of Atlanta's most relaxing getaways. After what Natalie had put herself through concerning Iverson, she felt that she needed it. The previous night's events drained her and she felt as if she needed to be rejuvenated. Soft music provided a soothing ambiance as the ladies sat and talked.

"I don't believe you told him," Alicia squealed.

"What I don't believe is how well he took it."

"He knew who you were the entire time. That is so funny. You put yourself through all of that for nothing."

"Gee thanks. You sure know how to make a girl feel good about herself."

"You have to admit. It is kinda funny. I wish I coulda been a fly on the wall when he walked in with those pictures. I bet that was priceless. What I wanna know is what made you tell him last night?"

"Everything was cool until we got ready to leave his house…"

"You were at his house? You are such a slut." Alicia clowned.

"Like I was saying…Iverson started saying all these wonderful things to and about me. The thing that got me the most was when he chose which car he wanted to drive. He chose the one that he said was fit for a queen."

"What did he choose?"

"He chose the Rolls Royce Phantom."

"I bet you felt like a queen."

"Queen is an understatement. You should have seen how people were looking at us. The night couldn't have been more perfect but the more perfect the night seemed, the worse I felt. I couldn't even enjoy it."

"The important thing is that you finally got it off your chest and things went better than you thought."

"I couldn't agree with you more."

The internet dating sites are like gambling. Sometimes you win but most of the time you lose. Then there are those people that win but don't quit. That can be defined as an addiction. For some, an addiction can be confronted but in some cases, it is usually undetected or denied because most addicts won't admit that they have a problem.

Iverson sat at his desk at Future Records waiting for his right hand man to make it to the office. As he sat going over his monthly numbers an instant messenger box popped up bearing an unfamiliar name.

KandeeGyrl: Ivy?

Thinking that it was just someone that found his profile on ebonyworld.com, he ignored it. Two minutes later the box popped back up.

KandeeGyrl: Iverson Shamar Davenport!

That caught Iverson off guard because only a few people, outside of his family, know his full name. He wanted to respond but he knew that if he did, it may not lead to anything positive. There is this thing called curiosity that gets people in trouble — often.

> **KandeeGyrl:** I guess you don't have time for an old friend...
> **Ivy_Dav:** who is this?
> **KandeeGyrl:** OOOH! Now you respond...I'm an old acquaintance
> **Ivy_Dav:** how old of an acquaintance?
> **KandeeGyrl:** you knew me by a different name
> **Ivy_Dav:** and what name was that?
> **KandeeGyrl:** I don't know if I should tell you right now...I'm probably not one of your favorite people in this world.
> **Ivy_Dav:** the way my world has been lately, you could be anybody
> **KandeeGyrl:** according to BET, MTV, Black Reign and VH1... ur doin' pretty good these days.
> **Ivy_Dav:** business is great but that wasn't what I was talking about.
> **KandeeGyrl:** u must be referring to ur love life

Ivy_Dav: could be…but unless I know who u r, I'm not going to discuss it
KandeeGyrl: if you behave urself…you might find out.
   Ivy_Dav: to be honest…it doesn't matter who u are. I'm happy and that's what matters to me.
KandeeGyrl: I guess that means I'm a lil 2 late.
Ivy_Dav: I guess it does.
KandeeGyrl: ITS NEVER 2 LATE!!!!!!!!!!
   KandeeGyrl has logged out

T-Bizzy walked into the office to find Iverson blankly staring at his computer monitor. Iverson noticed his friend and snapped out of it.

   "Nice of you to join us?" Ivy remarked.
   "What's good?"
   "I need you to get Black on the line and set up a meeting with him and the girls."
   "That's a dolla' bet. I take it you're new talent scout gave Purrfection a good review."
   "Man! Let me tell you about that. I didn't tell you who she really was."
   "Who she really was?"
   "Remember me telling you about that fine ass point guard that played for the Diamonds?"
   "You talkin' 'bout Natalie Simms?"
   "Yeah. That's Dymond."
   "You bullshitin'!"

"She confessed last night."

"Let me get this straight…she was posing to be someone else but you knew who she was the hold time. That's crazy."

"That's the girl that played for Tennessee that is hanging on the wall in the studio at the crib."

"Wow. You have all the luck."

"It's not luck, pimp. Its skill."

"So are you gonna keep kickin' it wit her?"

"Hell yeah! Why wouldn't I."

"She lied. And if I'm not mistaken, Mr. Iverson Davenport has this big thing about dishonesty."

"This is different. She wasn't dishonest with me to take advantage or get close to me for personal gain. She was only protecting herself so I can't fault her for that. You lie to me all the time and I still keep you around."

"You got a point," T remarked as he pressed the intercom button on Iverson's phone. "Michelle…"

"Yes?"

"I need you to call Black and set up a meeting for tomorrow at 8 o'clock at Spondivots."

"Don't you have a secretary?"

"Michelle, don't act like that."

"You know I don't deal with Black."

"Michelle," Iverson spoke.

"Yes, Iverson…"

"Can you set up the meeting for me?"

"No problem, Ivy."

"Thank you, Mami."

"How in the hell do you do that?" T asked.

"Because I'm Iverson's assistant," Michelle answered. "Not yours."

"You do me so dirty, Michelle."

"I still love you, Papi."

"I love it when she calls me Papi." T-Bizzy laughed.

"You love when a woman calls you anything other than a slut."

"You know what?" T paused.

"You right!"

At a relaxing spa in the heart of Atlanta, Natalie and Alicia sat with their feet submerged in water as they were getting pedicures. Relief is so refreshing. Natalie's aura was glowing due to last night's events and confessions. She could not help but to smile.

"Are you ever going to stop smiling?" Alicia clowned.

"You just don't understand. I think I've finally found my King."

"Who?"

"Iverson!" Natalie laughed.

"Oh, him. He's aiight. Now that you've told him, what's the next step?"

A huge smile spread across Natalie's face as she said, "To get inside the master bedroom."

"Natalie! You are such a slut!"

"I'm not talking about like that! When he gave me a tour of his house last night, he showed me every room in his house except for his bedroom."

"Why?"

"He said that his bedroom is his palace and only a woman fit to be his queen will ever see those walls."

"He's runnin' game on you."

"He is not runnin' game. I think it's very noble."

"Ok, noble. He's trying to get you in his bed."

"He is not," Natalie giggled. "I'm trying to get in his bed."

"I knew you were a slut."

"Girl its been seven months. Messin' wit me, we might not make it to the bedroom."

"O-Kay!" Alicia hi-fived Natalie.

"But seriously, you're not going to sleep with him just because you've finally told him, are you?"

"No I'm not. I'm going to go with the flow and take it one step at a time and when those steps lead to the bedroom, so be it. But until then, I am going to take the time to get to know Iverson."

"Sounds like you have it all figured out. You just make sure you take care of that good man cuz you know they are hard to find."

"I'm not letting this one get away like I did the last one."

"But I thank you for letting that one go."

Iverson and T-Bizzy were still sitting in Iverson's office going over the particulars of the deal they wanted to offer Purrfection. They discussed money, tours, and number of albums. T wanted to lock them down for three albums but Ivy wanted to be a little more conservative. He was thinking more along the lines of one album to see how the fans responded.

"If we only do one album," T began. "We run the risk of losing them after the contract is up."

"I'm doing the same thing with EL GEE and ATP. As long as we keep our artists happy, they will remain loyal."

"Why not just lock them in and not have to worry about that."

"You are not looking at both sides. True, they are a hit in Atlanta but what about the rest of the country."

"Their fan base is bigger than just Atlanta. It starts in North Carolina and extends down the east coast to Florida. They can go multi-platinum in those four states alone. One of the girls is from North Carolina, one is from Miami and the lead singer is from here. That's love in three states."

"I knew there was something I wanted to talk to you about."

"I promise you," T assured holding up both of his hands. "It wasn't me?"

"Calm down, Shaggy. It's about the group. You said that the group was a mix of Amerie, Jennifer Lopez and LeToya Luckett, right?

"Right."

"Dymond said that they were a mix of Amerie, J Lo and Aaliyah."

"Aaliyah? That can't be right."

"You and I both know that there's a big difference between the two."

"Maybe they pulled a Destiny's Child."

"That's the same thing Natalie said."

"Natalie?"

"Dymond."

"Oh yeah. So they changed group members. It happens all the time."

"Yeah but that may mean more work. If the missing member contributed any songs that the group wants to use, that could get messy. We have to go back and re-record all songs containing her vocals on it."

"Ivy, you're putting the cart before the horse. Let's just have the meeting and go from there. We'll give them a tentative offer and then discuss the terms of the contract before they sign."

"I knew I kept you around for something."

"That's what I do. Now if you'll excuse me, I'm hungrier than a hostage. I got a lunch date with Alexa."

"Alexa? Who is she?"

"Remember Luda's party?" Ivy nodded.

"Alexa was in the group of girls that came to see you."

"You talkin' about the light-skinned girl with the body? I thought she was too plain for you?"

"That's what I thought until I got to know her."

"Since when did you start getting to know women?"

"I guess you're rubbin' off on me."

"Wait a minute. That party was about two months ago. You been seeing shorty for that long?"

"We're just kickin' it."

"Ok, just kickin it. You're in a relationship."

"Shhhhhhhhhh!" T hushed and looked around. "That's how rumors get started."

"Boy you a fool," Ivy laughed.

"But to be honest with you, I like spendin' time with her. We actually have a lot in common."

"Like what? You both like the same sexual positions..."

"See, that's why I don't tell you nothin'. I'm tryin to be serious and you're clownin'."

"Damn," Ivy replied with a look of surprise on his face. "You really diggin' this girl."

"This is all new to me. I haven't been in a relat..."

"Stop! You are not gettin' ready to say the dreaded R-word."

"You know what? I'm leaving. I thought you were my boy."

"I am ya boy T but you don't give me much to work with. Since I've known you, I only remember one relationship you've ever been in. Just take the same advice you gave me. Take it slow."

"Aiight man. I'll get at you later."

T-Bizzy left the office as Iverson pulled up his Internet Browser. Curiosity would not let him get **KandeeGyrl** out of his mind. He typed into the address bar: www.ebonyworld.com. In seconds the hottest African American website popped up. After logging in, Iverson placed his cursor into the **Member Search** box and typed KandeeGyrl. The screen went blank and then returned a member profile, with no picture, that read:

WHAT UP, EBONYWORLD! THIS IS THE SWEETEST GIRL IN THE WORLD…KANDEEGYRL. I RECENTLY MOVED BACK TO ATLANTA IN ORDER TO PURSUE MY SINGING CAREER. AT ONE TIME I WAS LIVING THE GOOD LIFE WITH THE MOST WONDERFUL MAN IN THE WORLD BUT JEALOUSY MADE ME THROW IT ALL AWAY.

*******TO ALL THE WOMEN*******
BELIEVE ME WHEN I TELL YOU THAT
A GOOD MAN IS TRULY HARD TO
FIND. WHEN YOU HAVE A MAN
THAT TREATS YOU LIKE A QUEEN,
HOLD ON TO HIM… ESPECIALLY
WHEN HE HAS GIVEN YOU NO
REASON TO DOUBT HIM.
SOMETIMES WE GET CAUGHT UP IN
THE THINGS WE HAVE TO DO TO
KEEP FROM LOSING HIM, WE FAIL
TO PERFORM THE THINGS NEEDED
TO KEEP HIM. WHEN YOU ARE
BLESSED, RECOGNIZE AND BE
THANKFUL. IF YOU FIND YOURSELF
IN BROKEN RELATIONSHIP AFTER
BROKEN RELATIONSHIP, STOP
BEING SO QUICK TO POINT THE
FINGER AT YOUR COUNTERPART
AND TAKE A LITTLE TIME FOR SOME
SELF ASSESSEMENT. NOT ALL MEN
ARE
DOGS!!!

*******TO ALL THE MEN******
PLEASE ALLOW ME TO
APOLOGIZE ON BEHALF OF ALL
WOMEN THAT LET FOOLISH
THOUGHTS AND HEARSAY ALLOW

US TO LOSE PERSPECTIVE OF WHAT'S REALLY GOOD. WE SOMETIMES ACT ON EMOTION INSTEAD OF FOLLOWING OUR HEARTS. IN OUR DEFENSE, SOME OF US HAVE EXPERIENCED A FEW LESS THAN MANLY MEN BUT IN OUR ERROR, WE TAKE OUT PAST EXPERIENCES ON PRESENT ENDEAVOURS. NO ONE SAID THAT THIS THING THAT WE CALL LIFE WOULD BE EASY BUT WE DO THE BEST THAT WE CAN.

WE ALL MAKE MISTAKES BUT THE ADMISSION OF OUR WRONGS AND THE WILLINGNESS TO MAKE IT RIGHT, DETEMINES A GOOD MAN/WOMAN FROM A BAD ONE. IF THERE IS ANYONE FEELING ME, PLEASE FEEL FREE TO HIT ME UP AND LET ME KNOW HOW YOU FEEL.

UNTIL WE MEET AGAIN, REMEMBER: THERE'S NOTHING SWEETER THAN KANDEE!!!

The words of a wounded soul pouring out her heart in search of an apology seemed to speak directly to Iverson. Sympathy filled his

heart as if this were directed toward him. Due
to his past relationships, he felt that he could
relate. It was hurt like this that made him
cherish what he was building that much more
with Natalie — or did it?

Sometimes the internet can be
deceiving. The deceitful that parade around on
the internet as helpless victims or the *born-
agains* – people that have done wrong, by a
man or woman but have changed their ways —
are known as web predators. These predators
are skilled at what they do. They use words in
a way to draw the attention of the sympathetic
and soft at heart. In the cyber world there is no
room for weakness. Those that don't take
words for what they are leave themselves to be
easily consumed. After the bait is laid, some
people don't know how to leave well enough
alone.

If Iverson had a downfall, it would be
the humanitarian in him. He tries to help
everyone that he can. That is not a bad thing
but it can get sticky sometimes. In those words
he saw a cry for help. His humane side told
him to at least give a few words of
encouragement. Reality reminded him that this
person knew who he was. Still he felt
compelled to reply. He clicked on the Message
icon and was redirected to a pop-up. He placed
his cursor in the Subject box and typed:

Subject: APOLOGY ACCEPTED!

Message:
ON BEHALF OF ALL THE MEN TO WHICH
YOU SPEAK...I ACCEPT YOUR APOLOGY
BUT IN ORDER TO BE FORGIVEN BY THE
ONE IN WHICH YOU HURT, YOU MUST
FIRST FORGIVE YOURSELF. SOMETIMES
WE GET CAUGHT UP IN MOMENTS AND
LOOSE FOCUS ON WHAT IS AT HAND. I
FEEL WHAT YOU ARE SAYING AND WANT
TO TELL YOU TO HOLD ON AND KEEP
BELIEVING. THE MAN THAT IS FOR YOU IS
FOR YOU AND NO ONE ELSE. I HOPE MY
WORDS FIND A PLACE WITH YOU AND
REMEMBER TO KEEP YOUR HEAD UP!

IVY_DAV

Bait taken—hook, line, and sinker.
Iverson was oblivious to the clues that were
right in front of his face. It was evident who the
author was but to Iverson, it remained a
mystery. A rude awakening was in store for
the CEO and Founder of Future Records.

The digital ring tone of Janet Jackson's
"I Get Lonely" circulated through Natalie's
SUV.
"You really need to do something about
that ringtone," Alicia laughed.
"Can you reach into my bag and hand
me my phone?" Natalie asked Alicia reached

into Natalie's gym bag and fished out her phone.

"It's Iverson," Alicia squealed like a teenager. Natalie reached for the phone but Alicia answered it. "What's up, Mr. Davenport?"

"Hello?"

"How are you today?"

"I'm fine," Iverson hesitated. "To whom am I speaking with?"

"You can drop the professionalism. It's me, Alicia."

"Hey Alicia, What's up?"

"Nothin much. We just left the spa."

"That's what's up. Where's Dymond?"

"Hold on. She's right here. Nice talkin' to you again."

"Same here." Alicia passed Natalie the phone.

"Hey, Boo!" Natalie greeted.

"How's my Diamond?"

"Feeling brand new. What are you up to?"

"Nothing much. Me and T just got finished going over the deal that we're going to offer Purrfection."

"You're going to sign them?"

"I think so. We have a meeting set up for tomorrow night at Spondivots."

"Oh Spondivots. Sounds fun."

"You like seafood?"

"Like it? I love it!"

"Would you like to join me tomorrow night?"

"I don't know. You guys are gonna be handling business. I don't want to be a distraction."

"A distraction? If it weren't for you, I might not be signing them. You deserve to be there."

"Since you put it like that, how can I turn it down? I'd love to go."

"Great! Pick you up at seven."

"Which one are you going to? The one in Buckhead or the one on Virginia?"

"Buckhead."

"I live in College Park. How about I meet you at your house so you don't have to come out here?"

"It's okay now. I know you live in a Mansion. You don't have to keep me away anymore."

"I'm not," Natalie laughed. "I was just trying to look out for you. I don't care how many millions you have, gas is expensive."

"I appreciate that. I guess I'll see you at seven. Well, babe…I gotta run. I'll hit you up later on tonight if you're not too busy."

"Okay, sweetie. Talk to you later."

"One."

"What was that all about?" Alicia inquired.

"Iverson invited me to the meeting he is having with Purrfection tomorrow night. He's going to sign them."

"Purrfection?"

"The group I told you we went to check out Thursday night."

"You better get ready because you are getting ready to become the First Lady of Future Records. Next thing you know, you'll be all up in the videos with ya ass in a thong lettin' Ivy pour Cristal all over you."

"I will most certainly not! I am not one of those video skeezers."

"So you mean to tell me that if Iverson asked you to be in a video you wouldn't."

"I'm not saying I wouldn't but I don't believe that Iverson would ask me to be in a video if I had to do something degrading."

"On the serious side, be careful. I feel that Iverson wouldn't do anything to disrespect or hurt you but he is in the music industry. You know women throw themselves at him left and right and will do it in front of you if they get the chance. Be open-minded and command respect."

"I've been thinking about that and that's something I'm going to have to work on because I don't know whether I told you or not but I have a small jealous streak in me."

"All women do but you can't let it get the best of you. I had to deal with the same thing when me and Dré got back together. You know how he had tricks all over him."

"How did you handle it?"

"I trusted him and didn't jump to conclusions. I knew that when he left home, he was mine. While he was out, he was mine and when he came back home, he was mine."

"If I never needed anyone before in my life, I'm going to need you. I don't want to lose this one."

"I got ya back, MC Cataract!"

"Who is MC Cataract?"

"I have no idea. That's somethin' I picked up from my crazy ass husband."

"That figures." The two laughed as they continued on their way.

The 10 o'clock hour found Iverson and Natalie in two different locations in the city joined by a broadband connection — via Instant Messenger. Judging how Natalie and Iverson talked to each other and carried on, one would have thought they had known each other for years.

Ivy_Dav: u can not b serious!!!!!
Dymond4eva: I am...Kobe Bryant is by far the best physical athlete in the game
Ivy_Dav: better than D Wade?
Dymond4eva: yes better than D Wade. Wade can't score like Kobe, he doesn't have the jumper that Kobe has and he can't take over a game like Kobe
Ivy_Dav: u r the first woman that has ever taken up for Kobe
Dymond4eva: I'm a baller so I look at his game and not his personal life....

speaking as a woman, I would haven't handled the situation as well as Vanessa took it. I couldn't have been at that press conference sittin' at the same table.

Ivy_Dav: y not?

Dymond4eva: cuz everytime I thought about what he did, I prolly would have swung at him....lol!

Ivy_Dav: lmao! That's y he's married to a woman that's not all the way black!

Dymond4eva: rofl...u know! Can I get serious 4 a min?

Ivy_Dav: whatz on ya mind?

Dymond4eva: am I wrong for being nervous about us?

Ivy_Dav: its about what I do, isn't it?

Dymond4eva: yes...being around entertainers and people in the music industry

I have a slightly tainted view about the industry.

Ivy_Dav: I know where this is going so we'll lay it all out now...the music industry is my job and a major part of my life but its not my whole life...I know

how to separate myself from my work. I want you to be a major part of my life & I want you to experience it all with me...the good and the bad...as I want to experience your world with you...

Dymond4eva: then do me one favor

Ivy_Dav: What's that?

Dymond4eva: don't just say what ur gonna do, do what you say ur gonna do
Ivy_Dav: I can respect that bcuz I respect you and I would neva do anything 2
intentionally disrespect or hurt u…u know the nature of the biz…I am constantly approached by women…sum wit real intentions of tryin 2 pursue music and sum with the intentions of pursuing status. I've been doin this long enuff to distinguish the two. Just keep an open mind…
Dymond4eva: all u need to know is that I'm wit u
Ivy_Dav: that's all I need 2 hear…but this also works both ways…as a ball player, u spend a lot of time on the road. I know how star-studded the arenas can be. Promise me u won't leave me for Jack Nicholson…lol!
Dymond4eva: Jack Nicholson goes to c the Lakers not the Sparks…but if he did show up at a game…u might b in trouble! Lol!
Ivy_Dav: u can have jack if I can have Alicia Keys…
Dymond4eva: that's not fair…u might work wit her one day…make it Macy Gray and you got a deal…lol!
Ivy_Dav: throw in Kelly Roland and you got a deal!

Dymond4eva: throw in Kid Rock and its poppin!

Ivy_Dav: I knew it! You ball players are all alike…get a lil money and u get u a white dude…lol!

Dymond4eva: Kid Rock is a sexy 4 a white guy…lol…WOW! Where did the time go? I have to get up 4 church n da mornin'

Ivy_Dav: cool…u have a good nite and enjoy church…I'll see 2morrow.

Dymond4eva: ok boo! u have sweet dreams…ttyl

Chapter 15

"As I look over the congregation,"
Pastor Harris began. "I feel deep grief in my
spirit this morning."

"Come on, Pastor!" one of the members
cried out.

"God has ordained me as the Shepard of
this flock, thus meaning that when my sheep
hurt, I hurt. When my sheep are down trodden
and heavy laden, I feel your pains. When there
is grief and despair, you have to remember that
God is right there. All you have to do is reach
out. Call his name because he is a CAN DO
GOD! I had a message prepared this morning
but I feel like God is leading me in another
direction. Do you mind if I speak on it this
morning?" A barrage of approvals rang out
over the sea of faces that sat in attendance.
Among the members in attendance were
Natalie, André and Alicia. "There is a great evil
that is spreading through out our community
and city. This evil knows no age, race or
gender. It sits in every hotel, business, office
building and almost every one of your homes.
This evil is known as the World Wide Web or
internet, for short." The church began to gasp
and chatter. "I see some of you looking at me
and saying to yourselves, 'Pastor, how is the
internet an addiction?' Let me give some

clarification before I lose somebody this morning. It's not the internet that is evil but the activity that goes on. As some of you may know there are websites that people who call themselves church folks, don't need to be on. The internet can be a useful tool or a deadly addiction. It will break up homes cause stress and strife. It is often used to exploit and degrade our women. Let me say to you church, DO NOT GET CAUGHT UP IN THE DEVIL'S WEB OF DESTRUCTION!"

A warm feeling came over Natalie's body but the one who needed to hear this particular sermon was not in attendance. With open ears and an open heart, Natalie sat and listened as if the Pastor was speaking directly to her. She made up her mind that if things did not work out between her and Iverson, she would not use the internet to find another companion.

Across town at Iverson's estate, he and TyQuan sat going over the particulars for their meeting.
"Do you think they'll go for this deal?" T-Bizzy inquired.
"What we're getting ready to offer them is probably the best deal they've seen so far. Besides, I'm not that pressed. Either they take it or leave it."
"I guess your right. But on the real, what's up wit you and Dymond?"

"Everything is everything. We've been taking our time with it. As each day goes by, we get closer. I don't want to speak too soon but I think I've finally found my queen."

"I know I give you hell all the time but speakin' as your homeboy and best friend, I'm happy for you man. You're a good dude and you deserve it."

"I 'preciate that. That means a lot knowing that my boy has my back. So what's good wit you and Alexa?"

"We're doing good but she's a tough cookie."

"What do you mean?"

"Alexa is a good girl. She's a successful real estate agent and she has it all together. Her only problem is dealing with me and the industry. She says that she trusts me but it's the other women that she don't trust. Its cool now but what happens when we hit the road?"

"I've experienced it first hand when a woman lets her insecurities get the best of her. It was partly my fault for not making her feel more secure but believe me when I tell you, I've learned my lesson. You don't wanna make the same mistake I did. Now is the time to capitalize if you really want to be with her. You have to be on the straight and narrow and give her no reason to think that she has anything to worry about. Spend a lot of time with her and show her TyQuan and not T-Bizzy."

"I don't understand."

"Look at it like this, even though we own the label, we're not behind the scenes like a lot of label execs are. We're like Dame and Jay, Diddy and JD. We chose to be in the public eye instead of behind the scenes. Out in public, we're T-Bizzy and Ivy. That is how everybody knows us. Off the scene, we are Iverson and TyQuan. Not too many people know who we really are as people. When you spend time with Alexa you have to show her the side of you that people in the industry don't see. That's what I do with Natalie."

"Who?"

"Dymond. When we spend time together I don't let her call me Ivy. She calls me Iverson. That's how you build the separation between the real you and the person that is apart of the industry."

"I think that's been my problem the whole time. I didn't know how to separate myself from what I do. That makes sense."

"Take tonight for instance, Natalie is going to be at the meeting with us. Tonight is huge because we are signing a female group. This meeting is going to show her that business is business regardless of what sex the artists are."

"Smart man."

"If you're going to get serious and settle down with Alexa, you need to introduce her to your business side as well because just like Natalie, your girl probably has a lot of misconceptions about what you really do in the industry."

"You know what, Dog? I may clown around a lot and give you hell but I really appreciate what you've done for me. I woulda never thought that a country boy like me would have ever been in the position I'm in now."

"It's all good. I'm just glad I got my homeboy by my side through my success."

"Aiight, Aiight! Enough of this mushy shit. I gotta go get ready for tonight. Eight o'clock, right?"

"No doubt."

"I'll see you at Spondivots."

"Aiight homie, be easy and don't be late."

Iverson walked TyQuan outside. They exchanged pounds and T was on his way. Iverson returned inside and went upstairs to check his messages and email. Once in his office and positioned in front of his computer, he logged into his email account. He noticed that he had received a couple of messages on EbonyWorld. Iverson double-clicked the link and in seconds he was logged into his EbonyWorld account. In his inbox, he saw there was a reply from KandeeGyrl. The message read:

Subject: Re: APOLOGY ACCEPTED!

Message:

I APPRECIATE YOUR KIND WORDS
AND TO BE HONEST, I NEVER
THOUGHT THAT YOU WOULD FEEL
THAT WAY. THANK YOU FOR
TAKING THE TIME TO STOP BY MY
LIL SPACE IN THIS WORLD. DON'T
BE A STRANGER. TTYL!

THEE SWEETEST GYRL IN THE
WORLD

Iverson was kind of confused by her words. She spoke to him as if she knew him. He let the thought pass and continued to check the rest of his messages. As he sifted through the mass messages, an instant messenger box popped up.

KandeeGyrl: Ivy…u there?
Ivy_Dav: WZUP?
KandeeGyrl: how r u 2day?
Ivy_Dav: I'm cool…gettin' ready for a bizness dinner 2nite
KandeeGyrl: That's u…all bizness all the tyme
Ivy_Dav: I don't mean 2 b rude, but do we know each other?
KandeeGyrl: yes we do… we know each other real well
Ivy_Dav: how?

KandeeGyrl: in due time…well gotta run…I just wanted to speak
Ivy_Dav: wait a minute
KandeeGyrl has logged out

Now Iverson was really confused. She seemed to know a lot about him but anybody could found out anything about anybody they wanted to. All they had to do was to do a Google search. For about fifteen minutes, Iverson racked his brain trying to figure out who this female was but kept coming up with nothing — except the obvious.

Around 6:45 Natalie arrived at Iverson's place, dressed to impress. That night she wore her hair curly. Her ensemble was amazing. Natalie displayed a dark blue, denim Moschino outfit with a pair of Donna Karen stilettos. Sitting on top of her head were a pair of silver, wide-framed Dolce & Gabana Shades to accent her white gold Tiffany's necklace and bracelet. Iverson had his silver, Lexus LX470 parked out front. As Natalie pulled up, Iverson was coming out of the door. He walked over to Natalie's SUV and opened the door for her.

"What's up, beautiful?" Iverson greeted as she stepped out of the vehicle.
Hugging Iverson, "I'm good. How are you today?"
"Fine now that I see you."

"You're too much." Natalie giggled like a school girl as the two exchanged lips.

"Are we going to have a drink before we go?"

"We don't have time. I have to run by the office and pick up the contracts. I was in a rush when I left yesterday and forgot to grab them off of my secretary's desk."

"That's cool. You ready?"

Iverson escorted Natalie to the passenger side of the Lexus and opened her door once again.

"Thank you, kind sir."

Iverson walked around the back of the car and listened as Natalie unlocked his door.

"I guess you are a great one," Ivy remarked as he entered the truck.

Iverson's reference to Natalie being a great one comes from the movie *A Bronx Tale*. In the movie, the mob boss told his young protégé that a man was only allowed three great women in his lifetime. In being a great one, the woman can not be selfish so you had to put her through a test. When a man picks up a woman, he gets out of the car and locks his door. After he opens her door and she's inside, he walks around the back of the car. If the woman unlocks his door, that means she's not selfish. If she doesn't that means she is and should be dumped on the spot.

"What number am I?"

"You've seen Bronx Tale?"

"Seen it? I own it and love it. It's one of my favorite moves. So, what number am I?"

"If in fact you are a great one, you're number 3."

"Number 3, huh? That means if we don't work out, you've come across all three of your great women and you're doomed to settle with someone lest than great?"

"That's if you believe everything you see in a movie. Who's to say that we won't work out?"

"Nobody knows that but you, me and God."

"Good answer." Iverson and Natalie swung by the office and then headed to the restaurant. In less than twenty minutes they were in the parking garage next to Spondivots. It was around ten minutes to eight. Just as Iverson was opening the door for Natalie, TyQuan pulled up with a passenger in his black Dodge Magnum sittin on 22" chrome rims.

"Whoa, Whoa, Whoa!" Iverson began as he got out of the car. "When did you get this?"

"I bought it yesterday."

"I think I'm paying you too much," Iverson laughed.

"I'm just tryin' to get on your level."

T walked around the car and opened the door for his companion. Out stepped Alexa.

"Ivy, you remember Alexa don't you?"

"How you doin, Alexa?"

"Good to see you again," she replied.

"Alexa Herrington meet Ms…," TyQuan tried to introduce.

"Oh my God! I can't believe it. You're Natalie Simms! I'm a huge fan."

"Thank you so much. I didn't know you had such good taste in women, T."

"Again wit the jokes," TyQuan laughed.

"Come on y'all," Iverson began. "Let's get inside and get to our table before Black and the group gets here."

As they walked towards the building Natalie whispered into Iverson's ear, "If I hadn't come clean already, that would've blown everything." The two laughed as they entered the restaurant. They were greeted by a short biracial girl that looked to be around 21 years old.

"Hey Ivy!" she greeted. "Good to see you again. Your table is ready."

"You act like Ivy is the only one that comes here to eat," TyQuan remarked.

"Hello, T-Bizzy," she greeted with no emotion. "Right this way." They followed the hostess to the back of the restaurant where a table was set for seven guests.

"I'm sorry," Ivy apologized. "The original reservation was for 7 but we added one more."

"That's no problem. TyQuan can eat outside."

"Hold up...," Ty began to get upset but Iverson interrupted.

"Could you please just get us another chair and place setting."

"Anything for you Ivy." The hostess pulled a chair from another table and pushed it up to the table. "Anything else, Ivy?"

"That's fine."

"I'll bring the rest of your party back when they get here."

"Thank you, Cassandra."

"You sure have a way with the ladies," Natalie laughed as they sat down.

"What was that all about?" Alexa inquired. "If you don't mind me asking?"

"Nah, it's cool," TyQuan began.

"I met Cassandra at a wrap party after we finished shooting one of our artist's videos. She told me she wanted to be in a video and that she'd do anything to be in one. To make a long story short, we started seeing each other and within a week she told me she loved me. I ceased all contact with her and she's been mad at me every since."

"That's what you get when you promise a woman something, sleep with her and don't keep your promise," Alexa persecuted.

"I deserved that but you have to believe that every man can change."

"I'm not the type of woman that will hold your past against you. I judge you by what you do to me and how you do it to me."

"If that's the case, then..."

"Alright!" Ivy interrupted before T had a chance to say the wrong thing. "How about some drinks."Right on cue, the server arrived to the table to take the groups drink order. Their server was a young, medium height, slim brown-skinned girl with her hair pulled back in a ponytail and glasses.

"Hello everybody," she greeted. "My name is Phyllica and I'll be taking good care of everyone tonight. Our catch of the day is blackened Mahi Mahi served with a shrimp and scallop crème over it. It is served with rice pilaf and fresh steamed broccoli. Our featured drink is a *Futurama*. This drink is dedicated to Iverson and Future Records as our way of saying thank you for your patronage to our restaurant."

"Are you serious?" Iverson asked.

"A lot of celebrities come through here and we wanted to show our appreciation for your business and the mentions of us in some of your songs. The bartenders created the drinks based on what you order when you come in."

"Who else has a drink named after them?" Natalie pondered.

"Ludacris has the *Disturbing Da Peace*, OutKast have the *3000* and the *Stankonia* and Young Jeezy has the *Snowman*."

"Well then let us get four Futuramas, and two orders of Calamari."

"Ok, I'll get those drinks for you and put in your appetizers." Their server walked off towards the bar.

"That's hot," Natalie remarked. "If my girl was here she would definitely have the Disturbing Da Peace."

"That is right," Ivy began. "Alicia does have that thing for Ludacris."

"Wait until I tell her. She'll probably bring me here just so she can have a drink." Natalie and Iverson laughed.

"I thought ya girl was married," T remarked.

"She is but who is to say that a woman can't have a secret crush on a celebrity?"

"Just like the crush I have on Brian White," Alexa added as she fanned herself.

"Who?" TyQuan's voice went up a couple notches.

"You know, the pretty boy from *Mr. 3000* with Bernie Mac," Iverson explained.

"Who?"

With passion and a slight moan in her voice Alexa replied, "T-Rex Pinnabaker."

"And who might you have a celebrity crush on?" Iverson asked Natalie.

"My crush is not an actor but an athlete."

"Who Girl? Kobe, D Wade, Vince Carter?"

"Steve Smith, Wide Receiver for the Carolina Panthers."

"Why him?" Ivy wanted to know.

"He is sexy and low key. He is not outspoken like other athletes like T.O., Chad Johnson and Randy Moss. His game play speaks for him."

"So you're telling me if Steve Smith walked in here right now, you'd leave me."

"Of course not. That's why its called a crush. Besides, he's too short for me."

"But I'm only a few inches taller than he is."

"Are you serious? You damn near a foot taller than him."

"Good answer."

"What about you TyQuan?" Alexa pressed.

"Who is your celebrity crush?"

"I'd have to say it's still Sanaa Lathan. She's beautiful, sexy and down to earth."

"You met her?"

"Yeah. We met at Diddy's all white party in the Hamptons Labor Day last year."

"Iverson?" Natalie nudged. "Your turn."

"I haven't really developed a new crush since mine died."

"Who?" Alexa asked. "Aaliyah?"

"That would be correct. She was the total package. She was sexy, talented, she was a good dancer and she was also very down to earth. I met her here in Atlanta for R Kelly's birthday party the year before she passed away."

"And no other celebrity has caught your eye since she died." Alexa interjected.

"There is one but I don't know about her."

"Who, Dog?" T asked.

"Natalie Simms."

A huge smile lit Natalie's face as she replied, "You are too sweet."

"Sweet enough to make your teeth rot," T mumbled.

"Green is not your color, TyQuan." The group laughed and continued on with conversation. The server dropped off the drinks they waited for Black to arrive. Before long 8:30 came and went and 9 o'clock was approaching.

"Where's ya boy?" Iverson looked at his watch.

"I have no clue." At that statement, TyQuan's cell phone rung displaying Black's name. "Speak of the Devil." He flipped open the phone and answered. "T-Bizzy, you're live."

TyQuan excused himself from the table and walked towards the bathroom because he couldn't hear. Five minutes later he returned.

"He'll be here in five minutes but he only has two of the girls."

"That's why I didn't want to deal with Black. He knows that you can't sign contracts without all parties involved present."

"Just calm down. We can make the offer and then set up another meeting to sign."

"See what happens when you try to deal with colored folks."

Five minutes passed and Iverson looked up to see the hostess escorting Black and two females to the table. Iverson and TyQuan didn't bother to stand as they approached. Apologies were the first thing that came out of Black's mouth as he and the girls sat down.

"My bad fellas," Black began. "It's been a crazy past couple of hours..."

"Black," T-Bizzy scolded. "You really makin' me look bad. I went out on a limb for you and this is what you do. You show up over an hour late and on top of that, you're missing a group member. Seriously, this is not how you start off."

"I know and I'm sorry. The meeting was kinda short notice and the other girl had a prior engagement."

"Ladies," Iverson began. "Do you realize how important this is for you? Do you realize that the absence of your third member could possibly cost you a deal? How can we count on you to be in place when we need you if you can't even get everybody here on the night you meet the label that could potentially sign you?"

"In our defense Mr. Davenport," One of the girls spoke up.

"We just found out about the meeting around one o'clock this afternoon. Our other member has been out of town since Friday. She was supposed to be back this morning but we haven't heard from her. We've been trying to get in touch with her since Black called us this afternoon."

"You just found out about this meeting this afternoon?" Iverson turned to Black. "That's not good management technique. I admit it was short notice on my part but you knew about this meeting since yesterday morning."

"I know, Ivy. Let me explain."

"I don't need anymore excuses. Despite how I felt about trying to work with you, I did my man a favor. I came to see the girls perform and didn't get to see them. I went off of the word of this young lady here because she said the group had what it took to compete in this industry. This isn't about you, Black .This is about the fact that you're letting people down that went to bat for you. Ladies, I don't doubt that you're talented but your management decisions are hurting you."

"Mr. Davenport," the other of the two girls began. "Can you excuse us for five minutes? We need to have a word with our manager."

"You have five minutes, exactly." The ladies excused themselves from the table as Black followed them outside. The group watched and laughed from inside as Black seemed to be receiving the cussing out of a lifetime. In exactly four minutes and forty-five seconds, the ladies returned to the table without Black.

"I'm so sorry," the young lady that favored Amerie began. "I know we were late and have wasted a lot of your time but can we please start over?"

"Where's your manager?" Iverson asked.

"I regret to inform you that we are no longer affiliated with EnTouch Management and are currently seeking new management."

"Ladies, let me be the first to tell you that that was one of the wisest decisions you ever made. Please introduce yourselves."

"I am Katina Walker known on stage as Miss Kitty. I sing most of the lead vocals."

"I'm Rolanda Fernandez, known on the stage as Daddy's Lil' Girl. I sing back up vocals, do choreography and I'm the stylist of the group. I do our hair, make-up and make our outfits."

Rolanda was the member of the group that favored Jennifer Lopez.

"How'd you come up with the name Daddy's Lil' Girl?" Natalie asked.

"My father took full custody of me when I was about 5 years old. My mother was in an abusive relationship. Not only did he abuse her but he abused me. I went to school one day with bruises on my arm and the next thing I know, my father came to pick me up and the state gave him custody of me."

"I'm sorry to here that."

"Please don't be. If I hadn't of went to live with my dad, I probably wouldn't be here right now."

"How so?" Iverson asked.

"My dad was a keyboardist in a band until I was about 17. He used to take me to his shows with him. Sometimes he would sit me onstage beside him when he performed. That's where I gained my love for music."The group's server returned to take their order. Everybody paused from the conversation and placed their dinner order. Once the server left, Iverson continued the conversation.

"How long have you been singing?"

"I started singing when I was about 8. Just like a lot of singers, I started out in the church choir. That's where I met Katina. We've been together for a long time."

"When did you start singing R&B?"

"Wow," Katina began. "When we got to high school, I started dating this guy that sang. One day he asked if me and Rolanda would sing back up for him in a show. That was the first time we sung in front of people without the rest of the choir. We saw how the crowd reacted towards him and we wondered what it would be like if they were cheering and clapping for us. That night we decided that we wanted to be a group and that's when we formed Purrfection but quickly found out that either we had to start writing our own songs or add another member because there weren't many two-girl groups out there so the songs were limited."

"When did you add the third member?"

"The girl that is a part of the group now just joined the group about 2 months ago after our third member decided she wanted to go solo. We met our original third member when she transferred to our school. She was a singer and an MC. She fit perfect because TLC and Destiny's Child were the hottest girl groups out at the time. Being from Atlanta, we've done a ton of shows here and have been building our fan base for a long time."

"TyQuan brought it to my attention that your fan base stretches from North Carolina all the way down to Florida. How'd that happen?"

"That's how we met Black," Rolanda took over. "We were at an audition to be an opening act for Ginuwine's tour after he dropped *100% Ginuwine*. He told us that if we would get down with him, he could get us on the tour because he said he knew the promoters. Being young and naïve, we agreed. To our surprise, he actually came through. We got on the tour and they loved us. When he saw how well we did, he started getting us shows throughout North and South Carolina, Georgia and Florida."

"Then why is he messing things up now?"

"Black has a habit. It didn't start off as a habit though. He said he bumped a little every now and then. We didn't pay it no mind because we figured it was an industry thing. It started becoming a problem when we started missing gigs and the money started coming up short."

"When did this start happening?"

"About a year ago."

"Why wait until now to drop him?"

"I guess it was loyalty. Black did a lot for us but we were still on the verge of leaving him. We've been shopping for a deal for the past three years. Every time we come close, something mysteriously happens. We started putting two and two together. Our original third got wrapped up in the same habit that Black has. Black started filling her head up with nonsense making her think that she was bigger than the group."

"She caught that Bobby Brown disease," TyQuan laughed.

"Exactly. We told Black he had one more chance to make things right or we were going to walk. That's when he ran into T-Bizzy at Club Blaze. He said that him and T-Bizzy went way back and that he could get us a deal with Future. We told him that if he didn't come through with this deal, we were going to walk. He told us that he had us sold as the next TLC so if we were going to perform for you, we had to replace our missing third member. That's when we found Candace."

In the midst of the conversation, Iverson missed the name that was said.

"What happened to the deal with Capitol?" Ivy asked.

"What deal with Capitol?"

"Black told T that you didn't like the deal that Capitol was trying to offer you."

"That's news to us. We never heard anything about a deal from Capitol."

"I can't believe ya boy lied. You can't trust anybody these days. Listen ladies, this has been a very informative meeting. Unfortunately, we can't discuss any further business pertaining to the group without the entire group being present."

"Does this mean we don't get the deal?" Rolanda asked.

"Not necessarily. I tell you what I'll do and this is only because I'm not going to hold your former manager's negligence against you. If you can have the entire group in my office Wednesday afternoon at 3 o'clock, we'll talk about it then."

"Thank you so much, Mr. Davenport."

"Until then, business is adjourned. Now let's eat, drink and be merry."

"Here, here!" TyQuan remarked as he raised his glass. "I'd like to propose a toast." Everyone raised their glasses. TyQuan looked into Alexa's eyes. "To the Future."

"The Future!" the group responded as they clanged glasses together.

The four ladies and two gentlemen continued to laugh and talk the rest of the night away until they realized that Katina and Rolanda rode with Black and he was gone. Natalie offered Katina a ride since she lived on her way and TyQuan offered Rolanda a ride. After all was settled, they each went their separate ways. Katina sat in awe as they pulled up in front of Iverson's house.

"This is amazing," Katina complimented.

"Thank you. This is the product of hard work, determination and desire. You can have one too but you have to want it."

"I've never wanted anything more than to be a famous singer. I eat, sleep and breathe music."

"Good because that's what its going to take."

"Is that your truck, too?"

"That's mine," Natalie replied.

"What do you do?"

"I'll tell you in a minute. Can you excuse me and Iverson for a minute? You can wait for me in the truck."

"Ok. Good night, Mr. Davenport."

"Good Night, Miss Kitty." Katina hopped out of Iverson's truck and into Natalie's.

"You never cease to amaze me, Mr. Davenport."

"What do you mean?"

"At first I thought you weren't going to sign them."

"I haven't singed them yet."

"But you're going to sign them, aren't you?"

"I'll know that on Wednesday."

"Come on, Iverson. You see how bad these girls want this. You need to sign them just because they put up with Black all these years."

"I'll see what they got on Wednesday."

"Business is over for the night. You can put Ivy away so I can have Iverson back for a good night kiss." Iverson laughed as he and Natalie exchanged lips.

"I'll talk to you tomorrow."

"You sure you don't want me to take her home, it's not a problem."

"If I have to leave my man now, so does she."

"Nobody says that you have to leave." Natalie paused for a moment and looked Iverson deep in the eyes.

"Let me go before I get in trouble." Natalie kissed Iverson once again and proceeded to exit the vehicle. "Nite, baby."

"Good night."

Chapter 16

Under a full moon, Natalie and Katina
cruised the expressway bound for College
Park. The night's events could not overpower
the beauty that shined from the City of Atlanta.
From the auburn lights of the underpasses on
the I-85/I-75 connector to the bright whites,
blues and reds that danced from building to
building. Even the clarity of the black sky
allowed the stars to twinkle and glistened as
they hung in their designated positions.
Atlanta dazzled in the darkness begging for
someone to take notice. Conversation was
paused as Ne-yo's soothing voice filled the
luxury Sports Utility. Two strangers sat in
silence reflecting on the night's communion. In
one mind, thoughts of a complete relationship
loomed and in the other, the thoughts of a
dream on the brink of demise.

"Okay, Ms. Simms," Katina began.
"We're in the car now. What do you do for a
living?"
"I'm a professional basketball player."
"Really?"
"I play for Diamonds."
"What's it like?"
"Basketball has always been my life. I've
been playing since..."
"Not playing basketball, being a star."

"I am far from a star. I've only played professional for one season."

"You are a star. You play in front of thousands of people. When you're on the court, all eyes are on you. What you do sets the mood of the audience. Just like singers do. If you play good, the crowd cheers for you but if you don't play good, the crowd shows it's dislike. Its kinda like being a singer."

"I never looked at it like that."

"How do you look at it?"

"Me playing for the Diamonds is my reward for my hard work, determination and my refusal to give up on making my dreams come true."

"Did you always want to play basketball?"

"Growing up, I was Daddy's lil' girl. My father coached an inner city, high school girl's basketball team. He always wanted my older brother to play ball, like he did, but he just wasn't into sports. All he wanted to do was hang out with his friends and get in trouble. I wasn't really into sports but I loved being with my dad. Everywhere he went, I was right on his hip. Needless to say, I grew up going to basketball games whether it was high school, college, or NBA. Since my brother didn't want to play basketball he decided to see if I would like it. When other girls got their first Barbie doll for Christmas, I got my first basketball."

"But you started liking it after you started playing, right?"

"Not at first but as long as my Daddy was happy, I kept playing. The next thing you know, I got pretty good at it. By the time I got to high school things got pretty rough. My brother started hanging out with the wrong crowd. I come from one of the roughest cities in New Jersey so when I say wrong crowd you know what I mean."

"Sound like 'dem Bankhead boys."

"Camden started gettin' real crazy. People were gettin' robbed and shot on the regular. My mom wanted to move but my dad loved coaching for Camden High for some odd reason. Even though he didn't want to leave, he didn't want me and my brother there. Right before my first season playing varsity as a freshmen, my brother got shot walking home from school. I usually walked home from school with my brother but that day, I had practice."Natalie had to pause for a minute.

"Are you ok?"

"I'll be alright. It's still hard for me to talk about sometimes."

"You don't have to talk about it anymore if you don't want to."

"It's cool. The more I talk about it, the easier it gets. I couldn't even get this far before." Natalie wiped the tears from her eyes and continued on. "My family didn't have a lot of money but they wanted me to go to college. The only way I was going to be able to go to a good school was to either get an academic scholarship or an athletic scholarship. That's when I started seeing basketball as my way out. The worse Camden got, the harder I worked on my game. By the time I was a senior, I caught the attention of a lot of big name schools. My dad wanted me to go to Rutgers or UConn but I was tired of the city so I chose to come down south to play ball."

"What school did you go to?"

"I went to the University of Tennessee."

"You played for Pat Summit?"

"You like basketball?"

"I like NBA but my sister played ball in high school and always talked about going to Tennessee and playing for Pat Summit."

"Did she get a chance to play ball after high school?"

"Nah. She got pregnant her Senior year and couldn't play."

"That happens to a lot of girls."

"Yeah. It was messed up but she still went to school. She just couldn't go to Tennessee. She's graduating from Georgia Tech next fall."

"She couldn't play for Georgia Tech."

"She didn't have time. She had to work and take care of her daughter. My parents helped her pay for school but they said she had to make her own living. I guess that was supposed to be her punishment."

"I don't think it was punishment. I think it was more along the lines of teaching her to take responsibility for her actions."

"That's the same thing they said. But when did you know that you wanted to play basketball professionally?"

"My mom was a corporate woman. She was the business suit, briefcase type. She sat in an office eight hours a day. Her life was routine and predictable. I never wanted my life to be like that. Basketball was exciting for me because every time you stepped on the court, you never knew what to expect and I loved that aspect of the game. The WNBA was just gettin' up and runnin' when I got to college. Finally, a female basketball player could go to the next level after college. When I got to Tennessee the first thing Coach Summit told us was that if we thought that just because we came to play for the University of Tennessee, we were going to make it to the WNBA, we were wrong. It was going to take a lot more to make it. That's when I began to live basketball."

"But you don't look like a basketball player."

"What's a basketball player supposed to look like?"

"All I know is, the girls that played ball at my school, including my sister, dressed like boys."

"Like boys?"

"You know, they always had on basketball shorts and high tops or either something that had to do wit' basketball and they always had their hair pulled back in a ponytail except for a special occasion."

"Sounds like a couple of my teammates," Natalie laughed. "That was never me. Even though I play, I'm still a lady. I like getting my hair and nails done, going shopping and looking cute. You know, girl stuff."

"You know what, Ms. Simms? You're a real cool person."

"Thanks. Now let me ask you a question."

"Sure."

"Are you going to be able to make it to the meeting on Wednesday?"

"I hope so."

"Why wouldn't you make it?"

"When Black told us that we had to have a third person in order for him to get us a shot at a deal with Future, we rushed to find the first female we could find that could at least hold a note. They do an open mic night at Apache on Wednesday nights. Me and Rolanda went down there because one of our homeboys told us about this girl that performs there on the regular. When we heard her sing, she sounded a lot like our original third member so we approached her with the idea of joining our group. She was kinda hesitant until we told her about us possibly getting a deal with Future. She was all for it after we told her that. She sent me a text while we were at the restaurant and told me she was back in town.

I'ma give'er a call when I get home to tell her about Wednesday."

"I'm sure she'll make it."

"The only thing I'm concerned about is the fact that we don't have a manager. I don't know a lot about the business but I do know we have a good group. Mr. Davenport seems like he's all business but I don't wanna be taken advantage of."

"Iverson's not like that. I believe that he'll do right by the group."

"I know that's your man but with all due respect, when it comes to the music industry, its hard for a female to trust a man."

"I can understand where you're coming from I feel that way sometimes about the men I work for. I don't know what I'd do without my agent."

"See what I mean?" As they talked, Katina had been giving Natalie silent directions to her house. "I'm right up here on the left."

Natalie pulled into a government housing project. As she slowly rolled through, she began having flashbacks of home. There were addicts walking around, drug dealers scattered about watching her every move, and other project inhabitants "out and about," for no reason at all, at 1 o'clock in the morning.

"You don't have to be scared," Katina comforted. "You're with me and everybody knows me around here."

"Scared? This is what I left behind in New Jersey. Don't let the Navigator, the clothes or the diamonds fool you. Underneath it all, I'm still a project chick. The only difference is, I fought my way out and so can you."

"You can let me out right here. I live in that building right there."

Natalie pulled out her cell phone as Katina opened the door, "What's your number?"

"404-555-1420"

"I'm going to call you tomorrow night so be on the look out for my call. I'm letting you know now; it'll be from a private number so answer it."

"Ok, I will." Katina hopped down out of the SUV. "Thanks a lot, Ms. Simms."

"Please, call me Natalie."

"Thanks, Natalie."

"Oh yeah, make sure you get in touch with the other member of your group before tomorrow night."

"I'll make sure I talk to her if I have to go to her house."

Katina thanked Natalie once again and closed the door. Natalie waited for her to get upstairs and in the door before she drove off. Once she was inside, Natalie made sure all her doors were locked and headed for home. As she drove she thought about how much Katina's situation and environment reminded

411

her of her own past life. She seemed to be so close to getting out; she just needed a helping hand.

When Natalie arrived home, she peeled of her clothes and entered every woman's sanctuary…The Master Bathroom. In nothing but a towel, Natalie leaned over and turned the knobs for the water to come rushing out of the faucet. The water's rumble began to soothe her because she knew that it was the prelude to relaxation. Once the water reached the appropriate temperature, Natalie added her menagerie of bath oils and bubble bath. For no apparent reason, Natalie decided to replace the existing candles that surrounded the bathtub with new ones. Once the bath water was ready and the candles were ignited, Natalie dimmed the lights and the prelude to Natalie's symphony of relaxation was complete.

Upon submergence into the water, Natalie could feel her pores open and the process had begun. Before laying her head back on her aqua pillow, Natalie reached for a remote control that sat just in arms reach on a small ledge. With the push of a button, her collection of timeless, love songs began to play. First up to soothe and relax was a familiar tune by Mariah Carey, *Love Takes Time*, floated about Natalie's sanctuary setting her mood to relax, relate, and release.

Once the entire relaxation process was complete, Natalie finished her nightly primping and retired to her boudoir. She engulfed herself in her Ralph Lauren, down comforter and turned on the television. As she flipped through the channels she found a familiar face once she landed on MTV. It was Iverson in The Southern Sunz video for *Where You From?* A huge smile crossed her face as she watched her man. Thoughts of Ivy filled her head moving her to give him a call.

"Hello," Ivy answered in a relaxed voice.

"Did I wake you?"

"Nah, I was just layin' here watching TV."

"That's what I'm doin'. I just saw you on BET. That's what made me call you."

"Word? That's what's up? I didn't get a chance to ask you but did you enjoy yourself tonight?"

"I always enjoy myself when I'm with you."

"I need to ask you a question."

"What's on ya mind?"

"Was I too harsh with the girls tonight?"

"At first I thought so but you mellowed out real quick and kept it professional."

"That's been bothering me since we left the restaurant. I knew it wasn't the girl's fault but they have to understand that business is business."

"I think they got that part. Me and Katina talked on the way home. She was a little discouraged."

"About getting the deal?"

"That and the fact that they don't have a manager."

"You know me, as long as they do right by me I'll do right by them."

"That's the same thing I told her but you know how it is when it comes to women dealin' with men in the industry. It's not always business."

"I feel that."

"I want to talk to you about something but I have to talk to Alicia about it first."

"Why do you have to talk to ya girl about it first?"

"You know how us women are. Before we make a decision, we have to talk it over with our girlfriend."

"Can I at least get a hint?"

"Nope. If I give you a hint, you'll know what its about."

"You suck, yo."

"I do very well thank you."

"See, that is not nice." They laughed.

"I won't make you wait long. I'm going to talk to Alicia in the morning and then I'll call you by noon. Deal?"

"I guess I can accept that. Only because you're cute, though."

"You are so silly," Natalie giggled. "Well, I guess I'll go and try to get some rest. I got a long day tomorrow."

"Aiight, baby girl. You have a good night."

"Sweet dreams, baby."

Natalie hung up the phone and turned her television's volume down. In less than twenty minutes, she was asleep.

The bright, morning sun rushed through Natalie's 2nd story window as the birds sung the day's first song. Natalie poked her head from under the covers. The brightness of the sun caused her to squint as she looked toward the clock to see the time. It was 9:57, time for her day to begin. The Atlanta Diamond pulled herself up and out of bed and into the bathroom to start her morning. Once again she grabbed the remote and turned on the stereo in the bathroom. Instead of the soothing love songs that played the night before, she opened her day with a little *get crunk* music. First up to bat was DJ Unk's remix to *Walk it Out* featuring André 3000, Jim Jones and Big Boi. Natalie danced her way through the bathroom as she prepared for her day.

Once her morning ritual was complete, Natalie stood inside of her huge, walk-in closet trying to decide on what to wear. While in deep thought about her day's ensemble, her cell phone went off. She walked out of her closet and over to her nightstand to see who beckoned. It was Alicia.

"What's up, Chick?" Natalie greeted. "I was just about to call you."

"Stop lyin'," Alicia laughed.

"I was. I have to talk to you about something."

"No! I am not going to a release party, a birthday party or a concert."

"That is not what I was going to call you about. I have a serious matter to discuss with you."

"Now you goin' all AKA on me talkin' about a serious matter."

"That's why I can't stand you or your husband," Natalie joked. "Y'all always got jokes."

"I'm sorry, girl. I'm just in a good mood today."

"Dré must've broke you off somethin' decent this morning."

"Okaaaay!"

"But on a serious note, have you ever thought about doing a side gig?"

"Like what?"

"I was thinking about starting a management company."

"What type?"

"For artists."

"Musical artists or visual artists?"

"Musical."

"And where is this coming from?"

"Do you remember the group I told you about that I went to see with Iverson?"

"You talkin' about Purrfection, right?"

"Exactly. Last night they had a meeting with Ivy and T. Ivy wants to sign them but their manager screwed some things up for them and they were missing one of the members because she was out of town. During the meeting, they fired their manager..."

"And now you want to represent them."

"Yeah. I was talking to one of the girls last night and she reminds me a lot of me. She's on the brink of one of the biggest breaks of her life and I want to help her."

"Isn't your season getting ready to start up in a few months?"

"That's why I need your help. I need somebody I can trust to make sure things get done when I'm on the road."

"We don't know anything about the music industry."

"We don't have to. I'm pretty sure Iverson will help me out."

"Have you talked to him about it?"

"I told him I had something to talk to him about but I had to talk to you first."

"If Iverson's cool with it, I got ya back. Just remember that we have careers. This is a side venture. Don't be trying to sign everybody."

"I got you. Let's just start with this one and see how it goes. Deal?"

"Deal. Now where you taking me for lunch?"

"Oh yeah, before I forget. Ludacris has a drink at Spondivots."

"A drink?"

"Yeah. A couple of rappers that frequent that particular location have drinks named in honor of them as a thank you for their business."

"What's it called?"

"Disturbing Da Peace."

"Damn right! He can disturb my peace any day."

"Alicia! I will not have you talking like that. I am telling your husband!" The two ladies laughed.

Since Iverson met Natalie, he hadn't been on the internet much — with the exception of the short conversations he had with KandeeGyrl. In all honesty, there was no need. He'd found what he was looking for. Be that as it may, the internet is still an addiction and sometimes when you stop an addiction cold turkey, it has the tendency to creep back up on you. There's something about that thing called curiosity. It'll get you every time.

The eleven o'clock hour found Iverson fastened to his desk in his downtown office. He sat struggling with what to do about Purrfection. On one hand he wanted to sign them despite Black's foul up's and the fact that he was doing TyQuan a solid, but on the other hand, he wanted to wash his hands of the entire situation. While reading over the contracts, he realized that Black's name was on them and the girl's names weren't. They had to be redone. He wasn't pressed because nothing could be decided until he met and talked with the entire group. Iverson's thoughts were broken by the tone of an Instant Message. He wiggled the mouse to get rid of the screensaver. It was KandeeGyrl. He started to ignore it but once again, there is something about that thing called curiosity.

> **KandeeGyrl:** u there?
> **Ivy_Dav:** I'm here...what's good?
> **KandeeGyrl:** u
> **Ivy_Dav:** seriously
> **KandeeGyrl:** I am being serious
> **Ivy_Dav:** listen...due 2 da fact that I don't know who u r...I have a lot to
> do and I don't have time to play these games with u.
> **Ivy_Dav:** if u know me like u say u do... u know I'm a busy man
> **KandeeGyrl:** u don't have to get no attitude...I was just jokin'
> **Ivy_Dav:** u know what...ur rite. I'm sorry...I just got a lot goin on rite now
> **KandeeGyrl:** like I said...nothin's changed...ur the same ol' ivy...wanna
> talk about it?

Ivy_Dav: sorry but I make it a point not to discuss business or personal
matters with complete strangers

KandeeGyrl: I keep tellin' u I'm not a stranger...u know who I am

Ivy_Dav: like I said unless ur going to tell me who u r...u r still gonna be a
stranger to me

KandeeGyrl: and like I said....n due time....Peace!

KandeeGyrl has logged out

"I hate it when people do that," Ivy mumbled.

"Do what?" TyQuan asked as he walked in.

"Do you ever knock?"

"The door was open. You must be doin somethin' you ain't got no business doin," T laughed.

"I'm sittin' here goin' over this Purrfection deal."

"What about it?"

"To be honest wit you, I don't really wanna do this deal."

"Come on man. The group is hot. Even ya own girl says they're hot."

"I know but I'm lookin at it from the business aspect. I didn't get to see them perform, since you last saw them, they changed members. To top it all off, we set up a meeting to discuss a potential deal and we get two members and now they don't have a manager. I'm not in the mood to baby sit. We got other shit to do."

"Like what?"

"Do you realize that the summer is coming? The Southern Sunz's summer tour with Ludacris and OutKast starts in June. We got Buddah Rhatt and Lucky Twelve getting' ready to drop their compilation album which means another tour and Legacy getting ready to drop her second album which means..."

"Another tour," T interrupted. "Ivy, I know all of this. This could be our biggest summer ever. We've never dropped three albums in one summer or had four tours. Since we're lookin' at the big picture, picture this..."

TyQuan stood up in front of Iverson's desk and made the motions of big words in the air.

"*The Summer of the Future*. We have an opportunity to set the tone. We can do it. If we drop three albums and at least a single for the Southern Sunz, we will be all over the radio and TV and if I'm not mistaken, you did say you wanted to do it big this summer. Did you not?"

"That is what I said."

"Then what's the problem?"

"With Purrfection having no manager, we add more to what we're already trying to do."

"Just admit it. You don't wanna sign Purrfection."

"It's not that. It's just a lot to think about. When will you or I have the time to manage the group?"

"We won't."

"That's what I'm trying to stress to you."TyQuan hung his head as he sat down on the couch. "Don't look like that. I tell you what. We still got the meeting on Wednesday with them. We'll tell them if they can find a legitimate manager, we can do business. Is that fair?"

TyQuan perked up, "Are you for real?"

"I'm serious. We'll give them a deadline and if they come through, I'll sign them."

"That's what's up. I knew you'd come through for ya boy."

"But all of this is tentative provided the whole group shows up to the meeting."

"That's fair."

"Ivy," Michelle called via intercom.

"Yes Michelle?"

"Natalie's here to see you."

"Send her in." Ivy turned his attention back to T-Bizzy. "I wonder what she's doing here?"

"You know how women are. They like to just pop up to make sure you're not doin' anything you ain't got no business doin'."

"Hey baby," Natalie greeted as she walked passed T and went around Ivy's desk to give him a hug and a kiss.

"What's good, boo? What you doin here?"

"AHEM!" T cleared his throat. "Ivy's not the only one in here. Didn't ya mother teach you no manners."

"And didn't your mama teach you not to interrupt when grown people are talking?"

"Again wit the jokes."

"I'm just playin'," Natalie laughed as she sat down on the couch beside T. "What's up T?"

"Coolin'."

"Ivy I need to talk to you."

"That's my cue," T remarked as he began to stand up.

"No, T. I need you here, too."

"Okay." T sat back down.

"Ivy you remember when you asked me about being apart of the industry?"

Ivy's eyes lit up, "You droppin' an album?"

"Not yet but I'll do you one better. I want to manage Purrfection."

"YES!" T-Bizzy shouted as he jumped up off the couch.

"How are you going to manage a group? Isn't your season starting in a few months?"

"That's why I told you I had to talk to Alicia first. She got my back on this. This is going to be our side venture. I know you have a lot going on but I was wondering if you can help me out in the beginning?"

"If this is something you want to do, I got ya back."

"I got ya back too, Nat."

"You guys are the greatest."

"So what's the name of your management company?"

"Name?"

"Yes. Every company has a name."

"I didn't think about that. How about Simms Management?"

"C'mon, boo. This is the music industry, you gotta be a lil' more creative than that."

"I got it," TyQuan interjected. Natalie and Iverson looked at T. "How about Dymond in da Ruff Management?"

A wide smile lit Natalie's face, "That's kinda hot."

"I like that," Ivy added.

"Natalie Simms, CEO and Founder of Dymond in da Ruff Management. I really like that name, T."

"Then it's settled," Ivy began. "You both get what you want. I get to work with a manager I know and trust and T gets to sign a group that he discovered. Is everybody happy now?"

"Yes," Natalie answered.

"Ecstatic," TyQuan answered as Ivy and Natalie stared at him."What?"

"Ecstatic?" Ivy laughed. That's a pretty unusual word coming from you."

"Hellooooo! I did graduated from college." The trio laughed.

"Okay baby," Natalie stood up.

"I gotta run. I have to meet my lawyer in an hour."

"Let me walk you out?" Iverson walked from around his desk, grabbed Natalie's hand and walked her downstairs.

"Are you sure about this?"

"I've never been surer in my life. These girls have worked hard to get where they are now. They've put up with a lot of unnecessary bull and I think they deserve a shot."

"If that's how you feel, do ya thing."

"When will you have time to squeeze me in for some me and you time?"

"I'm tied up for the rest of the day and pretty much all day tomorrow. How about we get together Wednesday night?"

"That's cool because I got a lot to do today and I gotta meet with the girls tomorrow. Wednesday sounds good."

"You wanna go out or what?"

"Since you have been a good boy, I'll cook for you. Dinner at my place."

"Can you cook?"

"I learned a little bit over the years. You like Italian?"

"Love it."

"Then I'll have to make my famous Chicken Parmesan."

"I feel special."

"You are special. If to nobody else, you are to me."

Natalie moved her lips up to meet Iverson as he came down with his.

"Aiight, Boo. Call me if you have any questions."

"You know I will."

Iverson stood and watched as his Diamond walked down the street and around the corner.

"Thank you," Iverson whispered as he looked toward the sky and smiled.

The days end found Natalie on I-285—stuck in rush hour traffic. If you've never been to the city of Atlanta, there are keys times that you do not want to be caught on any interstate—the morning drive from 7-9 and the evening ride home from 5-7. They call them expressways but, at the aforementioned times, there's nothing express about those ways. Natalie was trying to wait until she got home and was comfortable before she called Katina but it looked like it was going to be a minute before she got there. Traffic was at a stand still as she reached into her purse to grab her cell phone. She scrolled through her numbers until she found Katina and dialed. After 30 seconds of listening to Chris Brown, someone answered.

"May I speak with Katina?" Natalie asked.

"This is Katina."

"Katina, this is Natalie."

"Hey!"

"Did you get a chance to talk to your other group member?"

"Everybody's right here. Want me to put it on speaker?"

"That's cool." There was a brief rumble and then it stopped. "Ok, Natalie."

"What's up, ladies?"

"Hello!" the other two greeted.

"Are you ladies ready for Wednesday?"

"We're ready," Rolanda answered.

"Only problem is, we still have no manager."

"That's why I'm calling."

"You found us a manager?" an unfamiliar voice asked.

"How would you ladies like to be the first group signed to Diamond in da Ruff Management?"

"Who would our manager be?" Katina asked.

"Me and my business partner, Alicia Marshall."

"Are you serious?" Rolanda squealed. "I don't believe this." Natalie began to hear the sounds of three girls jumping and screaming through the phone.

"Ladies! Ladies! Calm down! I know you're excited but I need you to keep it together for a minute."

"I'm sorry Natalie," Katina replied calming herself and the girls down. "Its just that were so happy!"

"We don't have the deal yet but it can possibly be. Now listen. I need to meet with all of you, and I do mean all of you, tomorrow night at the Cheesecake Factory at the Cumberland Mall. Can you be there?"

"Just give us the time and we're there," Rolanda answered.

"8 o'clock and please don't be late."

"We'll be there," Katina responded. "Do we have to get dressed up?"

"You can dress casual. This is just a meet and greet and we'll sign the management contract. Katina, pick the phone back up. I need to talk to you for a minute."

"I'm here."

"Is it just me and you?"

"Yes."

"Katina I need you to listen very close. I am going out on a limb with this. I see how bad you want this and I want to help you. You are the lead vocalist in the group so I need you to take control. I believe in you but you have to show and prove."

"I got it all under control."

"Alright, I'ma hold you to that. I'll see you tomorrow night. Don't be late."

"We won't."

Traffic began to move a little faster. Before long, Natalie was moving at a normal speed. Fifteen minutes later, she was home and in the house. She didn't know what she was getting herself into but she believed that she was up for the challenge.

Chapter 17

It was a cool, mid-March, Tuesday evening in the city of Atlanta. The sun was drifting off to sleep as a full moon awoke to light up the night sky. It was half past seven. Natalie had just picked up Alicia and the two were leaving Buckhead on their way to Cobb Parkway for their meeting with Purrfection. Rush hour was over so the roads were clear to move freely.

"Do you really think we can do this?" Alicia asked.

"I really do. I was thinking about it all last night. Ivy said he had our backs and I believe him."

"Then that's all I need to know. Speaking of Ivy, how are things with you two?"

"Everything is good. He got a little busy but he still manages to make time for me. I invited him to my place for dinner tomorrow night."

"Aww suki suki now! Don't be tryin' to seduce that man once you get him to the mansion."

"I am not trying to seduce Iverson," Natalie laughed. "Every time we've been together we've always been out and about the city. I think it would be a nice to just chill at home for a change."

"I can feel you on that. It was hectic with me and Dré because of how successful *Matters of the Heart* was at the time. Every time I turned around, we were going to a gala, a banquet or a business dinner."

"It's really gonna be rough when the season starts back."

"You'll be ok. I'm pretty sure Iverson's time will be occupied while you're on the road. Hell, he might even travel with you when he can."

"Oh my gosh! Do you know how that would make me feel to know my man is in the stands watching me play? That's like a dream come true."

"Desmond never went to any games?"

"Who? I was lucky if Desmond came to see me any other time than when he wanted sex."

"Wow! You can't be serious."

"Last man that saw me play ball was Dré and even he wasn't there to see me at first."

"You can't be talking about when he went to Houston to see Shawna?"

"Yup. It's all good though. I think I got a winner this time."

Natalie and Alicia arrived at the Cheesecake Factory with five minutes to spare. The business partners went inside and took their table to await Purrfection. Right on schedule, Katina, Rolanda and their third member were walking back to their table. If the group had one thing, it was the look. Even off stage, the three bombshells looked like a group. The three ladies exchanged pleasantries as they sat down to get down to business.

"Ladies," Natalie began. "First, I'd like to thank you for your punctuality. It seems small but that is a positive step in the right direction. This is Alicia Marshall. She is my business partner and she'll be assisting me with the management of your group. Before I let you introduce yourselves, Alicia will you introduce yourself to the ladies and tell them a little about yourself."

"As Natalie said, I'm Alicia Marshall. Natalie and I have known each other for a couple of years. I am the Vice President of Marketing for Bower and Powell. We do all the marketing for the Hawks, Falcons and the Thrashers."

"Can you introduce me to Josh Smith?" Rolanda interrupted.

"I might just be able to set that up but we'll talk about that later. I guess that's all about me for now. I'll turn it back over to Natalie and she can continue."

"Okay ladies. Your turn. Katina we'll start with you."

Katina was a short, fair complexioned girl. She was a black and Asian mix which was easily detected by the shape of her eyes and roundness of her face. She had long, curly, black hair that extended to just below her shoulders. Though she was short, at 5'3", she was not small framed. She was built like a video vixen—medium size chest and a curvaceous bottom half.

"I'm Katina Walker, know to on stage as Miss Kitty. I sing most of the lead. We see ourselves as equals so there is no leader of the group. I've just always acted as the contact and voice of the group because of the relationship we had with our previous asshole, I mean manager."

"That's rule number one and two," Natalie interjected.

"Rule #1: You are a group and you are a whole. No one is better than the other. It takes each of you to make it happen. Rule #2: You will conduct yourselves as ladies at all times meaning you will have to watch the things you say—especially in public. Your turn Rolanda."

Rolanda was the *butter pecan Rican*. She was spicy, sassy and confident. She was the tallest of the trio at 5'7" and Puerto Rico ran all through her veins. She, too, had long black hair but hers was straight. She favored Jennifer Lopez in the aspect of her body, small chest and shapely bottom, as well as her choreography and fashion sense.

"My name is Rolanda Fernandez a.k.a Boricua Especial b.k.a Daddy's Lil' Girl. I am the stylist and choreographer of the group. I add that Latin flava to the group. If our group was a bowl of arroz con pollo, I would be the hot sauce that gives it spice."

"I like her," Alicia laughed.

"Last but not least," Natalie began. "The mysterious third member."

Purrfection's third member was every bit of Aaliyah. She stood about 5'5" with silky, black hair that she wore over her left eye. She was nicely shaped but small framed.

"First of all, I'd like to apologize for my absence at the first meeting. My name is Candace Conner but everybody calls me Cee Cee. On stage I'm known as Unique. I do a little bit of everything. I help Kitty with the lead vocals and I help Rolanda with the choreography. I've sang back up with a few independent artists from Georgia to Florida. I've done a couple of videos and I am a song writer."

"Thank you, ladies. Now let's get down to business. The reason for this meeting is to prepare you for tomorrow. I have the inside track but I'm not going to speak prematurely. If you ladies can show and prove tomorrow, you could possibly be the next big thing to come out of the Future Records camp."

"How do you have an inside track?" Candace probed.

"Let's just say Iverson and I are pretty tight."

"How tight?"

"If you don't mind, I'd like to keep my business and personal lives separated."

"I'm sorry. Didn't mean to pry."

"It's okay. I don't know what tomorrow holds exactly but you need to be ready to perform, if asked, being that Iverson has yet to hear the group. The keyword for tomorrow's meeting is confidence. Walk in like you have the deal already. Show them that you want this and you deserve it."

"I was talking to my husband last night and as a favor to me, if you get signed, you ladies will be featured on *Hotlanta Live* when your first album drops and if your popularity is great, which I know it will be; you could possibly make a couple cameos on a couple shows on Black Reign."

"Are you serious?" Katina asked.

"This is real," Natalie took over.

"Because of our inside connections, you can be huge but it's all up to you. All we can do as your managers is put you in the right positions, the rest is up to you."

For the next hour, Natalie and Alicia went over business plans and marketing strategies with the group. The girls seemed to be at ease due to the fact that they were working with females. Even though Natalie and Alicia were new to the business, they spoke as professionals. Everything was straight to the point. At the close of the meeting, a serious question arose from one of the groups members.

"All of this sounds good," Candace began. "But what if, by chance we don't get this deal? Are you still going to shop us with other labels?"

"Of course. If we don't get picked up by Future, I'm sure there is another record label that would love to have you. But like I said, this deal depends on you and how bad you want it. Alicia and I can only do so much. You have to do your part."

"I can respect that." Once the meal and the meeting were over, Purrfection went their way and the two business partners went theirs.

The large, black, blur of Natalie's luxury SUV blazed down I-75 south toward Buckhead. Alicia and Natalie laughed and talked the entire way to Alicia's. Once they arrived, Alicia raised a couple of questions to Natalie.

"Is Iverson really going to do this deal?" Alicia asked as she reached in the backseat for her purse.

"I don't see why not. He said that the only reason that he didn't want to sign them was because they didn't have management. Now they do."

"You know I like to play devil's advocate, right?"

"Yes you do."

"What if he doesn't sign them? Are we still going to go through with this management thing?"

"Honestly, I don't know about that. I'm making a sacrifice to help them get this deal with Iverson. If it doesn't work, we can still shop the group but we they'll have to wait until after the season."

"Think they'll wait?"

"If they want to be represented by us, they have no choice."

"Girl, you sound just like Suge Knight," Alicia laughed. "Hopefully everything will go well tomorrow. What time is the meeting again?"

"Tomorrow night at eight. I'm picking the girls up from Katina's at around quarter after. That should put me downtown by quarter 'til."

"I'll be coming from home so I'll meet you there." With the close of the conversation, André walked out of the front door and called to the women from the porch.

"Alright, Natalie!" André shouted from the porch. "Can I please have my wife back?"

"Dré, go back in the house and stop hollerin' in these white folks neighborhood," Natalie responded from the truck.

"I'll talk to you tomorrow. You know he get crazy when he don't get his mid-evening lovin'."

"Y'all nasty. I'll call you around lunch time."

"Ok, girl. Talk to you tomorrow."

"Good night, big head," Natalie joked with Dré.

"Next time have my wife home at a respectful hour."

"Its only 10 o'clock."

"That's right and ain't nothin' open after nine but legs. Now take yo' fast ass home."

Natalie laughed as she tooted the horn and backed out of the driveway. Thirty-five minutes later she was back home in College Park. Once inside Natalie trotted upstairs to her office/library to check her email. Ten minutes into it, a messenger box popped up. It was Iverson.

Ivy_Dav: Hey pretty lady!

Dymond4eva: Hey handsome!

Ivy_Dav: how'd the meeting go?

Dymond4eva: it went good…all the girls were there

Ivy_Dav: so what do u think about the group?

Dymond4eva: they're a good group of girls that have been through a lot. u

would not believe some of the things they've been through dealing wit Black

Ivy_Dav: I told u this industry was a beast. I hope ur ready

Dymond4eva: did u forget where I'm from? If I can handle growin up in Camden I can handle anything...lol!

Ivy_Dav: rofl...u do got a point

Ivy_Dav: did u tell them that they are going to have to sing tomorrow?

Dymond4eva: 2 steps ahead of u

Ivy_Dav: u my girl and all but I can't sign a group w/o having heard them 1st

Dymond4eva: I feel u

Ivy_Dav: what's the name of the other girl?

Dymond4eva: Cee Cee but her stage name is Unique

Ivy_Dav: so we got daddy's lil girl, ms. kitty and unique...I like that!

Dymond4eva: they haven't been 2gether long but they have a good chemistry

they also conduct themselves as ladies at all times...an occasional cuss word

slips out every now and then but we all do that when in a comfortable setting

Ivy_Dav: how do they speak...u know, for interview purposes

Dymond4eva: Kitty has a degree in Sociology and she does most of the talking

Rolanda is a licensed cosmetologist and Cee Cee is a student at Clark.

Ivy_Dav: r u telling me that I get to work with people that have sense?

Dymond4eva: lol! u are so silly

Ivy_Dav: ur laffin...I'm serious...u'd be amazed at the people that come up

to me about getting a deal and can't spell or pronounce the word deal

Dymond4eva: lmao! U don't have to worry about that with Purrfection

Ivy_Dav: seriously...it makes shit a lot easier when u don't have to keep

explaining something over and over and over and over

Dymond4eva: I GET IT! LOL!

Ivy_Dav: what do u have to do in the morning?

Dymond4eva: my day doesn't start until after 1 2morrow...y?

Ivy_Dav: I want 2 c u

Dymond4eva: in the morning?

Ivy_Dav: no 2nite

Dymond4eva: do you know what time it is?

Ivy_Dav: yes...lets go for a ride

Dymond4eva: where 2?

Ivy_Dav: meet me at the studio in 30 mins

Dymond4eva: r u serious?

Ivy_Dav: as a heart attack.....see u in 30... u might wanna grab a jacket PEACE!

Dymond4eva: Ivy wait!

Ivy_Dav has logged out

"What in the world is this man up to?" Natalie thought aloud.

Spontaneity should definitely be an element in any relationship. Without any further thought, Natalie slipped out of her business suit and into a pair of dark, blue jeans and an Atlanta Diamonds sweatshirt. After pulling her hair back into a ponytail, she galloped downstairs and out of the house. A certain feeling of excitement built up as she headed downtown once again.

When she got to Iverson's office, she noticed that Iverson's Phantom was parked out front with the hazard lights on. She pulled behind it, got out and locked her truck. Iverson was walking out as she walked towards the entrance. They exchanged hugs and lips then Ivy escorted her to the car and opened her door for her. Once inside Ivy asked her to put a blindfold. Natalie was hesitant for a split second but obliged his request. Once blindfolded, Iverson pulled off and they were on their way. The sounds of Legacy, one of Ivy's artists, floated through the Phantom as they rolled up I-85 North. Natalie was cool for the first fifteen minutes of the ride, then she started to ask questions.

"Where are we going that requires me to wear a blindfold?" Natalie inquired.
"To the Bat Cave," Ivy joshed.
"Very funny."
"I'm taking you some place special."
"Are we there yet?"

"Twenty more minutes and we'll be there."

"Are you taking me to kill me?" Natalie laughed.

"Damn! You caught me. Nah. I'm taking you to a special place."

"How special?"

"Let's just say that you'll be the first woman that I've dated to experience this place."

"Really? Wow!"

"Now sit back and enjoy the ride."

"I could enjoy it a little more if I could see," Natalie laughed. Twenty minutes was over and Iverson made a left turn off of the main road onto a narrow dirt road. After traveling the dirt for about a minute and a half, the slender path opened up to reveal a cabin sitting on a lake.

"Are we there?" Natalie asked as she felt the car stop.

"Yes we are but don't take the blindfold off." Iverson turned the car off, got out and walked around to help Natalie out of the car. He guided Natalie past the cabin towards the dock that jutted out into the lake. He sat Natalie in a lawn chair.

"Sit right here for like three minutes. I'll be right back."

Iverson left Natalie sitting and ran into the cabin. Once inside, he grabbed a couple of blankets, a bottle of wine, two glasses and a lighter. He darted back outside and out onto the dock. On his way to the end of the dock, he lit Tiki torches that were placed about five feet apart on each side of the dock that was about seven feet wide. After the torches were lit and he spread a blanket on the end of the dock, he returned to Natalie. Because he was rushing, he stopped about ten feet in front of her to catch his breath.

"You ready?" he asked as he grabbed her hands to stand her up.

"I was ready 20 minutes ago," Natalie joked. Iverson walked behind Natalie and began to untie the blindfold.

"Welcome to my Paradise." Natalie stood in silence as she took in the entire scene. No man had ever done anything this romantic for her. Iverson grabbed her hand and led her towards the dock.

"You like it?"

"I love it. Iverson this is so beautiful."

"When things get hectic for me and I need to get away for a minute, this is where I escape to."

"I need a place like this."

"Anytime you want to come out here with or without me, it's yours."

"You are too good to me."

"Only for my Queen."

"I'm your queen, now?"

"Only if you want to be."

Iverson and Natalie stood at the end of the dock and engaged in a deep passionate kiss that seemed to last for a lifetime in the minds of all parties involved. At the completion of the lip lock, Iverson and Natalie took their places on the blanket. Iverson was sitting with his legs stretched straight out. Natalie placed her head in his lap and looked up at the stars. They sat in silence for about five minutes as they basked in the moment. Iverson looked down at Natalie and noticed that she had her eyes closed and a smile on her face.

"What's on ya'mind?"

"You just don't know how good I feel right now. I've never had anybody do anything this romantic for me."

"You haven't?"

"I've never really had time for relationships. Basketball has been my life since high school. If I wanted to get out of Camden, I had to be focused."

"What do you mean?"

"I used basketball as my way of getting out of Camden. I didn't have time for relationships. True, I dated but nothing was ever serious. I couldn't afford for anything to stop me from getting a scholarship so when things started getting too serious, I had to let it go. I know I hurt a few people but that was a small price to pay to get outta the hood."

"Would you like a glass of wine?"

"I'd love a glass." Iverson popped the cork on a bottle of Cabernet Sauvignon from Chateau Davenport and poured two glasses.

"When was your last real relationship?"

"Thank you," Natalie expressed as she sat up and leaned on Iverson.

"Last year. After things didn't happen with me and Dré, I met Desmond."

"Why have I heard that name from you before?"

"Which one, Dré or Desmond?"

"Dré."

"Dré is Alicia's husband that works for Black Reign."

"You dated your best friend's man?"

"That is a long story so I'll give you the short version. I met Dré at Club Blaze the night I signed my first contract with the Diamonds. Him and Alicia had just got together after being friends since fourth grade."

"Fourth grade? That's crazy."

"I know. He was up front about her so we were just friends. We went out a couple of times and I really started feeling him. He treated me like no man had ever treated me to that point."

"So what happened?"

"Things got outta control when one of my teammates lied to me about him tryin' to talk to her. He told me the truth when I asked him but that let me know that I was really fallin' for him. I had to take a step back. I had no contact with him until we ran into each other in Houston. That night I told him that Shawna had lied and I was too embarrassed to call him because of the way I overreacted. We reconciled our friendship and we've been tight every since."

"What about Desmond?"

"Me and Desmond broke up about eight months before I met you. He couldn't handle my friendship with Dré."

"Its hard for some men to accept the fact that his girl is close friends with another single guy."

"That's just it. Dré and Alicia got married about a month after we got together."

"So Money just had issues."

"The crazy part is, I lost a good friend because me and Alicia were getting cool and now he's dating her. Talk about being spiteful. I was a good friend to her and a good girlfriend to him. I don't know why people choose to treat me the way they do."

"That's because they fail to realize what a good thing they have in their life."

"Are you trying to get me naked?"

"What?"

"I'm just kidding," Natalie laughed. "So, what about you Mister pink motorcycle in the garage?"

"That Motorcycle belonged to my ex. I met her online a while back. Just like your ex, she didn't realize what she had. I never gave her any reason not to trust me. I went on tour in Latin America with this Latino artist we signed. The next thing I know, I'm getting a phone call telling me that my condo was flooded. I come home and my place was ruined. Apparently she stopped up all the drains in the sinks and tubs, cut the water on and left. I haven't seen or heard from her since. Crazy thing about it is...I don't know why."

"I just don't understand some people. They stay faithful to the ones that treat them like dirt but screw over the people that care about them."

"That's what happens in this crazy thing that we live called life."

"Thank you. Let me ask you a question?"

"Sure," Iverson answered as he poured more wine.

"We've known each other for about five months, correct?"

"Correct."

"Out of those five, we've been exclusive for about two. Where do you see us going?"

"I've never met a woman like you. You are beautiful, you have a good career, you have a good head on your shoulders and I love spending time with you. I don't want to jinx it but honestly, I see us going all the way. You possess qualities that men only dream of finding in a woman and since you are my third great one, I can't see myself letting you go. What about you?"

"I enjoy every moment that we spend together. These past couple months have been absolute bliss. The thing I love the most about you is the fact that not once, has sex come up nor have you come on to me."

"To tell you the truth, that's been the hardest part."

"How so?"

"I love sex just as much as the next man does, if not more, but its one of those things that doesn't run my life. Contrary to popular belief, men in the music industry don't just have sex on the brain. Sometimes I have to portray it for business purposes but there's a lot more to me. In the little time that we've known each other, you know more about me than anybody. On top of it all, I brought you to my special place. No woman in my life has ever set foot on these grounds."

"And that reason alone, makes me and you that much tighter. At this moment I couldn't think of any other place I'd rather be other than with you, right here, right now."

Natalie finished the last bit of wine in her glass, sat it to the side and turned to face Iverson.

"You have no idea how special you are to me."

Natalie repositioned and was now straddling Iverson's lap. She put her arms around his neck and pulled him into her lips. Passion screamed through the silence of night as Iverson wrapped his arms around Natalie. As she kissed him deeply, she ran her fingers through his dreadlocks. Iverson slid his large hands up and down her back as she released quiet but passionate moans. Natalie leaned forward onto him to get him to lay back and continued to kiss his lips then moved to his neck. While kissing Iverson's neck, she pushed her hands up under his sweater and ran them across his rippling abs and chest.

In a sly motion, Natalie used her arms to push Iverson's shirt up to his neck and over his head. Once his shirt was off, she sat up, removed hers — leaving her bra on — and pressed her body against his. The night was a little chilly but with the heat that was being created on that dock, the cool air couldn't manage to extinguish it. The couple was rounding first base on their way to second. Natalie paused for a second to sit up and pull the second blanket over their bodies. They continued to kiss and caress each other. Iverson ran his hands down Natalie's bare back sending chills down her spine and warmth to an area that was already on fire. With all of the rubbing, touching and caressing, Iverson never once touched her breasts nor her backside. That drove Natalie crazy. Even in the beginning stages of a sexual act, Iverson continued to treat Natalie like a lady. Pinned up sexual suppression caused Natalie to cry out.

"I can't take it anymore," Natalie released in a whisper moan. "I want you so bad." Natalie sat up once again only this time she felt a large lump in Iverson's pelvic region. She grinned a devilish grin as she reached for Iverson's belt.

"Wait! Wait! Wait!" Iverson whispered as he grabbed Natalie's hands.

"I don't have any condoms."

"It's okay," Natalie explained as she reached for his belt buckle once again. "I'm on birth control."

"I don't doubt that," Iverson sat up.

"It's just that I told myself that I'd never go that far with a woman unless she was my fiancé or my wife."

"That far meaning?"

"Meaning, I can't have unprotected sex with you unless you are my fiancé or my wife. It's not that I don't trust you, that's just one of my beliefs. I hope you understand."

"I guess I don't have a choice, do I?"

Iverson put his arms around Natalie's body and pulled her close to him as she buried her head in his shoulder. Natalie started to feel her nose burn foreshadowing her on-coming tears. No matter how hard she tried she could not manage to suppress them. It wasn't until the second sniff and the warm drop he felt on his bare chest that he realized Natalie was crying.

"What's wrong?" Iverson asked with major concern.

"I'm fine. I promise. It's just that*sniff* I've never felt this way about any man before. You mean so much to me right now. I hope I didn't offend you?"

"Everything is cool. Believe me when I tell you that sticking to my beliefs was a hard thing to do just now."

"Not to mention another hard thing," Natalie laughed.

"I didn't anticipate this happening tonight that's why I wasn't prepared. I just wanted to spend some time with you away from everyone else. The little time that we have spent alone was always right before we went out."

"It's funny that you say that. I just had this conversation with Alicia earlier today. That's why I wanted to cook for you tomorrow night so it could just be me and you."

"I guess great minds do think alike."

"That they do."Iverson laid back with Natalie clinging to his chest.

"Can we just stay here like this forever?"

"If it were only that simple but like I said, you can come out here whenever you want to, with or without me. I keep a spare key on top of the porch light."

"You know what, Iverson Shemar Davenport?"

"What's that Natalie...," Iverson paused for a second to try to remember if she had told him her middle name.

"It's Nicole."

"Thank you. What's that Natalie Nicole Simms?"

"I am so blessed. I'm living my dream, I have a strong, black man in my life that treats me like a queen and I'm half naked on a pier on a lake in the middle of nowhere. I've died and gone to heaven."

After lying and talking on the dock for another hour, Natalie slid her top back on and the two gathered the items that were spread about on the pier. Iverson extinguished the tiki torches as they walked back towards the cabin. Instead of spending the night at the cabin, Iverson and Natalie drove back into the city. Once at the office, Ivy and Dymond exchanged lips and went their separate ways. In thirty minutes Natalie was back home in her bed and Iverson was fast asleep in his King-size, soaked in the memory of a good night.

With a new day, comes a new series of events. Fresh off of the memories of the previous night, Iverson and Natalie were set in two different areas of the city. In College Park, the morning found Natalie intertwined with her Ralph Lauren comforter as 8:30 found Iverson asleep in his Buckhead estate. In the mind of his fair maiden, Iverson stood more chivalrous than any knight to ever hold a seat at King Arthur's round table — or any round table for that matter.

When it comes to women and their men, women have a list of qualities that her desired man must possess in order to have a fighting chance at winner her heart. Do not let a woman allow you to think for a moment that looks do not matter because they do. There has to be a physical attraction for a woman to allow herself to be approached by said male. As you ponder this, keep in mind that what is attractive to one, may not be attractive to someone else. The category of looks falls in different rankings on each individual woman's list but trust, it is close to the top if not at the top.

Two more qualities that a man must have are the abilities to communicate and listen. It is no secret that women love to talk but what a woman loves more than talking is to be listened to. Due to the abundance of women that abuse the talking part — which turns out to be on some occasions just plain nagging — men have learned to turn a deaf ear to the words that are uttered from the mouths of our queens. For a man that will genuinely listen, her words go from those categorized as being the equivalent to riot noises to the sweet sounds of a woman — true and fascinating. In most cases women find a man that will listen and not talk or they find man that will talk with no intentions on ever listening. On the rare occasion a woman finds a man that can do both, that is two stars in the boxes of *things a man must have to be a husband.*

What other qualities should a man possess? In addition to looks and communication there are a couple more things such as: honesty, fidelity and loyalty. Don't get it twisted; these three things are not the same. A faithful man is not always a loyal man. An honest man is not always a faithful man and a loyal man is not always honest. Many women use the age old expression: *men are dogs.* That is not a bad thing. As a matter of fact you would hope that your man would have in him a few qualities that a dog has. A dog is the most loyal and faithful creature on the face of this vast planet. A canine will stand beside his master until death. If his master walked across the street and punched his neighbor in the eye and a fight broke out, the dog would come running to the aid if its master despite his master's wrong doing. That's loyalty and fidelity. If a man had to be away for 2 years and left his dog with a friend, upon his return the dog would be excited to see him and leave with him. That is loyalty and fidelity. Make no mistake, some men have a tendency to have the negative qualities that a dog has such as raising his leg all over the neighborhood, or sniffing every tail that comes by, but as said before, you would hope that he possesses some canine qualities, not all.

When it comes to men, each womans list is going to be different but if you ask 50 respectable women to list the qualities they look for in a man, on each list, you'll see looks, the ability to communicate, honesty, loyalty and fidelity — not necessarily in that order. For any upstanding man, those qualities are a must and if a man does not have them, then he is merely a boy posing as a man.

Chapter 18

Lunch time in downtown Atlanta found Natalie and Alicia at a deli on Peachtree Street. Natalie was enjoying a roast beef on rye bread with a thin spread of Dijon mustard and Alicia was indulged in a turkey and bacon club, hold the tomatoes with an extra pickle spear, and a bag of Lay's plain potato chips. The two chattered on about their business venture until a very heated subject was brought to the table.

"What you do last night after we left the restaurant?" Alicia asked as she slid a potato chip into her mouth.

"If I told you," Natalie paused and took a sip of her Sprite. "I'd have to kill you."

"I knew it! You are so nasty! You slept wit'em didn't you?"

"Shhh! No I didn't sleep with him."

Natalie leaned in towards Alicia and whispered, "He didn't have protection."

"What?"

"Iverson is the most romantic man I have ever met. I think he might give Dré a run for his money."

"Nobody is more romantic than my Dré Bear."

"Picture this. A cabin by the lake, 20 or more tiki torches, a pier, two blankets and a bottle of wine."

"Really?"

"You should have seen it. We were chattin' online when out of the blue he says he wanted to see me. Before I had the chance to tell him that I was tired, he tells me to meet him at his studio in thirty minutes and logged off. Before he logged off he told me that I should bring a jacket. I was caught off guard but I figured he had somethin' up his sleeve. I met him at the studio. When I got there guess what was parked outside."

"Don't tell me the Phantom?"

"Yes girl, the Phantom."

"You know I'm hatin' on you right now, right?"

"The next thing I know he puts me in the car, blindfolds me and drives off."

"And he's kinky," Alicia laughed.

"We rode for about 30 minutes before we finally stopped."

"I know you were scared at first."

"I wasn't really scared. I would say that I was just a little nervous and anxious."

Alicia stopped eating and gave her the *yeah right* look.

"Okay, I was scared as hell. I was blindfolded going God knows where with a man that I've only known for about five months and it was the middle of the night. But because it was Iverson, I was cool with it. The next thing I know we stop and he helps me out of the car. Before he let me take the blindfold off, he left me sitting in a chair for five minutes.

Believe me when I tell you that when he took that blindfold off, it was worth every minute that I waited. Iverson has a cabin by the lake somewhere off of 316. Behind the house was a dock that stretched out in the water. The dock was lined with tiki torches that Iverson had lit."

"That sounds so romantic but enough with the ambiance. Tell me about when you almost had sex."

"And you call me nasty," Natalie joked as she bit into her sandwich. "You know how us girls do it."

"After I calmed down a little bit we sat down on a blanket that he had on the edge of the dock. We talked as we drank and Iverson started saying all the right things. It wasn't like he was trying to impress me or come onto me, though. He was just being himself and that is what turned me on the most. Giiirl, the next thing I know I had him out of his shirt, I was out of mine and I was ready."

"Just like a slut," Alicia clowned.

"Do you know how long its been since I've felt a man? Too long. Even after we didn't have sex, just because I was with Iverson, I was satisfied."

"Girl I woulda been wetter than the lake."

"How did you know?" The two women laughed as the waitress brought the bill.

"I got this one," Alicia reached for the check. "I'm glad you're happy and I mean that from the heart. I know the last couple of years have been rough but you hung in there. Sounds to me like you've found your great one."

"You've seen *A Bronx Tale?*"

"You know that's one of Dré's favorite movies."

"That is right. Iverson says the same thing about me."

"What? That you're his great one?"

"Yeah."

"Believe him. I did when Dré said it about me and look at us now. We're happily married goin' on three years."

"Things are good now but like I've said before, the true test is gonna come when the season starts."

"You'll be okay. You know how the summer is for music and I'm sure that Iverson will have enough to do to occupy his time while you win another championship."

"That's another thing."

"What?"

"One night last week me and Iverson were playin' around in the studio and he recorded me. He said that I had talent and wants me to drop a CD."

"Are you gonna do it?"

"The deal is if I win the championship or make league MVP again, I drop an album. If we don't make the playoffs, I have to work as an A&R for his label. The only way I can get

459

out of either one is if we make it to the playoffs but don't win it all."

"With us managing Purrfection, you get to see first hand how things will be."

"That's the part I'm scared of."

"You never know. You might be the next MC Lyte."

"I learn more and more about you everyday."

"What? Because I mentioned MC Lyte?"

"Yeah."

"You know me and Dré grew up on hip hop. He gave me my first homemade mix tape. You know the one that was recorded off the radio?" Natalie and Alicia laughed.

"I know Dré loves Hip Hop but I wouldn't have thought you were into is as much as he was."

"I've been around Dré all my life. If you haven't noticed it yet, I'm like a female version of him. In college everybody told us that the movie, *Brown Sugar* was made about us."

"That's probably why we click so well."

"You think so?"

"I know so."

Alicia and Natalie continued to chatter for the remainder of the hour. Before long, 1 o'clock spun around and Alicia had to return to the workplace. The two women went their separate ways and Natalie found place at her second home, the gym.

Just up the street from where the two women were dining, Iverson arrived to the office. He was greeted by Michelle with his daily messages and bottle of Evian. Once settled in he called a meeting with TyQuan, KD and Will. In less than ten minutes, the four men were gathered in Iverson's office.

"What's the word, Boss?" T-Bizzy asked as he took his place on the couch.

"T you know what's going on tonight but I need to fill Will and KD in on what's going on. We might be signing a new group this week."

"C'mon, Ivy," Will complained."We got enough going on as it is."

"I know but we are tryna do it big for the summer. Plus, you know how I work. If anyone finds valid talent, I'll give it a shot. T found a group and I'm going to give them a shot provided all goes well tonight."

"For real Ivy," KD began. "I have a lot of plans for the summer."

"First of all, you and Will's work will be done before the summer hits. Me and T will be the ones on the road the whole summer. You already know that we have to work on Legacy's second album and the Lucky Twelve compilation. In addition to that, The Southern Sunz second tour is coming up this summer and we hope to have a new single out for them for the summer, as well. It's time for Future Records to do it on a whole new level. I know there is going to have to be some sacrifices but I promise you it'll be worth it."

"Worth it how?" Will inquired.

"I tell you what, Will. If we pull this summer off, I'll give you what you've been asking me for."

"A Phantom?"

"Your own label."

"Are you serious? Don't be playin' with my emotions."

"What do I get?" KD asked.

"You actually get yours before the summer. If we sign this new group this week, I'm giving you your shot. I'm going to let you Executive Produce their album."

"And if they don't sign?"

"You get Will's job after he gets his own label and you get to oversee the all aspects of the studio."

"If I'm gonna be doing two jobs do I get two checks?"

"I don't care how white you are, you's still a nigga." Ivy laughed.

"I'll give you a pay increase."

"Aiight, my turn," TyQuan stood up.

"What's up, I know you got somethin' good for ya boy."

"You got yours already."

"What?"

"I'm giving you Purrfection. You are responsible for everything that has to do with the group."

"I got that. What about after we pull off the *Summer of the Future*?"

"You get to keep your job," Ivy clowned.

"That's bullshit."

"You know I got you, bruh. We'll talk about that later. Alright fellas, lets have a productive day. Face, Buddah Rhatt and Encore are coming in around three to lay down the first single off the Lucky Twelve compilation. Will I need you to run by So So Def some time today and pick up those tracks that JD has for me. T-Bizzy, I need you to get on the phone and start getting us some songs for Purrfection's album. With all that being said, everybody...Get out."

The rest of the day breezed by and Iverson's evening appointment was approaching. At 7:45, Iverson was sitting in his chair, at the head of the table, in the meeting room. As always before he signs a potential artist, he gets nervous. Because this was his grind, he treated every potential artist as if he was signing his first artist. To allow himself to calm down, he liked to sit alone prior to any meeting. He swiveled from right to left engaged in deep thought for five straight minutes. Just as his nerves were setting themselves to calm, his silence was broken by the arrival of T-Bizzy.

"What it do, bruh?" TyQuan greeted as he sat down at the table. "You alright?"

"I'm good. Just getting ready. Question is are you ready?"

"I got this. I've been going over ideas since I first saw them perform at Club Blaze. I'm serious about this. I know I've played around a lot and left a lot of the load on you but now its time for me to get it together."

"Who are you and what did you do to the TyQuan I know?" Iverson laughed.

"I'm serious. Since me and Alexa been together, she's shown me some things that I've never noticed."

"Like what?"

"Things like my future. I couldn't be completely successful at the rate I was going. I think its time for me to learn how to separate my personal life from my work."

"I've been telling you that for the past three years."

"I know but its something about hearing it from a beautiful female that's diggin' me for me and not what I do or have. Feel me?"

Before Iverson had the chance to answer, Natalie and Alicia walked into the meeting room dressed in business suits and carrying briefcases. They took position on each side of the door.

"Gentlemen," Natalie began. "Dymond in da Ruff Management would like to grace your presence with Purrfection."On cue, the women began to harmonize. Iverson and TyQuan sat up as they heard Purrfection's sound. "First I'd like to introduce the founder of the group. She hails from Atlanta, Georgia. Gentlemen I present to you, Ms. Kitty."Katina walked in as she continued to sing her part.

"Next up," Alicia introduced. "This diva is another native of Atlanta and the one responsible for the group's style and fashion, Daddy's Lil' Gyrl." Rolanda strutted in and took her place beside Katina.

"Last but definitely not least," Natalie announced. "Straight out off the South Coast, this young lady is the final piece that completes this puzzle we like to call Purrfection. Gentlemen I present to you, Unique."

Cee Cee walked in and took her place on the other side of Katina. Iverson sat in shock. After two years, his past had finally come back to haunt him. Standing before him was Candace Conner — known to him as Unique Pleazures. For the first time since she ruined his condo while he was on tour, the two were face to face and Candace seemed to be enjoying every minute of it. The only person in the room that knew Candace was T-Bizzy but for some reason, he hadn't caught on to who she was. Iverson gained his composure and stood up and carried on with business as if he didn't know who she was.

"Welcome ladies," Iverson greeted. "It's a pleasure to have all of you here. Please have a seat."

The entire time Iverson spoke, Candace had her eyes locked on him watching his every move. Iverson tried to continue but couldn't manage to keep his composure.

"Excuse me for a minute. T can I see you in my office for a minute?"

Iverson walked out of the room followed my TyQuan. When T got to the office Iverson was sitting behind his desk with a distraught look on his face.

"Dog, what's up?"
"Do you not know who that is?"
"Who?"
"Cee Cee."
"Her face looks familiar but I can't place her."
"That's Candace."
"Candace who?"
"My Candace." TyQuan paused for a minute and it came to him.
"I knew she looked familiar."
"This is bad. I can't sign them."
"What! Come on man, that was two years ago. Business is business."

"It's hard for business to be just
business when your new girlfriend is the
manager of your ex-girlfriend's singin' group."

"Does Natalie know?"

"Not yet?"

"Good. Let's just conduct the meeting
and you can talk to her tonight. I know I asked
for this but if it might cost you ya girl, I
understand if you wanna pull out."

"I can handle working with her. The
question is: can her and Natalie handle it?"

"Just do ya thing. Don't offer them the
deal tonight. Talk to Dymond about it and go
from there."

"But I promised you this."

"It's okay. There are exceptions to every
rule. If you don't sign'em, just remember you
owe me. Get yourself together and let's get
back to the meeting."

As difficult as it was, Iverson
maintained his cool and continued the
meeting. Candace continued to seduce him
with her eyes as well as her comments and
questions. Natalie began to pick up on the vibe
that her client was hurling at her man. A
barrage of questions and answers were slung
back and forth between the executives of
Future Records and the members of
Purrfection and their management team. At the
close of the meeting, the Oscar went to Iverson
for best performance under pressure. Iverson

thanked everyone for coming, their time and efforts but offered no deal.

"Ladies," Iverson began as he sat back in his high-backed leather chair. "I would like to thank you all for coming. Your talent is extraordinary and your look is amazing. I like the way you conducted yourselves. You definitely have the poise of a group that can compete and be successful in today's industry."

"Do we get the deal?" Katina blurted.

"My associates and I have some further details to discuss. I will be in touch with your manager as soon as we have an opportunity to convene and come to a final decision. You ladies have a wonderful evening." Iverson bid his goodnights and walked out of the meeting room and into his office. After Iverson left the room, Purrfection sat and shot the breeze with Will, KD and TyQuan. Natalie excused herself and walked to Iverson's office. From the other side of a closed door, Natalie knocked three times. At Iverson's command of "come in," Natalie poked her head in the door.

"Are you okay," Natalie asked as she slid the rest of her body into the office.

"I'm good," Ivy replied with a strange expression painted on his face. "I just needed a lil' time to myself."

"We're still on for tonight, right?"

"Of course we are."

"Okay. Well, I'm getting ready to take the girls home. See you in about an hour?"

"It's a date."

"Alright, Boo. See you then." Natalie blew Iverson a kiss and returned to the meeting room to gather her passengers. Once everyone was gone, TyQuan straightened up the room, turned the lights off and journeyed to Iverson's office.

"Was that crazy or what?" T-Bizzy exhaled as he flopped down on the couch in Ivy's office.

"The crazy thing is…I still want to sign them."

"Are you serious?"

"I have never heard a group of voices that blend together that good. They can be big?"

"What you gonna do?"

"I can't make a decision until I talk to Natalie and Candace?"

"Together?"

"Hell no! I'ma talk to Natalie first and then handle it from there."

"You should talk to Dymond first but have her there when you talk to Candace."

"That's what I'm leaning toward."

"All the times I've wanted to be you," TyQuan laughed. "Now is not one of those times." Iverson couldn't help but laugh.

"I don't think I wanna be me right now. The only thing I can do is be open and honest with Nat. We just had a conversation about Candace last night."

"About what."

"Natalie asked me about our relationship and I told her all about it."

"I think you'll be alright. Natalie seems like she has a level head." TyQuan stood up and reached in his pocket for his keys.

"I'm gettin' ready to bounce. Enjoy yourself tonight and whatever you decide to do, I got ya back."

"Aiight, kid. Be safe."

TyQuan reached over the desk and dapped Iverson up before he left. Iverson leaned back in his office chair and took several deep breaths before he got up to leave. As always before leaving, Iverson did his nightly walk through. He checked all doors and trotted downstairs to make sure all of the necessary studio equipment was off. Once his security check was done, Ivy made his way outside. The sound of a familiar voice overpowered the jingling of Ivy's keys as he approached his car.

"Hey stranger," Candace called as she walked from around the corner.

"Candace Conner."

"Not the greeting I expected but I guess it'll do."

"You tell me how I'm supposed to greet the woman that ruined my home and vanishes into thin air?"

470

"Look, I'm not asking you to take me back or nothing like that. I just want a shot at this music. As I recall, while we were together you told me that when I was ready, you were ready."

"As I recall, that was before you pulled a disappearing act."

"Iverson, I know things ended bad between us and I'll be the first to admit that it wasn't your fault. I had no idea that when I joined this group that we'd end up in your office on the verge of a deal. That's why I didn't come to the first meeting. I needed a little more time to get my head together before I faced you for the first time."

"Where is this going?"

"I guess what I'm tryna say is that if your going to be mad at somebody, be mad at me. Don't take it out on Rolanda and Katina because they deserve this shot. They have no idea about our past. I'm not here to start any trouble. I just wanna sing. I give you my word on that."

"Your word?" Iverson chuckled to himself. "That's funny. Unfortunately I can't make this decision on my own. I have to discuss it with my girl, who just happens to be your manager."

"I kinda figured that. I just ask you keep one thing in mind while making your decision."

"What's that?"

"People can change." Candace turned and walked down Peachtree Street as Iverson hopped into his ride.

Life has a tendency to throw a person a curve ball every now and again. Never in a million years did Iverson expect Candace to come back into the picture on these terms. Iverson was the master of separating his business and personal lives but this was going to be a crucial and grueling situation. By his side was a woman that possessed everything that he looked for in a woman. New to the picture was the woman that he would have given the world but in the blink of an eye, she was gone without a trace.

Iverson played a dozen different scenarios in his mind as he road to Natalie's place. Deep down in his heart he knew that Natalie would understand the situation but the question that arose was would she be willing to work with her? The last thing Ivy needed was to get caught up between his present companion and an ex as he was on the verge of his biggest summer ever. Once he arrived to Natalie's he tried to push those thoughts to the back of his mind until the time was right for him to talk to Natalie about it. Ivy stood outside and gathered his thoughts as he waited for his lady to open the door.

"Hey baby," Natalie greeted as Iverson entered her domain. "Come on in." Natalie closed the door behind Iverson and immediately wrapped her arms around him as the two exchanged lips.

"This is nice," Iverson expressed his approval as he looked around.

"Just a little something I picked up. I'm thinkin' about sellin' this place and moving downtown."

"I used to live down there. It was cool but I think it's too congested."

"I just think this is a bit too much for just me."

"I think its perfect for you. A classy crib for a classy lady."

"You're too sweet," Natalie complimented as she kissed him once again. "Thirsty?"

"I could stand to partake of a beverage or two."

Natalie grabbed Ivy's hand and lead him into the living room. Iverson's house was indeed fit to be viewed on MTV's cribs but Natalie's estate was no slouch, either.

"Before we drink let me give you a tour. This is the living room."

Natalie's living room was huge. In the middle of the room was an enormous, overstuffed, graphite gray, u-shaped sectional. In the middle of the floor, a contemporary, glass coffee table sat on a Persian rug. In front of the sectional was the fireplace. On the mantle, Natalie had a couple of her awards and trophies on display. Above the mantle was a large team picture of the Atlanta Diamonds posed with their championship trophy. The walls were painted a light shade of bone and were accented by an array of colorful floral arrangements scattered about the room.

Off of the living room was the dining room draped in the colors of bluish-grey. In the middle of the room sat a smoked glass, 12 seat table—completely set. The high-backed chairs were covered in the same colors as the walls. The table's center piece was laced with Easter lilies and was about three feet in circumference.

"This is where I throw down from time to time," Natalie introduced as they walked into the kitchen. Once in the kitchen Natalie pulled a bottle of wine out of a sterling silver, champagne bucket, poured two glasses and handed one to Ivy.

"I know it's not Chateau Davenport but it'll have to do."

"I guess I can make an exception," Iverson laughed as he took a sip of the wine. "This is good wine. What is it?"

"Alicia and her husband brought this back from their honeymoon in Italy. I've been saving it for someone special occasion but I guess you'll have to do."

"You just full of jokes," Ivy laughed.

"I have to get you before you get me."

"Indeed you do."

"You wanna see the rest of the house or do you wanna eat first?"

"Let's eat first."

"Okay. You can wash your hands here and then take your seat in the dining room." Iverson washed his hands and returned to the dining room to have a seat.

Natalie remained in the kitchen to prepare two plates of her famous *Chicken Parmesan ala Natalia.* Iverson's diamond entered the dining room carrying two covered dishes. She placed one in front of Iverson and one at her place setting.

"I can tell you worked in a restaurant."

"How?"

"Because you have the forks and knives rolled in the napkin," Iverson teased.

"I guess old habits die hard." Natalie lifted the cover from Iverson's entrée. The aromas of marinara sauce, parmesan cheese and chicken danced in Ivy's nostrils.

"This smells delicious. What restaurant did you get this from?"

"And you say I got jokes," Natalie remarked as she took her place. "Will you say grace?"

"Sure." They bowed their heads.

"Dear Lord, thank you for the food that we are about to receive. We ask that you bless it to be nourishment and strength for our bodies. I ask that you bless the hands that prepared it. Lord I would also like to thank you for blessing me with such a special woman that is beautiful, intelligent and understanding." Natalie smiled as her head remained bowed. "May your way guide our lives. Amen."

"Amen."

"How was that?"

"Beautiful."Natalie reached for the wine to pour Iverson another glass of wine but he intercepted the bottle.

"Allow me."

"Where did you come from and where have you been all my life?" Iverson snickered to himself.

"What's so funny?"

"Life."

"What do you mean?" Natalie asked as she pushed a fork full of pasta in her mouth.

"We both grew up in the same city and had to come all the way to Atlanta to meet each other."

"I think about that sometimes. The only thing I can come up with is timing."

"Timing?"

"Yeah. We met when we were supposed to meet. If we'd met back in Camden, I probably wouldn't have given you the time of day."

"Really?"

"I told you. When I was in school, I was focused on basketball and school work. Guys were the last thing on my mind."

"I feel you on that. I probably woulda never stepped to you anyway."

"Why not?"

"I was shy in school."

"You? Shy? For real?"

"I was a late bloomer. I wore glasses and had braces until the summer before my senior year in high school. When I went back to school that fall, everybody thought I was a new student."

"Wow! That's crazy. I wore glasses and braces until my sophomore year in college. I was straight busted."

"I was busted. I was 6' 2" and skinny as hell. I wasn't just skinny, I was lanky wit it. I'll have to show you some pictures next time you come over."

"Let me tell you somethin' crazy. My dad said he made me wear glasses and braces so no boys would talk to me so I could stay focused on school and basketball."

"Now that's wild."

"You tellin' me."

"Do me a favor," Iverson paused and took a sip of his wine.

"Next time you talk to your dad, tell him I said thank you."

"Stop that," Natalie giggled. "I'm too light to be blushin'."

Iverson and Natalie continued to engage in small talk as they continued their meal. The way he carried himself, one could never tell that Iverson's mind was still racing from the nights previous events. Once dinner was over, the couple took their plates in the kitchen and walked upstairs to Natalie's den.

Iverson stood in shock as he entered Natalie's shrine. This room was state of the art. On the right wall was a 62" Sony High-Definition television — with Dolby surround sound. Below it was a video gamer's dream. Natalie had all the latest video game systems — Playstation 3 and an Xbox 360. On the right of the television was a bookcase that had seven shelves and stood about six feet tall. Instead of books, Natalie used the case to house her DVD's and games. On the wall straight in front of him was the bar. The wall looked like that of a club due to the mirrors and shelves that held a host of liquor bottles. At the far end, coming out of the wall were three draught beer taps. On the left wall was Natalie's personal shrine. The entire wall was a trophy case. Among the many trophies that Natalie had accumulated over the years, the four that meant the most to her were on display — her WNBA MVP award, her Championship trophy, her National Title trophy that she won with Tennessee and her high school state championship trophy. Scattered about the walls were large photographs of her from high school, college and the pros.

"I didn't know that Camden High girls won state in '93."

"I was a sophomore that year. We only lost one game that year and that was the first game I started."

"Who'd you lose to?"

"Woodrow Wilson." That was Iverson's high school alma mater.

"My bad," Ivy chuckled. "That was one of the three games they won that year."

"Wait a minute. I was at that game. Me and some of my homeboys from Howard came up for the game. I don't remember you."

"That was over ten years ago. Plus, I told you that I was busted. I was the short girl with the long ponytail and the goggles."

"Number 22 was you?"

"You remember?"

"One of my boys was trippin off you," Ivy laughed.

"That is not nice!" Natalie clowned as she punched Iverson in his left arm.

"Just for that you can fix your own drink."

Iverson wrapped his arms around Natalie from the back and kissed her on the neck, "Don't act like that. You were a cutie pie." Natalie folded her arms and poked out her bottom lip.

"That is not going to work." Ivy gently kissed and sucked on Natalie's neck.

"Is that working?"

"I will not stand here and be seduced."

Ivy continued to kiss Natalie on the neck until she finally turned around and engaged in a deep kiss with her man. Before the wine kicked in and things got steamy, Iverson stopped and looked Natalie in her eyes.

"We need to talk about something."

"About what?" Natalie inquired as Ivy let her go and led her to the couch. After Natalie sat down, Iverson walked over to the bar and fixed their favorite drink — Hennessey and Coke with a side of Grand Mariner.

"About Purrfection. We have an issue."

"Talk to me. What's up?"

"Remember last night when I told you about Candace?"

"Your ex-girlfriend, right?"

"Yeah."

"What about her?"

"Candace is Cee Cee."

"Cee Cee?" Natalie paused for a second and thought about it. "My client Cee Cee?"

"Yes. Cee Cee, Candace Conner a.k.a Unique."

"Are you serious?"

"I almost fainted when she walked in the room. That's why I had to excuse myself for a minute. I had to get it together enough to continue the meeting."

"Wow...that's crazy."

"You tellin' me. The crazy thing is that she says she's not trying to start any trouble, she just wants to sing."

"When'd she tell you that?"

"Tonight. She was waiting outside after everybody left."

"That explains why she didn't leave with us," Natalie paused and took a swallow of her drink.

"So, now what?"

"That's why I wanted to talk to you."

"You don't want to sign them now."

"That's just it. I want to sign them but I don't know if the three of us can work together."

"Listen," Nat began. "I don't know what you're used to or have dealt with in the past. I'm not a jealous woman but I do hold close to me what's mine. If it's me you're worried about, don't be. I know business is business and I trust you. If you want to sign them, I will still manage them but she has to know and understand that."

"She did manage to make a valid point. She told me if I was going to be mad, to be mad at her and not take it out on Katina and Rolanda. To be honest, I like the group's sound and style. They fit well together and I think they have what it takes to be hot. If you say you can deal with it, I trust you. Knowing Candace, all I ask is that you be on your toes."

"I have one question."

"What's that?"

"Are you over her?" Iverson sat in silence for about five minutes before he answered the question. "I wasn't before I met you but as we spent time and got to know each other, I let it go. I'm happy and I want to make you happy."

"That's all I need to know."

"I knew you'd understand."

"We're in this together. Let's go platinum." Natalie and Iverson toasted to the journey that was ahead of them.

"But don't get it twisted...I will drop her like it's hot if she steps outta line." Natalie had the most serious look on her face for about 30 seconds before she busted out in laughter.

Over the next hour, Natalie and Iverson participated in a game of NBA Basketball on the Xbox 360. It was the Los Angeles Lakers versus the Miami Heat. Through the laughter and fun, Iverson was fascinated by Natalie. He had never met a woman that enjoyed ALL of the things he enjoyed — even video games. Despite the fun and games, time still rolled on. Before long, it was 1 o'clock in the morning. Being the gentleman that he was, Iverson took the glasses and placed them in the sink under the bar and helped Natalie straighten up.

"Well, Mami," Iverson began as he pulled his keys out of his pocket. "I guess I'll be headin' to da crib."

Natalie stood up, draped her arms around Ivy's waist and buried her face in his chest, "I don't want you to go." With both hands, Iverson gently grabbed Natalie's head under her ears and lifted her face to him.

"Are you sure?" Natalie nodded her head in a positive motion. Natalie reached up and pulled Iverson's hands down in front of her. Like a school girl she smiled and led him out of the den. Hand in hand, they walked down the long upstairs hallway. Natalie had it made up in her mind that it was time for her to experience all that Iverson had to give her. For Iverson, the thirty seconds that it took to walk from the den to the master bedroom seemed to take forever. With ease, Natalie pushed the slightly cracked door open that led to the queen's lair. The Atlanta Diamond's bed sat tall in the middle of the far wall. On each side were over height, dark wooden nightstands that held Tiffany lamps. Her bed looked like a king-sized cloud due to her linen selection.

When their steps ended, Iverson and Natalie were standing beside the bed. Once again Natalie turned to face Iverson. The couple began to kiss with passion and desire. Iverson could feel how nervous Natalie was through her hands as they touched his face, neck and body. The countdown to pleasure had begun. Before he started to undress her, Iverson paused and looked into Natalie's eyes.

"Are you sure about this?" he asked.
"I'm yours."

Iverson reached for the top button of his queen's blouse and one by one, unfastened them. Starting at her lips, Ivy kissed down her neck as he slid his hands down her back sending chills up and down her spine. He pulled his hands from around her back and on to her stomach, back up over her chest — taking her shirt off, as he slid his hands over her shoulders. Natalie returned the favor by helping him remove his. Using the gentle touch of a woman, Natalie kissed Iverson's chest and ran her tongue down his muscular stomach and back up.

After the tops were removed, Iverson reached down and slowly pulled Natalie's skirt to the floor leaving her standing in black, lace bikinis. Never had Natalie looked so beautiful to him. In amazement and awe he lifted Natalie up and placed her on the bed. Before climbing into the cloud, Ivy removed his jeans and sneakers — along with the rubber band that held his dreads in a ponytail. Once in the bed he pushed Natalie onto her back and started on a familiar path.

Iverson positioned himself between her legs, which were open to accept him. He held himself up and looked down at his Diamond. From the light of the dimly lit lamps and Natalie's complexion, he could see her smile as he gazed at her. Body to body, Iverson began to kiss her obsessively. Stuttered breaths and sexy moans came from Natalie as Iverson made her body temperature rise. From her lips, he moved to the neck down to the peaks of her perfectly shaped breasts. Natalie squirmed with desire as he ran his tongue around each nipple in a circular motion while the ends of his dreadlocks tickled her body. Once Ivy felt that each breast had been attended to he continued on his way. From down in the valley of Twin Peaks, he moved towards the Mason Dixon line. Using his teeth, he pulled her panties down to her ankles and off. That tactic began to drive Natalie crazy and Iverson knew it.

On his way back up, Ivy kissed her ankles, her calves and the insides of her thighs. The closer he moved to her southern hospitality, the more she moaned. Lying in the V of her open legs, Iverson began to please her in a way that only a real man could. With each lick and kiss Natalie rolled her hips and arched her back. It had been too long since Natalie's body experienced that type of ecstasy. Twenty minutes, which seemed like forever to Natalie, passed as she felt her first climax readying itself for release. Iverson could feel Natalie's body begin to tremble from the oncoming orgasm. At explosion, Natalie grabbed Ivy's head and moved him as her legs closed and her body began to convulse.

Natalie gained her composure but she was still breathing heavily. Phase one was complete and now it was time for phase two. Iverson sat up on his knees and looked down at his damsel in sexual distress. Not knowing whether Iverson was prepared or not, Natalie rolled over and reached in to her nightstand for a bit of protection. She handed Iverson a gold package indicating how ready she was. Once he was equipped, Ivy opened Natalie's muscular, yet soft, legs once again. Upon insertion, Natalie's body tensed. He paused to make sure she was okay and after her confirmation, he continued.

The first stroke was long and slow. Natalie released more stuttered breaths for each inch that Iverson slid into her soaked flesh. Now that he was all the way inside, he continued to stroke in the same manner he began — long and slow. Iverson made love to Natalie gentle and calm. Once he pressed his body down against hers, Natalie wrapped her long legs and arms around his waist and back. Passion and pure bliss filled the room as Natalie received what she wanted the previous night at the lake. The couple continued to exchange moans, Ooo's, Ahh's and yeses as they sealed their relationship. Before long, Iverson sped up the pace of his stroke and sent Natalie into overdrive. In the blink of an eye, Natalie turned from the classy and sassy lady that he paraded with around the city of Atlanta to the lusty vixen that all men desire to have in their beds.

Without allowing Iverson to exit her southern entrance, Natalie rolled over and was now on top of her CEO. Up and down she slid taking it all with every downward motion. Iverson could feel her body jump every time he found her spot when he pushed inside of her as she came down. Just like Iverson when he was on top, Natalie started off slow but before long, she was engaged in an all out sprint with him inside of her. At first she was using Ivy's stomach to brace herself until she interlocked her fingers with his. Before long, Iverson sat up with Natalie still on top of him. Natalie latched onto him and squeezed his body tight lightly pressing her nails into his back. Feeling her second orgasm coming on she let Iverson go and pushed him back onto the bed and began to ride him like she was in a rodeo. Her sudden change of motion began to bring on Iverson's climax.

As any man would, Iverson tried to suppress his sexual noises but it felt too good. Before long, Natalie and Iverson reached a dual orgasm that caused their souls to collide.

Out of breath and energy spent, Natalie collapsed on Iverson's chest with him still inside of her. Like an infant Natalie tucked her arms under her body and put her ear over Iverson's heart as if she were listening to what it was saying. Still semi-erect Iverson pulled out of Natalie and rolled her onto the bed as he hopped down and walked into the bathroom. Through the door, Natalie told him where the towels and wash cloths were.

Natalie perked up when she heard the shower cut on. Once again she grinned a devilish grin and crept into the bathroom. In her bathroom was a stand alone shower incased in glass. She could see Iverson's body through the steamed glass as she walked toward it. Iverson had his back to the door so he had no idea that Natalie was in the bathroom with him. With cat-like stealth, Natalie eased into the shower. Iverson jumped when Natalie put her arms around his soapy body.

"You scared the hell outta me," Ivy laughed. "You can't just walk up on black folks like that when they butt naked."

"I'm sorry baby but you forgot something."

"What's that?" Natalie moved from behind Iverson and positioned herself in front of him. With the water gushing from above, she slowly descended to her knees and filled her mouth with Iverson. In no time, he was at attention and ready for action. For a man there is no greater feeling than looking down at a beautiful woman as she is pleasing you. The eroticism of the water flowing over their bodies sparked Round 2. Natalie engaged in Iverson as if she had been starving for months. Due to the pleasure, Ivy felt his legs becoming weak and he had to lean against the shower wall to keep him from falling down. Being pleased orally was a beautiful thing but there was nothing like the feeling of being inside of a woman.

Iverson gathered his thoughts and reached down and lifted Natalie back up. As he did to lift her on to the bed, Iverson hoisted Natalie up onto him and turned her back to the wall. Forgetting about what he said about not having sex with a woman unprotected, Iverson pushed inside of Natalie and began to stroke her once again. Natalie latched onto him and held on tight. The scene that was set was like that of a movie — two bodies engulfed in steam and soaking wet. It might not seem like much but this was a huge statement for Natalie and Iverson. Just by them making love in this manner showed that Natalie trusted Iverson and Iverson trusted her.

When Iverson felt he couldn't hold her up anymore, he put Natalie down, turned her to face the shower wall and took her from behind. The expressions on Natalie's face were that of zeal and infatuation. Never had a man made love to her in this way and she loved every second of it. In her mind she felt that she had found the man she had been looking for all her life. In the eight months she spent with Desmond, her ex, she only had two orgasms and was now on her way to her third in one night. People try to say that sex doesn't have a lot of bearing on a relationship but it does. If a man treats a woman like a queen and can make her body feel like it's never felt before, nothing but good can come out of the relationship — or can it?

In the aftermath of Natalie's third orgasm and Iverson's second, they stood under the water as it washed away all of their past experiences with other people and made way for the new life that they were set to experience. Once the actual shower was complete, covered in nothing but towels, Iverson carried Natalie into the room and placed her in bed. To the other side he walked and climbed in. Before he had a chance to get settled in, Natalie migrated to his side of the bed as if she was magnetically attracted to him. Iverson put his arm around her as she laid her head on his chest and the two drifted off into Mr. Sandman's world, satisfied and exhausted.

Chapter 19

Deborah Cox released a song entitled *The Morning After*. This song embodied the true feelings that two lovers experience after they have reached sexual bliss between them. This song can only be felt by those that are trying to achieve something deeper than one night of passion. Now that the line of friendship has been crossed, what does the next plateau hold? Now comes the time to answer the question of: *Where do we go from here?* For those on the journey for stability and true companionship, the morning after marks the eve of confirmation. When the separate paths of two people searching to find that one that will please them in every way finally come together, the merger can be a little turbulent but as rough roads extend, they eventually become smooth again.

For a week strong, Iverson fought a serious inner battle. Sometimes things can be easier said than done but in Iverson's case, it was a lot easier said. Without flinching he told Natalie that if she could work with Candace then so could he. He found that to take that initial step was more difficult than he thought. It had been seven whole days and he still hadn't given anybody a definite answer concerning the future of Purrfection. The

window of time was getting smaller and
TyQuan felt that it was time for some answers.

Knocking on Iverson's office door as it
sat open, "You got a minute, homie?"
"Yeah, T. What's the deal?"
"I was just looking over our proposed
update to our summer schedule of events and
its telling me that if we want to stay on track,
we need to get Purrfection signed, yesterday?"
"I know, kid. This is one of the hardest
decisions I ever had to make. Feel me?"
"Trust, Ivy. I'm wit you that's why I
haven't said anything. That was the friend
part. Now comes the business part. We rollin'
up on the end of the month. I got a whole
album for the group waiting in the wings. KD
is done with seven tracks for the album. I
cashed in a couple of favors and got two songs
from Ne-yo, one from Tosha Scott and I'm
getting tracks from Timbaland, Pharell and Lil'
Jon. I already have the first single picked and
me and Shakeem already been shootin' ideas
back and forth for the video. I'm ahead of
schedule but I need a group."
"Sound's like you been busy as hell."
"Maybe you don't understand how
serious I am. Everything I learned about the
industry I learned from you. You put up with
shit from me 'cuz I'm ya boy. I've let you down
more times than I wanna talk about and on top
of everything, if it wasn't for me askin' you to

go out to see the group, nothing woulda ever happened to the 300. So in a way, I owe you."

"C'mon man, what happened to my car wasn't your fault."

"Just let me have that one," TyQuan laughed. "I was rollin' at the time. I know how serious this situation wit Natalie and Candace is but if you're gonna sign Purrfection; they need to be signed by Friday. That gives you three more days to think it through."

"I'll give you my answer Thursday morning. Fair enough?"

"I'm not a hard man to please. Thursday it is. Now if you'll excuse me, I have a lunch date with Alexa. I'll be back around 2. We got a meeting with Legacy and her manager at 3:30."

"You really done stepped ya game up. You must be tryna get a raise."

"Is it that obvious?" Ivy laughed as his ace left his office and realized that he was wrong in his assumption of his business partner and best friend. TyQuan's track record wasn't the best of things but it looked like he had his mind set on business. Iverson's thoughts were interrupted by the digital sound of two lips kissing. Someone was sending him an instant message. Wiggling the mouse, Iverson found that it was KandeeGyrl.

KandeeGyrl: Ivy!
Ivy_Dav: what's good?
KandeeGyrl: this kandee...lol!!!! j/k how r u?

Ivy_Dav: I'm good.

KandeeGyrl: I know you think I'm crazy b/c I won't tell u who I am but

I have good reason. When the time is right I will tell you who I am.

Ivy_Dav: u know what? It's really not that serious to me anymore.

KandeeGyrl: u don't have to be rude about it ☹

Ivy_Dav: its not bein' rude...its being real...I have much more important things

2 do than 2 play guessin games with some random chick on da net

Ivy_Dav: so for me to remain civil the best thing for u to do is leave me be

KandeeGyrl: r u serious?

Ivy_Dav has logged out

Afternoon found Natalie at Freedom Arena in a team meeting. Technology was truly a beautiful thing. As one of the assistant coaches was going over some unnecessary information, Natalie and Alicia were engaged in a meeting of their own—via their Sidekicks.

Drewifey: has ivy said anything about signing the girls?

Dymond4eva: not yet

Drewifey: what is he waiting on?

Dymond4eva: this is a hard decision for him to make

Drewifey: what's so hard about it? He has a talented group... sign'em!

Dymond4eva: OMG! I forgot to tell you the inside story…

Drewifey: WTF? inside story?

Dymond4eva: about ivy and cee cee

Drewifey: ivy and cee cee? now i'm really confused

Dymond4eva: I'm in a team meeting… let's do lunch

Drewifey: Fox Sports Grill in about an hour

Dymond4eva: c u there

Natalie put her Sidekick back in her purse and continued to scribble in her note pad as the coach continued to ramble on. A smile crossed Natalie's face when she realized what she was doing. Like a high school girl, she was doodling *Iverson & Natalie* all over the page. Things like that are what relationships are made of. Even when you don't realize that person is on your mind, he or she manages to pop up. The meeting adjourned and Natalie was making her way to the parking garage she was joined by a familiar face.

"Hey Natalie!" a voice called from behind her. Natalie recognized Shanice's voice and stop just to see what she had to say. "You got a minute?"

"You got one minute."

"Look. I know we haven't had much to say to each other these days but I wanted to take this chance, while I got it, to apologize. I know what I did was wrong and I'm sorry."

495

"You know what? I am so over that. I've moved on with my life and beyond those high school games you and Desmond playin'." There was nothing Shanice could say. "All I want to know is what did I do to you?"

"That's just the thing…you didn't do anything but be a friend. When we started out as teammates last season, I never thought that I'd find a friend like you. You reminded me of the girls I grew up playin' ball wit. You always shot me straight and that's what I always liked about you. To make a long story short, what you said to me that day in the car about us being confused as being lesbians really struck a soft spot with me."

"I don't understand."

"As long as we've been friends, I never told you that I was gay."

"Then what were you doing with Desmond."

"Being spiteful. It has always been me and you. I've never had to share you with anybody. When Alicia came into the picture I got jealous."

"You're makin it sound like we were a couple or somethin'."

"In some twisted way, in my mind, we were."

"Are you serious? Why are you telling me this?"

"It's just something I wanted to get off my chest before I go."

"Before you go?"

"I got traded. I'm not a Diamond anymore. I got traded to Detroit for their first round pick next year and some chick they drafted this year."

"Wow! That's crazy."

"I guess karma's a bitch sometimes. I'll see you on the court." Shanice turned and gingerly walked away.

"Shanice, wait." Natalie walked over to her and put her arms around her. "All is forgiven." Shanice broke down in tears as the one she wronged accepted her apology.

"Thank you so much," Shanice sniffled. "It sounds so cliché but, everything happens for a reason. I don't know what the reason was or is and to be honest, some things are better left unsaid."Shanice gathered up as she let go of Natalie.

"Remember, no matter who you play for, you'll always be a member of the Atlanta Diamonds...WNBA Champions."

"And you'll always be my Diamond." Shanice kissed Natalie on the cheek and walked away.

Despite everything that had happened between Natalie and Shanice, Natalie was saddened by the loss of a good teammate. On the court Natalie and Shanice were like Scottie Pippen and Michael Jordan. Everything that Natalie saw during the game, Shanice saw. Her role on the court was going to be a hard one to fill but a true team player can play ball with anyone — or could they?

Memories of the good times they had ran through Natalie's mind as she made her way to Atlantic Station to meet Alicia for lunch. When she got there, Alicia hadn't arrived yet. Natalie got a table and ordered drinks because she knew that her friend wouldn't be far behind. Alicia walked in and found Natalie sitting with her head propped on her hand aimlessly stirring her drink.

"Who died?" Alicia joked as she sat down.

"Hey, girl."

"What's wrong? You look like you just lost ya best friend."

"I did. Shanice got traded this morning."

"I'm sorry. You okay?"

"I'm cool. I know we weren't really talkin' to each other but I figured one day we'd get over it. I'm just glad we managed to clear the air before she left."

"Who's she playin' for now?"

"The Detroit Shock. The same team we beat in the conference finals to play for the championship."

"Look at the bright side, you still got me to put up with?"

"That's why I'm so depressed," Natalie laughed.

"That is not funny."

"Anyway, let me fill you in on what's going on. He hasn't said anything to me but I believe that Iverson hasn't signed the group yet is because he used to date Cee Cee."

"Are you kidding me?"

"They used to live together and everything. One day out the blue while Ivy was on tour, she floods his condo and leaves. He hadn't seen her until the night we had the meeting at the office."

"Seriously?"

"He said that if I could work with her considering their past, then he was okay with it. I think he's still going to sign them, its just taking him a minute to get prepared for it."

"Have you asked him about it?"

"I'm not stressin' him about it. When he feels its time to make a decision, he will."

"I'm surprised at how well you're taking it."

"I'm like this, Iverson and I have been together for going on six months. In these six months, he has not given me any clues to lead me that he wants to be with any other woman but me. I'm confident in that and I trust him."

"You have to. I don't have to tell you what me and Dré been through. He knew a couple women before we came back together. Take Vanessa for instance."

"Vanessa?"

"You know the one that lives in Jerome's apartment building, Taylor's godmother."

"Oh okay. I know who you're talking about."

"She had the serious hots for Dré until he cut her off. They ran into each other later on down the road, they talked about it and now they're friends. She's a beautiful girl but it doesn't matter because I know that André is mine. You have to remember, if you don't have trust, you don't have nothin'."

"I trust Iverson."

"Then that's all that matters. Plus, she know I got ya back so it really ain't nothin' happenin'." The ladies laughed as they ordered their lunch and set themselves to participate in idle girl talk.

Thursday rolled around and it was time for Iverson to give TyQuan his answer. He informed his friend that he would be meeting with him, Natalie and Cee Cee that afternoon. For hours he sat in his office alone. When time for the meeting came, Iverson put his game face on. Natalie, Cee Cee, and TyQuan were waiting for him when he finally made it to the conference room. Iverson greeted everyone as he took his seat at the head of the table. Before he had a chance to get the meeting started, Cee Cee opened up.

"Before you even get started," Cee Cee began. "I already know what this is about. I've come to the conclusion that since the other girls aren't here, this has everything to do with me and Ivy's past relationship and your current relationship. Am I correct in my assumption?"

"Absolutely." Iverson replied.

"Miss Simms, I'll tell you the same thing I told Ivy, I know me and him have a past but it's exactly that, the past. I'm not here to start any trouble, I just wanna sing."

"I just want to make sure that all parties involved know that. This is business and as long as we keep it just that, we'll all be fine."

"Since we're all being open," Natalie interjected. "Cee Cee, I am fully aware of what you and Iverson had. I don't know everything but just so you know, your past with Iverson has no bearings on me nor do I feel threatened by you. You are a client and as long as you do right by Diamond in the Ruff, Diamond in da Ruff will do right by you."

"And why am I here?" T-Bizzy asked raising his hand.

"I'll get to that in a minute. I don't know if the other girls know what's going on but I'm going to leave that up to you. It's your choice whether you tell them or not. I would just in case something may happen down the road, they won't be caught off guard."

"I don't have anything to hide. I'll tell them. I just didn't feel that it was any of their business just yet considering we haven't signed yet."

Reaching over to the phone and pressing the intercom button, "Michelle?"

"Yes, Ivy?"

"Are they on the line?"

"Yes they are."

"Thank you." Iverson pressed a couple buttons on the phone. "Ladies are you there?"

"We're here," Katina answered.

"I'm sitting here with your manager and Cee Cee. I had my secretary to call you because I have to ask you a question."

"Ask away, Papi," Rolanda shouted in the background.

"I love it when they call me Papi," Iverson laughed. "How would you ladies like to be the newest group to sign to Future Records?" A barrage of high-pitched screams jolted through the phone's speaker. "Is that a yes or a no?"

"Yes! Yes! Yes!" the girls screamed sounding as if they were jumping up and down.

"Your manager will have the contracts. I need them signed and back in my office in the morning. Provided that happens, Monday will start the rest of your lives. Welcome to the family."

"Thank you so much!" Rolanda screamed.

"Cee Cee," Iverson began as he turned off the intercom. "Welcome to the family."

"Thank you," Cee Cee replied as she stood up. "I guess I need to go have a talk with my girls. Miss Simms...I'll be hearing from you soon?"

"I'll call you girls in about an hour so we can get these contracts signed."

"We'll most likely be at Katina's house."

"Okay. Talk to you later. I guess I need to be going too. I have to run by Alicia's while I'm over this way." Natalie stood up, leaned down and gave Iverson a kiss. "Call me later."

"I will."

As children, everyone was taught that if you play with fire, you're bound to get burned. People can change but it is not always good to see if they have. Iverson made a decision based on loyalty and business. TyQuan was Ivy's ace and business partner and his loyalty to him had the potential to be something dangerous. The last time Iverson laid eyes on or even spoke to Cee Cee was the day he left for that tour in Latin America. On that day Candace told him that she would always be there for him no matter what. Two years later, the label is good, Candace seemed to be out of his system and now she's back in the picture. With Cee Cee's return, also comes the painful memory of a condominium and a relationship left in shambles.

Just like they do every night, Iverson and Natalie were either on the phone with each other, like two high school sweethearts or either chatting away online. On this particular evening, Iverson and his Diamond were engaged in a conversation via instant messenger.

Ivy_Dav: u r out of your mind! En Vouge was the female group of the 90's

Dymond4eva: so ur tellin' me that TLC is not as good as En Vouge

Ivy_Dav: that's exactly what I'm sayin....left eye, chili and t-boz can not

sing as good as teri, maxine, cindy or the other light skinnded one..lol!

Dymond4eva: u know what? this conversation is over cuz ur trippin'!

Ivy_Dav: lol! forgive me if I'm biased but I've been in love with them

every since I saw them on the *Born to Sing* tour back in da dayz

Dymond4eva: whatever! Anyway...I need to get serious for a minute

Ivy_Dav: aww hell...what I done did now? Lol

Dymond4eva: hold on...

Iverson's cell phone rang as he maximized his Free Cell game he's put on pause. What ever it was that Natalie wanted to tell him, she had to say it to him.

"Hello?" Ivy answered.

"Hey boo," Natalie replied.

"Now what was so important you had to call me?"

"I don't have to have a reason to call you, sir. Maybe I just wanted to hear your voice?"

"Excuse me, Ma'am," Ivy laughed. "But on the real, what's up?"

"I just wanted to say thank you for what you did."

"What did I do?"

"You put aside personal issues and signed a talented group."

"Oh that. I'm a firm believer in forgiveness and second chances. I know things weren't exactly cool between me and Candace but it wasn't just her. When I looked in Katina and Rolanda's eyes, I saw the same thing that I saw in all of my other successful artist's eyes."

"To be honest, you only know the half of what those girls have been through. Me and Katina have really had some deep conversations and I'm glad me and Alicia decided to manage them. I believe that if they had got hooked up with another male to handle their careers, they would have broke down."

"What do you mean?"

"These girls have dealt with the sleaziest of club owners, promoters and other riff raff in the industry."

"Don't be naïve. It's still a hustle. In this industry some people say any and everything they can to get ahead. These girls were raised in Southwest Atlanta and on Bankhead. Some women from those particular areas of town are born with larceny in their hearts. They have hustler mentalities so watch yourself. They've been in the industry for a minute and they know how to play the game. Not saying that they are but just be careful."

"Don't think that just because I play ball, that I'm not hip to what's goin' on. It's shady people in all areas. I know how women use their emotions and mind tricks to play on men's sympathies. That doesn't work from woman to woman. Trust me. If there is somethin' shady in the mix, it'll come out."

"Oh no doubt. Just because I chose to work with Candace, doesn't mean I fully trust her. She has a long way to go to regain my trust. As long as she does right by you and the group, we're good."

"I have a question."

"What's that?"

"Do you still have feelings for her?"

"Before and when I first met you, I did. Since I've devoted all my time and efforts into you, Candace is the furthest thing from my mind. You are who I want to be with and nobody, and I mean nobody, can change that. The only person that can change that is you. Feel me?"

"I do and that's all I wanted to hear. I've been through a lot of bullshit and I just don't want to end up playin' the fool."

"What we have is special in every way and the last thing I want to do is loose you. I believe it when they say Diamonds are forever."

"You are too sweet," Natalie complimented as a huge smile spread across her face. "Out of all the chicken heads, sluts and skeezaz runnin round half butt naked on Ebony World, you chose me."

"I'm just thankful you allowed yourself to be chosen."

"You always know what to say, don't you?"

"I try. Listen, I got some people I want you to meet."

"That's cool. Just let me know when and where."

"Tonight on Just4kickz.com."

"Excuse me?"

"I been kickin it on this website for awhile. It's a video chat room. I've never dated anybody from the site but I have gotten attached to a few people. Their kinda like family."

"Are you serious?"

"Yes I am. I hope you don't think of me as being strange but these people mean a lot to me. A couple of them have been in video shoots and some of us have partied together. Remember the guy from North Carolina that I introduced you to at the last album release?"

"You talking about Teddy?"

"He's one of my people from just4kicks."

"Wow. These people must be like family."

"They were around for a lot of the crazy shit I've been through but no matter how bad my day is or what I'd been through before I log on...I always log out in a better mood. These people are hilarious."

"They sound like a good group of people. What do I have to do?"

"Go to just...the number 4...kickz...k-i-c-k-z dot com. Join the site. Give me ten minutes to run to the rest room and to the kitchen and I'll be right back."

"Ok."

Natalie was hesitant at first but Iverson really seemed excited about her meeting his internet friends. Natalie went to the site and opened her account. Ten minutes later, Iverson hit her on the IM.

Ivy_Dav: finished settin upp ur account?

Dymond4eva: almost...

Ivy_Dav: what is ur screen name?

Dymond4eva: I put Dymond down temporarily

Ivy_Dav: that's cool...let me forewarn u...these people are a trip...people are
going to hit on u...and women might make some crazy comments when I first

log in...I haven't been on since we've made it official...I wanted u to b there

Dymond4eva: that is so sweet...i'm finished...now what?

Ivy_Dav: click on video chat...when the name list comes up...double click

On ***Mami*Dearest***...if u don't get in the first time...keep trying...I'll

Have Mami get rid of some people so u can get in if I get in before u

Ivy_Dav: by the way...in there I'm known as Futurama

Futurama has entered the room

<Thyk2Def> I THINK I JUST SAW A GHOST...LOL

Dymond has entered the room

<*Mami*Dearest***>** HEY STRANGER!

<Teddy Pinned*Her*Ass*Down> ITS MY DUDE! WHAT IT DO CUZIN!

<City Ave Diva> HEY FUTURE BABY, I MISSED U!!!!

<MACK Truck> SUP CUZIN!

<Mrz*Pinned*Down>HEY FUTURE!!!!!

<Futurama> WHO IS THAT?

<Mrz*Pinned*Down> ITS ME....CHOCO LATTE!

<Thyk2Def> U HAVE BEEN GONE FOR A MINUTE!@FUTURE

<Futurama> BEFORE I GO ANY FURTHER I WANT TO INTRODUCE EVERYBODY TO THE 1ST LADY OF FUTURE RECORDS...PLEASE MAKE HER FEEL

WELCOME....I'D LIKE YOU TO MEET
DYMOND

<Dymond> HEY EVERYBODY!

<Da Ice Cream Man> hey Dymond!

<City Ave Diva> WHAT'S UP HOMEGIRL!

<***Mami*Dearest***> ANY FRIEND OF
FUTURE'S IS ALWAYS WELCOME
HERE...WITH OR WITHOUT HIM!!!! LOL!

<Teddy Pinned*Her*Ass*Down> IS THAT
THE ONE YOU INTRODUCED ME TO AT
THE PARTY@FUTURE

<Futurama> YEAH@ TED

<Dymond>HEY TEDDY...GOOD 2 C U
AGAIN? TALKED TO CIARA LATELY? LOL!

<MACK Truck> AND SHE COMIIN IN WIT
JOKES...SHE'S GONNA FIT IIN JUST
FINE...LOL!

<Got'em Hatin> SO WHAT DO U DO FOR A
LIVIN TO BE WIT A RECORD EXEC?

<Futurama> DAMN@HATIN'...SHE JUST
GOT HERE...LOL!

<Dymond> ITS COOL@FUTURE... I PLAY
PRO BALL AND I HAVE A MANAGEMENT
COMPANY THANKS TO FUTURE

<Da Ice Cream Man> what team u play 4?@
Dymond

<Dymond> I PLAY FOR THE ATLANTA
DIAMONDS

<Da Ice Cream Man> leave it to future to
bring the enemy up in here

<Futurama> LOL...MY BAD ICE CREAM

<Dymond> I DON'T GET IT

<Da Ice Cream Man> I'm from Michigan

<Dymond> SORRY@ICE CREAM
<Da Ice Cream Man> its cool...see u in the playoffs this year
<Futurama> NOW BACK TO THIS MRZ PINNED DOWN THING...WHAT'S THE DEAL WIT DAT CUZIN?
<Mrz*Pinned*Down> I LIVE IN NC NOW@FUTURE
<Got'em Hatin> I'M STILL MAD AT TEDDY FOR TAKIN MY GIRL AWAY FROM THE 619
<Teddy Pinned*Her*Ass*Down> WELL NOW SHE'S REPPIN THAT 910
<Mrz*Pinned*Down> I'M STILL 619 TO THE HEART@HATIN
<Da Ice Cream Man> what position do u play@dymond
Mr.SexxyB-Baller has entered the room
<Thyk2Def>SEXXXXXY!!!!!!!!!1
<Dymond> POINT GUARD@ICE CREAM
<Futurama>ICE CREAM WILL U PLZ STOP HITTIN ON MY GIRL
<Da Ice Cream Man> sorry future...lol
<Mr.SexxyB-Baller> WHAT'S UP E'RYBODY...WHO'S A POINT GUARD
<Dymond> LEAVE ICE CREAM ALONE@FUTURE
<Teddy Pinned*Her*Ass*Down> SEE WHAT HAPPENS WHEN U INTRODUCE YA GIRL TO YA FAMILY...SHE TURNS ON U...LOL
<Futurama> U C DAT CUZIN...LOL
<Dymond> I AM@SEXXY
<Teddy Pinned*Her*Ass*Down> ALL THE NAMES TO CHOOSE FROM AND SHE

CALLS HIM SEXXY...FUTURE U BETTA WATCH YA GIRL

<Da Ice Cream Man> what college did u play for@dymond

<Thyk2Def> ICE CREAM SHE DID NOT COME IN HERE TO BE INTERVIEWED

<Futurama> HOW LONG U BEEN IN NC@CHOCO

<Dymond> MIND YA BUSINESS TEDDY

<Mr.SexxyB-Baller> DAMN TEDDY...SHE KNOW U ALREADY...LOL

<Mrz*Pinned*Down> I BEEN OUT HERE FOR ALMOST A MONTH

<Teddy Pinned*Her*Ass*Down> AIN'T DAT A BITCH...LOL

<Futurama> HOW U LIKIN DA SIMPLE LIFE

<Got'em Hatin> SHE HATES IT AND WANTS TO COME BACK

<Mrz*Pinned*Down> I LOVE IT...NO MORE TRAFFIC...I DON'T HAVE TO LEAVE HOME 2 HOURS EARLY TO GET TO WORK 5 MINS LATE

<Mr.SexxyB-Baller> WHERE U WORKIN AT@CHOCO

<Teddy Pinned*Her*Ass*Down> AT MY HOUSE...LOL

<Mrz*Pinned*Down> TEDDY...SHEEEDUP!

<Futurama> LOOKS LIKE YA WISH CAME TRUE CUZIN!

<Mrz*Pinned*Down> I WORK ON FORT BRAGG

<Da Ice Cream Man> u never answered my question@dymond

\<Mr.SexxyB-Baller\> U LIVIN WIT TEDDY?

\<Dymond\> I'M SORRY@ ICE CREAM...I PLAYED AT TENNESSEE

\<Mrz*Pinned*Down\> I GOT MY OWN PLACE FOR NOW...I HAVE TO SEE HOW TEDDY'S GONNA ACT NOW THAT I'M IN TOWN

\<Teddy Pinned*Her*Ass*Down\> I TRIED TO GET HER TO STAY WIT ME CUZIN BUT SHE SAID SHE DIDN'T KNOW ME LIKE DAT

SlicK has entered the room

\<Teddy Pinned*Her*Ass*Down\> AWWW SHIT...HIDE DA WEED AND THE WHITE WOMEN... SLICK IS IN DA BUILDIN!

\<MACK Truck\> TEDDY U A FOOL!

\<Dymond\> WHEN U AND YA GIRL COMIN TO VISIT US IN ATLANTA@TEDDY...SINCE U DIDN'T BRING HER TO THE PARTY

\<Teddy Pinned*Her*Ass*Down\> GET YA GIRL@FUTURE

\<Mrz*Pinned*Down\> YEAH TEDDY...WHEN U TAKIN ME TO ATLANTA?

\<Teddy Pinned*Her*Ass*Down\> WHENEVER U WANNA GO MY CHOCOLATE DROP

\<Got'em Hatin\> I THINK I'M GONNA BE SICK!

\<Da Ice Cream Man\> green is not ur color@ got'em hatin...lol!

\<City Ave Diva\>WHAT'S IT LIKE DATIN FUTURE@DYMOND

<Thyk2Def> THAT'S WHAT I WANNA KNOW

<Dymond> FUTURE IS A PERFECT GENTLEMAN, HE'S ROMANTIC AND HE KNOWS HOW TO MAKE A WOMAN FEEL LIKE A WOMAN...IF U KNOW WHAT I MEAN LADIES!!!! LOL!

<Got'em Hatin> HEEEEEEEEYYYYYYYY!!!!!!!!!

<City Ave Diva> I'VE KNOWN FUTURE THE LONGEST AND LET ME TELL U GIRL...U GOT A GOOD ONE!

<Futurama> THANX DIVA!

<City Ave Diva> ITS NOT TOO MANY BROTHAS LIKE HIM OUT THERE...U BETTER HOLD ON TO HIM

<Dymond> U AINT GOTTA WORRY BOUT DAT@DIVA

<Teddy Pinned*Her*Ass*Down> SOUNDS LIKE SOMEBODY GOT SOMEBODY ON LOCK DOWN....CLINK! CLINK! LOL!

<Thyk2Def> LOL!

<Futurama> LOOK WHO TALKIN...SOUNDS LIKE DA POT CALLIN DA KETTLE BLACK IF U ASK ME

<Da Ice Cream Man> he got u on that one@teddy

<Got'em Hatin> EVERYBODY KNOW MY GIRL RUN DAT SHIT

<Teddy Pinned*Her*Ass*Down> FOR FEAR OF HAVIN MY SEXUAL PRIVLEDGES CUT OFF I CHOOSE NOT TO COMMENT ON THAT

<Mrz*Pinned*Down> DON'T LET TEDDY FOOL Y'ALL...HE HAS YET TO TASTE THIS CHOCOLATE GOODNESS!

<Futurama> WOW!

<Dymond> LOL!

<Thyk2Def> AND Y'ALL DON'T LET CHOCO FOOL U INTO THINKIN TEDDY AIN'T BEATIN HER BACK OUT...NOT ONLY DOES HER NAME SAY IT BUT WHAT WOMAN MOVES FROM COAST TO COAST FOR A NIGGA SHE MET ON THE INTERNET?

<Teddy Pinned*Her*Ass*Down> I'M GLAD SOMEBODY ELSE KNOWS THAT!

<Mrz*Pinned*Down>******PLEADIN' DA FIF*********

<Dymond> WHAT MADE U MOVE FROM CALI TO NC@PINNED DOWN

<Teddy Pinned*Her*Ass*Down> DO U HAVE TO ASK? LOL!

<Got'em Hatin> I KNOW THE ANSWER TO THAT QUESTION

<Thyk2Def>WE ALL KNOW THE ANSWER TO THAT QUESTION

<Mrz*Pinned*Down>WHEN TEDDY SHOWED ME THAT HE REALLY WANTED TO BE WITH ME

<Futurama> HOW'D U DO IT CUZIN

<Teddy Pinned*Her*Ass*Down> I SHOWED UP AT HER DOOR UNANNOUNCED

<MACK Truck> U DIDN'T TELL US ALL THAT@CUZIN

<Thyk2Def> WHAT I WANNA KNOW IS WHAT DID UR MAN SAY?

<Mrz*Pinned*Down> HE WASN'T HOME WHEN TEDDY CAME OVER. I DIDN'T KNOW HE WAS IN TOWN...HE SAID HE NEEDED MY ADDRESS B/C HE WANTED TO SEND ME SOMETHING...AN HOUR LATER HE WAS STANDING AT MY FRONT DOOR WITH A DOZEN PINK ROSES

<City Ave Diva> AWWWWW....HOW SWEET!

<Mr.SexxyB-Baller> THAT'S SOME PIMP SHIT RIGHT THERE CUZIN TED!

<Thyk2Def> WHEN DID U TELL YA MAN U WERE MOVIN TO NC?

<Mrz*Pinned*Down> THAT NIGHT

<Thyk2Def> WOW!

<Da Ice Cream Man> that damn teddy!

<Mrz*Pinned*Down> TEDDY TOOK ME OUT THAT NIGHT AND WHEN WE GOT BACK HE WAS HOME. I CAME IN WITH TEDDY AND TOLD HIM THAT I HAD FOUND A REAL MAN THAT WAS GOING TO TREAT ME LIKE A REAL MAN IS SUPPOSED TO TREAT A LADY AND THAT I WAS MOVING TO NC

<Dymond> DID HE KNOW U MET TEDDY ONLINE?

<Teddy Pinned*Her*Ass*Down> HE KNEW WHO I WAS

<Futurama> HOW DID THAT HAPPEN?

<Mrz*Pinned*Down>I FORGOT TO LOG OUT ONE DAY AND HE LOOKED

THROUGH HER MESSAGES AND SAW
EVERYTHING
<Thyk2Def> WHAT DID HE SAY?
<Mrz*Pinned*Down> THERE WASN'T
MUCH HE COULD SAY…MY MIND WAS
MADE UP AFTER HE INVADED MY
PRIVACY
<Da Ice Cream Man> my mama always told
me to be careful when u go lookin for
something….u just might find it
<Got'em Hatin> I CAN TESTIFY TO THAT
ONE!
<City Ave Diva> DID HE CRY?
<MACK Truck> WHAT IS IT ABOUT
WOMEN AND A MAN CRYIN?
<Mrz*Pinned*Down> NOT THAT NIGHT
BUT HE DID THE DAY I LEFT
<Da Ice Cream Man> teddy is a
homewrecker!!!!!
<MACK Truck> THAT'S MY CUZIN!
<Mrz*Pinned*Down> NAH ICE
CREAM….TEDDY IS A
HOMEMAKER…SINCE I'VE BEEN IN
FAYETTEVILLE… HE'S MADE ME FEEL
LIKE THIS IS WHERE I'VE ALWAYS
BELONGED
<City Ave Diva> WHERE DID U AND
FUTURE MEET@ DYMOND
<Dymond> I MET HIM ONLINE BUT I SAW
HIM A COUPLE TIMES BEFORE WE
ACTUALLY MET
<Futurama> 4 REAL? U NEVER TOLD ME
THAT

<Dymond> WELL ACTUALLY I SAW U FIRST AT CLUB BLAZE AT LUDACRIS'S PARTY AND RIGHT AFTER WE MET ONLINE I SAW U IN LENNOX

<Da Ice Cream Man> sounds like a stalker to me...lol!

<Thyk2Def> SHUT UP@ICE CREAM

<Da Ice Cream Man>***HANGING HEAD*** yes ma'am

<Futurama> U LEARN SOMETHIN NEW EVERY DAY...LOL...WELL Y'ALL I GOTTA BE OUT...I GOT SHIT TO DO IN DA MORNIN

<Dymond> I GUESS THAT'S MY CUE TOO...NICE MEETING EVERYONE...EVEN U TEDDY!

<Da Ice Cream Man> nite Dymond...lata Future!

<Teddy Pinned*Her*Ass*Down> DAMN CUZIN...U NEED TO START SIGNIN COMEDIANS CUZ YA GIRL IS HILARIOUS...LOL

<Dymond> AND I LUV U 2 TEDDY!

<Futurama> SPEAKING OF SIGNING....BE ON THE LOOK OUT FOR MY NEWEST GROUP...PURRFECTION...THEY ARE DYMONDS CLIENTS

<City Ave Diva> AIN'T NUTTIN LIKE A WOMAN AND HER MAN GETTING DAT MONEY 2GETHER...YOU GO GIRL!!!!!!

<Dymond> LOL! NITE EVERYBODY!

Ivy and Natalie logged out together. Before Natalie had a chance to make it to her bedroom, her cell phone was ringing.

"Have a good time?" Ivy asked.

"Oh my God! Those people are so fun!"

"I knew you'd like'em."

"I have not laughed that hard in ages. I didn't know Teddy was that funny."

"Teddy's real cool people. I hope everything works out for him and Choco."

"I can't believe she moved all the way from California to North Carolina to be with a man she met on the internet."

"That does seem a little crazy but when you're diggin' somebody, you do crazy things."

"Like blindfold a woman and take her into the middle of no where and seduce her?"

"Exactly," Ivy laughed. "Well, Mami. I just wanted to say goodnight. We got a lot to do tomorrow."

"I know. You have a good night and I'll talk to you mañana."

"Nite, Dymond."

"Sweet Dreams...Futurama."

Chapter 20

Friday morning all the necessary contracts were signed and Purrfection were official members of the Future Records family. Everything was in place and it was now a race to the summer. Iverson prepared himself for any and every thing that could possibly happen. The first two weeks started off fine. The girls came in to record. Iverson interacted with them just as he did any group. Cee Cee behaved like a perfect angel but Natalie still had her eyes on her. It was only natural. In a relationship, if you don't have trust you don't have anything.

One late Wednesday evening found Iverson, TyQuan, and the girls in the studio listening to tracks trying to find which one they wanted to use for their first single. The quintet sifted through tons of tracks. They were passed the forty or fiftieth track before TyQuan remembered that he had a couple of track CDs on his desk in his office.

"Damn," TyQuan interrupted "I got some more tracks on my desk. I'll be right back."

T got up and walked out of the studio leaving Ivy and the girls. At the same time, Katina's cell phone rang and Rolanda excused herself to go to the bathroom. Iverson continued to scroll through tracks as Cee Cee sat on the table behind him.

"Am I behaving myself good enough for you?" Cee Cee asked.

"To be honest, I had my doubts but things have gone good, so far."

"I told you Ivy, all I want to do is sing."

"Can I ask you a question?"

"Why'd you leave me the way you did?"

"I know it wasn't that long ago but I was young and dumb. I didn't realize what I had — like all women do when they lose a good man."

"Then why didn't you just leave? Why'd you have to destroy my crib?"

"Listenin' to my girls. Remember how we used to use songs to describe a certain situation?" Ivy nodded in a positive manner. "The song to describe that situation would be *Chick With No Man*, by *Somethin' For the People*. Every time I turned around, they had somethin' negative to say about our relationship and like an idiot, I felt for it."

"What brought you to your breakin' point?"

"They kept tellin' me that they were seeing you on TV surrounded by all these women. I didn't believe them until I saw you in an interview with Mysterio. Y'all were in a hotel and you were sitting on the bed with some Spanish chick rubbin' all over you."

"Are you serious? You know that was just for show."

"I knew it but I had my homegirls in my ear telling me I told you so. I guess I just lost it. I know your people had a few choice words about you signing us."

"Surprisingly, no. The only person that knew about us was T. Natalie didn't know until I told here. I told her about you the night before I saw you for the first time."

"She seems like she's a good girl. I wish you two the best of luck and I mean that. I had my chance and I blew it."

"Thanks. That means a lot to me."

"I'm just happy to have you back in my life even if it is just business. I gotta tell you though, if she ever slips up, I got you."

"Oh really?"

"Yes...really," Cee Cee replied as everybody came back into the studio.

"You two been behavin'?" T-Bizzy clowned as he placed one of the CDs in the CD Rom drive. "These two tracks are from one of Buddah Rhatt's people."

Once the music began to play, the ladies started bobbing their heads to the track. After close analysis, Ivy approved the first track for the album. The second track was hot but with the concept of the album that was chosen, it wasn't going to fit. Ty removed that CD and replaced it with another one. He notified the group that the track was made by Lil' Jon. The track began and was on for about 30 seconds before it got approved.

Now that the track was selected, they began to throw songs back and forth to come up with the first single. TyQuan lifted a single sheet of paper off of a stack of papers. It was a song list. The title of every song that was in the stack was on that sheet. Whenever a title came up that was of interest, somebody read the lyrics to the song. As they were rifling through songs, Cee Cee came up with a good idea.

"I have a suggestion," Cee Cee interrupted. "Since we are a group composed of three different styles and voices, I think we should each get a solo on the album to really showcase our group's talent."

"That's a good idea," Katina remarked.

"Whoever is being showcased, the others will sing back up."

"That's what I call a group," Ivy smiled. "You ladies have the makings of something special. Well ladies, I think its time to call it a night. Take the song list and highlight the songs you want to check out. Each one of you list twenty and we'll compare the lists and see what songs the three of you agree on and we'll take it from there. The first single needs to be decided on by Monday so you can put it together and start working on it by next Thursday or Friday. Natalie will have your itinerary for the next two months finalized by

Monday. Keep in mind that every event has to be executed in a timely manner. We got a lot of work to do in a little bit of time but I think you can do it. If you don't think you can, let me know and we'll wait until after the summer. Y'all have a good night."

"After the summer?" Cee Cee questioned. "That's not even an option. Purrfection will drop this summer."

"Don't talk about it, be about it."

The ladies gathered their belongings and headed out for the evening. TyQuan was going in their direction so he offered to give the ladies a ride. Iverson returned to his office to shut down for the night. After he logged off of his computer, he walked downstairs and out onto the street. He arrived to the parking garage to find that once again, after everybody else was gone, Cee Cee stayed behind.

"What you gettin' ready to do?" Cee Cee asked as she appeared from between a mini van and an SUV.

"I'm going home. I'm tired as hell."

"Let's go to the Silver Dollar."

"I don't think that's a good idea."

"C'mon Ivy. Nothing says that two friends can't go have a drink. We are friends aren't we?

"Well..."

"And don't try to tell me you don't go out with your artists because I know better than that."

"I don't think Natalie will be cool with that."

"Who says Natalie has to know?"

"See, its shit like that…"

"I'm just kidding Iverson, damn. Just one drink. I'll behave. I promise." Iverson paused for a minute and gave it some thought.

"One drink, that's it."

Candace climbed into the passenger seat off Iverson's SUV and they were off. Five minutes later they arrived at the Silver Dollar Sports Bar. Happy hour was over but it was still crowded. The bar was full so Iverson and Candace took a table in the back of the bar. Their waitress took their drink order and in no time, returned.

"I learned a little bit about the business from you while we were together and I know it takes longer than 3 months to put an album together."

"Not really. We just give ourselves a larger window to work with. Most of the time the work that is done on the album can be wrapped up in three months. This just means that there's no time for bullshit. Y'all gotta be on top of it."

"We got this."

"Okay, we got this."

"I'm serious. We'll have the first single picked out by tomorrow. As far as those individual lists are concerned, that's something that we're gonna do together to cut out all that excess time. When you get twenty songs from us, they'll be songs that we all agree on."

"Sounds like you got it all figured out."

"I have to be honest with you. I wasn't down with joining a group but when Katina and Rolanda approached me talkin' about possibly signing to Future, I jumped at the chance. Now a days, groups don't stay together long. I don't wish nothin' bad on our group but that's just how it is. You know that and I know that. By the time we get to our third album, I'll have established my voice and then I'm going to push for a solo career like Beyonce. I'll still be a part of the group but I've always wanted to do the solo thing."

"Who says you'll make it to your third album?"

"The fact that we have talent says that we'll make it to our third, fourth and fifth album."

"I like that," Ivy smiled.

He raised his glass to propose a toast.

"To longevity."

"To longevity," Candace replied as she touched her glass to Iverson's.

"Besides, I heard ya girl, Legacy. She can't touch me."

"I don't know. Her first album went multi-platinum. Do you think Purrfection has what it takes to sell more than 3.5 million?"

"If you promote us the right way, we can sell close to a million, if not a million in our first couple of weeks. Legacy only sold 364,000 in her first two weeks."

"You remembered."

"I also remembered how happy and excited you were when she went platinum the first time. Your passion for what you do is what has always attracted me to you."

"So money had nothing to do with it?"

"Money? That was the last thing on my mind when I met you. When I met you, I had just broke up with Julius Peppers."

"Julius Peppers from the Carolina Panthers?"

"I met Julius at a Models and Bottles party in Charlotte. We hit it off and dated for about 9 months before I got tired of being the girlfriend of a NFL player. I didn't even like football. When I met you on Ebony World, I had just moved back to Miami. At the time I was trying to get my modeling career on track."

"Why didn't you tell me about you and Julius Peppers while we were together?"

"I didn't think it was important. I didn't want you to think I was one of those chicks that ran around chasin' athletes and entertainers."

"Been there and done that."

"I never asked you but what attracted you to me?"

"The fact that you remind me a lot of Aaliyah."

"Really?" Candace inquired sipping her drink. "How so?"

"Everything about you reminded me of her. The way you looked, your style and your whole demeanor."

"Why am I just finding this now?"

"You never asked until now."

"Good answer."

Candace put her drink down and placed her hand on top of Iverson's.

"Since we're being so honest tonight, I have to tell you that out of all the relationships I've been in, nobody treated me the way you did. You always treated me like a lady and I've been beating myself up every since I did what I did."

Sliding his hand from under Cee Cee's, "You live and you learn. Some people just have to learn the hard way."

"Believe me, I know." Candace sat back and stared at Iverson for about two minutes without saying a word.

"Did you miss me?"

"I'd be lying if I said that I didn't. For two months, I waited for you to come home or call but you didn't. Eventually I started dating again. The first couple of females didn't work out because I wasn't over you but as more time passed, it got easier."

"You're telling me that if I would've come back within the first few months, you woulda took me back."

"I'm not saying that I would have or wouldn't have. All I know is that your chances were greater in those first few months."

"You have no idea how bad I wanted to come home but I thought the damage was done. I really crossed the line with what I did."

"That you did but I felt that what we had was far more precious to me than anything material that I owned. I just wanted you."

"It's funny how things come out after the fact."

"Life's a trip that way."

"At least we can still be friends. Can't we?"

"I don't have a problem with it as long as you respect my relationship with Natalie."

"Fair enough." Candace raised her half empty glass. "To friendship."

"To friendship."

Iverson touched his glass to hers and then finished his drink.

"I'm glad we had a chance to sit and talk."

"Looks like my one drink is finished. You sure we don't have time for one more?"

"What the hell. I don't have anything to do."

Iverson ordered another round of drinks for him and Candace. The more they drank the more they talked about their past relationship. As they talked, Iverson realized that they had a hellavah lot more good times than bad times. In fact, the only bad time they had was when Candace left him while he was out of the country. The conversation also reminded Candace of how perfect their relationship was until she got caught up in what her no-man-having-ass friends were saying. Time slipped away and before long it was ten o'clock.

"Wow!" Ivy exclaimed looking at his Jacob.

"It's gettin' late."

"Ten o'clock is not late," Candace replied looking at her watch.

"We used to kick it into the wee hours."

"Just like you said, we used to kick it into the wee hours. I don't hang out like that no more."

"Just a little while longer," Candace whined. "We're having so much fun."

"I'd love to but I gotta get home."

The alcohol began to toy with Ivy's feelings and emotions. To keep himself out of trouble, he decided that ending the evening was the best thing to do. He paid the tab and the two of them left the bar and headed back to the office. Iverson turned down the volume on the radio as they pulled into the parking garage.

"Which one is yours?" Ivy asked as he slowed down.

"The black Mercedes."

"I guess I know what somebody did with some of her advance money."

"Not even. Julius bought me that for my birthday."

"I thought y'all broke up?"

"Right before we met, I went back to Charltotte. We tried to give another shot but things just weren't the same. I gave up and went back to Miami."

"I feel bad. All I bought you for your birthday was a motorcycle."

"Speaking of which, do you still have it?"

"It's still in my garage."

"Can I have it back?"

"I don't know. I have to see how you act." Iverson laughed.

"You can't do nothin' with a pink bike."

"I'll make you a deal..."

"Here we go. You and your freakin' deals. Why is it that when somebody asks you for something, you can't just give it to them? You have to make a deal."

"You can't get somethin' for nothin' these days but if Purrfection releases their album on time, you can have it back."

"What if something happens beyond our control?"

"I'll take it into consideration. Do we have a deal?"

Iverson reached his hand out to shake Cee Cee's but instead of extending her hand she pushed her lips to his.

"Come on now!" Iverson exclaimed as he pushed her off of him. "See what I mean!"

"I'm sorry," Candace replied with a grin on her face.

"It won't happen again."

"I'm serious. Things like that can ruin what we're trying to do. Don't make me regret my decision."

"Ok, Ivy. I get it! Damn!" Candace grabbed her purse and opened the door to hop out. "It's just business."

Candace slammed the door, jumped in her car and sped out of the parking deck. Iverson shook his head as he pulled off and headed home. The night's events let him know that he couldn't just be friends with Candace. It was going to cause problems — especially when alcohol was involved. In less than fifteen minutes, Iverson was turning into his driveway. The alcohol finally crept up on him and fatigue started to set in. He took a shower and crawled in bed. Just as he was about to doze off, a tone alerting him that he had a text message interrupted his drifting.

Ivy,

Just wanted 2 say good night and let u know I was thinkin bout u. I know you had a long day cuz mine was long too. We need 2 get up b4 sunday 2 go over the final itinerary. Call me sum time 2morrow. Nite Nite! Sweet Dreams! ttyl

Dymond4eva

The weeks end found Iverson at his normal place — sitting at his desk in his downtown office. Iverson instructed Michelle to have T-Bizzy bring him his draft of the itinerary. Ten minutes later, TyQuan walked into Ivy's office. He placed the papers on his desk and took his seat on the leather sofa.

"What happened Wednesday night?" TyQuan asked as Ivy flipped through the pages.
"Excuse me?" Ivy paused his reading.
"When I left, I only left with two girls. Cee Cee stayed behind. I paid it no mind because I knew she had her own car. I had to come back to pick up my laptop and I saw your Truck parked at the Dollar."
"Me and Cee Cee went out and had drink."
"Don't do it, bruh. It's a set up."
"A set up?"
"She's tryna work her way back in."

"Stop trippin'. It's nothin' like that."

"Does Diamond know you had drinks with her?"

"No and that's how I intend to keep it."

"And you say I'm trippin'."

"I appreciate what you're trying to do but I got this."

"Aiight. Do ya thing."

"Seriously, I got this. I just had a few things that I wanted to talk to her about. Nothin' more, nothing less."

"Just be careful."

It may seem redundant but there is something serious about curiosity. Think about it like this: the majority of horror movies start off with what? Curiosity. The movie begins with a guy and a girl — they're usually white...lol! — wandering along, minding their own business. Take the movie *Jeepers Creepers,* for example. The couple was driving down a country road and they look over and see someone dumping something that looked like a body into a tube. There would not have been a movie if it were not for what? Curiosity. Instead of paying it no mind, they decide to turn around and investigate. The next thing you know, the plot for a horror movie begins but it all started with what? Curiosity.

The part of it you don't see is the reality of what curiosity causes. The young couple could have had the world in front of them. He could have gone on to be a renowned surgeon and she could have discovered the cure for the common cold. The point that is trying to be conveyed is the fact that they seemed to have nice lives before they decided to turn around and see what was being dumped into that tube on that day. That day, curiosity changed their lives. Not saying that all curiosity is bad, it's just that some things just need to be left alone.

Mid-afternoon in Atlanta was live as always. Ryan Cameron was rockin' the box on V-103, along with the beautiful Elle Duncan. Natalie tore through traffic on her way home from a team workout. Rush hour hadn't begun but one false move on any given expressway in the ATL could cause maximum chaos. Natalie was laughing at something Ryan Cameron was saying when her cell phone rang.

Still laughing as she answered the phone, "Hello?"

"What are you laughin' so hard at?" Alicia asked.

"Girl, I'm laughin' at Ryan Cameron's crazy ass."

"That's the only thing I hate about working in the office, I have to be careful what I listen to at work. Them white folks'll think I'm crazy if I just start laughin' in my office."

"Them people already know you silly as hell."

"That's what you think. When I'm at the office, I have to be Ms. Corporate America. They ain't ready for the Alicia you know." Natalie laughed.

"Anyway, where you headed?"

"I just left a team workout. I'm on my way home to shower and relax."

"No Iverson tonight?"

"He's coming by later on tonight so we can finalize the itinerary. We gotta get things moving."

"You're really taking this well."

"Taking what well?"

"This whole Iverson and Cee Cee thing."

"I am not worried about Iverson and Cee Cee. We've talked about it and I trust my man."

"I hope he knows what he has. Girls like you don't come around often. Let you had been Shaquan. As soon as Ivy woulda told you him and Cee Cee used to be together you probably woulda been ready to fight."

"I admit when I first found out I was a little skeptical because I know how these lil' young girls like to play games."

"I don't think I woulda been able to do it."

"This is a business venture. A stranger than usual business venture but a business venture none the less. You mean to tell me if you had the chance to make money with a client that just so happened to have dated your husband, you wouldn't do it?"

"It's not enough money in this world to move on something that could potentially cause problems between me and my husband."

Natalie was silent for a moment.

"That's just me. I'm jealous as hell when it comes to Dré. I've always been that way about him even when we were just friends. We go back. Thing is, Dré knows that and I don't think he would want to put me in that situation."

"Do you think I'm making a mistake?"

"Just because I said I probably couldn't do it doesn't mean you can't. To be honest, if Dré had my back like Ivy has yours, there's a chance that I would take a risk but I'd keep my eyes wide open. When I say wide, don't go lookin for that petty stuff cuz you'll turn nothin' into somethin' if you do that."

"What would you consider petty?"

"Things like her paying a lot of attention to Iverson, times when it might just be the two of them in the studio alone or something like the two of them sleeping together. You know...petty stuff."

"WHAT!"

Busting into laughter, "I was just jokin' about that one."

"You almost made me run off the road."

Alicia continued to laugh.

"But you never answered my question."

"No, I don't think you're making a mistake. I've been checkin' y'all out and from what I've seen and what you've told me, you have nothing to worry about. When it comes to Iverson, you're the only Diamond he's concerned about."

"Hold on for a minute."

Natalie pulled the phone away from her ear to see who was calling.

"That's Iverson."

"Speak of the devil."

"I'll call you later."

"Bye, girl."

"Bye."

Natalie pressed a button and switch lines.

"Hey boo! I just talked you up."

"For real? Wit' who?"

"That was Alicia."

"Oh okay...that's what's up. What you up to?"

"On my way home to take a shower and relax before you come over tonight."

"Relax? What you been doin'?"

"We started our workouts this week. Remember?"

"That's right. My bad."

"I know you got a lot goin' on so I forgive you."

"You're too good to me. I might have to give you a massage for that."

"Don't threaten me wit a good time."

"Stop bein' nasty," Ivy laughed.

"What you gettin' into for the rest of the afternoon?"

"I'll be here until later on this evening. KD has the flu so I have to man the studio today."

"Can't T do it?"

"T's been handling business for Purrfection all day."

"He's excited about this, isn't he?"

"Excited is not the word. This dude is like a kid in a candy store. You would think he's workin wit' Beyonce or somebody."

"Hard work is its own reward. Besides, you never know. One of those girls could turn out to be as big as Beyonce."

"Let's hope so. To be honest, I really don't know how to act. T's actually working and I don't feel like I'm runnin' this label by myself. He shoulda met Alexa along time ago."

"Looks like he's finally found a girl to whip him into shape."

"And I'm loving every minute of it."

"Well babe, I'm home. Call me later."

"Ok Mami."

"Behave yourself and have a productive rest of the day."

"Don't I always?"

"Bye boo."

"Later babe."

There wasn't an artist due to work in the studio until five so Iverson found himself with a little free time on his hands. Because of everything that had been going on, Ivy had neglected to check his emails and messages over the past week. When he logged into his messenger he found that he had 65 messages from the FutureRecords.com, 12 from friends and family and one from EbonyWorld.com. Since he and Natalie got together, Iverson didn't go onto the site much. He paid it no mind, at first and continued checking his other emails. Once Iverson sifted through and read all the messages that needed to be read and deleted all the ones that needed to be deleted, he saved the message from Ebony World for last. The message read:

Subject: Only If U Really Wanna Know!

Ivy,

Its been a minute since we were last in touch and I've been thinking about you. If you really wanna know who I am, you can catch me at *just4kickz.com*. My screen name there is Kandee. It's a video chat site. I think you'll enjoy it. The room that I kick it in with all my friends is run by a chick with the screen name Lil' Big Girl. Its not one of those sex sites so don't worry about that. It's actually entertaining. You'd be surprised by some of the things that go on. It's free to join. I hope to see you there soon.

KandeeGyrl

PS: The best time to come in the chat room is after 10. That's when it starts poppin! Don't be afraid to Cam Up!

Iverson thought that the suspense of his mystery woman was finally over. All he had to do was logon to the website and go to her profile. From the home page, he was lead to a profile page. The page had Kandee's name, her location — which was Atlanta, Ga — a few other particulars such as race, age and interests but no picture. In the box that was supposed to house her picture was the silhouette of a female and the words Discreet Profile. In smaller letters under those two words indicated that only her VIP friends could view her pictures. Just for kicks, no pun intended, Iverson read her *About Me* section.

About Me:

What up, everybody? This is the ATL's sweetest treat blazin through to give Just4kickz.com a couple cavities...lol! I'm one of the coolest females you'll ever wanna meet or talk to. I'm not lookin to hook up with anybody but if I just so happen to meet some cool people, we might be able to hook up and kick it locally. You never know. I guess this is where I'm supposed to tell you a little about myself. Honestly, there's too much to put in this little ass box...lol! Anything you wanna know just hit me up in the chat room(Lil' Big Girl's Room) or leave me a message. Oh yeah. Before I forget…**NO PIC, NO LOVE!!!!** Until later….Be Easy!

Rats!!! Foiled again. Iverson began to get a little frustrated with the cat and mouse game KandeeGyrl was playing. Before he knew it, time had flown and it was almost time for him to hit the studio. Iverson laughed to himself as he closed the internet browser.

Ten o'clock met Iverson at Natalie's estate in College Park. The night was clear and the stars danced in the sky as the CEO walked from his car to the front door. Natalie greeted her man with hugs and kisses as she led him to the living room. Iverson and Natalie engaged in idle chatter over a couple of drinks before any mention of business.

Iverson spent the next hour explaining Natalie's duties as a manager to her. By the time business came to a close, Natalie had a blank expression on her face. Ivy assured her that it wasn't as bad as she thought. To ease her mind he said that he would hire an intern from one of the local colleges to be a personal assistant for her. The Purrfection project was a lot of work but between Iverson, TyQuan, Alicia and Natalie, it would get done. When the conversation switched from Natalie's duties to the actual group, Cee Cee's name came up and Iverson felt the need to get something off of his chest.

"Baby," Ivy began as he pulled his flash drive out of the USB port. "I need to tell you something."

"What's up?"

"I don't really know how to say it so I'm going to just come out wit' it."

"Okay."

"The other night, T and I were in the studio with the girls listening to tracks and goin' over songs. After we closed up shop for the night, me and Cee Cee went to the Silver Dollar for a drink. Before you say anything, just let me finish. The only reason I did it was because I needed some answers. Candace left me without a word or a reason then almost two years later she pops back up as an artist. I tried to just let it go but I couldn't. I'm sorry for not telling you sooner."

"Come here," Natalie commanded. Iverson got up from behind the computer, walked over to the chaise, where Natalie was curled up, and sat down. Natalie sat up and wrapped her arms around Iverson.

"I know how some women can be but I'm not an overly jealous female. Remember when you told me that it was all about me? I believe you and I appreciate you being honest with me. At first I had my doubts about the whole situation but after we talked about it, I was fine. I understand that this is a crazy situation for you to deal with and I'm patient. As long as you respect me, I'll be fine."

"I would never do anything to disrespect you."

"I may not know a lot about the industry but since I've been with you, I've learned a lot about Future Records. I know that you guys are a family and you treat your artists better than most labels do. You are my man and I care a lot about you. All you have to do is look me in my eyes and tell me that nothing is going to happen between you and Candace that is going to jeopardize this relationship."

Turning to look Natalie in her eyes, "Nothing is going to happen between me and Candace to jeopardize this relationship. You are my Diamond and at this moment in my life, I couldn't be happier with anybody else."

"That's all I needed to hear."

Natalie looked over Iverson's shoulder to the clock on the wall that displayed 11:45.

"It's almost twelve o'clock. I have to workout in the morning. You stayin' the night or you goin' home?"

"What do you want me to do?"

"I'd like for you to stay."

"Then I guess I'll stay." Natalie and Iverson exchanged lips.

Natalie stood up, grabbed Iverson by the hand and escorted her CEO to the bedroom. After getting undressed, Iverson and Natalie climbed in bed and engaged in pillow talk until they fell asleep. The next morning the two parted ways for the day. Iverson headed home to shower and change. Natalie hopped in the Navigator and went to her team workout. Around eleven o'clock, Iverson fell into the office to get the days activities on the road. Upon arrival, he was shocked to find TyQuan already hard at work. He tried to walk past him, and leave him be, but he just couldn't help himself.

"I think I've died and gone to heaven," Ivy laughed as he leaned into T-Bizzy's office.

"I'm telling you," T-Bizzy began looking up from what he was reading. "Between you and ya girl, we might need to start signing some comedians cuz y'all got mad jokes."

"You know I gotta fuck witcha. But on the real, what it's lookin like for the day?"

"We're supposed to decide on the first single with the girls, Legacy has a photo shoot and we have to be at the Cumberland Mall at 3 o'clock."

"Why do we have to be at the Cumberland Mall?"

"You're kiddin' me, right? We have the model search at 4."

"I thought that was next week."

"Nah, bruh. It's today. Is there a problem?"

"Nah. I got it."

"No doubt."

On the way into his office, Iverson picked up his messages from his secretary. Once settled behind his desk, Ivy turned on his computer and began to read his mail. As soon as the computer booted and all his messengers automatically logged in, he received an email notification. Ivy continued to read his mail and made a few phone calls before he checked his emails. Before he had a chance to read them, he was interrupted by his secretary.

"Ivy," Michelle called via intercom.
"Yes Mami?" Ivy replied.
"You have a visitor."
"Who is it?"
"She says she doesn't wasn't me to tell you because it'll ruin the surprise."
"Send her in." In less than a minute, a very familiar face walked into Iverson's office. "Shelby Cortez."
"Hello, Mr. Davenport."
"What do I owe the pleasure of this visit?"
"I just left a meeting and I was passing by the office and saw you walking in. How you been?"
"I'm good."
"Good? From what I see on BET, MTV and Black Reign, you're doing better than good."
"I've been blessed."

"That's good to hear." There was a moment of awkward silence. "Listen. I stopped by because I wanted to really apologize…"

"That's not necessary," Iverson interrupted.

"Please let me say what I need to say."

"I'm sorry. Please continue."

"I know that nothing I can say or do will take back what I did. It was immature and completely uncalled for. I let my ill feelings towards my ex-husband involve somebody that only tried to be there for me."

"Ex-husband?"

"Calvin divorced me shortly after."

"I'm sorry to hear that."

"I'm not going to take up anymore of your time because I know you're a busy man but I just felt that for my own sanity, I needed to get that off my chest. I hope that you're not too mad at me anymore."

"I'm over that. Life is too short to stress things that we have no control over sometimes. I accept your apology and I hope that things work out for you."

"Well, I guess I'll be going." Shelby got to the door, paused and turned around. "Who's the lucky lady in your life now, if you don't mind me asking?"

"Natalie Simms."

"I kinda figured that. You two look cute together. I hope she knows what she has. Take care, Iverson."

"You too, Shelby."

Just when a person thinks that his love life has beat him to the ground, things start to level off. The sign of a successful relationship to come is manifested when those small curiosities that linger in the back of the mind begin to fade away due to answers and sometimes genuine disregard. For Iverson, his lingering *what if's* diminished. One by one he began to receive closure — from WifeyMaterial, XoticMami and now Unique Pleazures, also known as Cee Cee. Men have the tendency to think that men don't need it because they are supposed to be built mentally to get over past relationships and failed companionships. It is those same unanswered questions that cause people to lose focus on the task at hand. If not careful, one can allow everything they worked so hard to build, to be destroyed.

Chapter 21

Memorial Day had arrived. Iverson and his entire camp were at Centennial Park in Downtown Atlanta to kick off *The Summer of the Future* at their annual *Future Fest*. All of their hard work had paid off. The Lucky 12 Compilation was complete, Legacy's second album was complete, and the first single was climbing up the charts. The Southern Sunz were two weeks away from embarking on their second tour and had three singles ready for the summer — each artist had a solo single ready to fall into rotation as well as one as a group. To top it all off, Purrfection's album was complete and the first single was hitting the radio that night at 6 o'clock on Gregg Street's show.

In the middle of the park was a huge stage surrounded by screaming fans chanting for somebody to hit the stage. Backstage, Iverson stood on top of a speaker crate getting ready to address his camp. As he looked out over his family he saw an array of diverse faces and backgrounds that have all put in the necessary time and efforts to fulfill their dreams. To his right side, as always, was TyQuan and at his left stood the lady in his life. TyQuan motioned for everyone to cease chatter as Iverson readied himself to speak.

"First of all," Ivy began. "I'd like to thank everyone for what you have done to make this all possible. Give it up for yourselves!"

Everyone under the sound of Iverson's voice erupted with cheers and applause.

"This is a historical day for us because today marks the end as well as the beginning. For some of you it marks the end of all the hard work that you have put forth in these past months and for all of you, it marks the beginning of the biggest summer of your careers. As you all know, we signed a group three months ago that were so ready to put an album together they did it in two and a half months just so they could have the opportunity to perform on the same stage with those who have been down with the camp for a while. For those efforts, I'd like to applaud Ms. Kitty, Daddy's Lil' Girl and Unique…Purrfection, ladies and gentlemen!"Once again the group cheered for their newest family members. "As we do every year for those who haven't been with us that long, we decide who performs when by last years sales. The order in which you will be performing goes as follows…The newest members of the camp, Purrfection will open the show. They will be followed by Buddah Rhatt, Face and the rest of Lucky 12. Legacy bats in the third spot and this year's headliners are the Southern Sunz who are only

100,000 units away from the five million mark." Iverson was interrupted by cheers once again. "In the midst of all this madness, I know some of you have seen this young lady to my left around the studio. For those that don't know, this is Purrfection's manager, Natalie Simms of Diamond in da Ruff Management. In addition to being their manager, she is also the number one lady in my life. The big headed high yella lady standing behind her is her business partner, Alicia Marshall."

"That is not nice, Iverson!" Alicia laughed. "Iverson before you go any further I have an announcement to make that concerns the Future family." Iverson stepped down off of the speaker crate and helped Alicia up. "I was going to wait until after the show but I think now is a good time. My husband, André, is an Executive Producer at Black Reign Networks. He has chosen Future Records for a reality show that he has created called *The Opening Act*. The show is their competition for *American Idol*. Unlike Idol, the competition isn't just limited to singers. It is a competition for rappers and comedians as well as singers both solo and group."

"How will the contestants be chosen?" Ivy asked.

"As we speak, my marketing firm is designing a website for people to upload their auditions to. A panel will choose 11 sets of 12 contestants to compete for a shot to open for one of your concerts. Each weekly winner will be placed in a competition the show before the finale. The viewers will then vote on who they think should open for the season finale but the opener will not be revealed until that night."

"What does the overall winner receive?" EL GEE inquired.

"The overall winner will earn a spot as the opening act for the next tour that Future Records puts together. In addition to that, Iverson has extended a possible one album recording contract. In the event that a comedian wins, they get a one hour live stand-up on Black Reign's hit show, the *Dirty South Comedy Showcase*. So on behalf of my husband and Black Reign networks, this should be considered as a reward for all of your hard work. Congrats!"

Alicia stepped down to applause as the fans outside began to get louder and louder.

"Thank you Alicia," Iverson replied as he stepped back onto the crate. "Aiight, y'all. This is it. Today marks the beginning of the *Summer of the Future*. When you hit the stage today...I want you to show everybody in Atlanta what Future is all about. Purrfection you're on in ten. If there are no questions...Let's do this!"

The crew dispersed to get prepared to hit the stage. Many artists had rituals that they went through before a performance and others chose to be by themselves to get focused. Natalie and Alicia left the backstage area to take their place on the VIP platform which was next to the stage.

Iverson and TyQuan stood on the two different sides of the stage but off the stage far enough to remain unseen. In the middle of the stage, was a platform where the DJ was set up. Upon command from Iverson, the DJ dropped the instrumental to one of Buddah Rhatt's first singles and the crowd went ballistic. From backstage Iverson shouted into the microphone, "A-T-L! Make some noise!" as he and TyQuan made their appearance on stage. Along with Iverson and T-Bizzy were four beautiful young ladies wearing short black shorts, and black T-shirts, that were tied in a knot between the breasts, with Future Records printed in white letters on the front. The ladies threw T-shirts and hats into the crowd as Iverson and T-Bizzy continued to get the crowd ready for the show.

After about 10 minutes of whipping the crown into a frenzy, Iverson introduced Purrfection. Purrfection hit the stage. To represent the City of Atlanta, the ladies wore renditions of each of Atlanta's professional sports team's jerseys. Miss Kitty represented the Falcons by wearing a Michael Vick jersey dress, Daddy's Lil girl payed homage to the Hawks with her Josh Smith jersey dress and

Unique hit the stage wearing a Natalie Simms, Atlanta Diamonds Jersey dress—how ironic. Once Purrfection began their first song, Iverson made his way to the VIP platform to check on Natalie.

"Looks like you got a new fan," he laughed.

"I think it's kinda flattering."

"After they finish performing, we can walk around and enjoy the festival until the Sunz get ready to perform later on tonight."

"I'll be right here. Just come and get me when you're ready."

"Before I forget," Iverson turned to Alicia. "Tell your husband I said thank you."

"He's on his way. You can thank him for yourself."

"That's what's up. I'll see y'all later." Iverson gave Natalie a kiss and returned to the stage with Purrfection and T-Bizzy. Once Purrfection had performed, Ivy and Natalie accompanied Alicia to meet André at the front. Alicia ran to greet her husband like a high school girl meeting her boyfriend at the fair. After they exchanged hugs and kisses, Alicia brought André over to meet Iverson.

"This is the infamous Iverson Davenport," Alicia introduced.

"Pleasure to finally meet you," André began as he shook Ivy's hand. "My sister talks about you all the time."

"I hope you don't hold that against me," Iverson joshed.

"Trust me, I don't believe a word she says."

"Hey, man…I want to thank you personally for choosing us to do the show with."

"You deserve it. Future has done a lot for the entertainment industry as well as the community. It's the least we could do. You exemplify what hard work can produce."

"Whenever you're ready to sit down and go over the particulars, let me know."

"No doubt. You should be hearing from us in about a week or two."

"Okay boys," Natalie interrupted. "We're here to have fun. We can talk about business later."

The two couples started their enjoyment at the Tilt-A-Whirl. From there they rode the Gravitron, the Zipper, and the Scrambler. They tried to ride the swings but André's fear of heights put a halt to that one. Through the park they wandered and frolicked like high school kids. As they walked, Iverson passed a few familiar faces. The first person Ivy saw was Shayla — also known as 2much4U — followed by Shelby Cortez and her new man. It must have been a day for past experiences because Natalie had a run in with a familiar face. Iverson and André left the ladies sitting at a picnic table as they walked over to a vendor to get ice cream. Out of no where, Desmond walks up to the table. Judging by the way he was wobbling, he was intoxicated.

"Well if it ain't Miss Natalie Simms," Desmond spoke as he approached.

"Hello Desmond."

"Not the reception I expected but I'll take it. How've you been?"

"What do you want, Desmond?"

"I want you to stop acting like you don't know me and talk to me for a second."

"Desmond you're drunk. I have nothin' to say to you."

As he reached for Natalie's arm, "Why you ackin' like dis…"

"Desmond she asked you to leave her alone," Alicia interrupted.

Iverson and André traded jokes as they turned to make their way back to the girls. Iverson was the first to notice the male figure that looked to be harassing their companions. As they neared the women, André recognized him and informed Iverson of who he was. The men were about ten feet away from the girls when Desmond pushed himself on Natalie and pinned her down to the picnic table. Iverson dropped the two ice cream cones he was carrying and ran to Natalie's rescue. Forceful but careful, Iverson grabbed Desmond by the back of his shirt and slung him to the ground.

"What the fuck is wrong with you?" Iverson barked as he made a motion to stomp Desmond.

"Ivy no!" Natalie screamed as she wrapped Iverson up from behind. "He's not worth it!"

"Who is this clown?" Security noticed the altercation and made their way towards it.

"This is my ex I was telling you about."

"You just don't quit, do you?" André laughed. "Hasn't this happened before?"

"Fuck you, nigga!" Desmond replied as he fell back to the ground after his attempt to stand had failed.

"Is there are problem here?" One of the officers asked as they stood between Iverson and Desmond, whom was still on the ground.

"Yes, Officer. I'm Iverson Davenport and I put this event together. I would appreciate it if you would remove this clown from the premises."

The officer asked for Iverson's ID and used his radio to confirm his position. Once the requests were confirmed, the officers helped Desmond up and escorted him away.

"You alright?" Iverson asked as Natalie walked around him.

"I'm cool."

"Ya' boy was about two seconds away from havin' front row seats to a stompfest."

"I know baby but he's not worth the effort."

"Maybe not but I don't take too kindly to strange men puttin' they hands on you."

"I had to do the same thing to Money awhile back," André interjected. "He's the type of dude that can't hold his liquor and it winds up gettin' em in trouble."

"He's done this before?" Ivy inquired.

"Last summer we had a cook out for my birthday," Dré began. "Homeboy had one too many and started actin' ill towards my sis. I was gettin' ready to tune his ass up but Nat wouldn't let me do it."

"Desmond might act like he's crazy but he ain't stupid."

"Same thing a friend of mine said a week before she was found dead in her apartment. Her boyfriend was the same type dude."

"It's all over now," Natalie exhaled. "Can we please go back to enjoying the festival?"

"What time is it?" Iverson asked as he reached for his cell phone.

"Almost 4 o'clock," Natalie answered. "Why? What's up?"

"I gotta get back to the stage. We have to announce the winners of the contest."

"What contest?" Natalie inquired.

"As people came in, they entered in a drawing to win a night on the town with the Future artist of their choice."

"Damn right!" André stated as he pulled out his ticket stub.

"Sir!" Alicia scolded. "You did not enter that drawing."

Putting his ticket back in his pocket, "That's right. I did not enter that drawing."

The four laughed as they made their way back to the stage. As they neared, Iverson noticed that there was no one on the stage. He picked up the pace until he was backstage. When he got to there, he found a huge altercation involving the entire Lucky Twelve camp and a couple of other guys. T-Bizzy, ATP and EL GEE stood as a wall between the men that were trying to get at each other.

"What now?" Iverson asked himself as he pushed his way through the crowd. "Yo! Yo! Yo! Everybody chill the fuck out!" All members of the Future Records family calmed down and began to back away from the confrontation. "I leave for an hour and I come back to this. T...what happened?"

"Rhatt and Lucky 12 were on stage and they started pullin' girls up..."

"That's when this bitch ass nigga jumped on stage," Buddah Rhatt roared.

"Who the fuck you think you talkin' to like that?" the guy that had jumped on stage replied as he tried to push through TyQuan the other guys.

"Rhatt...chill out. Please? T go ahead."

"One of the girls started dancin' wit Rhatt and that's when dude jumped on the stage and started pullin' her away. Face tried to stop the dude from pullin on ol' girl the way he was and he pushed Face. That's when EL GEE and ATP ran out on stage to help me get the two of them back stage so we could keep the show rollin'. That's when the other three dudes jumped on stage."

"We was just makin sure nuttin' happened to our boy," one of the other guys exclaimed.

"Where was security when all this was happening?"

"If I knew, I would tell you."

"Alright, y'all. Let's break this up and get this show back on the road."

The mob dispersed and Ivy regained control of the situation. T-Bizzy went out on stage and apologized to the crowd as Lucky 12 readied themselves to finish their performance. The rest of the night went smooth and before long, *Future Fest* had come to a close. Iverson and Natalie were on Peachtree headed to Iverson's office to drop off some things as well as return Natalie to her truck.

"Was this a crazy day or what?" Ivy laughed as he shifted his car into Park. "In all my years of doin Future Fest, this has by far had got to be the craziest one."

"It was still fun…crazy yes…but fun none the less."

"I hope this is no indication of what the summer holds. If it is, I'm stayin in the house."

"I feel you on that one," Natalie laughed and then paused for a second.

"What's wrong?" Ivy asked as he noticed Natalie's change in expression.

"Do you know what next week is?"

"What?"

"The season starts."

"Already?"

"I knew it was coming but I was hoping I would have a little more time."

"Time for what?"

"Time to prepare."

"You've been practicing almost everyday for the past few months."

"I'm not talking about preparing for basketball. I'm talking about us spending most of the summer apart."

"I've been thinking about that, too."

"This will be my first time away from you for long periods of time."

"These are the lives that we chose to live. We knew it wasn't going to be easy but if we care about each other the way we say we do, we'll be okay."

"You promise?"

"We'll be fine. I was going to wait to tell you but I looked at our stops and the road games that you'll be on and I'll be at about fifteen of your road games." Natalie's eyes lit up and a huge smile spread across her face.

"Are you serious?" Natalie squealed.

"I want to be away from you as less as possible."

"Iverson Shemar Davenport," Natalie lulled as she put both of her hands on his face. "I love you."

"I love you, too." Natalie and Iverson engaged in a deep kiss.

"What are you doing when you get home?" Ivy asked as he wiped his bottom lip.

"It's been a long day so I'll probably just take a shower and chill."

"Okay. I'll probably drop in to check on the fam. You should pop in. They been askin about you."

"I might just do that."

Futurama has entered the room

<Got'em Hatin> TEDDY DON'T JUMP FLY JUST CUZ U GOT MY GIRL WHIPPED!

<Mrz*Pinned*Down> EXCUSE ME??????

<Teddy Pinned*Her*Ass*Down> GIRL STOP! LOL!

<City Ave Diva> HEY FUTURE!! HOW WAS FUTURE FEST?

<Futurama> IT WAS A LOT OF FUN DESPITE THE SMALL ALTERCATIONS

<Optimo Pryme>****GLOCKS OFF SAFETY**** WHO FUCKIN WIT U CUZIN?

<Da Ice Cream Man> ***loading sling shot*** I got ya back too Future!

<Teddy Pinned*Her*Ass*Down> YOU AIN'T GOT NOBODY BACK WIT DEM LITTLE ASS LETTERS...LOL

<Got'em Hatin> WHAT HAPPENED?@FUTURE

<Futurama> DYMOND HAD A RUN IN WIT HER EX AND I ALMOST HAD TO STOMP HIS ASS OUT

<Optimo Pryme> WORD?@CUZIN

<Thyk2Def> DID U GET IN A FIGHT??@FUTURE

<Teddy Pinned*Her*Ass*Down> CATS LIKE FUTURE DON'T FIGHT...

<Da Ice Cream Man> they pay other people to fight for him...lol!

<City Ave Diva> I WAS THINKIN THE SAME THING@ICE CREAM

<Futurama> NAH... SECRUITY HANDLED IT

<Mrz*Pinned*Down> WHERE'S DYMOND@FUTURE

<Teddy Pinned*Her*Ass*Down> TOLD U...LOL!

<MACK Truck> IF U EVER NEED ANOTHA BODYGUARD I GOT U@ CUZIN

<Futurama> SHE MIGHT STOP THROUGH LATER...WE HAD A LONG DAY

<Futurama> GOOD LOOKIN OUT@CUZIN MACK

Krystal Lyte and G Tizzle has entered the room

<Da Ice Cream Man> g tizzle??? Who is that?

G Tizzle has entered the room

<Krystal Lyte and G Tizzle> EVERYBODY I WANT Y'ALL TO MEET MY MAN...G TIZZLE

<Got'em Hatin> HEY TIZZLE

<Optimo Pryme> SUP HOMIE

<City Ave Diva> HEY KRYSTAL! HEY G TIZZLE!

<Futurama> ON TOP OF THE SHIT THAT HAPPENED WIT DYMOND...SOME DUDES JUMPED ON STAGE WHILE MY ARTISTS WERE PERFORMING

<Mrz*Pinned*Down> PLZ TELL ME NUTHIN HAPPENED TO FACE!!!

<MACK Truck> SUP DUDE@TIZZLE

<Futurama> HOW'D U KNOW FACE WAS ON STAGE WHEN IT HAPPENED?

<Teddy Pinned*Her*Ass*Down> WE GOTTA HAVE A LIL TALK ABOUT THIS WHOLE FACE THING@CHOCO

<City Ave Diva> WHAT HAPPENED@FUTURE

<Optimo Pryme> DAMN CUZIN...DO U NEED ME TO HEAD UP UR SECURITY TEAM?

<Futurama> THEY STARTED PULLIN GIRLZ ON STAGE BUT ONE OF THE GIRLS THEY PULLED ON STAGE WAS WITH HER MAN...HE JUMPED ON STAGE AND PUSHED FACE WHILE HE WAS TRYNA BREAK IT UP...TWO OF MY OTHER ARTISTS RAN ON STAGE TO BREAK IT UP WHEN HIS BOYZ JUMPED ON STAGE

<Mrz*Pinned*Down> IS FACE OK?

Dymond has entered the room

<Dymond>HEY EVERYBODY!!!!!

<Futurama> LUCKY FOR US NOBODY GOT HURT

<City Ave Diva> HEY DYMOND...WE WAS JUST TALKIN BOUT U!

<Mrz*Pinned*Down> WHAT'S UP DYMOND!

<Dymond> HEY GIRLS@ CHOCO, DIVA AND HATIN'

<Got'em Hatin> WHAT'S UP DYMOND GIRL!!!!!

<Teddy Pinned*Her*Ass*Down> WHAT NIGGA IN THE ATL GOT MY CUZIN BOUT TO STOMP HIS AZZ?@DYMOND

<Dymond> MY IGNORANT EX BOYFRIEND

<Futurama> I SEE U MADE IT@DYMOND

<Dymond> I TRIED TO LAY DOWN BUT I COULDN'T SLEEP

<Da Ice Cream Man> drink some warm brandy

<City Ave Diva> STOP TRYNA GET PEOPLE DRUNK@ICE CREAM

<Futurama> LOL!

<Dymond> SORRY ICE CREAM...I DON'T DRINK BRANDY

<Teddy Pinned*Her*Ass*Down> THAT'S PROLLY TOO STRONG FOR HER...SHE PROLLY LIKE DEM FRUITY DRINKS

<Futurama> I DON'T KNOW TED...MY GIRL CAN HOLD HER OWN

<Got'em Hatin> TELL'EM GIRL...REAL WOMEN DRINK LIQUOR!!!

<Teddy Pinned*Her*Ass*Down> WHAT U DRINK DYMOND....MALIBU, SMIRNOFFS OR ZIMAS

<Da Ice Cream Man> he said zima...lol!

<MACK Truck> WHAT ABOUT THEM ST IDES SPECIAL BREWS...LOL!

<Dymond> 4 UR INFORMATION MR PINNED HER ASS DOWN AND MR MACK TRUCK...I DRINK HENNESSEY

<Da Ice Cream Man> u took it back wit dat 1@mack

<Optimo Pryme> DAMN FUTURE...SHE'S THE REAL DEAL!!!!

<Futurama> I TOLD U!!

<Teddy Pinned*Her*Ass*Down> I WISH MY GIRL DRANK HEN WIT ME

<Krystal Lyte and G Tizzle> THAT'S MY DRINK TOO GIRL!!!

<Mrz*Pinned*Down> I DID DRINK HENNESSEY WIT U B4@TEDDY

<SoopaFly> ANYTHING WIT ALCOHOL IN IT IS UR DRINK@KRYSTAL

<Da Ice Cream Man> she drinks Hennessey on Monday, Tuesday, her birthday, Jesus birthday...hennessey...and she will take Remy as a back up

<Teddy Pinned*Her*Ass*Down> WHEN DID U COME BACK@SOOPAFLY

<Optimo Pryme> THAT'S THAT KATT WILLIAMS...LOL!

<Dymond> LOL@ICE CREAM

\<SoopaFly\> I LEFT MY NAME PARKED...I JUST GOT BACK

\<Futurama\> WHAT UP SOOPAFLY...WHERE DA WIFE AT?

\<***Mami*Dearest***\> THAT'S WHY PEOPLE HAVE A HARD TIME GETTING IN...IF U ARE NOT IN THE ROOM OR WILL BE GONE FOR LONGER THAN AN HOUR...PLZ LOG OUT

\<Got'em Hatin\> THAT'S RIGHT...MAMI DEAREST HAS SPOKEN

\<Dymond\> TEDDY STILL TREATIN U RIGHT?@CHOCO

Mr.SexxyB-Baller has entered the room

\<City Ave Diva\> SEXXXXXXXXYYYYYYY!!!!!

\<Got'em Hatin\> SEXXYYY!!!!

\<Mrz*Pinned*Down\> SO FAR SO GOOD....HE TRIED TO SHOW HIS ASS THE OTHER NITE BUT I HAD TO CHECK'EM

\<Dymond\> TEDDY R U MISBEHAVIN???

\<Got'em Hatin\> DON'T MAKE ME COME TO NC@TEDDY

\<Teddy Pinned*Her*Ass*Down\> ***HALO HANGIN OVER HEAD*** OF COURSE I AM

\<Mrz*Pinned*Down\> NAH..I'M J/K...TEDDY IS WONDERFUL

\<Dymond\> IF HE GETS OUTTA LINE U TELL ME AND I'LL GIVE HIM A GOOD SWIFT KICK...LOL!

\<Teddy Pinned*Her*Ass*Down\> NOT WIT DEM BIG ASS LEGS...U'LL NEVA KICK ME IN DA ASS...LOL!

\<**Da Ice Cream Man**\> ur boy iz kinda kwiet@Krystal

\<**Futurama**\> WATCH YA MOUTH@CUZIN TED LOL!

\<**Mrz*Pinned*Down**\> OH YEAH@DYMOND...ME AND TEDDY ARE COMIN TO ATLANTA IN JULY FOR HIS BIRTHDAY

\<**Teddy Pinned*Her*Ass*Down**\> U KNOW ITZ ALL LUV CUZIN

\<**Dymond**\> JUST MAKE SURE U LET ME KNOW AHEAD OF TIME...I HOPE U DON'T COME WHILE I'M ON THE ROAD

\<**Teddy Pinned*Her*Ass*Down**\> MY BIRTHDAY IS ON THE 9TH AND THATS ON A SUNDAY SO WE'LL BE IN THAT FRIDAY

\<**Futurama**\> I GOTTA CHECK MY SCHEDULE TOO@CUZIN TED CUZ I MIGHT BE ON THE ROAD TOO?

\<**Thyk2Def**\> DO U KNOW WHEN UR COMIN TO HOUSTON@FUTURE

\<**Optimo Pryme**\> I'M SUPPOSED TO BE IN ATLANTA THAT WEEKEND TOO...ONE OF MY CUZINS IS GETTING MARRIED THAT SATURDAY

\<**Thyk2Def**\> I WANNA GO TO THE WEDDING@OPTIMO

\<**Futurama**\> WE'LL BE IN HOUSTON IN JUNE...I'LL LET U KNOW THE EXACT DATE

\<**Optimo Pryme**\> ALL U HAVE TO DO IS ASK@THYK

\<City Ave Diva\> WHEN IS SOMEBODY COMIN TO PHILLY

\<Futurama\> I KNOW FOR SURE THAT I'LL BE IN PHILLY IN JUNE

\<Thyk2Def\> DON'T B BULLSHITTIN@OPTIMO...I'M SERIOUS

MRZ.SOOPAFLY has entered the room

\<SoopaFly\> WHAT'S UP BOO!!!!

\<MRZ.SOOPAFLY\> HEY BABY!!!

\<Optimo Pryme\> WE'LL TALK ABOUT IT LATER ON TONITE

\<Dymond\> I'M GETTING SLEEPY@FUTURE...I'M GETTING READY TO CALL IT A NIGHT

\<Futurama\> I'M NOT GONNA BE HERE MUCH LONGER MY DAMN SELF

\<Teddy Pinned*Her*Ass*Down\> SEE CHOCO...THAT'S HOW ITS SUPPOSED TO BE...WHEN I LEAVE U LEAVE

\<MACK Truck\> TELL'ER CUZIN

\<Mrz*Pinned*Down\> TEDDY...U HAVE NOT PUT IN ENUFF TIME TO BE TELLIN ME WHEN TO COME AND GO

\<Da Ice Cream Man\> ouch!

\<Got'em Hatin\> GET'EM GIRL

\<Mrz*Pinned*Down\> WHEN U PUT A RING ON THIS FINGER THEN U MIGHT BE ABLE TO TELL ME WHEN TO COME AND GO BUT UNTIL THEN....SHEEEEEED UP!!!!

\<Dymond\> DIDN'T U KNOW THAT WOMEN RULE THE WORLD TEDDY...U'LL LEARN ONE DAY...LOL!

\<Teddy Pinned*Her*Ass*Down\> I NEED SOME COUNCILIN@CUZIN FUTURE

\<Futurama\> SORRY CUZIN...THAT'S NOT MY FIELD...IF U NEED TO DROP AN ALBUM...HOLLA AT YA BOY...LOL

\<City Ave Diva\> LOL

\<Dymond\> NITE E'RYBODY!!!!

\<Mrz*Pinned*Down\> NITE GIRL...SD!

\<MACK Truck\> LATA MRZ FUTURAMA!!!!!

\<City Ave Diva\> G'NITE DYMOND!

\<Dymond\> LOL@MACK...I EXPECT THAT FROM TEDDY BUT NOT U TOO

\<MACK Truck\> U KNOW I SLIDE ONE IN EVERY NOW AND THEN

\<Got'em Hatin\> SO I'VE HEARD...LOL

\<Dymond\> OMG!!!

\<Futurama\> NITE BABYGIRL...I'LL TALK TO U IN THE MORNIN

\<MACK Truck\> AND WHAT IS THAT SUPPOSED 2 MEAN@HATIN

\<Dymond\> NITE MR. DYMOND...LOL

\<Got'em Hatin\> I KNOW HOW U TRUCK DRIVERS R

\<Optimo Pryme\> SAY IT AIN'T SO CUZIN@FUTURE

\<Futurama\> SHE CAN CALL ME WHATEVA SHE WANNA CALL ME AS LONG AS SHE CALL ME...LOL

\<MACK Truck\> NO I DON'T KNOW HOW US TRUCK DRIVERS R...TELL ME

\<Got'em Hatin\> RIDIN AROUND IN YA TRUCK SLINGIN DICK FROM CITY TO CITY...LOL

<Da Ice Cream Man>I guess she does know u@mack...lol
<Mrz*Pinned*Down> LOL
<Futurama> LMAO...AIIGHT Y'ALL...THAT'S MY CUE...MY BABY IS GONE SO I GUESS I'LL BE GONE TOO...BE EASY!!!!!!

People often say that when you go looking for love, you seldom find it. When you least expect it, the right one crosses your path. Natalie and Iverson seemed to be a match made in heaven. They both had lucrative careers and had gone through pure hell before finding each other making them wiser and more understanding to toward the other. Having experienced heartache due to relationships was the best thing that could have happened to them because experience is the best teacher. It's hard to be empathetic of someone's past tribulations if the empathizer has yet to endure a couple of failed relationships.

Never in a million years did Iverson think he would have found a woman like Natalie on the internet. Many frown on internet dating and relationships but if you look at it, meeting someone on the internet is just like meeting someone face to face. The same facades that people put on the internet are the same as the ones people put on when you meet them in person. Some attempt to argue the point of people online not being who they say they are. This is true but still no different from meeting someone face to face. It takes a very open-minded and adventurous person to web date. It's something about getting to know a person you've never met face to face.

For people like Iverson and Natalie, if you look at it, meeting someone from the internet makes it a little easier. With their status and wealth, the web allows them to slowly let people into their world — just like Natalie did Iverson. There is nothing wrong with a little honest deception to see where a person's head is. The one thing people have to remember about the internet is the fact that it is addictive. Even when people feel that they have found the one their heart desires, those innocent occasions when they find themselves "just looking around" can prove to be more than some people can handle and if not careful, it can bite you in the ass.

The next morning Iverson sat in his office looking over the tour schedules listening Legacy's new single. Due to the insanity of the past three months, Iverson didn't have much time to himself. He sat and reflected on all that he had endured to get to his current position. At that moment he realized everything he had accomplished. Through it all he managed to find the woman he had been searching for while making moves to embark on the biggest summer of his career. Life was good. Iverson smiled as he ran across the stars beside the dates that indicated the times he would be in the same city with Natalie. With his eyes locked on the computer screen, he didn't notice T-Bizzy standing in the doorway to his office.

"Damn," TyQuan laughed as he walked into the office and sat down. "I ain't seen you smile like that since The Southern Sunz went platinum."

"What it do, Cuzin?"

"I'm good. What's up wit' you?"

"Sittin' here lookin at these tour dates."

"Can I talk to you about somethin'?"

"What's up?" Ivy asked as he rolled his chair to the left to give his friend his undivided attention.

"I'm a lil' worried about this summer."

"Worried about what?"

"Me and Alexa. You know how life on the road is and you know how I've been in the past."

"I don't understand."

"As long as I'm around Alexa or know that she is just a phone call away, I'm cool."

"I see where this is goin' now. You're scared you're gonna cheat on her."

"This is the first real relationship I've been in, in a hot minute, and I'm actually enjoying it. I still have a hard time fightin' temptation even with Me and Alexa bein' in the same city."

"Bruh...that's all apart of being in a relationship. You get tested on a daily basis."

"And you know as well as I do, I'm not good at tests."

"Answer this for me. Do you love her?"

"We've been together exclusively for about as long as you and Dymond. I care a lot about her but as far as being in love with her, I don't know yet."

"Okay. I got another question. Have you had this conversation with her?"

"Are you crazy? Why you think I'm talkin' to you about it?"

"I think you should talk to her about it. If she cares about you as much as you do her, I'm sure she'll understand."

"Maybe you're right."

"I know I'm right."

"Now let me ask you a question. How are you gonna handle being on the road wit Candace?"

"Wow," Ivy laughed. "Outta all the questions you coulda asked, you ask that one. To be honest with you, I haven't really thought about it."

"I bet Natalie's thinking about it."

"She probably is but I don't think it's bothering her too much."

"I think I'm gonna ask Alexa to marry me."

"If it was bothering her...Excuse me?"

"I said I'm thinking about asking Alexa to marry me."

"Not the M-word. Are you serious?"

"If I don't I might lose her."

"How you figure?"

"Me and you feel the same way about the sanctity of marriage. I know that if Alexa and I are married, I won't cheat on her."

"Do you hear the words that are coming out of your mouth? We leave in two weeks to go on the road. I don't think you have enough time to plan a wedding and Alexa doesn't strike me as the justice of the peace type."

"Then what do I do?"

"Talk to her. Tell her how you really feel."

"You right," T replied as he stood up to leave. "I'm trippin'. I'ma talk to'er."

"Let me know how it goes."

"I'm tellin' you. If she leaves me after we talk, I'm blaming it all on you."

"And that's what I'm expecting. You blame everything else on me."

"You know what…you right." Ivy and T-Bizzy laughed as TyQuan went on his way. Contrary to popular belief, men do talk about things other than sports.

The day moved towards its closing time as the evening approached. Natalie and Alicia had just dropped the girls off and decided to stop off at Spondivots for a bite to eat. The ladies sat at a table in the back of the establishment awaiting the arrival of their server.

"Looks like the moment of truth has finally come," Alicia commented as she examined the specials.

"What are you talking about?" Natalie inquired looking over the top of her menu.

"The beginning of the season."

"Oh...that."

"Don't sit there and act like it's not a big deal."

"It's not."

"I'm ya girl. You ain't gotta lie to me."

"It's just another season. Just like last year."

"It's not just like last year. Last year you didn't have Iverson."

Putting her menu down," I know, girl. I don't know what I'm gonna do. I'm gonna miss him so much."

"Take it from a girl who's had first hand experience in being away from the man she loves, its hell."

"Thanks a lot," Natalie laughed.

"The best advice I can give you is to not dwell on it." Before Natalie had a chance to respond, a short brown-skinned girl approached the table.

"Hello, ladies. My name is Phyllica and I'll be taking care of you tonight."

"Hi, Phyllica," the ladies greeted.

"What can I get you ladies to drink tonight?"

"I'll have a Futurama and my friend will have a Disturbing Da Peace."

"Any appetizers?"

"Do you eat Calamari?" Natalie asked Alicia.

"I never tried it."

"You'll love it. Bring us an order of Calamari."

"Ok. I'll put that Calamari in for you and get your drinks."

"Thank you."

"What in the hell is a Disturbing Da peace?" Alicia inquired.

"That's Luda's drink I told you about."

"Does Ludacris come with it?"

"Keep it up. I'ma tell ya husband."

The ladies laughed and continued to look over the menus trying to decide on dinner. They sat in silence for about three minutes before Alicia hit a touchy subject.

"Can I ask you a serious question?"

"Depends on how serious."

"How do you feel about Ivy being on the road with Cee Cee?"

"I told you. I trust my man. Besides, Iverson's over her."

"But is she over him?"

"Whether she is or not doesn't matter. I trust my man."

"I was just checkin'."

"Where is all of this coming from?"

"The more I'm around Iverson, the more he reminds me of my husband. André is the type that likes to avoid confrontation so he'll allow things to happen that shouldn't happen just to keep the situation cool."

"I don't understand."

"You know how women flirt to see if they can get a bite. Dré used to entertain it because he was a flirt himself. It's that out of sight, out of mind mentality that men have. I'm not saying that Ivy would allow something to happen but something that seems so innocent can be taken the wrong way especially when the two that are flirting have a past."

"I never thought about it like that."

"I'm sorry. I hope that didn't come across the wrong way. I'm just tryna look out for you. Iverson's a good man but its something about Cee Cee that's not sittin well with me."

"How long have you been feelin' like that?"

"I picked up on a vibe about a month into the whole Purrfection project. She doesn't act the same way around us as she acts when she's around Ivy. It's like she's trying too hard to show you that she's not interested in Ivy when you're paying attention to her but when you're doing something else or not in the room, she's a totally different person."

"Really?"

"We're all going to be together Friday for the meeting about the tour. Just watch her. You'll see what I'm talking about."

Chapter 22

Excitement filled every square foot of Freedom Arena as the night Natalie dreaded and anticipated had arrived. It was opening night for the Atlanta Diamonds. Due to Natalie's involvement in the music industry, and with Iverson, there were more stars in the building than in the skies that night. Atlanta's hottest entertainers fell through to show Natalie love in the Diamonds' home opener. Iverson, his squad and a few of Future's artists sat courtside to cheer for the home team. A menagerie of Future hits spilled from the public address speakers as a shout out to the camp.

"Yo!" Iverson shouted over the music at TyQuan. "It's live as hell in here!"

"I know, kid! I don't see this many stars at Hawks games."

"That's cuz they ain't won no championships."

"Have you seen the girls?"

"Oh yeah, I forgot to tell you. They're singing the National Anthem tonight."

"Now that's what's up."

Wanda Smith, the voice of the Diamonds, hyped up the crowd before she introduced the team. At the flip of a switch the arena went black. The only lights visible were the flashes of the hoard of cameras spread throughout the building. A parade of yellow, red, blue and orange lights danced around the court floor as highlights of the Diamonds' championship season appeared on the giant screens attached to the scoreboard. In the tunnel that lead to the court, Natalie stood in the middle of a circle of her teammates.

"Alright ladies," she roared as the circle swayed from side to side. "We are now the defending champions of the WNBA and everybody's gunnin' for us. We are a team and we have to be able to look into the eyes of each and everyone under the sound of my voice and know that she's givin' 100 percent. I'm the team captain but no one is bigger than the team. Tonight let's show our fans why we are the Champions. Bring it in! Bring it in!" Natalie knelt to the floor as her teammates engulfed her. "Our road to repeat begins tonight. Like coach always says: 'Offense wins games, defense wins championships! Defense on three! One! Two! Three!"

"DEFENSE!" barked the ladies in unison.

The ladies lined up with Natalie at the head of the line.

"A-T-L! Make some noise!" the announcer bellowed. "It gives me great pleasure to introduce the defending WNBA champions! Your Atlanta Diiiiiiiamooooonds!"

The crowd went wild as Natalie led her team onto the floor and into lay-up lines. Enroute to the basket, Natalie smiled and blew a kiss to Ivy as she ran past him. After a period of warm-up drills and jump shots, the ladies huddled once again then took their places to await the National Anthem and the introductions of the starting line-ups.

"Ladies and Gentlemen will you please rise for the singing of our National Anthem. Here tonight to perform the Star Spangled Banner…Future Records recording artists…Atlanta's own…Purrfection!"

The trio took center court bathed in a single spotlight. Purrfection delivered an accappella rendition of the National Anthem that received a thunderous ovation upon completion. Once the performance was done they took their seats with the rest of the camp as the announcer introduced the visiting team's starting five.

"Atlanta here is the starting line-up for your Atlanta Diamonds! Starting at Forward from Franklin Memorial University…Precious Anderson! Starting at the other Forward from The University of North Carolina…Christina Cantrell! The Protector of all things down low…from The University of Maryland…Jacinda Wilson! Starting at Guard… from The University of

Connecticut...Chanel Maxwell! And last but not least...starting at the other guard...your team captain...WNBA MVP, Rookie of the Year and WNBA Finals MVP...From The University of Tennessee...Natalie Simms!"

Natalie ran bent over through a double line of her teammates giving low-fives and chest bumped Chanel as she brought her teammates into their final huddle. Once the rest of the team dispersed leaving the starting 5 to take their positions for the opening tip-off. In the middle of that Diamonds logo, center court, Jacinda Wilson stood eye to eye with the L.A. Sparks' center, Lisa Leslie. The twin towers loomed over the referee awaiting the first tip of the season. The referee tossed the ball into the air. Jacinda out jumped Lisa Leslie to tap the ball to Natalie — giving the Diamonds the first possession of their 97-81 victory. Natalie ended her first game with 27 points, 11 assists and 6 steals.

A mob of fans surrounded the player's exit to the arena in hopes of autographs from their favorite players. Over the span of 30 minutes the players exited through the back door of the *Diamond Mine*. Caught up in the moment, the young fans failed to notice that standing behind them, leaning against a concrete pillar was the CEO of Future Records, Iverson Davenport. Natalie was one of the last to file out of the building because of interviews and the post-game press conference. She stopped to sign autographs and take pictures until she noticed Iverson leaning on the pillar with a smile of approval on his face. After signing her last autograph, Natalie ran into the arms of her beau.

"You were great tonight," Iverson complimented as he squeezed his Diamond. "I knew you were good but you done stepped up ya game since last season."

"You're gonna make me blush," Natalie squealed. "I was shocked to see everybody that came out. Did you have something to do with that?"

"If I said I did, I'd be lyin'. You're apart of the ATL music family now and you know how we support each other."

"What about the girls singin' the National Anthem? I know you had somethin' to do with that."

"Nope. That was T."

"Well what the hell did you do?" Alicia laughed.

"I came out to support the number one lady in my life."

"Oh Ivy," the Diamond cooed as she kissed her man. "You don't know how much it means to me to finally have a man other than my Dad come see me play ball."

"You've never had a man come see you ball?"

"Never. Okay once but that didn't really count."

"I don't understand."

"Before he married Alicia, Dré came to a game in Houston but he wasn't there to see me at first."

"I still don't understand."

"At the time, we were in the aftermath of a fall out. He flew out to meet one of my teammates for a long distance booty call. We ran into each other in the bar of his hotel the night before the game."

"Drinkin' the night before a game...what kind of athlete are you?" Ivy joked.

"N-E way...over a couple of drinks, we reconciled our friendship, I got into a fight wit Shawna and Dré came to see me play the next day."

"Damn! Money had you fightin' over him?"

"It wasn't over him. Me and her just had some unresolved issues we needed to work out."

"Violence is not the answer young lady."

"Yes Daddy."

"Stop it," Ivy grinned. "You know I like it when you call me Daddy."

Playfully punching him in the arm, "You so silly."

"You ready to go?"

"Go where?"

"It's a surprise."

"I don't have to wear a blindfold again, do I?"

"Not this time." Iverson pulled his Sidekick from his hip and sent a text message. In less than five minutes, a limousine pulled up to the couple.

"What is this all about?" Natalie inquired as the driver got out and open the door for her.

"Just get in. Everything you need is in there. The driver knows what to do. I'll see you in a little bit."

Ivy kissed Natalie on her forehead, walked to his car and drove out of the garage.

Without any argument or further inquiry, Natalie ducked into the back of the limousine to a huge bouquet of red, pink, white and yellow roses. In a hanging bag was a white, Chanel party dress with thin spaghetti straps. On the seat in a box were the matching stilettos.

"What is going on?" Natalie thought to herself. Nevertheless, she changed into the dress because the last time Ivy had a surprise for her turned out to be one of the most romantic nights of her life. Once she slipped out of her post-game clothes and into the dress, Natalie pulled her hair out of the ponytail wrapper, brushed it down and applied her usual, minimal amount of make-up. Ten minutes after her transformation was complete, her sleek, black carriage came to a halt in front of Club Blaze.

Once again, the limo's driver walked to the back of the vehicle to open the door for Natalie to get out. His tip for his duties came in the form of an eyeful of Natalie's assets hugged by the fabric of the Chanel original. Dymond recognized where she was but wondered why she was at the club on a Tuesday night. Being an avid patron of the club, she knew that whenever something was happening at Blaze, it was always packed. She couldn't understand why the only person in the parking lot besides her and the limo driver was one guy, dressed in all black, standing at the buildings entrance. Knowing that this was all Iverson's doing, she approached the gentleman standing at the door. Music leaked through the club's doors as she stepped up.

"Miss Simms?" the man in black confirmed.
"Yes."
"Mr. Davenport is expecting you."

The muscular arm of the man extended to the door and flexed as he pulled it open. Natalie could hear Purrfection blaring through the speakers once the doors opened. The club wasn't packed like it normally was. There was a modest crowd inside dressed in all white engaging in drinks, conversation and dancing. Once she was all the way inside the club, she began to recognize her Atlanta Diamond team affiliates, Future Camp members and other Atlanta-based entertainers.

"Ladies and gentlemen," The DJ echoed on the mic and stopped the music. "Natalie Simms is in the building!"

Natalie was greeted with a barrage of applause, cheers, screams and whistles. Draped in all white linen Iverson emerged from a group of people holding a glass of champagne in his right hand.

"Hey sexy," Ivy greeted as he extended the drink to his precious gem. "Surprised?"

"That's an understatement. How'd you get all of these people get in here and there's no cars outside?"

"We shuttled everybody here from the arena."

"What is this for?"

"It's a victory party."

"What if we woulda lost?"

"Then I guess it woulda been an all black, you'll get'em next time party." They laughed.

"I never know what to expect with you Futurama Davenport."

"Speakin' of just4kickz, somebody wants to meet you."

Ivy took Natalie by the hand and led her upstairs to the room known as The Network. Natalie squealed with joy as Teddy Pinned*Her*A$$*Down approached her holding hands with an unknown dark-skinned female.

"What's up Teddy?" Natalie greeted as she hugged him. "This must be Choco Latte."
"When were in public she goes by Nikki."
"Hey girl!" Natalie and Choco exchanged hugs.
"So nice to finally meet you."
"I know right," Choco replied. "Girl you was killin'em out there tonight."
"Gotta give the fans what they paid for. How long y'all in town?"
"We'll be here 'til Sunday."
"How'd you get a week off?"
"I don't work anymore. I help my Teddy with his business."
"That's what's up, Cuzin." Ivy interjected.
"I tried to tell her she didn't have to work when she first came to da 'Ville but you know how some women are...I-N-D-E-P-D-E-F-G-L-M-N-O-P....Muthafucka...you know how to spell it!"

The quartet laughed as they made their way to their table. Natalie was greeted by her teammates and other celebs as they moved through the crowd. Once at the table, they laughed and partook in more champagne. After a few minutes passed, Ivy excused himself and made his rounds to make sure everything was running smooth downstairs. Once downstairs, Ivy made a quick stop at the bar and greeted a few guests. After all of his tasks were completed, he turned to go back upstairs but was intercepted at the bottom of the stairs by Cee Cee.

"Hey Ivy!" Cee Cee's words were slurred as she tried to put her arms around Iverson's neck.

"What's up, Cee Cee?" Ivy spoke in disapproval ducking her clutches. "Chill out." Her intoxication caused her to sway from side to side as she stood in front of her CEO.

"Wha you meeean shill out? I'm cool. You shill out."

"I think you had enough." Cee Cee slapped Iverson's hand away when he reached for her drink. "Look at you. This is not the way we act in public."

"I'm fiiiine," she giggled. "You think I'm shjrunk. I'm not shjrunk. I'm tip-see."

"I think you should call it a night. I'll get somebody to take you home."

"What I wanna go there for? You're here."

The Purrfection member lost her balance and fell towards Iverson. In doing so, Iverson had to lean down to catch her bringing the two of them face to face. Cee Cee tried to kiss Iverson's lips but he moved his face. Iverson sat his ex down in a chair while he went to get one of his bodyguards to take her home. What he didn't know was she was staggering right behind him. As soon as he stopped to talk to one of the members of his security team, he felt a pair of arms wrap around his waist and a face on his back. Ivy quickly grabbed her hands and removed her arms from latched to him.

Spinning her around swiftly and grabbing her firmly by her biceps, "Candace! Stop it! You're making a fool outta yaself."

"Ooooh! I see...Now that you're with Natalie...I'm a fool."

"That's not it and you know it," Ivy growled through his teeth as he pulled Cee Cee close to his face in order for her to hear him.

"Stop actin' like a groupie."

"Wooow...Now I'm a groupie." The way Iverson was positioned, Cee Cee's back was to the stairs. As he reprimanded Candace for her behavior, he looked over her left shoulder and saw Natalie standing at the bottom of the stairs. Seeing Natalie, Iverson let Cee Cee go and she stood wobbling.

"What's goin' on?" Natalie asked as she approached.

"This one's had a little too much to drink. I'm tryna get her situated so I can get somebody to take her home but I can't get her to sit still."

"Candace what is wrong with you?" Natalie scolded.

"Look...you not my mama...you my manasjer...what I do is my biz-ness."

"You're not a regular person anymore. Everything you say and do is a direct reflection on people other than yourself and right now you're not representing your label or yourself like you're supposed to." Cee Cee gathered herself enough to stumble away from Iverson and Natalie.

"I need some air," Ivy sighed. "You wanna step outside?" Natalie nodded and followed Iverson outside of the club. Ivy let out a deep breath as he leaned against the wall and put his head back to look into the sky.

"You okay?" she asked as she walked up to him and put her arms around him.

"I'm cool."

"She's not over you, is she?"

"Apparently not. This is why I was against signing the group."

"Iverson...listen to yourself. Purrfection is a hot group and they're doin well."

"Yeah but losing you is not a price I'm willin' to pay for the success of a group."

"I knew the possibilities of problems before we started this. I'm not worried about her petty advances. It's all up to you not to fall for it. Tonight marks a plateu in our relationship I was dreading."

"What do you mean?"

"My season started tonight. I have five more home games and then I'm on the road for three weeks. Three weeks away from the man I love. At the same time you go on tour with Purrfection. You're going to be going from city to city, hotel to hotel with a girl that you used to be involved with and judging from her actions tonight, a girl that still has a thing for you." Natalie reached up and put her hands on Iverson's broad jaw lines and pulled his face towards her to look into his eyes. "That scares the hell out of me but I trust you. Do you hear me Iverson? I trust you. Despite all I've been through, I promised you I wouldn't hold my past relationships out on you. Don't make me regret it."

"I would never do anything to intentionally hurt you. Like I told you before, you are the First Lady of Future Records meaning you're the number one lady in my life."

"I love you, Futurama."

"I love you too, Dymond." The couple engaged in a passionate kiss. In mid-kiss TyQuan poked his head out of the door.

"Come on man," Ty laughed. "How's the guest of honor outside swappin' spit wit the host?" Ivy and Natalie busted into laughter — in mid kiss.

"My bad T," Natalie apologized as she wiped the lipstick from Iverson's lips. "We're comin' right now." TyQuan held the door open as Natalie and Iverson re-entered the club. On the way to the stairs, Iverson noticed Cee Cee standing in a corner talking to a local Atlanta artist. Hand in hand Natalie and Ivy returned to the network and took their seats with Teddy and Choco Latte. Despite what had just transpired, Natalie and Iverson enjoyed their evening with their friends and colleagues. After a couple more hours, the night came to a close. Natalie and Iverson stood downstairs bidding their guests good night. Once the Club was empty Ivy chauffeured his Diamond back to the Arena to get her car.

"It's right around here," Natalie directed. "Oh my God! Where is my truck?" Natalie began to get hysterical. "Iverson...someone stole my truck!"

"Calm down."

"Calm down? Iverson did you just hear what just I said? Some-one stole my truck!" Iverson tried with everything he could to hold back his laughter but let a slight snicker go.

"This is not funny! Why are you laughing?" Iverson didn't answer her. Instead he drove up the ramp of the parking deck to the next level.

"Where's my phone? I gotta call the police. Damn it! My purse is in my truck!"

"Natalie Simms...calm down. Your truck is fine. It's at your house."

"What?" In the hysterics of the moment, Natalie wasn't paying attention to what was going on. The deck was empty with the exception of one vehicle hidden by a tan car cover. Iverson pulled up in front of the car and stopped.

"What are you doing?" Iverson put the car in Park, exited the vehicle and walked around the rear to open the door for Natalie. He grabbed her hand as she stepped out of the Chrysler. By the hand, Ivy led Natalie to the driver's side of the vehicle. Starting at the back of the covered car, Iverson removed the cover revealing a Bentley Continental GT Speed — Platinum in color and fully loaded.

"You like it?" Iverson smiled.

"Ivy, what is this?"

"Whenever an artist joins the family, I give them a chain with an iced-out Future Records logo medallion."

"But I'm not an artist."

"That's right. You are the First Lady of Future. The First Lady deserves more than just a chain. This is just a small token of my appreciation for all the work you've done with Purrfection and most of all, a symbol of my love for you." Iverson reached into his pocket and pulled out the key to the car. Natalie stood with her hands over her mouth and tears in her eyes.

"Iverson this is too much. I can't accept this."

"Natalie Simms...this is a gift. Had it been a bracelet would you have accepted it?" She nodded in a positive manner. "The price of the gift has no bearing. This is from the heart. Please...take it." Natalie held out her hand as Iverson dropped the key into her face up palm. After wiping her eyes, she pressed the button to unlock the car. The lights flashed as the driver's side door unlocked. Ivy opened the door as his First Lady slid into the vehicle. The Atlanta Diamond sat behind the wheel like a teenage girl behind the wheel of her first car.

"Crank it up," Ivy commanded as he closed the door. With the turn of the key, the engine began to sing its song of vehicle perfection. "Enjoy it and I'll talk to you tomorrow." Iverson walked to his car to grab Natalie's gym bag, put it in the back seat of the Bentley and turned to walk back to his car.

"Iverson," Natalie called as she rolled down the window. He turned to face his Diamond.

"I love you."

Every relationship has to cross certain points in order to move to the next plateau. Some plateaus are harder to cross than others. Natalie and Iverson's relationship seemed to be a smooth one, despite the situation they put themselves in. At times people allow themselves to get caught up in how they feel about each other and fail to look at the big picture. Take a moment to reflect on the duo of

Natalie Simms and Iverson Davenport. Iverson is a successful record executive and Natalie is a pro basketball player that met on the internet. This type of thing happens every day. Does it make a difference because of their status? Of course not. Everybody needs somebody and there is somebody for everybody. If you believe in the bible, this statement holds true. Though Adam didn't meet Eve on *inthebegining.com*, God saw fit to create a companion for Adam.

With that being said, now take a look at the big picture. Natalie and Iverson have added an element to their relationship for a number of different reasons believing that trust will see them through. All that's cool but the couple failed to take into consideration the motive of the x-factor, Cee Cee. Candace and Iverson, at one time, were in a relationship in which they lived together. Over a misunderstanding, Cee Cee removed herself from the relationship. When relationships end with looming questions unanswered wavering in the hearts of the parties once involved, the time spent apart allows the once involved to think about the past union disengaged. In Cee Cee and Iverson's case, they had a good relationship. When the two had an opportunity to sit and talk about what went wrong and why it went wrong, Cee Cee admitted that she had no true quorum with Iverson. She fell victim to listening to her friends instead of listening to her heart. Many times these revelations should have been discovered before the demise of the relationship but often don't. Now that she is back in Iverson's life as an artist with a history, how will she handle it? Only time would tell.

"He bought you a what?" Alicia screeched into the phone.

"You heard me. Ivy bought me a Bentley."

"Dré! Iverson bought Natalie a Bentley!" André picked up the phone in the room that he was in.

"Girl what did you do to this man for him to buy you a Bentley?" André inquired.

"That's what I've been asking myself since last night."

"Baby, why don't I have a Bentley?"

"Okay sis. It was good talkin' to ya. Love you! Bye Bye now!" Natalie laughed as Dré hung up the phone.

"I can't stand him sometimes but I love him so much," Alicia laughed. "Now back to you, Miss Lady. How did all this happen?"

"I don't know, girl. Iverson is so intriguing and spontaneous. Last night after the game, he threw me an all white party at Club Blaze…"

"Just out the blue on a Tuesday?"

"Same thing I said but before I get to the car, let me tell you about Miss Cee Cee."

"Uh oh."

"Uh oh is right. We were chillin' in the Network with a couple of friends when Iverson excused himself to check on things downstairs. He was gone for about fifteen minutes so I decided to go down to make sure everything was okay. When I get down there I see Iverson holdin' Cee Cee by the arms. When he saw me he let her go and she started wobblin'."

"Don't tell me she was drunk."

"She was so drunk she couldn't even talk straight."

"Wow. So what are you gonna do now?"

"I've been thinkin' about that too. I'ma let her slide this time cuz she was drunk but believe me, when I see her tonight, I got a few choice words for her. I'll be damned if I let this chick ruin my relationship cuz she hangin' on to the past."

"Before you get to hasty, think about it for a minute. Iverson is your man and you know that because why else would he buy you a Bentley? If you get upset or lash out at her, you're falling right in to what she wants you to do."

"You sayin' I should just let it ride?"

"Hell nah! Let her know what she did was wrong but you have to keep it professional. Remember, outside of her past with Iverson, she's a contracted client so you have to handle this situation with caution because she's a little more than the average ex-girlfriend."

"I see ya point."

"I know it's hard but you have to be the bigger person in this situation."

"I was the bigger person. I started to snatch her by the back of her head when I saw her all up in my man's face."

The instrumental track of Purrfection's hit single, *Second Time Around,* controlled the groups bodies as they rehearsed the song's choreography in the dancehall at Future Records. With Katina positioned in the middle of Rolanda and Cee Cee, the three danced with fluidity as they watched their moves in the mirror. In mid dance step the music disappeared. The ladies turned to see what the problem was and found Iverson walking toward them.

"Ladies," Ivy began as he was about 5 feet from them. "We need to talk."

"Sure Ivy," Katina replied picking up her towel off the floor. "What's up?"

"We need to talk about public behavior." Iverson glared directly at Cee Cee. "One thing you have to remember is that when you're in public, you represent more than just yourself. You represent your group, your management and most of all, your label."

"Papi," Rolanda interrupted. "Where is all of this coming from?"

"It's obvious that a certain group member can't hold their alcohol or their feelings."

"Uh, Iverson," Cee Cee stuttered.

"Feelings?" Katina and Rolanda questioned with confusion.

"You haven't told them, have you?"

"Told us what?" Rolanda asked. "Cee Cee what is going on?"

"Okay, okay. Me and Iverson used to be involved about two and a half years ago. In a jealous fit of anger, I ruined his condo and disappeared while he was out of the country on tour. Over time I realized I was wrong and wanted to make things right but didn't know how. Time kept passing and eventually I moved on but never got over him. When you approached me about joinin' the group I didn't want to until you told me it was with Future. I saw that as my way back to Iverson. Unfortunately for me, Iverson was taken and I didn't know how to deal with that. Last night I had a little too much to drink and made a jackass out of myself."

"Wow," Katina sighed.

"I should have told you before we got into this but I thought that I could control my feelings. I'm sorry."

"Ladies remember...we've all done things in our past that we're not proud of. The important thing is that we have to focus on what is at hand. In two weeks you go on your first tour. If there is anything that you need to get out, now is the time."

"How could you do this to us?" Rolanda stood up and walked towards the window.

"I said I was sorry. What more do you want from me? People make mistakes."

"Do you know what your mistake could have cost us?"

"Rolanda calm down," Katina pleaded.

"Calm down? Kitty, are you serious? You should be just as pissed as me! After everything me and you been through to get here and you want me to calm down?" Rolanda walked from the window towards Cee Cee causing Kitty to stand up. "We've performed in every hole in the wall in Atlanta, North Carolina and South Carolina. We put up with sleazy promoters more interested in gettin' us in bed than on stage not to mention putting up wit Black for the past 3 years..." Kitty had to stand between Cee Cee and Rolanda because she knew how Rolanda's temper was.

"Rolanda, that's enough. We're a group now. If it wasn't for Cee Cee we wouldn't be here right now."

"I'm not about to sit here and let my dream be crushed by somebody who can't let go of the past!"

"Look...I know I messed up and know your upset but you're not going to stand here and talk to me like I'm a child."

"A child?" Rolanda let out a sarcastic laugh.

"I said I was sorry. Why can't you just let the past be the past? We're gettin' ready to be the hottest group to come outta the A since TLC and Xscape." Rolanda calmed down and walked back to the window.

"Cee Cee," Ivy began. "Rolanda has every right to be upset right now. You're playin' with other peoples lives. When you first came to me you said that you didn't want any trouble. You said that all you wanted to do was sing. If that's the case, that's cool but the next time something like what happened last night goes down, the consequences might be a little more severe."

"I'm done for the day. I need time to think." Cee Cee grabbed her bag and stormed out of the dancehall. Iverson and Katina walked over to Rolanda to find her with tears in her eyes.

"You okay?" Iverson asked as he put his hand on her shoulder.

"I'm cool," she sniffled. "It's just that we've come to far to lose it over some bullshit."

"I understand. It's a crazy situation and if I stand here and tell you that coming to the decision of signing you guys was an easy one, I'd be lying. The first time I saw Cee Cee since she left was the night all three of you we're together in the conference room. I wanted to dead the whole deal but Natalie and TyQuan fought for you. To be honest with you, I couldn't deny your talent. That's why I gave you a shot knowing our past. I'm fully aware of the risks but if you look at it, I have the most to lose because I have the most invested in you. I know Cee Cee and all she ever wanted to do was be a singer. She's a good person. All I ask is for you to be patient with her. Don't worry about what what's between me and her. That's on me. I'll handle that. You just get ready for the tour."

"What about Cee Cee?" Katina asked.

"She just needs time to calm down. One thing about Candace...she's not a quitter. She'll be right back here tomorrow for rehearsal."

"I'm sorry I got a little heated," Rolanda apologized.

"A little heated?" Ivy laughed. "It's all good. I felt where you were coming from and I think she did too. Why don't y'all call it a day and start fresh in the morning."

"Okay."

The ladies gathered their belongings and walked out of the dancehall. Iverson let out a heavy sigh and returned to his office. What had he gotten himself into? With a mind racing a thousand miles a minute, Ivy returned to his office and plopped into his chair. A heavy sigh of confusion was released as he swiveled from left to right in his chair. As he opened his eyes to glance at the screen, an instant messenger box popped up.

Dymond: Ivy…u there?

Ivy_Dav: Hey mami…what's up?

Dymond: in a team meeting bored out of my mind

Ivy_Dav: maybe u need to pay attention…don't let last season go to ya head

Dymond: nah…its nuttin like that…some girls in practice were slackin and coach got mad and decided we needed to talk

Ivy_Dav: speakin of talk…ya girls got into it today

Dymond: what now?

Ivy_Dav: I found out today that Cee Cee didn't tell the girls about our past

Dymond: WHAT?!?! how'd u find that out?

Ivy_Dav: i wanted to talk to them about what happened last nite and Cee Cee tried to cut me off… when it finally came out… Rolanda went off!!! There was getting ready to be hot sauce flyin every where! Lol!

Dymond: what was the outcome?

Ivy_Dav: Rolanda told her str8 up that she had come too far for her to mess it up

Dymond: what did Katina have to say…

Ivy_Dav: Kitty was the mediator in the whole thing

Dymond: now what do we do?

Ivy_Dav: ignore her…I know how Candace is, she's used to having all eyes

her...it's the attention she's going after whether it be from me, the fans or
anybody else. When she calms down...it will be back to biz

Dymond: so I'm supposed to act like last night didn't happen...

Ivy_Dav: She's doin it to see what kind of reaction she can get out of you. If you
follow her up...she'll keep goin.

Dymond: ok...I'll let this one slide but I'm serious when I say this...she's
not going to just blatantly disrespect me.

Ivy_Dav: Baby... I know...I got it under control

Chapter 23

The episode that happened between Ivy and Cee Cee was only the beginning of the madness. With the WNBA season in full swing and The *Summer of the Future* launched, it meant some rough roads ahead for the newfound union of Futurama and Dymond. Bound by contract, there was nothing Iverson could do about Candace. He hoped that his constant rejections would steer her away from him. There was always something intriguing about a woman that persistently pursued a prize possessed by another.

As a rule of thumb, for your first tour as a member of Future Records, you didn't get the luxury of flying first class. That was a right of passage that had to be earned through success and record sales. Purrfection's first bus tour was nothing like the old, Motown days—when four or five acts packed on a raggedy ass charter bus. It may not have been a G5, or first class on Delta but the trio's chariot was laced more than some people's homes.

It was about seven o'clock in the morning when the girls arrived at Future Records, looking nothing like future R&B stars. Dawned in head scarves, night clothes and slippers, they drug themselves upstairs and

into the conference room. T-Bizzy was the first
to greet the ladies.

"Ladies!" T-Bizzy shouted full of
energy. "What's the deal?"

"You have too much energy this early in
the morning," Katina moaned as she lifted her
head up off of the table.

"Are you kidding me? You should be
exited! This is your first national tour."

"Trust me," Rolanda began. "I'm excited
but I can't express it until after twelve. Get at
me then and we can jump for joy." TyQuan
laughed as he bounced from singer to singer,
shaking them to wake them up.

"What time does our flight leave?" Cee
Cee inquired.

"Flight?" T-Bizzy fell into hysterical
laughter. "Now that's some funny shit! I don't
care who you are!"

"What's so funny about that?"

"I'll leave that one for Ivy." Meanwhile,
at Hartsfield-Jackson Airport, Iverson and
Natalie were saying their goodbyes as she was
set to embark on a thirteen game road trip and
Iverson on a 30 city tour. The couple acted as if
one of them had been deployed to Iraq. It was
that kind of cute that almost made you sick.
LOL!

"I'm gonna miss you sooooo much,"
Natalie whined as she buried her face in Ivy's
chest.

"Look at the bright side..."

"There is no bright side."

"Out of 13 games, I'll see you for 5 of them."

"What about the other 8? How can I go from seeing you almost every day to just 5 times in 3 weeks? Who's gonna spoil me?"

"I woulda said Shawna but she's gone," Ivy laughed.

Hitting him in the chest, "That's not funny! Its bad enough I have to see her when we play Detroit." Natalie lifted her head out of Iverson's chest. "I promise you. If she so much as bumps me wrong, I'm goin' to jail."

"Then you'll have plenty of women to spoil you there."

"You are not helping the situation, Sir!"

"You know I gotta mess with you."

"Flight 102 to New York," the airport announcer began. "Now boarding at Gate 12."

"I guess that's me." Natalie and Iverson engaged in more than a peck but less than a French kiss. "Behave yourself."

"You know I will."

"And you tell Miss Cee Cee..."

"Stop it," Ivy commanded. "Get it outta ya head. Right now."

"...and the rest of the girls that I said break a leg."

"That's not what you really wanted to say but I'll relay the message."

Iverson gave Natalie one last kiss on her forehead and watched as his Diamond disappeared into the tunnel leading to Flight 102. The ride from the airport to downtown was usually a short ride. Because of rush hour traffic, it took Ivy nearly an hour to get there. Once he arrived, he got his messages from Michelle and walked into his office with TyQuan not far behind.

"Big Baaaay-baaaay!" T-Bizzy shouted as entering Ivy's office.

"Man, if you don't stop makin all that noise this early in the morning," Ivy scolded. "Why are you so hype?"

"We're goin' on tour, Man!" Ty bounced around Ivy's office like one of those balls you get out of the bubble gum machines in the grocery store.

"You act like you've never been on tour before."

"I haven't. Not with a group that I discovered."

"What about the kid from Morris Brown that time?"

"You're kiddin' me, right? How long ago was that?"

"We were just getting off the ground."

"Exactly. That so-called tour was in clubs, not sold out arenas and coliseums."

"My bad," Ivy laughed. "I just thought about somethin' though."

"What's that?"

"This is the first time you're going on tour while...you ready? You're in a relationship." TyQuan's entire facial expression changed. "Shit ain't so funny now. Is it?"

"That's just like you. Always gotta spoil a nigga's fun."

"That's aight. We in the same boat."

"Guess what? Cee Cee asked me what time the flight leaves."

"Wow! You didn't tell'em they don't get G5 status until the third tour?"

"I didn't have the heart to. Besides, the way that bus is tricked out, they won't be complaining."

"These are females...they always complain. Remember when Legacy went on her first tour?"

"Damn it man! She was a trip. Now we got three of'em. You know what...I'm flyin'."

"Wrong answer. Your group, your tour. You get to ride shotgun and keep Candace away from me as much as you can."

"You a grown ass man. I ain't babysittin' no bod-ee."

"It's like that? Okay. You better not let me see you in no other female's face."

"You wouldn't"

"Try me."

Nine o'clock rolled in as Will, KD and a couple other Future employees hauled the girl's luggage outside. The bus hadn't arrived but by the time everyone got outside, it would be there. Right before they were escorted outside, Ivy broke the news to the girls that they wouldn't be flying. They mumbled, moaned and complained all the way downstairs. All the negative remarks turned into sheer awe once they laid eyes on their luxury coach.

The bus was huge. Iverson had it wrapped as a rolling billboard with the girl's pictures and names on both sides. On the back was a mural of their CD cover along with the cities and dates of the tour. There was enough room for 8 people to function without space issues. The bus had beds for naps and lounging, TVs, video game systems and a DVD player. If you could think of it, it was probably there.

"I can rock wit' dis'," Katina expressed as she touched everything she could.

"Look out TLC!" Rolanda danced in the middle of the lounge area. "Purrfection is on the move!"

"This'll do," Cee Cee approved. "A G5 would be nice but this will definitely do."

"I'm glad it meets your approval," Ivy began. "Just so you know this is just for getting from city to city. You'll have full luxury accommodations in every city. That's the least I can do. Without further adieu, I'd like to turn it over to the Captain of your tour cuz from this moment on…I ain't doin' shit else. Anything you want, need or desire, my man T-Bizzy will provide for you."

"What if T doesn't have or can't provide what I want, need, or desire?" Cee Cee looked at Ivy with a devilish grin.

"See," Rolanda interjected. "That's that bullshit."

"Rolanda!" Katina scolded. "No cussin'." Rolanda began to talk mumble to herself in Spanish. It wasn't understood what she was saying but whatever it was, she meant it.

"First of all," TyQuan started as he stood up. "Welcome to celebrity status. Based on our track record, Future has never had an unsuccessful tour and we hope to keep it that way. You've been briefed on Future's conduct policies and your managers have gone over the itinerary with you."

"Are we going on tour or to Iraq?" Katina clowned. "All this talk about being briefed and itineraries."

"Katina!" Iverson barked. "Behave."

Iverson winked his eye at her to let her know he wasn't trying to be an ass.

"Like I was saying…you should have received necessary information to make this tour go as smooth as possible. Now you can sit back, relax and in twelve hours…we'll be in Miami."

"Twelve hours!" the ladies cried.

For the first part of the tour, Katina and Rolanda asked Ivy and T a thousand questions. As Ivy sat and listened to the girls talk, he noticed how intelligent they were when the conversations surpassed more than just money, cars, clothes and superstar status. From politics to history, on to entertainment and current events, the three college grads and the cosmetologist engaged in some heated conversations and debates. Cee Cee wasn't interested in anything they talked about. She lounged in one of the beds with her IPod.

Due to traffic in certain cities and a couple of non-scheduled stops, Purrfection didn't roll into Miami until midnight. The Future camp checked into the Hilton. Having slept for the last five hours of the ride, the crew was wide awake and ready to hit the city. Just like New York, Miami was also a city that never slept. At about a quarter past one in the morning, two luxury SUVs carried Ivy and the crew to South Beach. Having been to Miami plenty of times, Ivy knew the MIA like he knew the ATL. On a Thursday night, the main strip was packed. With newfound fame and national exposure, it wasn't long before they were recognized. That's what 106 & Park can do for a career.

Because of Miami being Miami, there was a constant flow of athletes, entertainers and actors. The people of South Beach were used to seeing celebrities and mega stars. This enabled Purrfection to enjoy themselves with out a mob of fans. The ladies signed a few autographs and took pictures with fans as they walked up and down the strip going in and out of clubs and bars. With Iverson and TyQuan both being licensed to carry concealed weapons, there was no need for much security that night. It was going to be a different story once they hit the radio stations and the malls for promotions.

Around 2:30am the newness of the city wore off for Purrfection and the long journey there began to kick in. Ivy and his people retired to the hotel to call it a night. Ivy tried to go to sleep but couldn't. He tried to call Natalie. There was no answer. After 15 minutes of flipping through the same stations over and over, he couldn't cure his boredom. He sat up in his bed and looked around the room. He spied the leather bag that contained his laptop sitting in a chair on the far side of the room. In minutes he set up and was logged on to just4kickz.com

---

Futurama has entered the room
<Optimo Pryme> IT DOESN'T MATTER....SHE SHOULDA KEPT IT OUT DA ROOM IF SHE DIDN'T WANT NOBODY TO SAY NUTTIN ELSE ABOUT IT!!!
<City Ave Diva> FUUUUUUUUUTTTTUUUUREEEEE!!!!!!

\<Da Ice Cream Man\> this is a public chatroom…WZUP FUTURE…mang…lol!

\<Krystal Lyte\> FUUUUUUUUUUUUUUUUUTRE BABY!!!!

\<MACK Truck\> CUZIN FUTURE! WHAT IT DO?!?!

\<Futurama\> WHAT'S UP FAMILY?!?!?! FUTURE RECORDS IS IN THE BUILDIN!!!

\<Da Wife\> HEY BABYDADDY!!

\<Da Ice Cream Man\> I thought we was in a chatroom…lol

\<Dymond\> Watch it!@Wife   LOL!

\<Da Ice Cream Man\> Fight! Fight!

\<Futurama\> WHAT U DOIN IN HERE @ 3AM. I JUST TRIED TO CALL U@DYMOND

\<Optimo Pryme\> ITS MY POTNA IN CRIME…WHAT IT DO BIG HOMIE!!

\<Soopafly\> UH OHH!!! SOMEBODY IN TROUBLE…LMAO

\<Dymond\> I JUST CUT MY PHONE BACK ON. ITS BEEN OFF SINCE WE GOT OFF THE PLANE.

\<Teddy Pinned*Her*Ass*Down\> DON'T BELIVE IT CUZIN! IT'S A SET UP! SHE CREEPIN!

\<Futurama\> LOL! ITS ALL GOOD!

\<Mrz*Pinned*Down\> TEDDY…SHEEEDUP!!

\<Futurama\> WHAT IT DO CUZIN TED!

\<Dymond\> HOW'S MIAMI?@FUTURE

\<City Ave Diva\> WHENS THE NEXT TOUR@FUTURE

\<Futurama\> WE GOT IN AROUND 12 AND THE GIRLZ WANTED TO HIT SOUTH

BEACH....IT KICKS OFF TOMORROW
NIGHT@DIVA
<Teddy Pinned*Her*Ass*Down> WHEN U
COMIN TO NC?
<Optimo Pryme> HOW IN DA HELL U
COME TO MY CITY AND NOT TELL A
NIGGA! WHERE DA SHOW AT?
<Dymond> JUNE 15TH IN
CHARLOTTE@TEDDY
<Futurama> MY FAULT PRYME...SHIT
BEEN CRAZY
<Mrz*Pinned*Down> THAT'S RIGHT!!!
DYMOND KNOWS WHERE HER MAN
GONE BE AT ALLLLLLLL TIMES. LOL!
TEDDY DON'T GO NO WHERE UNLESS I
KNOW ABOUT IT.
<City Ave Diva> THAT'S WHAT I'M
TALKIN ABOUT!!
<MACK Truck> SAY IT AINT SO CUZIN
FUTURE
<Da Wife> YOU COMIN TO MICHIGAN?
<Futurama>ONLY REASON SHE KNOW MY
EVERY MOVE OF THIS TOUR IS BECAUSE
PURRFECTION R HER CLIENTS
<Da Ice Cream Man> who???
<Krystal Lyte> THAT'S RIGHT GIRL! GET
DAT MONEY WIT YO MAN!!!
<Teddy Pinned*Her*Ass*Down> I NEED A
WOMAN THAT'S GONNA MAKE ME SOME
MONEY
<Dymond> LOL! IT'S A GOOD
FEELIN@KRYSTAL

<Mrz*Pinned*Down> TEDDY...KEEP IT UP
AND U GETS.....NONE!
<Futurama> DON'T LET HER DO U LIKE
DAT CUZ
<Optimo Pryme> WHAT'S UP WIT SOME
TICKETS@FUTURE
<Teddy Pinned*Her*Ass*Down> DON'T LET
CHOCO FOOL Y'ALL...SHE KNOW THAT
DICK RUN THIS HOUSE!
<MACK Truck>TELL'EM CUZ
<City Ave Diva> DICK MAY RUN YA
HOUSE BUT PUSSY MAKE THE WORLD GO
ROUND
<Futurama> HOW MANY YOU NEED?
<Soopafly> AND MONEY MAKE YA GIRL
GO DOWN!!
<Da Wife> HEEEEEEEEEEYYYYYYYY!!!
<Da Ice Cream Man> shes such a
slut...j/k@Wife
<Optimo Pryme> CAN I GET 3? THYK IS
COMIN DOWN 4 DA WEEKEND AND MY
LIL SIS LOVES PURRFECTION.
<Dymond> THE TOUR COMES TO
MICHIGAN@ WIFE.... IT'LL BE AT THE
PALACE
<Futurama> I'LL CALL YOU
TOMORROW...YA NUMBER STILL THE
SAME??
Thyk2Def has entered the room
<Da Ice Cream Man> thyyyyyyyyk!!
<MACK Truck> THYYYYYYYYYYK..WHAT
UP MAMI!!!
<Optimo Pryme> YEAH@FUTURE

\<**City Ave Diva**\> HEY GIRL!!!

\<**Optimo Pryme**\> BABY!!!! GUESS WHAT????

\<**Dymond**\> BABY…I'M GETTING READY TO CALL IT A NIGHT

\<**Da Ice Cream Man**\> what's the date@ Dymond…me soopa and wife might come

\<**Futurama**\> I'M NOT TOO FAR BEHIND YOU. THIS 5 HOUR ENERGY SHOT STARTIN TO WEAR OFF…LOL

\<**Thyk2Def**\> WHATS THAT @ BABYDADDY

\<**Optimo Pryme**\> SHOULD I TELL HER OR U WANNA TELL HER@FUTURE

\<**Dymond**\> NITE ALL!!! S/D CALL ME WHEN U WAKE UP BABY & TELL THE GIRLS I SAID HELLO

\<**Da Ice Cream Man**\> I will@ Dymond..roflmao!

\<**Futurama**\> U TELL'ER CUZIN

\<**Thyk2Def**\> SOMEBODY TELL ME!!!!

\<**Dymond**\> LOL@ICE CREAM

\<**Soopafly**\> ICE CREAM TRYNA GET SHOT!!!

\<**Optimo Pryme**\>SATURDAY NIGHT…YOU ME AND LIL SIS GOIN TO SEE PURRFECTION COURTESY OF FUTURAMA!!!!

\<**City Ave Diva**\> WHEN U COMIN TO PHILLY???

\<**Thyk2Def**\> YAAAAAAAAAAYYYYYY!!! WHO ELSE IS GONNA B THERE?

\<**Futurama**\> T-PAIN AKON AND LIL WAYNE

<Mrz*Pinned*Down> IS FACE WITH U ON THIS ONE@FUTURE
<Da Wife> LIL WAYNE!!! SOOPA U GOTTA TAKE ME TO THE SHOW
<Futurama> NOT THIS TIME@CHOCO HE GOES ON TOUR IN 2 WEEKS WIT RHIANNA CIARA & CHRIS BROWN
<City Ave Diva> YA PEOPLE BE ON SOME GOOD TOURS
<Teddy Pinned*Her*Ass*Down> PLEASE TELL ME THAT ONE IS COMIN TO NC!!!
<Da Ice Cream Man> I forgot teddy got a thing for Ciara…lol
<Futurama> THAT ONE IS ACTUALLY COMIN TO THE FAYETTEVILLE CUZ
<Teddy Pinned*Her*Ass*Down> I'M THERE
<Mrz*Pinned*Down> EXCUSE ME??
<Da Wife> TEDDY BOUT TO GET IT!!!!
<Futurama> WE MAKIN ONE BIG CIRCLE@DIVA
<Teddy Pinned*Her*Ass*Down> I MEAN…WE'RE THERE!
<MACK Truck> TEDDY GOT PUNKED
<Futurama> AIGHT FAMILY…I'M ABOUT TO BE OUT. FOR EVERYBODY THAT WANTS TO KNOW WHEN THE TOUR IS COMIN TO YOUR CITY…HIT DA WEBSITE OR SEND ME A MESSAGE…BETTER YET…HIT DA WEBSITE…LOL
<City Ave Diva> NITE FUTURE
<MACK Truck> PEACE CUZ
<Optimo Pryme> I'LL HOLLA AT U TOMORROW@CUZIN

It was a gorgeous, summer day in Miami, Florida. The sun shined bright, the skies were clear and Purrfection had a full day of activities on the agenda. They had radio appearances, autograph signings at a few record stores, rehearsal and the Future Records signature stroll and shopping spree at the hottest mall in the city. All of the events were set to wrap around 8pm in order for the group to get back to the hotel and relax before the first show of their first tour.

There is a lot of truth in the old saying: an idle mind is the devil's workshop. As long as Cee Cee was busy, she didn't have time to get to Iverson. Once the day wrapped up and they were back at the hotel, her antics began. It seemed like there was no stunt that she wouldn't pull to get Iverson's attention. What she didn't realize was that they hurt her more than they helped her.

That night, as Ivy sat in the presidential suite, a knock came at the door. When Iverson answered, it was room service. He tried to convince the young, Cuban that he hadn't ordered anything but he insisted that it was a gift from someone staying in the hotel. With Natalie being in New York, he had no clue who it could be from. He sat on the edge of the couch staring at the large cart draped with a white linen cloth that fell to the floor. Atop the cart was a large arrangement of fresh flowers, a bottle of champagne, 2 glasses and an elaborate cheese and cracker display.

After about five minutes passed, Ivy chuckled and walked toward the cart. He was about two feet from it when he saw it move. Something strange was going on. Before he could take another step, the cart moved again.

"Alright," Ivy began in a stern voice. "Come out from under there."

He waited but no one came out. When he lifted the cloth, Iverson got the shock of his life. In his mind, he was expecting a fan or a crazed groupie. He was mistaken.

"I don't believe this shit." It was Cee Cee.
"Surprise!!!" she smiled as Ivy pulled her from under the cart by her arm. His grip was firm but nothing that would've hurt her.

As Ivy led her to the door without saying a word, she pleaded for a moment to speak to him. Her request was denied as he opened the door, put her in the hallway and closed it. Seconds later, the door opened. Cee Cee thought that he had changed his mind but it was only for him to push the cart into the hallway with her. Ivy's cell phone rang just as he stretched out across the bed to watch television.

"Hey babe," Natalie greeted with great enthusiasm.

"How's Miami?"

"Miami is Miami," he replied. "I always enjoy coming down here. How's NYC?"

"Hot as hell. I'm so glad I got my hair braided before I left. Are the girls okay?"

"They're havin a blast. Miami is showin them a lot of love."

"And Cee Cee?"

"Baby...you gotta get that off ya mind. I got it under control. Nothing is going to happen that is not supposed to happen."

"I know, Ivy. I can't help it."

"The only thing you should be worried about is winning as many games as you can."

"You're right. I told you that I trusted you and I'm going to leave it alone. How's T? Is he behaving himself?"

"So far, do good. He flew Alexa in for the show. She's on vacation next week so she'll be rolling with us until next Sunday and then she's flying back out until we get to New Orleans."

"That's good. Then I'll have another female to kick it with. Well babe, I'm gonna let you go. Me and Jasmine are going down to the bar for a drink before curfew."

"You're such an alcoholic," Ivy laughed.

"I am not! I'm a drunk. Alcoholics gotta go to them damn meetings."

"Alright Baby Girl…call me or text me to let me know you made it in."

"I will. Talk to you later." Iverson hung up the phone. Within five minutes, he was asleep.

The next morning Iverson awoke to a missed call and a text message from Natalie. As promised, she was just letting him know that she was back in her room. After lying there for a few minutes, checking out the news and weather, Ivy got up to shower and get dressed before he was to meet the crew. An hour later, T-Bizzy and the girls arrived.

"Ladies!" Ivy greeted as they drug themselves into the suite. "Come on now. You better get used to this. You got 29 more cities to go. It only gets worse from here."

"Worse?" Rolanda questioned. "How does it get worse?"

"Certain cities we come to," T-Bizzy began. "We like to chill for the whole weekend. From here it's going to be rough for the next couple of weeks until we get to New Orleans. It's gonna be in and out. I suggest you all get all the rest you can on the bus."

"I shouldn't have to tell you this but I would save your voices as much as you can. You got a lot of singing to do. Oh yeah…before I forget. I talked to Ms. Simms and she wishes

you all the best and she looks forward to
seeing you when we get to New Orleans."

"I didn't know New Orleans had a
WNBA team," Katina remarked.

"They got a team at the same time
Atlanta got the Diamonds. I believe they're
called the Masquerade."

"Shoulda been the New Orleans Girls
Gone Wild!" Rolanda laughed.

"With all of that being said…Get out!"
The ladies filed out of the room as Ivy stopped
TyQuan.

"Ya girl is off the chain."

"Who? Cee Cee?"

"Who else?"

"What she do now?"

"Last night she snuck in here hiding
under a room service cart."

"Stop lyin'!" TyQuan laughed.

"I thought it was a fan."

"I wish I coulda seen the look on your
face when you saw it was her."

"She gotta get a grip before this gets out
of hand. The last thing I need is a stunt like
that while Natalie's around."

"I don't think she's that crazy."

"This is Candace we're talkin' about."

After Miami was a success, surprisingly
enough, Cee Cee behaved herself for awhile.
From Miami they went to Orlando, Tampa,
Jacksonville and then Pensacola. As the tour
gained momentum, so did Purrfection's

success. Iverson, T-Bizzy and Natalie had a group to be proud of. With heavy radio and video rotation, the trio's self-titled debut CD was jumping off of the shelves. Every city got more and more hectic. From the time they rolled into a city, whether they were performing there or not, until the time they rolled out it was utter chaos.

Chapter 24

Fifteen cities into the tour found the Future Records camp in New Orleans, Louisiana — N'awlins. This was the first of 5 cities that he would have the chance to see Natalie. It was an early Thursday morning when the luxury coach rolled into the city. The girls got a chance to cruise down the world famous Bourbon Street while it was empty. Once the sun came up, all of that would change. Moments after they checked into the hotel, they crashed for the remainder of the night. The next morning Ivy was pulled out of his slumber by the digital tone of his cell phone.

"Hello," Ivy grumbled.
"Hey baby," Natalie greeted. "We just touched down."
"That's what's up. What time you comin' through?"
"We have a team meeting at ten and then I'm free until practice at 4. I should see you around noon."
"Sound good to me. Get some rest and I'll see you then."
"Okay baby. Go back to sleep."

Ivy was free for the day because of Natalie's arrival. He left all responsibilities on T to make sure everything got done. When the clock struck noon, Natalie was stepping out of a taxi in front of Iverson's hotel. When she arrived to Iverson's suite, he opened the door and greeted her with a hug and a kiss. The two of them crawled into bed for a little *I miss you* fun. An hour later, Natalie rolled off of Iverson, energy spent and out of breath.

"Damn girl," Ivy began through heavy breathing. "We need to be apart more often."

"That was amazing," Natalie responded as she pulled her braids back into a ponytail. "I don't know if I'm gonna be able to practice. So, what you got planned for the rest of the day?"

"Absolutely nothing. I set aside today for you."

"Really?"

"Yeah. We have reservations at one of the finest spots in New Orleans."

"You are too good to me."

"Only the best for my baby."

Natalie and Iverson took a shower together then left the room to enjoy some of the sights of The Big Easy. Once on Bourbon Street, they caught up with T and the girls. The girls looked like they had been on a massive shopping spree. Three o'clock crept around and Natalie had to get back to the hotel to catch the bus for practice.

Later that evening, Ivy, Natalie, T-Bizzy, Alexa and Purrfection were at one of the city's most exclusive and upscale restaurants. They laughed and talked as the girls talked about the experiences of their first tour. Everyone joined the conversation with the exception of you know who. It wasn't like she was being excluded; she chose to alienate herself. The more she was around Iverson; the more she learned that the feelings she had for him never died. It was hard for her to stomach seeing Ivy with another woman. Noticing that Cee Cee wasn't saying too much, TyQuan decided to try to bring her into the conversation.

"You okay, Cee Cee?" T-Bizzy inquired.

"I'm cool. I just got a lot on my mind."

"Anything we can do to help?" Natalie asked as she sipped her wine.

"Thanks but that's alright. It's just one of those things. I'm good."

"Before we go any further," Ivy began as he stood up and grabbed his wine glass. "First of all I'd like to give the girls props for all the hard work that they've done so far. Never have I seen a group put an album together as fast as you three did and it come out hot. I have to give a special shout to my right hand for everything he's done to get Purrfection to this point. To the First Lady of Future Records, Natalie Simms, thank you for believing in the group and helping them get this shot. It's definitely been worth it." Everybody began to clap and applaud. "Now for the big announcement. The album has been on the shelves for two weeks. One million units sold. Congrats ladies."

The ladies squealed with excitement as Ivy and the rest of the group applauded them. Katina stood up to speak on behalf of the group.

"On behalf of Purrfection, We'd like to thank you Ivy for giving us the shot despite everything that stood against us. We also wanna thank T for all his hard work in helping us get the album finished on time. Last but not least, to Dymond in da Ruff, thank you Miss Simms for believing in us. We love you."

The remainder of the evening was spent eating, drinking and being merry. That night the ladies behaved like superstars. The old saying always holds true: Hard work is its own reward. The evening came to a close. T and the girls went back to the hotel as Ivy escorted Natalie back to hers. Once at Nat's hotel, she and Ivy retired to her room for a night cap.

"I can't believe it," Natalie started as she took her shoes off. "Platinum in two weeks."
"That's crazy."
"I was doing some research on your artists about a week ago and found out that it doesn't take your artists long to go platinum when they do. Why is that?"

"It's all about how you put it together and the tours you do. If you notice, my artists go on tours with some heavy hitters."

"I see that."

"We take our time to put out a quality product and try our best to keep shit from leaking out on the internet. That's the hardest thing to do."

"I'm so happy for them. Did you see their faces when you gave them the news?"

"I love seeing that look. Every time one of my albums go platinum it feels just as good as it did the first time. It never gets old."

"I wonder what's up with Cee Cee. She didn't say much tonight."

"I have no idea. She'll be alright."

"Do you think it has something to do with us?"

"It could be but who knows. She's like that sometimes. She'll get in one of her moods for a minute then she'll snap out of it."

"I don't know how I would act or react if I had to constantly see an ex with another woman."

"That's life. Shit sucks sometimes but we gotta roll with the punches."

"Well spoken Mr. Davenport."

"Can I ask you a question," Ivy began as he stretched out across the king-sized bed.

"What's up?" Dymond crawled into the bed beside him and laid her head in the small of his back.

"Where do you see us in 5 years?"

"Wow. I didn't expect that one."

"Why not?"

"I've never got far enough in a relationship to have this conversation."

"Really?"

"Yup," Natalie replied gazing up at the ceiling.

"God willing, in five years I could see us married with at least one child."

"What about ball?"

"I always said that if I had the choice between having a family and playing basketball, I'd give ball up in a heartbeat."

"Are you serious?"

"As a heart attack. If there is a way to do both so be it but I've always wanted to be a wife and a mother."

"You don't hear that much these days."

"What about you?"

"I can see us married wit a shorty. I do a good job taking care of my money and when that time comes I won't have to work as hard. I do what I do now so I can relax later on and let the label run itself. Plus I got T. He knows that label inside and out. He'd love nothing more than for me to put him in charge and step back."

"As much as T clowns around, he really does a great job."

"To tell you the truth, I'm mad impressed wit my man right now. I didn't think he was gonna pull Purrfection off. He showed me a different side of him."

"I think Alexa has something to do with that."

"You might be right about that. When he's not runnin' around chasin' skirts, he stays focused. I might have to give her a job."

They laughed as they repositioned themselves. Iverson propped up against the headboard as Natalie curled up into him.

"Can you really see me as your wife?"

"For the first time in a long time, I'm happy. You're amazing; you understand me and what I do. What man wouldn't wife you up?"

"That's what I thought about myself but I couldn't seem to find a man that would reciprocate everything I gave to him."

"That's something that you don't have to worry about anymore. As long as you make me happy, I'll make you happy."

"Ditto."

Iverson and Natalie exchanged lips. Natalie pleaded for Iverson to stay but he had some business to take care of early in the morning. He knew that if he spent the night, he would be late for his meeting. He assured her that they would be at the game the next night and vanished into the night.

Back at the hotel, TyQuan and two of the three the girls were sitting in his suite going over the next day's activities when Iverson got there. He came in and took a seat in an empty chair and listen to what was being said.

"Where's Cee Cee?" Iverson interrupted.

"She left right back out after we came back from the restaurant," Katina informed.

"Does she know what's going on tomorrow?"

"She said she did."

"Did she say where she was going?"

"To visit an old friend is all she told us."

"Can you call her for me, Kitty?"

Kitty pulled out her cell phone and dialed Cee Cee's number. She quickly hung up.

"It went straight to voicemail."

"What you want me to do?" TyQuan asked.

"You good. She's cool. Cee Cee knows her way around. Alright y'all. I'm going to bed. I got shit to do in the a.m. If you need me, you know where I am." Everybody bid Ivy goodnight as he left the room. Just as he got to his door, his cell phone rang. He started not to answer it because it came from an unknown number. He answered it anyway.

"Hello."

"Ivy, I need you to come get me."

"Cee Cee?" Ivy could tell by her voice that something was wrong. She sounded like she was crying.

"Yes. Please come get me. I'm on Bourbon St. by that club we used to come to back in the days."

"You talkin' about Club VooDoo?"

"Yeah. Please hurry. I'm scared. I'm at that little store across the street."

"I'm on my way."

In a frantic rush, Ivy ran downstairs and hopped in the whip to go get his artist. On the way, he called to T to let him know what the deal was. In ten minutes, he pulled in front of the store. Cee Cee saw him and ran outside to the car. Before she could get the car, two guys came from around the building and grabbed her. Ivy jumped out of the car with his pistol in hand.

"Let her go!" Ivy barked.

"Fuck you, nigga!" One of the hoods barked back.

Ivy cocked his 9mm and pointed it in the direction of the guys. The gun caught them buy surprise. The guy that was holding Cee Cee by the arm let her go and stepped back. Ivy stepped from behind the door and walked to the front of the car.

"Get in the car," Ivy commanded. Candace ran to the car and got in on the passenger side. As soon as Ivy lowered the gun, one of the guys pulled out a gun. Ivy saw the gun and tried to jump out of the way as three shots let go.

"Ivy!" Candace screamed as she saw Ivy falling to the ground.

The two hoods fled the scene as Ivy lay on the ground clutching his shoulder. Candace jumped out of the car and ran to the driver's side. Blood was everywhere. Candace went into hysterics.

"Calm down," Iverson grimaced.

"Calm down! You just got shot!"

"I just took one in the shoulder. I'm good. Just get me to the hospital." Candace helped Iverson up and into the car. After she got Iverson in, she turned on the hazard lights and sped off in the direction of the hospital.

"Shit!" Ivy groaned as he tried to pull his cell phone off of his hip.

"Oh My God! Please don't die!"

"Just calm down and drive." Through the pain, Ivy managed to find TyQuan's number.

"What it do?" TyQuan answered.

"Son, I'm hit," Ivy moaned through the pain.

"What!"

"I just got shot! Go scoop Natalie and come to the Hospital right down the street from the hotel."

"Where's Nat?"

"She's staying at the Hyatt. You'll see it on the way to the hospital. You got her cell right?"

"Yeah. I'm on it." Ivy tossed the phone into the console and continued to moan in pain.

"What in the hell were you doing out by yourself and nobody knew where you were?"

"I'm sorry, Ivy! I went to visit a friend but she wasn't home so I decided to hit a spot for a drink."

"Come on, Cee Cee. You know better than that. You're not the same Candace you used to be. Anything coulda happened to you."

"I know! I know!"

"No you don't know. This is some serious shit."

Candace damn near ran three people over as she pulled into the breezeway at the Emergency Room. She helped Ivy out of the car and into the ER.

"Somebody help us! He's been shot!"

The nurses and orderlies rushed to get Iverson into a wheelchair and back into the back. Ivy gave Cee Cee his wallet so that she could get him signed in. The lady at the counter gave her some forms and a clipboard to fill out. Five minutes into filling out the forms, TyQuan, Natalie and the other two members of Purrfection stormed into the hospital.

"Where's my man!" TyQuan shouted.
"Over here, T."
"Where's Ivy?" Natalie asked in a frantic tone.
"They took him back about five minutes ago."

Natalie went to the desk to inform the lady behind the counter that she was with Iverson. She escorted her to the back. TyQuan tried to go but only one person could be with the patient. He began to make a huge scene in the Emergency Room. Kitty and Rolanda managed to calm him down enough to get him to move the car and come back in. In the back, Natalie sobbed uncontrollably.

"Baby, please calm down. It's not that bad."
"You're shot! How can I calm down?"
"I'm fine. I promise."
"What happened?" Ivy began to tell Natalie what happened. In the process, the doctor walked into the room.
"Mr. Davenport," he began. "Lucky for you, the bullet went straight through. We'll have you patched up and on your way in no time."
"See baby. I'm fine." Natalie grabbed Ivy's hand and began to rock back and forth as

the doctor cleaned the wound and stitched his shoulder. "Can you tell what kind of gun he shot me with?"

"It was something small. Looks like a twenty-two. Had it been something like a 9mm or .357, it could've been much worse." Thirty minutes later, Ivy was all patched up and walking into the lobby of the ER. There was a lot of noise coming from the far side of the waiting room. When they rounded the corner, they saw TyQuan standing between Rolanda and Cee Cee. Kitty was doing her best to calm Rolanda down.

"Yo!" Ivy yelled. "Chill out! I'm good. It's not her fault. It coulda happened to anybody. Let's go. T, you take Kitty and Rolanda in your car. Me, Natalie and Cee Cee will follow you in mine." Natalie gave Ivy a sharp glare. "Okay, new plan. T, you take Kitty and Cee Cee. Rolanda will ride with us. We'll be right behind you." Rolanda and Natalie helped Iverson into the back seat of the car. The passenger's seat was cover with Iverson's blood.

"This has gone far enough. This girl got you shot."

"She's nothin' but trouble," Rolanda added.

"She did not get me shot. This could have happened anywhere with anybody. She just made a bad decision that put us in the wrong place at the wrong time."

"Why are you defending her?"

"I'm not defending her. I'm just telling you the truth."

"If she hadn't been running around the city, unsupervised, this would have never happened."

"Exactly!" the Purrfection member interjected.

In a very calm voice, "Ladies, I got a hole in my shoulder. This shit hurts and I haven't got my prescription filled yet. Can we just let it go for tonight and talk about it tomorrow?"

"Okay baby. I'm sorry."

"Sorry Ivy."

"It's all good. I know you're just upset and concerned. When we get back to the hotel, I'll have T take you back to the Hyatt."

"That's a negative. I told my coach what happened and that I would be back in the morning for practice."

Sometimes we can take things for face value; how it looks is what it is. This situation may run a little deeper than that. What was Cee Cee really doing out on Bourbon St. by herself at that time of night? Only God knows. Iverson didn't want to talk about the night anymore. Natalie escorted him to his suite and they called it a night.

The next day, Kitty was in Cee Cee's suite using one of her curling irons. Cee Cee said something to Kitty as she was in the middle of a curl. She turned towards her to respond. The curling iron's cord knocked Cee Cee's make-up bag off of the counter. Kitty bent down to pick up the bag and noticed a small bag of white powder had slid out.

"Cee Cee," she called. "Come 'round here for a minute." With one shoe on and the other in hand, Candace walked up behind Kitty.

"What the hell is this?" Kitty held the bag of powder up to show Cee Cee

"Why you goin' through my shit?" Cee Cee snatched the bag from Kitty.

"I wasn't goin' through your stuff. I knocked the make-up bag off the counter with the cord. Drugs Cee Cee?"

"Don't worry about what I do. I'm grown."

"That's not cool"

"Get up off your high horse, Kitty. You act like you do no wrong. I watch how you and Rolanda run around kissin' Natalie and Ivy's asses. You ain't no better than me. I know about you. I been up in Club Ebony before."

"I used to strip...so what?"

"That ain't all you used to do. I know two dudes that used to serve you back in the day."

"Don't try to bring up my past to justify the shit you doin."

"You know what? Just get the fuck out!" Kitty tossed the hot iron onto the counter and stormed outta the room. As she exited, she ran into T-Bizzy almost knocking him down.

"What's wrong with you?"

"Ask David Ruffin," Kitty replied as she walked into her room and slammed the door.

"Who in the hell is David Ruffin?" The slam of the door caused Rolanda to stick her head out of her room.

"What was that?" She asked T.

"Somebody done pissed off Kitty. Go check on ya girl." After TyQuan watched Rolanda go into Kitty's room, he continued his trek to Ivy's spot. Ivy was struggling trying to open a pill bottle when T walked into the room.

"Lemme get that for you." Ivy tossed him the bottle of medication and walked over to the mini refrigerator to grab a bottle of water.

"What's good?" he asked as he bit down on the top to unscrew it.

"I'm still tryna figure it out."

"What you mean?"

"On my way up here, Kitty almost knocked me down mumbling somethin' about David Ruffin."

"David Ruffin?"

"It looked like she was coming from Cee Cee's room."

"Aww shit. Something's up. It takes a lot to piss Kitty off. I need you to get to the bottom of it and get to the bottom of it fast. We rolling good....15 cities left. Handle it."

"I'm on it, Chief."

"I'm serious."

"I'm on it, Gotdamnit! Shit!"

"T," Ivy called right before he got out of the door. "Stop cussin'."

"Do a push-up and I'll stop cussin'."

"That's cold-blooded." TyQuan left Ivy's room and made a B-line to Rolanda's room. When he got there Rolanda was pissed off. Every other word that came out of her mouth was either a cuss word or a Spanish word.

"What's the deal?" he asked. "I wanna know right now."

"I'm tellin' you T," Rolanda started as she tried to calm herself down. "She is really pushing us to the limit."

"Cee Cee?"

"Who else?"

"That shit she's been pullin' with Ivy is one thing but now she's gone to a whole new level."

"What happened?"

"I was just in her room doing my hair. I accidentally knocked her make-up bag on the floor and there was a bag of Cocaine in it."

"Are you bullshitin' me?"

"I wish I was, T." The President of Future Records released a huge sigh and slumped down into a chair.

"What are we gonna do?" Rolanda inquired.

"First of all, we're not gonna say anything to Ivy or Natalie right now. My man got a hole in his arm and he don't need the extra stress. I know this is serious but everybody has their bad habits. Unfortunately, that's how the business is."

"Are you saying we just ignore this?" Kitty asked.

"I'm not saying that. I'll handle it." Rolanda stood up and walked over to the mini fridge and grabbed a bottle of water.

After taking a sip, "You better handle it because if I handle it, we're gonna be looking for a new third member."

"I got it. Just chill."

T-Bizzy didn't know what to think or do after he left the girls room. The situation was so sticky. He knew they just couldn't get rid of her in the middle of a tour. Even if they wanted to, the legal repercussions could prove to be very serious. With a clouded mind and no set destination, T walked to the elevator and went to the first floor. When the doors open, the first thing he saw was the hotel's bar. In he went for a drink. As soon as he sat down at the bar, a familiar voice began talking to him.

"I guess you talked to Kitty and Rolanda." It was Cee Cee. T ordered his drink and joined her at the table.

"Talk to ya boy. What's really good?"

"You know this business T. Everybody has a habit of some kind."

"That's what I just told the girls."

"I'm not an addicted or nothing like that; I bump every now and then to ease my mind. You know how it is; you blaze like a chimney."

"True dat but 'Cane is different."

"If it will ease your mind, I don't do it while we're out in public, performing or handling group business. I only do it when I'm by myself after a performance or when we got some down time."

"I been in this biz for a long time. You know that. I've seen what it does to people. They start off wit' a bump here, and bump there, and the next thing you know, it controls their lives. I'm not tryna preach to you cuz I do my share of wrongs too. Just think about the people's lives that it could potentially affect if it gets out of hand. I know you and Ivy ain't seein' eye to eye right now but if you care anything about him, you should chill. He put aside all his beef and put his relationship on the line to sign y'all. Regardless of the past, he believes in this group. You've been successful to this point. Platinum in two weeks. I don't want to see it all go down the drain because of a bad habit."

Cee Cee sat in silence for a minute. She dipped her finger in her drink then ran her vodka soaked finger around the rim of the glass as she stared at it. She began to sniffle as tears started streaming down her face.

"It's my fault Ivy got shot."

"That wasn't your fault. That coulda happened anywhere and to anybody."

"No T, it was really my fault. I left last night to go holla at my homegirl over in the 5th Ward to find out were I could get a bag. She couldn't leave the house cuz she had her kids so she called her dude and he told me to meet him at Club Voodoo. When I walked in the club, the DJ noticed who I was and shouted me out on the mic. I guess when he realized I was a celeb; he wanted to do more than just serve me. Him and his boy started gettin' a little too aggressive after he sold me the bag so I started to leave. They followed me outta the club so I ran across the street to the store to call Ivy. When he came, that's when it all went down. If I hadn't gone out, this would have never happened."

By the time her story came to the conclusion, Cee Cee was in an all out sob. T moved closer to her and put his arms around her for comfort.

"It's alright," he consoled. "It's over. I know you didn't mean for it to happen. We'll get through this." Candace held on to TyQuan and cried for about five minutes then tried to get herself together. As she reached into her bag to pull out her mirror, she also pulled out the small bag of Cocaine tightly balled in her fist. She handed it to T.

"Take it and do what ever you need to do. I promise you that for the rest of the tour, I'll leave it alone."

"That's my girl. You're doing the right thing. Now let's go talk to ya group."

"Do I have to right now?"

"Yes. Let's get it over with. We got stuff to do today."

"Alright." TyQuan paid for the drinks and they headed back upstairs. Cee Cee took a deep breath as T knocked on the door. Rolanda answered the door. When she saw that her third member was with T, her whole expression changed.

"Alright ladies," T began as he sat down in a chair. "This is the deal. We are not going to argue and we're not going to get loud. We're all grown ass adults and we're going to talk this out. We got 15 more cities to do and I refuse to let this go any further. You are a group and you're going to talk it out as a group. We leave everything in New Orleans. Who's gonna start?" Nobody wanted to break the ice. "Okay then, I'll pick somebody. Rolanda, you start."

"Alright. Since we're leaving it all here, I'm going to get it all off my chest. Cee Cee, you got mad talent. That's why we asked you to join the group. We thought that you would be a good fit for us. If it wasn't for you, we might not be here right now. In the same breath, you been doin' some shady shit. You didn't tell us about you and Ivy, you disappear without us knowing and now you doin' coke. I'm the last one to talk about people's bad habits cuz I got plenty myself but I don't think about myself anymore, I think about the group. Me and Kitty been through too much to get here and I'll be damned if I sit and watch you fuck it off."

"Yeah Cee Cee," Kitty began. "You made a comment about me and Rolanda runnin' around kissin' Ivy and Natalie's asses. It ain't even like that. They gave us this opportunity and believed in us despite your past with Ivy and what it could potentially do to their relationship. It ain't about kissin' ass, it's about being grateful. For the past 5 years me and my girl have been through it tryna get in this business. True, you helped give us the last boost we needed to get us over the hump but it ain't like we haven't paid our dues. We deserve to be here. Since you've been a part of this group, you haven't been a part of this group. You're with us when we're on stage or in front of the cameras but as soon as all that's over, you cut us off. You haven't given us the chance to get to know who you really are or what you're about. I'm not sayin' you gotta be around us 24/7; at least chill wit' us sometimes."

"To be honest, everything's happened so fast for me. When you came to me and asked me to be a part of the group because Ivy was thinkin' about signing you, I jumped at the chance but it was for all the wrong reasons. I told you that. I know I haven't been the best person to work with but I really do love being a part of the group. It's a dream come true for me. I guess I stay to myself because I see how tight you two are and I don't know how to be a part of that. I'll be the first to admit that I've been doing some foul shit. It took for something tragic to happen to somebody I care about for me to see that the things I do are wrong and is putting innocent people in jeopardy. The feelings I have for Iverson aren't gone but now I see that I can't have him. It's time to focus on being a singer. I promise that I will make an effort to do better and to become a part of this group so that we can have much success for years to come."

"What about the drugs?" Rolanda interjected.

"I got that handled," replied TyQuan.

"I've always been a solo artist and for the most part, a loner. All I ask is that you be patient with me. I'll do better."

"And that's all we can ask for," Kitty responded.

"Alright," T exhaled as he stood up.

"Now that we got this Oprah moment outta the way, I'm going to check on my man and then we gotta hit it. We got an in-store in about an hour so get it together."

Chapter 25

There's an old saying: A leopard can't change his spots. It seemed as if Cee Cee was sincere in all that she said to her fellow group members. The girls took it all in but were they really convinced? Candace's rap sheet was a lot longer than anybody knew. The only one that knew was Iverson. He was the only one that really knew anything about her. There had to be some good in her because he signed the group despite the past. If you notice, Iverson is the only one that really knows how to deal with her. She responds to him. The others allow her to get under their skin and she thrives off of it. The more she sees that she can get to you, the deeper she digs in.

After the game that night, Iverson didn't hang around the arena to wait for Natalie. Pain was forcing him back to the hotel to get his meds. TyQuan, Kitty and Rolanda hit the New Orleans Friday night club scene. Cee Cee wasn't quite back to normal. Her guilt behind the previous night's event had her mentally and emotionally drained. TyQuan understood where she was coming from. Candace bid her group goodnight.

She walked out of the front entrance of the arena. Ivy was surrounded by reporters shoving tape recorders and microphones at him. They were asking him about the previous night's shooting. Security was pushing people back left and right as Ivy refused to comment. Cee Cee saw the limo pulling up and pushed her way through the crowd of people. She grabbed Iverson by the hand on his good arm and pulled him through the crowd into the car.

"These muthaphuckas do not quit." Ivy straightened his hat.

"You think you'd be used to it by now."

"Bad press is something you never get used to."

"How do you consider it to be bad press?"

"A black record label CEO involved in a shooting...sounds drug related to me. You know how the media is."Cee Cee felt a warm sensation rush through her body when Ivy said the words: drug related. "Wait a minute," Ivy paused. "What are you doing in here? I thought everybody was going to the club."

"Last night took a lot out of me. I'm drained. I just wanna go back to the room and lay down."

"How is it that you're drained and I'm the one that took the bullet?" Ivy laughed.

"You know what I mean, crazy." The limousine pulled in front of the hotel. Iverson and Cee Cee got out and walked in. They continued idle chatter as they headed toward the elevator.

"Do you mind if I come up for a little while and talk?" Cee Cee asked.

"Yeah. You can come up for a minute. Natalie won't be here for another hour or so." Once in the suite, Iverson handed his bottle of pills to Cee Cee to open for him. She laughed as she opened the bottle.

"What's so funny?"

"This reminds me of the time you got sick about three months after I we moved in together. You were pitiful."

"That ain't funny. I was sick as hell."

"You were cute though." Iverson tossed his hat onto the couch and pulled the rubber band that held his locs in a ponytail off.

"This is the first time I've seen you with your hair down since we signed. I didn't realize how long your locs were."

"It's been a minute. When we first met, they were barely down to my neck."

"I wasn't feelin' them at first but they grew on me. I almost didn't talk to you because of them."

"Really?"

"Uh huh. I never dated a man with long hair before. I always liked my men clean cut."

"Is that why you left me?"

"We're not going there."

"Seriously...why did you leave?"

"I was stupid. I got caught up listening to my jealous, no man havin' ass friends. Excuse me...ex-friends."

"As much shit as they talked about me, as soon as Melanie found out that you and I weren't together no more, she tried to holla at me. I told you to leave them girls alone."

"I shoulda listened. As much as they didn't want to see us together, they stayed around because of the money. When you used to give me money, I used to take them out to dinner, treat them to the spa and a whole lot of other crazy stuff."

"You spent my money on them tricks?"

"Like a fool. As soon as I did what I did and left, they kicked me to the curb. I let'em fool me into walking away from the best thing that ever happened to me."

"But you knew I would never cheat on you. I treated you like a princess."

"That's just it. They were saying that you treated me the way you did because you were guilty or trying to hide something. I knew how some niggas were in the industry and I automatically put you in that category."

"Why didn't you leave then?"

"I was young and you had money. I also saw it as a shot to finally get into the business."

"So you're telling me that you were using me…"

"Honestly, in the beginning I was. Then I got to know Iverson. That's who I fell for."

"Then what happened?"

"Future took off and I didn't see Iverson as much. It was always Ivy. I traveled all around this country with you smiling for the cameras and being that dime piece on your arm. I thought it would die down but it kept growing and Future got larger and larger. Then you pulled the Puffy on me."

"What?"

"You stopped being just the man behind the scenes. The next thing I knew, you were in videos and featured on songs. That's when the attention started. I understand that you were, are, and will always be the face of Future Records but it was too much for me to handle. We couldn't go out without you having hoes all up in your face. I was happy when you were more like Russell Simmons."

"What's that supposed to mean? More like Russell Simmons…"

"Everybody knows that he is Def Jam but Russell wasn't always in front of the camera. That's why I said you went straight Puffy on me."

"Okay…," Ivy took a long pause as he stared at Cee Cee. "Answer me this. Why are you just telling me this now?"

"Had I said something back then you would have thought I was trying to stop you from doing what you loved to do or trying to change you. I just let you do you. Like I said, I thought it would eventually blow over. On top of all that, I had chicks in my ear pouring salt on my relationship."

"Damn," Iverson leaned his head back on the couch and stared at the ceiling. "I never realized that all of that was going on. I thought we had the perfect relationship and it just ended. Never in a million years did I think that I was a part of what drove you away."

"When things used to go down, you used to tell me that everything happens for a reason. Maybe it wasn't our time. I know it was hard to juggle a relationship and be in this industry. The major thing that I learned was that you never realize what you have until its gone. I shouldn't have wrecked your crib like I did. While I was doing it, I knew I was dead wrong but I couldn't stop myself. I was mad, hurt and confused all at the same time."

"That is not a good combination." With that statement, Iverson heard the door open. Natalie opened the door. When she raised her head, she paused when she saw Cee Cee in Ivy's room. "Hey Baby. I didn't think you would be here for another half an hour or so."

"When you lose, the press doesn't really want to talk to you for that long." Natalie walked past Cee Cee and gave Iverson a kiss before she spoke to Cee Cee. "You're not out with the crew tonight?"

"I wasn't feeling it. Last night took a lot out of me. On top of that, I couldn't sleep and we had a full day."

"Oh okay."

"I guess I'll be going now. It was nice talking to you again, Ivy. I'll see you at sound check." Natalie stared Cee Cee down as she walked to and out the door. She turned to Iverson.

"Don't start."

"What?" Natalie laughed. "I wasn't gettin' ready to say nothin'." Iverson gave here the *Yeah Right* look. "I wasn't. Honest."

"Okay, honest."

"What happened to y'all tonight? Y'all got demolished."

"Gee thanks. I didn't come over here for you to rub it in. If I wanted that, I coulda went out tonight." Natalie kicked her shoes off and curled up on the opposite end of the couch. She gazed at Iverson for about two minutes without saying anything.

"Go ahead and ask me cuz you know you want to."

"Why was she here?"

"She rode back from the arena with me. When we got here, she asked me if we could talk."

"About?"

"We tripped about a couple of things that happened when we were together and then she finally told me why she left me. I've been waiting on that for almost three years."

"What did she say?"

"In so many words she told me that besides her listening to her jealous friends, it was hard for her to deal with me when the label took off. I didn't realize it but now that I look at it, I changed."

"How so?"

"You know how I told you that I wanted you to get to know Iverson and not Ivy?"

"Yeah."

"Ivy took over and didn't look back. I was so caught up in the label that I forgot to be her man."

"But you were doing what you loved. The label is how you make your living."

"I understand that but there has to be a balance and there wasn't."

"It wasn't your fault. She had to know what she was getting into when you got in the relationship."

"She was young back then. I thought everything was cool cuz she never said anything."

"What's done is done and you can't go back and change that. Things happen for a reason. You and I both know that. Not trying to sound mean but I'm glad she didn't know how to handle it. If she did, we wouldn't be together."

"This is true."

"I know it's a lot to take in but don't stress over it. We make choices in our lives; some good and some bad. She made her choice and we've made ours. I love you more than words can express and that love grows stronger everyday that you are in my life."

"You are too much. I love you too." Natalie picked up a folder that was on the table and fanned herself with it.

"All of this expression of emotions is makin me hot. We better stop before we get something started."

"What's stopping us? I took a bullet in the arm, not the..."

"Ivy!" Natalie interrupted.

It was finally over. Thirty cities were in the books and R&B's newest group was at the top of the charts. The remainder of the tour, Candace stayed true to her word. She took time to let the girls get to know her and they became a tightly bound group. To the naked eye, Purrfection looked like they had been friends for years. Rolanda no longer wanted to kill Cee Cee on a daily basis and Kitty stopped having to be the voice of reason and mediator. The crew was exhausted as they were in the last few hours of their ride back to Atlanta.

"You did it," Ivy began as he sipped his drink. "Thirty cities and a platinum plaque. I'm impressed."

"It still feels like a dream," Rolanda expressed.

"Its gonna be like that for a little while longer," TyQuan interjected. "This is just the beginning. My voicemail box is full of promoters ready to book you on more tours."

"That's what's up!" Kitty smiled.

"What's next?" Cee Cee inquired.

"Its time to take it to the next level. I have a meeting Monday with Natalie, Alicia and your publicist. Y'all gettin' ready to be large."

Ivy pulled his Sidekick from his hip.

"This message is from Alicia. She says that your publicist has been getting calls from The Tyra Banks Show, Jay Leno, Conan O'brian, the Apollo, Soul Train and the list goes on."

"I didn't know Soul Train still came on," Cee Cee laughed.

"I was going to save this until we got back but I got a call from the BET Awards committee. You guys are nominated for 3 awards and they want you to perform."

"Are you serious?" Kitty gasped.

"Hard work pays off. I wouldn't have signed you if I felt that you were gonna be fly-by-night, one hit wonders."

"Wow! The BET awards. This is too good to be true."

"Well believe it," TyQuan added. "Hard work is its own reward and you girls worked your asses off to get that album done. On top of all that, everybody wants to work with you. I'm gettin' calls from everybody."

"Like who?" Rolanda asked.

"Where do I start? Jazze Pha wants you to do a song for his compilation album. Big Boi called and said he wanted you on a song for his album. Chris Brown's agent called. T-Pain's people hit me...."

"With all of this going on," Kitty interrupted. "When will we have time to start on our second album?"

"You got plenty of time for that. Once the first one starts to die down, then we start working on the second one."

"Cool."

"Until then....welcome to the life!" The crew talked for the remainder of the journey home. Around midnight, they hit downtown Atlanta. It had been a hellavah road trip and they were happy to be home. They pulled in front of the building and unloaded. Purrfection's families and friends were there to greet them. Dressed in pajamas and riding clothes, the girls stepped off the bus to a huge reception. Cee Cee was the only one that didn't have anyone there to greet her upon arrival. All of her family was back in Florida. As Kitty and Rolanda walked off with their people, she followed Ivy and T into the building. She went to the restroom then made her way to Ivy's office.

"I need a favor."

"What's up?"Before she could say anything, TyQuan came in.

"I'm headin' to the crib. You coming in tomorrow?"

"Tomorrow's Sunday."

"That's right. You goin' to church in the morning?"

"I need to but I'm tired. I might just skip and go next Sunday."

"Was God too tired to bless you with all of this? Was God too tired to fill your life with success?"

"Alright, Creflo! I'll meet you at the 11 o'clock service."

"Thank you. Aunt Shelia's having dinner at her house at 2. She said you better be there and you better bring Natalie."

"Natalie has a game tomorrow afternoon but I'll be there."

"Bet. Holla at ya boy!"

"Peace," Ivy turned his attention back to Cee Cee. "You were saying?"

"I need a favor."

"I got that part."

"Can you take me home?"

"Why didn't you catch T?"

"You have to go right pass my place on the way to yours. T lives in College Park."

"I guess I can give you a lift."

"Thank you." Ivy piddled around on his computer for a few minutes longer then they left. The lights of Atlanta were blinding to their tired eyes. Ivy and Cee Cee sat in silence as they rode toward Cee Cee's place. They were about five minutes from her spot when she started searching her bag for her keys.

"Uh oh."

"Uh oh? What the hell is uh oh?"

"Fran has my keys."

"Where is Fran?"

"In Charlotte until tomorrow. I left my car with her."

"Are you serious?"

"I'm sorry. You can just drop me off at the nearest hotel. I'll stay there for the night. Fran will be back in the morning."

"This is going to go against my better judgment but you can stay at the house tonight."

"That's okay. I don't wanna get you in any trouble with your woman. You know she don't like me."

"What makes you say that?"

"She doesn't and you know it. Every since you told her about our past, she's been watchin' me like a hawk when I'm around you. She doesn't treat me the same way she treats Kitty and Rolanda."

"How does she treat you different?"

"Anytime she says anything to me she says it with a different tone. She talks to Rolanda and Kitty like they're old friends. You saw it for yourself when we were in New Orleans. When she came to your room after the game, she had this look of disapproval on her face when she saw that I was in your room. To top it off, she made it a point to come in and give you a kiss before she even acknowledged the fact that I was in the room."

"You trippin'. It ain't even like that. You know we hadn't seen each other in a couple of weeks. She was just happy to see me. Besides, you are her client. She doesn't have to like you as long as she does right by you and the contracts."

"I know but it just feels like she shows favoritism. That scares me as a client. It makes me feel like if a situation comes up and she has to choose single members to do certain things, she'll always choose them before me."

"You're a woman so you have to understand her position. How would you feel if your man and his ex were on the road together? How would you feel if you signed a client and then found out that the client and the CEO used to be involved? This is not an easy situation for any of us but we gotta make it work. As far as the favoritism thing goes, I'll talk to her about it."

"That's not necessary. I can fight my own battles."

"You sure?"

"Yes I'm sure." Ivy and Candace arrived at his Buckhead estate. Cee Cee was amazed. This was the first time she'd been there. It was definitely a step up from the condo they used to live in. Ivy pulled around to the garage and pulled in.

"Where's my baby?" Cee Cee asked as she closed the car door.

"It's over there." Cee Cee walked over to her motorcycle and sat on it.

"Where's the key?"

"Girl it is 1 o'clock in the morning. It still runs. Trust me. My sister rode it about 3 months ago."

"You let somebody else ride my baby?"

"Girl stop. Now let's go in the house."

"You know this is mine again. A deal is a deal."

"You're right. You can take it whenever you're ready."

Candace unmounted the bike and followed Ivy into the elevator. They arrived on the second floor. Iverson showed her where she would be sleeping then went into his room and closed the door. Candace put her purse and carry-on bag on the bed. She opened the small suitcase and pulled out something to sleep in. From her room, she walked to Iverson's room and asked for a towel and a tour. Ivy gave her a towel but declined the tour.

Candace went back to the bedroom and took a shower. After she took her shower and put on her sleeping attire, she got in the bed. She tried to go to sleep but she had consumed too much caffeine on the ride home. Candace got up out of the bed in search of a television.

"I guess I have to give myself a tour," she thought to herself. Candace began to roam around Iverson's home. She went from room to room in admiration. After about 15 minutes of walking around, she found the game room. She walked over to the shelf where the DVDs were to find a movie. She scanned Ivy's collection and found their favorite movie, *Love and Basketball*. She popped the disc into the player then walked behind the bar to fix a drink. Once she had her cocktail and her movie on, Candace curled up on the couch under a Chenille blanket that was thrown over the back of the couch. About twenty minutes into the movie, Cee Cee got hot and removed her bottoms. Thirty minutes later, she was fast asleep.

The next morning, Ivy walked to the room he's put Candace up in. He knocked on the door but there was no answer. He peeked his head in the room and saw that she wasn't there. He went from room to room looking for her. After he searched every room on that floor, he remembered that she had to have the television to fall asleep. He walked downstairs into the game room and found Candace wrapped up in the blanked with the opening menu of the movie playing on the big screen.

"Cee Cee," he called as he shook her. "Wake up." She began to stir.

From under the blanket, "What time is it?"

"9:30…get up."

"Are you serious?"

"Come on. I have to get you situated before I go to church."

"Alright. Alright." Candace unraveled from the blanket and sat up.

"Damn girl!" Ivy laughed. "I forgot how you looked in the morning."

"Very funny."

Candace stood up in a top that exposed her flat mid-rift and a black thong. For the first time in a long time, Iverson got a glance at the light-skinned, perfectly round ass that he used to love so much.

"Don't you think you need to cover yourself up?"
"Its just ass. Don't act like you ain't never seen it before."

Candace walked past him towards the room where here things were. Ivy was an involved man but he was still a man. He watched as Candace walked past him to the door. Candace could feel Iverson watching her. She put a little extra switch in her walk causing her backside to jiggle. When she got to the door, she paused and looked back over her shoulder. She gave him a devilish grin as she smacked her ass and walked through the door.

"If I wasn't a faithful man," Ivy thought to himself. "I'd tear dat ass up." He laughed as he shook the blanket and placed it back in its rightful place.

After church, Iverson went over to Aunt Sheila's house for Sunday dinner. TyQuan and Alexa were sitting on the couch in the living room. He dapped up his partner and greeted the other family members that were in attendance. Aunt Shelia was that typical southern woman. As soon as she came home from service, she put on her house dress and got dinner ready to put on the table. In the middle of a conversation with one of the sisters from the church, she noticed Iverson standing in the living room.

"Lord have mercy," She moaned as she pushed the woman she was talkin to to the side and started into the living room. "I prayed just last night and asked the Lord to send my baby to see me." She embraced Ivy and put that Auntie squeeze on him.

"How you doin' Aunt Shelia?"

"Besides a lil' high blood pressure, I'm fine now that I got my two babies together at the same time. Where's that pretty girlfriend of yours?"

"She wanted to come but she has a game this afternoon."

"Tell'er I forgive her this time but she better get round here and see me."

"Yes ma'am. I'll be sure to tell her."

"Tee Tee, go get Iverson somethin' to drink."

"Tee Tee?" Alexa laughed.

"That's right. I gave him that name when he was a lil' ole thang. When we was tryna potty train him all he used to say was 'Tee Tee, Auntie. 'Tee Tee'."

"Auntie! You promised me you'd stop tellin' people that story." Ivy and Alexa laughed.

"Boy hush and go get Ivy something to drink."

"Yeah Tee Tee, run along and get me somethin' to drink." Like a small child, TyQuan shuffled in the kitchen with a slight pout on his face.

"You better straighten up yo face boy. You ain't too old for me to put the belt to you."

"Get'em Aunt Sheila." Ivy teased.

"I tell you. It's so good to see you again. You gotta come around more often. You know I worry about you and Tee Tee. If you can't make it by, at least call an old woman and let'er know you alright."

"Things have been real busy lately but I'll try to do better."

"I know baby. I see you on the TV all the time. You doin real good for yourself. I know your family is proud of ya. I know we are."

"Thank you."

"I gotta get this food on the table. You know you home. Don't be in here actin' like no stranger."

"Yes ma'am." TyQuan was coming out of the kitchen as Aunt Shelia was going back in. She popped him up side the back of his head as he walked past her.

"What was that for?"

"For takin too long."

"Here man." T handed Ivy a tall glass of Iced Tea.

"Preciate ya." Ivy took a big swig of the tea then sat down in the recliner.

"If Uncle Earl come in here and see you in his recliner, it's over."

"You know me and Uncle Earl cool like that."

"Okay cool like that." With the close of that statement, a short, stout man waddled into the living room.

"Hey boy!" Uncle Earl hollered as he came in the room.

"Hey Uncle Earl," TyQuan greeted.

"I ain't talkin' to you, boy. I'm talkin to the man with the money."

"I swear my family treat me like I'm adopted."

"Niecy finally told you?"

"What?"

"Gotcha!" Once again Ivy and Alexa got a laugh at T's expense. "Let me hold somethin', Ivy."

"You know you can get it, Unc."

"Where that pretty girl that Sheila was tellin' me about?"

"She had a game today."

"I know why you ain't brought'er by. You know once she meet ya Uncle, she gone leave you."

"You know it, Unc," Ivy laughed.

"You know me. I'ma Ol' G. Look at my eyes…roll'em."

"Uncle Earl. How is that Ivy can sit in yo recliner and I can't?"

"Tee Tee...stop bein' a playa hater. Ain't that what y'all young boys say?"

"I told you, T. Me and Uncle Earl cool like that."

"Alright Earl," Aunt Sheila called from the kitchen. "Come on and bless this food so we can eat."

"Alright baby," Uncle Earl called back. "Y'all come on."

Ivy, TyQuan and Alexa followed Uncle Earl into the dining room. After Uncle Earl said the blessing, everybody dug in. It was a typical southern spread — macaroni and cheese, collard greens, rice, baked ham, potato salad, fried chicken, field peas, cornbread muffins and sweet potato pie for dessert. That's how it goes down in the Dirty Souf! Everyone in attendance stuffed their faces and enjoyed a good meal. After the meal was over, people started to leave. Uncle Earl and Aunt Shelia moved to the living room with Ty, Alexa and Ivy for conversation.

"You put ya foot in them greens, Aunt Shelia," Ivy expressed as he sat down on the floor.

"Thank you, baby. I know my babies like to eat. I fixed you some food to take home wit ya. Make sure ya lady friend get some."

"Thank you. I really appreciate that." As they continued to talk, Ivy's Sidekick went off. He had received a message from Natalie.

Ivy,

Can a sista get some time? I know you got in late and I had a game today but I need to see you....Tonite! Call me when you get a chance. Love You!

Dymond

"That must be the wife," T laughed.
"You know it."

After an hour more of conversation, Ivy gathered up to leave. Aunt Shelia gave him the traditional plates wrapped with aluminum foil. She told him that she gave him one of her good plates so that he'd have to come back to bring it to her. He hugged Aunt Shelia and left. By the time he left, Natalie's game was over. He grabbed his cell phone and called her.

"Hey baby!" Natalie answered. "What you up to?"
"I'm on my way home."
"You win?"
"89-86 in overtime."
"Damn...that was a close one."
"Detroit got a good squad this year."
"Stats?"

"Thirty-one, 9 assists and 5 steals."

"That's my girl."

"I dropped 17 in the 4th quarter to bring us back to tie it up and send it into OT."

"Do it, Kobe!"

"What about ya girl, Shawna?"

"You would ask about her. She fouled out in the fourth with 5. She got away wit a couple cheap shots on me. I got a tech in the third quarter."

"For what?"

"She elbowed me in the jaw while we were fightin' for a rebound. I snapped and ran up in her face."

"They T'ed you up for that?"

"I got mad cuz I didn't get the call and kept fussin' at the the ref."

"That'll get you everytime."

"Anyway...Can I see you tonight?"

"You know it. You want me to come over there or you comin' to da crib."

"I gotta drop some things off to Alicia so I'll be on that side. I'll just come to you."

"Around what time?"

"Give me a couple hours. I still got go home and change."

"That's two hours right there."

"Hush!"

"If you haven't eaten anything I got some good home cookin from T's Aunt today."

"What she cook?"

"Greens, Mac and Cheese, ham, chicken, rice, field peas and potato salad."

"Lawd have mercy. Thank you Jesus! I haven't had good soul food in a minute."

"It's slammin' too."

"I know it is. I'll see you in a little while."

"Okay babe."

"Love you."

"Love you back"

Natialie hung up the phone. As she drove, she thought about her current relationship and the situation within it. She and Iverson had been together for a good while. Everything was good. He treated her like a queen and they were doing good business together. Through it all she still couldn't help but to think about Iverson's past relationship with Cee Cee and their current business involvement. She wanted to let her guard down and let him all the way in. Because of Cee Cee she couldn't do that just yet. The conversation that she and Ivy had while in New Orleans kept running through her mind. All she could hear was him telling her about finally getting the answer he was looking for from Cee Cee.

This was a big deal. When a woman begins to express those types of things to an ex, it means there are still some feelings there. She just didn't know how strong Cee Cee's feelings for Iverson were. In saying that, she was still unclear of Ivy's feelings for Cee Cee—

especially after finding out that the ending of their relationship looked like a misunderstanding. She knew that he assured her that everything was over between them and he just wanted some closure. Some women don't know how to leave it at that. Natalie promised Iverson that she wouldn't let her past relationships dictate their current relationship. In a situation of this magnitude, a statement like that is easier said than done.

Chapter 26

Alicia and Natalie sat in her home office looking over some paperwork. As Alicia was flipping through a document, she noticed that Natalie was zoned out with an odd look on her face.

"Natalie," she called.

Natalie didn't respond.

"Nat-a-lie!"

"Huh?"

"What is wrong with you?"

"Nothing. Why?"

"You've been spaced out since you've been here. What's up? What's on your mind? Talk to your girl."

"I've been thinking about my relationship a lot lately."

"Are you and Ivy having troubles?"

"That's just it. It seems too perfect."

"Then what's the problem?"

"I don't know. Since we've been together, we haven't fussed, argued or had so much as a disagreement."

"And what's wrong with that? Me and Dré don't fuss and argue."

"Not since you got married but you two went through a lot before you finally got together."

"We have a relationship that can't be explained. We've known each other since we were kids runnin' around on the playground.

675

He's the only man I've ever loved. Even when I was in other relationships, the love I had for them was so much different from the love I've always had for him."

"Did you ever feel that you and him might not have got back together?"

"That day when he came back to South Carolina to break up with me, deep down inside I knew that he would still be mine. I didn't expect for someone to die in order for me to get my man back but I knew he was mine."

"How did you react when you saw him on ESPN with me?"

"I wanted to kill you both," Alicia laughed.

"When me and Dré started kickin' it, I knew he wasn't my man. As much as I wanted him to be, I knew he wasn't going to be the man in my life. He had all the qualities that I wanted but because I knew that you were #1 in his life, I tried not to let myself fall for him. The thing that hurt the most was when he broke up with you and chose Karen instead of me. I knew I was more his type than she was."

"God bless the dead but I still don't know what he ever saw in her."

"I think he was more less filling a void. When he said that she reminded him of you the first thing I thought about was how similar the two of you looked."

"I do not look like that woman."

"Yes you do, white girl."

"Anyway.....this conversation ain't about me. It's about you. What ever it is that's bothering you about your relationship, get it out your system. I don't know what you need to do to get it out because I don't know the full details but as a woman I know that if you let it fester, it's going to cause problems. The least little mole hill is going to turn into a mountain. Ivy is a good brother and you know it. I'm feeling that this has to do with him and Cee Cee's past involvement and this current situation. Ivy is your man. I know it's hard to have the ex in the picture but you gotta get a grip on what's real and don't let the past dictate your present or your future."

"Damn girl," Natalie laughed. "You sound just like your husband."

"We've always been the same person. That's why we get along. Now it's up to you to become one with Ivy."

"That's deep."

Time ticked away and it was time for Natalie to head over to Iverson's. No matter how hard she tried, Natalie couldn't shake those thoughts out of her head. Nothing in life is guaranteed — especially relationships. It is up to the people involved in it to put forth the effort to make it work and to make it last. Natalie and Iverson were a good couple but history can have a major effect on a relationship. The things that people endure from relationship to relationship can sometimes take a serious toll on a person's mentality.

Look at Natalie. In the past few years, she hasn't had much success with companions. André was the person that seemed to be the most compatible with her but she couldn't have him. When they met, someone already had his heart. That seems to be the ultimate smack in the face. Even though they agreed that a friendship was all that they could have between them, it's not easy to keep yourself from falling for someone that possesses all of the qualities that you've been searching for.

Desmond was the other person that was a part of Natalie's life. When they first met on into the beginning of their relationship, Desmond was the perfect man. He was financially stable with his own business, he was attractive in Natalie's eyes and he treated her with respect and like a lady. The thing that killed their union was the fact that they got physical too soon. We all know that there's no written rule that says when you should get intimate with a person. Natalie and Desmond got sexually involved about two weeks after they met. For some, that's ample time. Desmond's mental wasn't strong enough to handle it. This built their relationship on sex. That's never a good thing to do.

Before long, Natalie began to see that sex was the only thing that kept them together. She tried to take a step back but that never works. When she brought it up to Desmond, he didn't understand where she was coming from. He didn't understand why she wanted to slow down on the physical. She tried to have special romantic nights with no physical intimacy but when you're used to those things always leading to sex, it is difficult to stop during the time that's usually set aside for the physical. That's when Desmond got frustrated and his feelings and actions changed.

Natalie tried and tried to get the relationship on track. She failed at every attempt. Pretty soon, Natalie and Desmond were just going through the motions. This went on for about 4 months until Natalie couldn't take it anymore. In the last two months, the only conversations they had led to arguments. That's when Natalie found that Desmond wasn't the right man for her. When it all came to a head, Natalie suspected Desmond of cheating and those accusations caused Desmond to disappear. As much as he denied it, deep down inside, Natalie felt that her feeling was right. The only thing she could think about was the fact that what she wouldn't or wasn't doing, another woman would and was.

Now let's look at Iverson. Iverson has also had his share of relationship trials and tribulations. It all started with Cee Cee. Ivy and Cee Cee met on the internet right as he and T were putting Future together. Fresh out of the NBA, he was just a club owner and promoter. Cee Cee was just starting her modeling career and dabbled a bit in music. When she met Ivy, she saw him as a stepping stone into the industry. During a conversation, Ivy told Cee Cee that he could help her with her demo and let her perform at the club. Before that could happen, the label that was in the developmental stages started making noise. Once the buzz started getting larger about Future Records, Ivy sold the club and devoted all of his time to the label. Cee Cee knew that she was going to be a star. All she had to do was lock him down and hang on when the ride began.

Before you know it, Cee Cee uprooted her life and moved from Miami to Atlanta to be with Ivy. In the beginning of the relationship, Cee Cee became the eye candy for the label. Her face and body was plastered on every flyer and print ad. She was even on the CD covers of Ivy's first artist and in a couple of his videos. Ivy and Cee Cee's relationship became overshadowed by what was going on.

At that time, Ivy was oblivious to the troubles of his relationship because on the outside, everything seemed to be perfect. Candace never complained or showed Ivy any signs that she was unhappy. On top of that, Candace was young. They say women mature faster than men but that's not always true in every case. Cee Cee got caught up in living the good life and reaping the benefits of a record label CEO.

Once the glitz and the glamour of the music industry got old and Iverson wasn't moving fast enough with her music career, she wanted to fall back and enjoy her relationship. The rising success of Future Records prevented that from happening. In the whirlwind of multi-city tours, television appearances, and the constant barrage of hateration coming from her so-called friends, Cee Cee and Iverson's relationship got lost in the confusion. When Candace lashed out at Iverson by ruining his condo, she knew that her actions would sever all ties to Iverson and that bridge would be forever burned. Everything they went through could have been avoided had they just taken the time to sit down and talk about what was going on.

After Cee Cee's sudden disappearance Iverson walked around in a fog. Still caught up in what was going on with the rise of his label, Ivy couldn't find time to deal with his pain. Other than Future business, Ivy stopped going out. Iverson hid his pain so well that even T-

Bizzy didn't know what was going on. He figured that everything that they were doing with the business was so tiresome that when there was nothing going on, Ivy just wanted to chill. This is when Ivy stumbled onto just4kickz.com. That's where he found his comfort. The people were so cool. All of the regulars in the chat room took Ivy in and accepted him for who he was. Even after they found out who he really was, it didn't matter. To them, he was just Futurama.

Through that website and ebonyworld.com, Iverson met a few other women. After Cee Cee, he decided not to take anyone he met on the internet serious. When he stepped up to bat again, the World Wide Web threw him three quick strikes: XoticMami, 2much4u and WifeyMaterial. That should've been enough to cut it out but he wanted to step up to bat one more time. This time the Internet threw him the perfect pitch: Dymond4eva. Ivy knocked it out of the park. To this point, Ivy had the perfect relationship. The question was: Would Natalie talk to Ivy about what she was feeling or would she keep it inside in hope that it would pass?

Natalie pulled up to Ivy's around a quarter past eight. She was greeted with the plate that Ivy got from Aunt Sheila's and tall glass of Kool-Aid—the red kind. Natalie and Ivy engaged in idle chatter while she ate. Once

she'd had her fill, they walked down to the
game room.

"Whew!" Natalie exhaled.
"I am stuffed. I hadn't had food that
good in a minute."
"Auntie do her thing."
"Yes she does." Ivy walked behind the
bar to fix a drink.
"You want a drink?"
"Why not. We're off tomorrow."
"The usual?"
"You know it."

Iverson fixed Natalie a Hennessy and
Coke with a side of Grand Mariner and a
snifter of Hennessy for himself. Natalie kicked
off her shoes and stretched out on the couch.

"How did the rest of the tour go?"
"It was bananas. The show we did in
VA Beach almost got cancelled because of bad
weather. It broke about two hours before the
venue opened. DC was cool and Philly was
cool. The show in SC was a disaster. I don't
know what in the hell the promoters didn't do
but it was a mess. The house wasn't close to
being packed."
"Wow."
"I think the girls did like 3 songs and
that was it. The after party was hot though. My
man Blaze put it down. The club was smaller
than I expected but it was on swole."

"I'm curious as to why the promoters didn't do a show in the ATL."

"They wanted to but all the venues were booked on the days they wanted. The only way they coulda did a show here woulda been to do it during the week."

"Did Cee Cee behave herself?"

"C'mon babe. You gotta let that go."

"What? I'm just asked a question."

"She and I had an interesting conversation last night."

"About?"

"She asked me not to say anything."

"You brought it up. You can't stop now."

"Ok but this stays between me and you. She said that she feels that you don't treat her the same way you treat Kitty and Rolanda."

"What?!"

"I'm just telling you what she told me. She said that you talk to her different than you talk to them. With them it's like you all are old friends but you treat her like just a client."

"That is not true," Natalie defended. "I met Kitty and Rolanda before I met her because she was M.I.A. I had the opportunity to get to know them. The first time I met her was the night before you saw the group together. The next thing I know, you're telling me that she was your ex. How am I supposed to react to that?"

"I know babe. Calm down."

"I am calm."

"I'm just telling you what she told me. I know it's not an easy situation to deal with but let's just try to use some professional discretion."

"I don't have to treat her like a friend. She's a contracted client as far as I'm concerned. As long as I do right by her contract, that's all that matters."

"And that's what I told her. Now can we change the subject?"

"Yes. Please change the subject."

Natalie and Ivy sat in silence for about 4 minutes before Natalie finally spoke again.

"Do you still have feelings for her?"

"No. I told you that."

"I know but I just wanted to hear you say it again."

"Is something bothering you?" This was Natalie's opportunity to get out in the open the feelings she was having. Everything that she talked about with Alicia, she could now talk about them with the person that really mattered.

"No. I'm cool. Why you ask?"

"I was just wondering. You seem a little edgy."

"Maybe I'm edgy cuz I haven't had my fix of Futurama in a while."

"Is that so?" Ivy asked as he pulled Natalie toward him.

Natalie crawled on top of Iverson like a lioness approaching her king. Before she did anything she stopped and gazed into his eyes. A sly grin spread across her face. Natalie took her hand and swiped Iverson's locs from in his face. She slowly moved her lips to his. Before their lips touched, she diverted from her path and kissed Ivy on the cheek. She repeated the same motion then kissed him on his forehead.

"Why you playin' wit me?" Ivy laughed.
"Be patient. We have all night."

Once more, Natalie moved toward Ivy's full lips. Right before the point of contact, she paused then kissed him on the nose. Natalie giggled then planted her lips on his. As they were locked in a passionate kiss, Natalie slid her hands under Ivy's arms and between the cushions of the couch. She stopped because she felt something silky.

"What? Why you stop?" Natalie pulled the foreign object from between the cushions. It was a pair of female boxers.
"Who's are these?"
"They're not mine." Natalie quickly removed herself from on top of Ivy.
"I know they're not yours. Who's are they?"
"I don't know."
"Don't lie to me, Iverson."
"I'm serious. I don't know."

"You had somebody else here, didn't you?"

"No other female has been here besides you." Iverson sat up and tried to figure out who they belonged to. All of Natalie's insecurities and doubts were starting to control her emotions.

"I'm going to ask you one more time, Iverson. Who do these belong to?"

"Wait a minute…those are probably Cee Cee's."

"Cee Cee! What the fuck was she doing here and why did she have these on!"

"If you calm down for a minute, I'll tell you."

"How in the hell do you expect me to calm down and you had your ex-girlfriend here? I don't believe you. After all that I've sacrificed. I trusted you Iverson."

"It's not what you think…"

"It's never what I think! You probably woulda screwed her in New Orleans if I hadn't come in when I did."

"Now you're going too far."

"No! You've gone too far."

"Will you just let me explain?"

"Just save it." Natalie put on her shoes and stormed out of the room with Iverson right behind her. He was begging for her to stop and listen to him but she wouldn't. Right before she could get out of the door, Ivy grabbed her by her arms and shook her.

"Will you calm the fuck down and listen to me for a minute?" Natalie snatched her arms from him. "My bad. I didn't mean to grab you like that."

"You got one minute." Ivy could see the anger, rage and hurt in Natalie's eyes when he looked into them.

"When we got back last night, Cee Cee asked me to take her home. Before we got there, she realized that her girl had her keys because she had her car and wouldn't be back until this morning. She wanted me to take her to a hotel but I felt that wasn't necessary. I brought her here. She was supposed to sleep in one of the guest bedrooms but when I came down this morning, she was sleep on the couch. She fell asleep watching a movie."

"And I'm supposed to believe that?"

"It's the truth. I woulda done the same for any of my artists."

Natalie stared at Iverson for about a minute then walked out of the door without saying anything further. A flood of tears poured from Natalie's eyes as she tried to drive. Realizing that she couldn't see anymore, she made her way to Alicia and André's house. When she rang the doorbell, Dré answered. A look of deep concern hit his face when her saw that Natalie was crying. He pulled her inside and embraced her as she let it all go. Alicia heard the crying and walked in the room to see what was going on.

"It's okay, Sis," Dré consoled. "Whatever it is just let it out."

"Natalie...what happened?"

"I think Ivy's cheating on me," Natalie sobbed.

"What?" Dré and Alicia led Natalie into the living room. When she sat down on the couch, Alicia slid the box of tissues in front of her.

While pulling out three tissues, "I think Ivy's cheating on me."

"Can you give us a minute, baby?"

"No. Something happened to my sister and I wanna find out who's ass I gotta whoop."

"André please...give us a minute."

"You got one minute." Dré walked out of the room as Natalie tried to gather herself enough to talk.

"Now what happened?" Natalie began telling Alicia what happened. It took her awhile to get it out because the more she talked about it, the more she cried.

"What did he have to say about it?"

"He said that she spent the night there because her friend had her keys and wouldn't be back until today. He also said that instead of sleeping in one of the guest bedrooms, she slept on the couch."

"Why don't you believe him?"

"I don't know. It's like Desmond happening all over again."

"Ivy is not Desmond and you know that. You know that man loves you."

"Then why didn't he tell me in the beginning that she was there?"

"Ivy knows that you're already having a hard time dealing with the fact that they used to be together. I'm ya girl so I gotta shoot you straight. You pushed for him to sign Purrfection even after you found out what the deal was because of Kitty and Rolanda. He has done nothing to this point to show that he's being unfaithful."

"What about the night he got shot? She was there. I came to his room when we were in New Orleans and she was there. She just went on a 30 city tour with my man. She's always there. To top it all off, I found out that the end of their relationship was all a misunderstanding."

"But you are the one that he's in love with. They work together now. They are going to have one on one interaction. You both knew what you were getting into when he signed the group. You said you could handle it. Remember?"

"I know that's what I said but I don't think I can handle it anymore."

"So now what? You just let the best thing that ever happened to you go because of an incident you're not clear about? I don't think that Ivy cheated on you. I believe that he's telling the truth. I could be wrong but I don't think that I am.

"Part of this is my fault too. I had the chance tonight to talk to him about what we talked about earlier but I let it pass me by."

"Listen. What goes on in the dark will eventually come to the light. Go home. Pray about it and sleep on it."

"You're right. Thanks." The two business partners and best friends embraced as Dré walked into the room.

"You good?"

"Yeah. I'm good."

"I don't need to whoop nobody's ass do I?"

"Not just yet."

"Alright. You need us to take you home?"

"Nah. I'm cool. I think I can make it."

Natalie thanked her friends and made her way home. She was emotionally drained when she got there. After a hot shower, she said her prayers and went to sleep.

The next morning found Ivy sitting at his desk staring blankly at the monitor. He still couldn't believe what happened. He was torn between the questions of: Did she do it on purpose or was it an honest mistake? While deep in thought, the tone of his IM went off.

KandeeGirl: Ivy r u there?
Ivy_Dav: I'm here
KandeeGirl: how r u?

Ivy_Dav: who is this?

KandeeGirl: u know who I am

Ivy_Dav: if ur not going to tell me who u are don't contact me. Better yet how bout I not give a fuck and block u

KandeeGirl: no need for all of that...its me

Ivy_Dav: me who?

KandeeGirl: Cee Cee

Ivy_Dav: wtf?!?!? r u serious?

KandeeGirl: yeah...surprised?

Ivy_Dav: pissed off is more like it

KandeeGirl: what I do now?

Ivy_Dav: u got me fucked up...that's what you did. u lefta pair of shorts in the couch that you slept on last night and Natalie found them

KandeeGirl: damn...anyway...how'd ur day?

Ivy_Dav: r u serious? u might've cost me my relationship and u ask me how my day was. Go to hell Candace

Ivy closed the IM box and shut down the messenger application. He was heated. Ivy was so mad that he was shaking. There was no way he was going to get any work done. He told Michelle he was stepping out for awhile and left the building. When Iverson hit the street, he took a left and started walking. His mind raced with a menagerie of different thoughts. After about fifteen minutes, Ivy stopped and sat down on a bench. For a good while he just sat and watched the cars and people go by. Then he decided to call Natalie. He dialed her number. It rang four times then went to voicemail.

"Dymond. It's Ivy. We need to talk about last night. Give me a call when you get this message."

Natalie sat on her couch and watched the phone ring displaying Iverson's number and playing his personalized ringtone. She wanted to answer it but she couldn't bring herself to do it. When the voicemail notification came through she listened to the message. She tossed the phone onto the couch beside her. At that moment, Natalie was in a state of confusion. She didn't know if Ivy had cheated or not, and if he didn't, how was her overreaction going to effect their relationship going forward. She heard Ivy's side of the story but she had to get to the bottom of it. She picked up the phone and dialed Cee Cee's number.

"Hello," Candace answered.
"Candace, this is Natalie."
"Oh hey."
"Listen. We have a meeting this afternoon at Copeland's. Can you make it?"
"Yeah. I can be there. What time?"
"Three o'clock."
"See you then."

Natalie hung up the phone.

This was a dangerous thing that Natalie was doing. In her fragile state of mind, this could be exactly what Cee Cee needed to push Natalie and Ivy's relationship over the edge. Natalie really didn't know what she was going to ask her or how she was going to ask her. She also didn't know whether Cee Cee's answers were going to be the truth. The one thing she did know what that she had to confront the source of the problem.

Chapter 27

Natalie sat tucked away in a corner at Copeland's. In front of Natalie were a menu and a glass of ice water. She reached into her purse to check her phone for the time. The numbers of the cell phone's clock read: 2:57pm. Natalie lifted her head when she noticed that someone was sitting down at the table. It was Candace. Candace looked around and noticed that the table was only set for two.

"Where's Kitty and Rolanda?" Cee Cee inquired.

"This meeting has nothing to do with Purrfection. This meeting is about you and me."

"What about you and me?"

"Would you like to order a drink or something to eat?"

"I'm cool. Just get to what this is about."

"We both know all about your past relationship with Iverson," Natalie began as she sipped her water. "What I want to know now is what were you doing at Iverson's house last night?"

"Are you serious?"

"I don't think that the look on my face expresses anything other than seriousness."

"I asked Ivy to take me home because a friend had my car. In her having my car, she also had my house key. I asked him to take me to a hotel but he insisted that I stay at his house. No big deal."

"Okay but I'm having a hard time understanding why I found a pair of your boxers stuffed down in his couch."

"Look...I didn't come here to be interrogated. Honestly, what me and Ivy did at his house is none of your damn business."

"Anything that concerns my man is my business. I'm going to ask you again. What happened?" A smug grin curled in the corners of Cee Cee's mouth. She knew that she had Natalie right were she wanted her. All she had to do was make her move.

"Ask your man what happened. He seemed to really enjoy it." With that statement, Candace slid her chair back from the table. "And the next time you want to talk to me, don't front like its group business. That's very unprofessional. Good day, Ms. Simms."

Candace hoisted her Coach bag over her shoulder and walked out of the restaurant with a feeling of satisfaction. The crazy thing about it was that she knew that Ivy wasn't going to be her man if they broke up. Her satisfaction would be the fact that Natalie didn't have him either.

Ivy's midnight blue 300C pulled up in TyQuan's yard in College Park. TyQuan was in the driveway washing his Magnum while listening to music on his IPod. Iverson got out of the car and stood right beside him unnoticed. He tapped T on the shoulder and scared the hell out of him.

"Come on man! You know I got bad nerves. You can't be sneakin' up on black people like that."

"You shouldn't be livin' ya life wrong. You wouldn't be so jumpy."

"Anyway...what's good?"

"The shit done hit the fan. Cee Cee stayed at the crib the other night..."

"Stop right there. What the fuck were you thinking?"

"That's just it. I wasn't."

"Did you smash?"

"No. She asked me to take her home right after you left. We get close to her crib and she realizes that she doesn't have her keys."

"Why didn't you take her to a hotel, man?"

"I was so tired that all I wanted to do was get in the bed. To make a long story short, Dymond found a pair of shorts that Cee Cee left on the couch."

"If you didn't smash, why would she be assed out in yo crib?"

"Bruh, I have no idea. I showed her to the room she was supposed to sleep in. The next morning I find her asleep on the couch. When she got up all she had on was a thong and a shirt. I was so focused on the ass that I didn't think to check the couch. I figured that's how she came down."

"You need to get yo shit together. What did Dymond say when she found them?"

"She went off. I tried to tell her the truth but she wasn't tryna hear me."

"Maybe she just needs to cool down. Give her some time."

"I'm so shook right now. If I lose this girl over some bullshit...Ughhh!" In frustration, Ivy kicked over T's bucket of soapy water.

"Come on, man! That bucket has done nothin' to you."

"My bad."

"You need to go to the crib and chill. Don't stress it. The truth will come out."

"Aight man. I'll holla at you later."

"As a matter of fact, take the day off tomorrow. The girls are gonna be there and you don't need to be."

"I'm good."

"No you're not. You just assaulted an innocent bucket of soap and water. Get ya mind right. Just chill."

"Whatever man."

"And don't go callin' that girl a thousand times." Ivy shot his ace the bird and pulled out of the driveway enroute to Buckhead.

"How could I have been so stupid?" He asked himself.

The next day, Natalie was at practice. It wasn't a good day for her. It seemed like she just couldn't get it together. She was missing shots that she usually made, getting the ball stolen from her and turning the ball over excessively. Those things rarely happened to her. Coach blew her whistle.

"Bring it in ladies!" The team jogged to the sideline and huddled around the coach. "What's the problem, Simms?"

"Sorry Coach. I'm just having an off day."

"Off days don't cut it around here. We can't expect to repeat as champions having off days."

"I know, Coach."

"What ever it is that's on your mind, get it together. I can't have my star player out there making petty mistakes."

"Can you get up off me please!? I have one bad day and you're all down my throat. I told you I got it."

"You're done for the day, Simms. Take it in."

"Excuse me?"

"You heard me. Get off my court."

Natalie snatched her towel then kicked over the Gatorade cooler as she left the court headed for the locker room. When she got there, she flopped down in her chair and put her towel over her head, her face in her hands and began to cry. Two minutes later, Jasmine walked in. She tried to find out what was wrong with her friend but Natalie wouldn't say a word to her. After a few minutes of trying to get her to open up, Jasmine returned to the arena as Natalie was packing her things to leave. Coach walked into the locker room.

"What has gotten into you today, Simms?"

"I'm sorry, Coach. I shouldn't have lost my cool like that. I just got a lot on my mind right now."

"I understand that but as the leader of this team, I expect more out of you. I don't want to send you home but I have to show the team that I will not be disrespected."

"I understand. It won't happen again."

"Thank you. Now I've been coaching for a long time and I know when my players are having certain kind of issues. I don't like to get too involved in my player's lives. Whatever is going on between you and that man you're with can be fixed. You just have to wanna fix it."

"How do you know it involves a man?"

"Being a coach is like being a mother. Mother always knows." Coach winked her eye at Natalie as she turned to leave.

"Coach," she called.

Turning around as she got to the door, "No need to thank me. Just get it together. I need you."

When you've gone through as many broken relationships as Ivy and Natalie have, one's defense mechanisms have a tendency to be a little more sensitive than the average person's. In Natalie's case, her lashing out at Iverson was her natural way of trying to protect herself from what may be.

A relationship is like an equation. All of the variables have to be correct in order to get the right answer. Any shift or input of the wrong information can throw the answer off and it will be far from correct. $A+B=C$. Natalie+Iverson= A Match made in Heaven. Now that a different variable has been added to that equation, only heaven knows what the outcome will be. $A+B(X)=Y$. Natalie+Iverson(Cee Cee)=Disaster. For the greater good of $A+B=C$, A and B have to figure out a way to get X out of the equation to avoid Y.

It was noon and Iverson was sitting in his office at home. The intercom buzzer went off. He pressed a button on the panel on the wall beside his desk.

"Yo!"
"Its Cee Cee. I came to get my bike."
"Meet me at the garage." Ivy pressed another button to open the gate. Minutes later, he was opening up the garage. When Candace walked in, Ivy was opening the key box to

701

retrieve the key to the pink and white motorcycle.

"Ya girl interrogated me yesterday."
"What?"
"Yeah. She had me to meet her down at Copeland's to ask me what happened when I was here."
"What did you tell her?" Cee Cee took the key from Iverson and started the bike. Before she answered she slid the pink helmet over her long, black hair and flipped up the visor.
"I told her that what me and you did over here that night was none of her business."

After that statement she tried to ride off. Ivy pressed the button in the garage to close the gate before she got there. When he walked from around the back of the house, Cee Cee was sitting at the gate.

"Why would you say something like that?" he asked.
"Because it's true. I'm her client. She doesn't need to be all up in my business. I don't care who that business is with. Now open the gate."
"That's some bullshit."
"It might be but if she woulda came to me like a woman instead of frontin like we had business to handle for Purrfection just to get

me down there, I might have told her the truth."

"You're going to tell her the truth."

"I don't have to do shit."

"Get off the bike."

"No. This is mine. We had a deal." Ivy snatched the key out of the ignition.

"Deal's off. Bounce."

"This is bullshit and you know it, Ivy!"

"Call it what you wanna call it. Haul ass before I have you arrested for trespassing." Ivy pressed the button on the console to open the gate.

"I'm not leaving here without my bike. Give me back the key."

"Kick rocks."

Candace let down the kickstand and dismounted the bike. She tried to take the key away from Ivy but all of her attempts failed. As she tried over and over again to get the key, her attempts became funny to Ivy. On her final attempt, Natalie pulled to the gate. Iverson didn't notice her because he had his back turned. When Candace noticed the Black Navigator, she stopped, smiled then continued to playfully advance toward Ivy. She made it look like they were standing in his driveway having a grand old time.

Natalie blew the horn causing Ivy to turn around. When he looked into her eyes, she was not a happy camper. She threw the car into reverse and sped off.

"Natalie wait!" Ivy yelled. "You knew she was behind me didn't you. That's some foul shit." Ivy took the key to the bike and threw it on the ground beside the motorcycle.

"Take the bike and get the fuck on."

"Don't act like that Ivy," Cee Cee playfully consoled and mocked. Ivy turned his back and walked toward the house. Once again, Candace mounted the bike then rode off down the street.

Iverson pulled his cordless phone out of his back pocket and dialed Natalie's number. Not recognizing the number at first, she answered the phone.

"Hello?"

"Natalie, don't hang up. We really need to talk."

"I can't. Not right now."

"Natalie please…"

"We can't talk right now but I need you to listen."The Atlanta Diamond took a deep breath then exhaled. "These past couple of days have been rough for me. I feel that you are the best thing that has happened to me. I love you and I want to believe that you would never cheat on me but I'm being shown otherwise. I know Cee Cee has had it out for you from day one. What I don't know is: are you falling for it?"

"Diamond...."

"Please just listen."

"Go ahead."

"I know I pressed you to sign the girls because of Kitty and Rolanda. In doing so, I had to be ready for everything that was going to come. I told you I trusted you and I meant it but I just feel like that trust is being pushed to the limit. I also told you that I wouldn't take it out on you for what happened to me in my past relationship and I haven't. I never told you but that relationship ended because Desmond was cheating on me. I'm not saying that you are. I just need some time to think. I promise you if you just let me calm down and get my head right, we can work it out. Right now this is affecting my game and I can't let that happen."

"Alright," Iverson sighed. "You know where I'm at. Whenever you're ready, get at me."

"I will.

For the next two weeks, Iverson and Natalie experienced one of the toughest periods of their young relationship. Situations get very sticky when legal documents are binding. Because Candace was a part of a group contracted by both Diamond in the Ruff and Future Records, she couldn't be easily removed from the equation. Iverson had a ton of money invested in Purrfection. He had to tread carefully. Even with her clouded and fragile state of mind, Natalie had to do the same.

The only person involved in the situation that was able to live a normal life was Cee Cee. Every chance she got to dig the knife in deeper, she did. One evening while flipping through the channels, Natalie came across Iverson, T and the girls on 106 & Park. Candace was draped all over Iverson. To add insult to injury, she sent Natalie a spiteful shout out.

"Is there anyone you'd like to shout out before you go?" Rocci asked the girls.
"Yes," Candace spoke up. "As always we'd like to thank God for all of his many blessings and our fans for all the love and support. A special thanks to our CEO right here, Iverson Davenport; we couldn't be happier anywhere else. To the man that discovered us, T-Bizzy and the whole Future Record Camp. Big shouts to Lucky 12. Alicia Burroughs and Natalie Simms of Diamond in the Ruff Management. We appreciate all your efforts and hard work."

At the close of her acknowledgements, Candace kissed Iverson on the cheek and winked into the camera. Natalie clinched her teeth together as she changed the channel. In a

matter of minutes, her cell phone erupted.
Natalie ignored call after call until she saw
Alicia's number pop up.

"Hey girl," Natalie answered.
"What you up to?"
"Sittin' here wishing there was a way to
jump in the television."
"You okay?"
"I'm cool."
"Natalie…its little shit like that that
should tell you that nothing happened
between Cee Cee and Iverson."
"How can you tell?"
"Look at how she was draped all over
him. She was on national TV so she knew there
wasn't a thing he could do about it. She's
doing this to piss you off."
"Well she's doing a damn good job at
it."
"Have you talked to Iverson yet?"
"Not yet."
"It's been two weeks."
"I know but every time I get ready to
talk to him, I keep having setbacks like that."
"Ok. This shit has gone too far."
"What are you talking about?"
"I've sat back and tried to hold my
peace and quietly support you but I can't take
it no more. I'm your girl so you should be able
to take everything I'm getting' ready to say as
love. You've let this silent treatment go on far
too long."

"But Alicia…"

"But Alicia my ass. You need to get your shit together and stop actin' like you in high school before you mess around and lose a good man cuz you 'round here following up some lil trick that you know Iverson doesn't want. I know everything you went through in your past relationship based on what you and Dré have told me. I know there are some similarities and I know it hurts but what it all boils down to is; Iverson is not Desmond. He's far from Desmond and you know it. You knew what you were getting into when you pressed Ivy into signing Purrfection. I stood right behind you because I'm your girl. You said you could handle it. Me and Iverson took you at your word. Now that shit is a little difficult, you wanna renig on everything. It is time for you to stop falling for these childish games and be the woman in this situation. If you wanna let him go, tell him that and stop leaving him in suspense and let him move on with his life. I know a hundred women right now that want to see this relationship fail and Cee Cee ain't even included in that number."

Natalie sat in silence. There was no rebuttal because everything Alicia said was the truth—rugged, but true. In all her years, Natalie had never had a friend put her in her place like that.

"You know what," Natalie began breaking her silence. "I've never had anyone check me like that."

"I didn't mean to come off so abrasive but I don't want you to lose out on a good thing."

"You're right. I have been acting childish. I'll talk to him."

"Better sooner than later."

"Thanks girl. Like it or not, I needed that."

"That's what real friends do for each other."

"That just showed me that I've never really had a real friend in my life."

"I resent that statement!" André interrupted.

"André Marcellus Marshall....How long have you been on this phone?"

"Long enough to hear you cuss my sister out," André laughed.

"I deserved it."

"Now you see what I go through. Everything may seem sweet on the outside but I'm in a very abusive relationship."

"I figured she was beatin on you," Natalie laughed.

"On the real though Sis, I ran into ya boy at the network the other day. He's goin through it. We chopped it for a minute and I can tell that he misses you. I know dudes that cheated on their women and got caught. They don't act like ya boy was acting. He's showin all the signs of a man accused of a crime he didn't commit."

"For real, Dré?"

"Yeah. I know Money like damn…I shoulda got da ass." André laughed as Alicia scolded.

"André! That is not nice."

"He's right though, Alicia. I let my anger and past experience put him on trial and convict him without giving him a chance to plead his case."

"Well now you know what you have to do."

"I'm gettin' ready to go get my man."

"Do Dirty!"

"Thanks guys. I love you."

Natalie hung up the phone and immediately dialed Iverson. The phone rang four times then went to voicemail. She decided not to leave a message because she figured he would see the number and call her back. Natalie felt that once she started talking, it was going to be too much for a voicemail to hold.

Chapter 28

An entire day passed and Natalie was still waiting on Iverson to return her phone calls. She tried not to press him but she was getting a little nervous. To ease her mind she decided to grab her laptop and relax by the pool. Once she came downstairs with her computer, she stopped in the kitchen to fix a drink. In black, satin, pajama bottoms and a white tank top, Natalie stretched out in a lounge chair beside her massive pool. The night was warm but a cool breeze floated past her from time to time. After about 30 minutes of checking email messages and web surfing, she decided to check in on some old friends.

<Got'em Hatin> WHO IN DA HELL DO SHE THINK SHE IS?!?!? I WILL COME TO VA AND SNATCH HER ASS INSIDE OUT!!!!!
<MACK Truck> LOL!!!!!
Dymond has entered the room.
<Da Ice Cream Man> lmao
<Gucci*Girl> TRICK PLZ! YOU AIN'T GONNA DO SHIT BUT RUN YA MOUTH LIKE U DOIN NOW
<Dymond>WZUP EVERYBODY!!!
<Mr.SexxyB-Baller> CAN'T WE ALL JUST GET ALONG?!?! LOL
<City Ave Diva> HEY DYMOND!

<Got'em Hatin>WHO IS THIS CHICK ANYWAY

<Da Ice Cream Man> u know thats Optimo's girl

<Thyk2Def>*****VOMIT*****

<Dymond>WHAT DID I ROLL UP ON

<Gucci*Girl> U JUST JEALOUS OPTIMO DROPPED YA AZZ FOR A REAL WOMAN@THYK

<SoopaFly> UH OH...THIS SHIT FINNA GET GOOD

<City Ave Diva>STOP INSTIGATIN@SOOPA

<Da Ice Cream Man>I'm not sayin no names but somebody's not welcome back in Michigan!!!!

<Thyk2Def>FIRST OF ALL NOBODY DROPPED ME...I JUST GOT TIRED OF THE LONG DISTANCE RELATIONSHIP. IF U WERE TRU 2 DA FAM U'D KNOW THAT

<Dymond>I'M SORRY ICE CREAM BUT WE HAD TO DO IT!!!

<City Ave Diva>WHAT R U TALKIN BOUT@ICE CREAM

<MACK Truck>HEY DIAMOND....WHERE'S MY CUZIN?

<Da Ice Cream Man>Dymond and the Diamonds came to Detroit and murdered the Shock. The only reason I watched the game was because I wanted to see Dymond play. I started to go to the game but I aint got money like Future

<Dymond>WE NOT VIBIN RIGHT NOW@MACK

<Gucci*Girl> MAN FUCK Y'ALL
HOES....I'M OUT DIS BITCH
Gucci*Girl just left the room.
<City Ave Diva>WHAT DID FUTURE DO TO
YOU?!?!
<SoopaFly>HOW U JUST ASSUME THAT IT
WAS FUTURE...DYMOND MIGHT BE LIVIN
FOUL...LOL J/K
<Thyk2Def> IF DYMOND WAS IN THE
WRONG SHE WOULDNTVE COME IN HERE
WITH ALL OF HIS FRIENDS....WOMEN
DON'T DO SHIT LIKE THAT
<Da Ice Cream Man> that is a valid point
<Got'em Hatin>THAT'S TRUE..ONLY
DUDES DO STUPID SHIT LIKE
DAT
<Mr.SexxyB-Baller>U WOMEN KILL ME...U
TALK ALL DAT SHIT BOUT US BUT U STILL
FUCK WIT US
<Da Ice Cream Man>and that is a valid point
too
Teddy Pinned*Her*Ass*Down has entered the
room.
Mrz*Pinned*Down has entered the room.
<MACK Truck>AWWWW HELL THE RIGHT
ONE IS THE ROOM NOW...YALL WOMEN
FINNA GET IT!!!!
Optimo Pryme has entered the room
<Da Ice Cream Man> double trouble is in da
buildin!
<Teddy Pinned*Her*Ass*Down>LADIES
AND GENTLEMEN HAVE NO FEAR...THE

LEGENDARY TEDDY PINNED HER ASS DOWN IN HERE!!!!! WHAT IT DO FAM!!!!
<Thyk2Def>
TTTTTTTTTEEEEEEEEEEEEEEEDDDDDDDD DDDDYYYYYYYYY!!!
<Got'em Hatin> HEY Y'ALL!!!!
<City Ave Diva>HOLD ON DYMOND…ITS GETTING READY TO GET REAL IGNANT IN HERE
<Mrz*Pinned*Down>TEDDY DO U ALWAYS HAVE TO ACKA ASS EVERYTIME YOU COME IN HERE??? CAN'T YOU JUST SAY HELLO…LOL
<Thyk2Def>HEY CHOCO!!!!
<Da Ice Cream Man> this must be a special occasion…its people in here we ain't seen in a minute…is it my birfday???
<Teddy Pinned*Her*Ass*Down>I COULD BABY BUT THAT WOULDN'T BE ME!!!!
<***Mami*Dearest***> WELCOME TO MY ROOM EVERYBODY BUT YOU KNOW THE RULES….THIS IS A VIDEO CHAT ROOM SO YOU NEED TO CAM UP OR BOUNCE!!!
<MACK Truck> I KNOW RIGHT@ICE CREAM…WE GOT DYMOND, TEDDY AND CHOCO
<City Ave Diva>I THOUGHT I SAW OPTIMO COME IN TOO
<Da Ice Cream Man>he did…he prolly tryna outdo teddy
<Dymond> HEY CHOCO AND TEDDY!!!!!
<Thyk2Def> U PROLLY RIGHT@ICE CREAM
<Mrz*Pinned*Down> HEY DYMOND!!!!

<Teddy Pinned*Her*Ass*Down> OH SNAP! WZUP DYMOND!!! WHERE MY CUZIN AT???

<Optimo Pryme>THIS IS SOME BULLSHIT!!! I BEEN KICKIN IT WIT Y'ALL FOR DAMN NEAR 4 YEARS...A WHOLE YEAR LONGER THAN TEDDY AND CHOCO. WE ALL COME IN AT THE SAME AND ALL YOU MUTHAPHUCKAS SPEAK TO TEDDY AND CHOCO AND DON'T SAY SHIT TO YA BOY!!! I'M HURT

<Da Ice Cream Man> told you! lol

<Got'em Hatin>FIRST OF ALL DON'T COME IN HERE GOIN OFF ON NOBODY

<Thyk2Def>SECOND OF ALL U NEED TO KEEP UR HOES IN CHECK

<MACK Truck>ROFLMAO

<Teddy Pinned*Her*Ass*Down>WHAT I MISS???

<Optimo Pryme>WHAT HOES?

<Mrz*Pinned*Down>BABY WE'VE MISSED A LOT...WE BEEN GONE FOR A MINUTE

<Got'em Hatin>THAT BITCH GUCCI

<Teddy Pinned*Her*Ass*Down>WHO IS GUCCI???

<Thyk2Def>OPTIMOS TRICK OF THE MONTH

<Mr.SexxyB-Baller>WOOOOOOW!

<City Ave Diva>LOL

<Optimo Pryme>THAT WAS COLD BLOODED@THYK

<Da Ice Cream Man>that was a low blow

<Teddy Pinned*Her*Ass*Down>I AM LOST AS HELL!!!! WHO IS GUCCI AND WHY IS SHE FUCKIN WIT OPTIMO? WHAT HAPPENED TO OPTIMO AND THYK???

<City Ave Diva>A LOT HAS CHANGED TEDDY

<Mrz*Pinned*Down>WHERE'S FUTURE@DYMOND

<Optimo Pryme>I THOUGHT WE WERE COOL@THYK

<Dymond>WE GOIN THROUGH IT RIGHT NOW

<Teddy Pinned*Her*Ass*Down>NOOOOOOO NOT MY CUZIN TOO!!!!

<Mrz*Pinned*Down>WHAT DID HE DO???

<Thyk2Def>WE'RE COOL OPTIMO BUT THAT CHICK DON'T KNOW ME LIKE THAT...YOU BETTA CHECK HER

<Teddy Pinned*Her*Ass*Down>HOW U JUST ASSUME IT WAS FUTURE???

<City Ave Diva>THIS IS THE CONVERSATION WE WERE HAVIN WHEN U 2 CAME IN

<Dymond>WE DIDN'T BREAK UP...ITS JUST BEEN A MISUNDERSTANDING

<Teddy Pinned*Her*Ass*Down>SOMEBODY ELSE IS MISSIN.....WHERE'S MY BABY MAMA???

<Mr.SexxyB-Baller>SHE CAME IN AT THE SAME TIME YOU DID

<Mrz*Pinned*Down>TEDDY DON'T GET HURT

<Teddy Pinned*Her*Ass*Down>NOT HER...I'M TALKIN BOUT DA WIFE AKA MRZ.SOOPAFLY BKA BUTT NAKED

<Da Ice Cream Man>damn teddy...u have been gone for a minute

<Got'em Hatin>SHE GOT MARRIED@TEDDY

<Mrz*Pinned*Down>MARRIED???? TO WHO???

<Teddy Pinned*Her*Ass*Down>NOOOOOOOOOOOO OOOOOOOOOOOOOOOO!!!!!!

<MACK Truck>LOL

<City Ave Diva> U WILL NEVER GUESS

<Mrz*Pinned*Down>UR SHITTIN ME!!!!

<Got'em Hatin>SHE GOT MARRIED ABOUT 2 MONTHS AGO

<Teddy Pinned*Her*Ass*Down>WHO DID SHE MARRY????

<Thyk2Def>SLICK OF ALL PEOPLE

<Mrz*Pinned*Down>WHAAAAAAT!!!!

<Teddy Pinned*Her*Ass*Down>****FAINTED****

<Da Ice Cream Man>u stoopid@teddy

<City Ave Diva>YUP...THEY HOOKED UP ABOUT A WEEK AFTER U 2 DISAPPEARED....HE MOVED TO MICHIGAN AND EVERYTHING

<Mr.SexxyB-Baller>THEY POP IN FROM TIME TO TIME BUT WE HAVEN'T SEEN THEM IN ABOUT A MONTH

<Teddy Pinned*Her*Ass*Down>OK I'M BACK...NOW BACK TO WHAT WE WERE

TALKIN ABOUT…WHAT HAPPENED WIT
YOU AND FUTURE@DYMOND
Futurama has entered the room
<Thyk2Def>DAMN! WE TALKED HIM UP!
HEY FUTURE BABY!!!
**<City Ave
Diva>**FUUUUUUUUUUUUUUUUUUUTTT
TTTTTTTUREEEEE
<MACK Truck>CUZIN!!!!
<Got'em Hatin>HEY FUTURE!!!!!!
<Mrz*Pinned*Down> Y YOU SO
QUIET@OPTIMO
<Futurama>WHAT'S GOOD FAM!!
<Optimo Pryme>I'M COOL@CHOCO
<Dymond>HEY BABY
<Teddy Pinned*Her*Ass*Down>WHAT IT
DO CUZ!
<Futurama>OH I'M YA BABY NOW
<City Ave Diva>NO SIR! FUTURE YOU WILL
NOT ACT LIKE THAT TOWARD YOUR
WOMAN
<Dymond>ITS COOL DIVA…I DESERVED
THAT
<Mrz*Pinned*Down>COME ON NOW…IT
WAS YOU 2 THAT HELPED BRING ME AND
TEDDY TOGETHER AND NOW U 2 ARE
NOT HOW I REMEMBER
<Got'em Hatin>YEAH FUTURE…WHAT
GIVES
<Futurama>TO BE HONEST…..I HAVE NO
IDEA WHAT'S GOING ON RIGHT NOW
<City Ave Diva>MAYBE YOU TWO
SHOULD TALK OFFLINE

<Teddy Pinned*Her*Ass*Down>YEAH CUZ...WHAT EVER IT IS...IT CAN BE WORKED OUT...AIN'T THAT WHAT YOU USED TO ALWAYS TELL ME

<Da Ice Cream Man>that's what he used to tell you teddy

<Futurama>UR ABSOLUTLEY RIGHT CUZIN BUT I CAN'T WORK IT OUT BY MYSELF...TWO WEEKS?@DYMOND

<City Ave Diva>OFFLINE FUTURE...THIS IS NOT THE VENUE

<Dymond>ITS COOL@DIVA...U GUYS ARE LIKE FAMILY

<Mrz*Pinned*Down>DIVAS RIGHT U 2 SHOULD TALK ABOUT IT OUTSIDE THE CHATROOM

<Got'em Hatin>U TWO HUSH!!!11I'M ALREADY POPPIN POPCORN

<SoopaFly>I'M BACK!!! WHAT I MISS?

<Thyk2Def>SHHHHH@SOOPA

<Dymond>I CAME IN HERE HOPING TO FIND YOU. I JUST WANT TO SAY TO YOU IN FRONT OF ALL OF OUR FRIENDS THAT I WAS WRONG AND I APOLOGIZE. I DID TO YOU EXACTLY WHAT I PROMISED YOU I WOULDN'T DO. WHEN YOU SIGNED PURRFECTION, I TOLD YOU THAT I TRUSTED YOU. I DID AND STILL DO. I JUST ALLOWED MYSELF TO GET CAUGHT UP IN THE GAME SHE WAS PLAYING. I KNOW THAT YOU LOVE ME AND WOULDN'T DO ANYTHING TO HURT ME OR JEPORDIZE THIS RELATIONSHIP. I'M SORRY FOR

ACTING CHILDISH THESE PAST TWO WEEKS. I LOVE YOU. CAN YOU FIND IT IN YOUR HEART TO FORGIVE ME???
<City Ave Diva>WOW
<Da Ice Cream Man>****crickets chirping****
<Thyk2Def>I THINK IM GONNA CRY
<Mr.SexxyB-Baller>I AIN'T NO PUNK BUT SHE GOT ME MISTY EYED UP IN THIS BITCH
<Teddy Pinned*Her*Ass*Down>CUZIN???
<Optimo Pryme>NOW THAT'S HOW U APOLOGIZE
<Mrz*Pinned*Down>SOMEBODY SAY SOMETHING
<Futurama>DON'T PUT THE BLAME ALL ON YOU BECAUSE IT TAKES TWO. I PUT MYSELF IN SOME COMPRIMISING SITUATIONS KNOWING FULL WELL WHO I WAS DEALING WITH. I'M THE TYPW OF PERSON THAT TAKES A PERSON'S WORD. CALL IT A FLAW BUT ITS JUST ME. SHE TOLD ME ALL SHE WANTED TO DO WAS SING AND I BELIEVE HER. THE GIRLS HAVE BEEN SUCCESSEFUL BUT I DIDN'T WANT IT TO COME AT THE EXPENSE OF OUR RELATIONSHIP. I FORGIVE YOU IF YOU FORGIVE ME.
<Optimo Pryme>Y'ALL BETTER NOT SAY NOTHIN TO ME ABOUT PARAGRAPHS EVER AGAIN...LOL!!!!
<Mr.SexxyB-Baller>DA YOUNG AND THE RESTLESS AINT GOT SHIT ON JUST4KICKZ!!!!!

<Da Ice Cream Man>lol

<Dymond>I FORGIVE YOU BABY!!!!!

<Teddy Pinned*Her*Ass*Down>SOMEBODY GETTING SOME BOOTY TONIGHT!!!! AND ITS GONNA BE THE BEST YOU EVER HAD!!!!!!

<Thyk2Def>YOU KNOW!!! AIN'T NUTTIN LIKE MAKE UP SEX!!!!

<Futurama>LMAO!

<Dymond>CAN I SEE YOU TONIGHT???

<Da Ice Cream Man>I'LL BE ON THE FIRST FLIGHT!!! GIMME ABOUT 3 HOURS!

<Futurama>YOU WOULD USE CAPS TO HIT ON MY GIRL! LOL

<Teddy Pinned*Her*Ass*Down>I WAS THINKIN THE SAME THING...ROFL

<Da Ice Cream Man>my bad future...I thought she was talkin to me...lol

<Teddy Pinned*Her*Ass*Down>THIS IS ALL FINE AND DANDY BUT I GOTTA BE NOSEY...WHAT GIRL???

<Futurama>YOU KNOW WHAT GIRL TEDDY

<Mrz*Pinned*Down>CIARA??? AIN'T SHE LIKE 12?

<Da Ice Cream Man>green is not ur color@choco

<Teddy Pinned*Her*Ass*Down>I'M SORRY CUZ BUT I'M LOST....

<Futurama>EVERYBODY IN HERE KNOWS HER

<City Ave Diva>YOU WAS MESSIN WIT ONE OF THE GIRLS FROM PURRFECTION!!!!!!

<Optimo Pryme>WAIT AMINUTE....I KNEW ONE OF THEM CHIKS LOOKED FAMILIAR!!!!

<Futurama>Y'ALL REMEMBER MY EX UNIQUE_PLEASUREZ

<Got'em Hatin>I THOUGHT THAT WAS HER!!!!

<City Ave Diva>HOW DID THAT COME ABOUT?

<Futurama>I'LL HAVE TO FILL YOU IN ANOTHER TIME

<Mr.SexxyB-Baller>WOW...U NEV NO WHO YOU MEET IN A CHATROOM. WE KNOW A PLATINUM SELLING RECORD LABEL CEO, A WNBA CHAMPION AND SOMEBODY WE USED TO CHILL WIT IS APART OF ONE OF THE HOTTEST GROUPS SINCE TLC....WHY AM I STILL BROKE!!!!!

<Got'em Hatin>LMAO!

<Da Ice Cream Man>don't forget WNBA MVP and Rookie of the Year@Baller

<Dymond>THAT'S RIGHT ICE CREAM...SET HIM STR8

<Futurama>WELL MY PEOPLE...THANKS FOR BEING THE TRUE FRIENDS THAT YOU'VE ALWAYS BEEN

<Teddy Pinned*Her*Ass*Down>U KNOW WE GOT U CUZ!!!!

<Dymond>THAT GOES FOR ME TOO...THANKS GUYS!!!!! MUAH!!!

\<**City Ave Diva**\>THAT'S WHAT FAMILY IS FOR...WE LOVE YOU TWO

\<**Mrz*Pinned*Down**\>UR JUST4KICKZ CUTEST COUPLE NEXT TO ME AND TEDDY OF COURSE...LOL

\<**Futurama**\>UR PLACE OR MINE@DYMOND

\<**Thyk2Def**\>MINE!!!!!!

\<**Dymond**\>LOL..I LOVE YOU THICK BUT I WILL CUT YOU!!!!

\<**Futurama**\>AS A MATTER OF FACT...I'LL BE THROUGH UR SPOT...I GOTTA MEET T@SPONDIVIOTS TO DROP SOMETHING OFF

\<**Teddy Pinned*Her*Ass*Down**\>THAT'S MY SPOT!!!!!!!

\<**MACK Truck**\>WHAT IS THAT@TED?

\<**Mrz*Pinned*Down**\>IT'S A SEAFOOD SPOT IN THE ATL

\<**Teddy Pinned*Her*Ass*Down**\>AND IT IS OFF THE HOOK!!!

\<**Mr.SexxyB-Baller**\>IS THAT THE SAME SPOT JEEZY BE TALKIN BOUT?

\<**Futurama**\>YUP

\<**Dymond**\>OK BABY..CAN YOU BRING ME SOMETHIN TO EAT???

\<**SoopaFly**\>ALL THIS TALK ABOUT FOOD....I'LL BRB!!!!

\<**Futurama**\>I GOT YOU...WHAT YOU WANT?

\<**Dymond**\>BLACKEND MAHI AND A BAKED POTATO

\<**Optimo Pryme**\>THAT SOUNDS REAL GOOD RIGHT ABOUT NOW

\<Mrz*Pinned*Down\>BABY CAN WE GO TO THE PEADEN'S

\<Futurama\> DAMN GIRL!! MAHI??? YOU ACT LIKE I'M BALLIN LIKE DAT..WJAT HAPPENED TO THE DOLLAR MENU??? LOL!!!

\<Teddy Pinned*Her*Ass*Down\>I WAS THINKIN THE SAME THING BABY@CHOCO

\<Dymond\>LOL…I'LL SEE YOU WHEN YOU GET HERE

Gucci*Girl has entered the room.

\<Futurama\>AIGHT FAM……I'M OUT!!!!

\<MACK Truck\>AWWWW SHIT…IT'S POPPIN NOW!!!!

\<Thyk2Def\>BYE FUTURE!!!!

\<Teddy Pinned*Her*Ass*Down\> AYE CUZ…CALL ME WHEN YOU GET A CHANCE…I NEED TO HOLLA AT YOU ABOUT SOME BIZZNAZZ…

\<MACK Truck\>PEACE CUZIN

\<Dymond\>BYE BABY…SEE YOU SOON!

\<Da Ice Cream Man\>uhhh dymond…ur man is leaving…that's ur cue

\<Futurama\>AIGHT TED…I'LL CALL YOU MONDAY AFTER LUNCH

\<Dymond\>EXCUSE ME ICE CREAM BUT I'M GROWN PLUS MACK SAID ITS POPPIN NOW! LOL!

\<City Ave Diva\>OOOOOKAAAYYY!

Futurama has left the room.

In order to move forward, sometimes a man and a woman have to take it back a few steps. Natalie knew how close Iverson was with his friends on just4kickz. She made a bold move by apologizing to Iverson in the chat room. She had no idea how he felt or how he would react. That move could have blown up in her face. When you love someone you have to take risks—just like the risk Natalie and Iverson took when Ivy signed Purrfection. Then again, love makes you do crazy things.

When Iverson arrived to Natalie's, she rushed out of the house and jumped into his arms. In the middle of the driveway, Natalie and Iverson engaged in a deep, passionate kiss that lasted for about ten good minutes. When it was over the two stood face to face and stared into each other's eyes.

"I'm so sorry," Natalie apologized.
"I'm sorry, too."
"I promise you that I'll never act like that again."
"Good cuz that was kinda 12th grade," Ivy laughed.
"Aww hush," Natalie giggled. "Did you bring my food?"
"Nope. I came to get you so we can go back and eat."
"You're kidding, right?"

"I'm serious. T called me and told me that he was meeting Alexa there. I thought it would be fun if we all chilled out for awhile."

"Look at me! I'm a mess."

"We got time. They won't be there for another hour. I know its asking a lot for you to get dressed on short notice but I need you to try your best."

"You just full of jokes tonight."

"I got two weeks worth saved up."

"Very funny. Come on in the house."

"I gotta run meet Michelle wit some money. She had a lil emergency. I'll be back in less than 45 minutes. Be ready."

"Okay, Papi. I will." Natalie kissed Ivy once again then turned to walk back in the house. Ivy slapped her on her ass as she turned around.

"You got on thong?"

"Nope."

"G-string?"

"Nope."

"The hell wit Michelle..." Ivy walked toward Natalie.

"Go handle your business."

"That's what I'm tryna do!"

"Bye, silly." Iverson hopped in his car and backed out of the driveway. A huge smile was spread across Natalie's face as she walked back in the house. Just as she got to the door, she stopped and looked toward the sky.

"Thank you!"

As usual, Spondivot's was buzzing with their evening crowd. Ivy, Natalie, Alexa and TyQuan sat tucked off in a quiet corner. They enjoyed drinks and appetizers as they waited on the main course to be prepared. Natalie and Ivy looked like the happy couple they once were.

"I'm glad you two got everything straightened out," Ty began as he sipped his drink. "This dude was gettin' on my nerves. You shoulda seen'em. He looked like a sad ass puppy."

"Here we go," Iverson laughed.

"Its okay," Natalie consoled. "If it's any consolation, I wasn't doin' too good myself."

"You're right. I saw that game against LA. You can't make another run for MVP wit seven points and two assists."

"I know! When everything first went down, I had a few bad days in practice. I thought I coulda shook it off by game time but I was pitiful. I even went off on my coach."

"That ain't nothing," Ty interrupted. "Ivy almost got arrested for assault."

"Assault?" Natalie inquired.

"Yup. He assaulted an innocent bucket of soap and water."

"You just full of jokes, ain't you?"

"As much hell as you give me. I don't get many opportunities to get you back so I gotta take advantage of them."

"All jokes aside though. I'm glad the three of us are here. We need to talk about our next move with Purrfection."

"What you got in mind?" Ty asked.

"We signed them for one album. That album is released. I think its time to switch it up a little bit. Do you think that we can find a valid replacement for Cee Cee?"

"You thinkin' about pullin' a Destiny's Child?"

"I'm thinkin about it. Kitty does most of the lead vocals. Rolanda is good with choreography, backup vocals and she can MC. Cee Cee did her thing but I feel that she can be replaced. What do you think?"

"Wow," TyQuan exhaled. "We're still going to have to pay her royalties from the album."

"I don't have a problem with that. It's a small price to pay to have her out of our lives. The thing that I'm concerned about is the management contract. Are there any loopholes in it?"

"I'm not sure but I believe there is. The management contract coincides with the deal you gave them. It's for the span of one album with an option to be extended or renegotiated along with any new deal that you offer the group."

"How do you think the girls are gonna react to this?" TyQuan pondered whole stirring his drink.

"Honestly, I don't think Kitty and Rolanda will have a problem with it."

"What about Cee Cee?"

"She'll have to get over it. Let me ask you Alexa. I'm pretty sure T has told you some of what's been going on. What do you think about the situation?"

"No offense but this sounds like its more personal than business. As a woman, I understand that you would want to do whatever you can to protect your relationship. There are so many angles you have to look at in this situation. You have to think about the negative PR that could possibly come out of it. Groups in the past have changed members and it's worked for them. If you feel that you can handle the possible repercussions of it then by all means, do what you feel is necessary. Just remember that no matter what Cee Cee has done, she's going to play the victim once everything goes down."

"I feel what you're saying and yes, it is personal. That's how she made it. I tried to be professional in every aspect. I feel that in order to protect my investment, some tough decisions have to be made. I would love to keep the group together but I can't go through this. It's not only about me and Natalie; it's also about Kitty and Rolanda. They don't deserve to have to go through the things that they've went through. They've already gone through enough. I have the final say in what happens but I'm going to leave the decision up to them. After all, they built Purrfection. Cee Cee just happened to be in the right place at the right time."

"I think that's the best thing to do," Natalie interjected. "Now can we change the subject?"

The conversation switched from business back to pleasure as the food arrived. They enjoyed a feast of crab legs, shrimp and lobster. The meal was occasionally interrupted by Atlanta Diamond fans asking Natalie for autographs and wanting to take pictures. Without hesitation, Natalie obliged every request. Every true athlete and entertainer knows that it's always about the fans.

Chapter 29

"That was amazing," Natalie expressed as she rolled off of Iverson and onto the bed. "I should stay away for another two weeks."

"Let's not get carried away," Ivy laughed.

"I can't believe I allowed myself to fall for her games."

"All that's over now. Its back to how it's supposed to be."

"So what's the next step?"

"For what?"

"Purrfection."

"I guess the next thing we need to do is talk to Kitty and Rolanda to see where they're at with all of this. I can't make any moves until I know how they feel."

"How do you think Cee Cee is gonna take it?"

"Knowing her like I do, she's probably gonna make a big deal about it at first. Then she'll go on her way."

"Do you think she'll try anything crazy?"

"Probably not. She might be a lil' twisted at times but she ain't no fool."

"I just don't want to have to walk around lookin' over my shoulder and peeking around corners."

"If you want, I can loan you a bodyguard."

"I hope it doesn't get to that point but I'll keep it in mind."

"Good. What does your day look like tomorrow?"

"I have practice in the morning and then I have to do a commercial for a chiropractor's office."

"A local office?"

"Yeah. I'm doing it as a favor for Coach. It's her nephew."

"Oh okay. Do me a favor. On your way to practice, call Rolanda and Kitty and have them come by the office around two."

"Do you need me there?"

"Not for this one. Depending on how it goes, you'll have to have your own meeting with your clients."

"What about her replacement?"

"Me and T gotta put our heads together. We might need to talk to ya boy."

"Talk to who?"

"Dré. He's the man over at Black Reign, right?"

"Please don't tell me you're thinkin about a reality show."

"You know me so well," Ivy laughed.

The beginning of another work week was on the horizon. The building that housed Future Records was already buzzing at 9 o'clock in the morning. Artists, especially hip hop artists don't usually work early in the morning. With the anticipation of his latest album growing stronger, Buddah Rhatt was already in the studio with a couple of other members of Lucky 12.

"Uncle Buddah," Ivy greeted. "What's good?"

"Business as usual."

"That's what's up. Where we at on the album?"

"Two more songs. I know I told you one but I was listening to something last night and it set the wheels in motion."

"Talk to me. Tell me what's up."

"Remember that song, *Life on the Road*?"

"The one you cut from your 3rd album. Yeah. I remember."

"I pulled it cuz I said something was missing. I found what was missing…A female."

"A female MC?"

"A singer. I reworked the hook and we're gonna lay it over a track my man Encore made for me awhile back."

"Who's gonna sing the hook?"

"What's up Buddah," Cee Cee greeted as she entered the studio. "Sorry I'm late." A cold sensation shot through Ivy's body as Cee Cee entered the room.

"You right on time. I was just tellin Ivy about the song."

"Hello, Mr. Davenport."

"I'm putting Unique on the hook. I was listening to that song, *Later for You*. I didn't realize that she had skills like that. I think she'll be a perfect fit."

"Aight then...do ya thing. I got some things I need to handle. Before you get ready to leave or when you get a chance, drop by my office. I need to talk to you about something."

"No doubt...I'll get at you in a lil while."

"Bet." Iverson left the studio and went upstairs to his office. On his way in, he told Michelle to have TyQuan come in as soon as he got in. About fifteen minutes after he settled in behind his desk, TyQuan walked in the office.

"What's up?" T asked as he sat down on the couch.

"This is the deal. Kitty and Rolanda will be here at two. Once I talk to them, then I'll know what we need to do from there."

"Do you think they want Cee Cee out the group?"

"I don't know but after everything that's gone down, they might feel how I feel."

"What about her replacement?"

"I got a meeting with Dré over at Black Reign."

"About what?"

"A reality show."

"Reality show? Are you serious?"

"As a heart attack. Purrfection is hot right now. Reality shows are hot right now. Why not? This is a way to counter any negative press that Cee Cee might try to throw our way. I talked to our lawyer this morning. He said we're in the clear on this. The only thing that we are obligated to pay her is royalties. I don't have a problem with that."

"Looks like you really did your homework."

"That's why I'm the boss," Ivy laughed.

"What if the network doesn't want to do the show?"

"Then we execute Plan B."

"What is Plan B?"

"The same way you found Purrfection, you find a replacement. We got plenty of time. They probably won't be ready to start on a new album for another 4 to 6 months."

"I already got a couple girls in mind."

"Good." In the middle of discussing Purrfection's future, Cee Cee poked her head in the door.

"Ivy," she began. "Can I talk to you for a minute?"

"Yeah. Come on in. Can you excuse us for a minute, T?"

"No doubt. I'll be in my office."

"What's on your mind?"

"I'm not happy."

"Why not?"

"This group thing is not for me. It was never for me. The only reason why I agreed to it was because I thought it was a chance for me to get back to you."

"So what are you saying?"

"I wanna go solo. We signed a contract for one album. That album is done. It's time for me to do my own thing."

"What about Kitty and Rolanda?"

"They'll probably jump for joy. I'm sure you won't have a problem finding a replacement."

"Is this you're formal resignation from the group?"

"Yes. I want out."

"Kitty and Rolanda will be here at two, you can tell them then."

"No problem. Now let's talk about my album..."

"Your album?"

While pulling a note pad out of her purse, "Yeah. I have about 6 songs finished but they need tracks. I talked to a couple of people about some songs and some tracks..."

"Hold on...back ya bus up. You think that you're going to release you're album on Future? That's not gonna happen."

"Excuse me? Why not?" Ivy stood up and walked from behind his desk. Once he closed the door he sat down on the couch beside Cee Cee.

"I was going to wait but I think now is just as good a time as any. You know I've always kept it 100 with you, right?"

"Yeah."

"You as a member of Purrfection wasn't working for me either. You looked me in my eyes and you lied to me. You told me that you weren't here to cause problems, you just wanted to sing. Against my better judgment, I signed the group anyway. From the time you signed the contract, you've been nothing but problems. It was because of you that I almost lost the best thing that's ever happened to me. On top of that, because of you I got shot."

"That wasn't my fault."

"Not your fault? You ran around New Orleans tryna find Cocaine, got hymned and called me to come to your rescue. I defended you. Kitty and Rolanda wanted you out the group that night. I plead your case for you not knowing the true reason why everything went down. I tolerated your childish games, the petty advances and all your selfishness. I didn't hold our past against you. I looked past a lot and gave you a second chance. Kitty and Rolanda are coming here at two to discuss Purrfection's future and the possibility of you not being a part of it. As far as I was concerned you were done but I have to respect the other members of the group and see what they want to do."

"So just like that you kicked me to the curb. That's real fucked up, Ivy."

"That's how you made it."

"I thought you were more man than this. This is not your decision because I know you. I was there before all of this shit ever came about. This has everything to do with that bitch you call a girlfriend!"

"Watch ya mouth."

"Fuck you, Iverson Davenport!" Cee Cee's emotions began to take over. Her face became flushed and tears formed in her eyes.

"Once again you use me and throw me away."

"Use you? How did I use you?"

"Don't play stupid. I was your Perfect 10. Iverson's eye candy. I stood by you when you didn't have shit. I smiled for the cameras and never complained. I sat at home while you were on the road wondering if you were thinking about me or were you screwin some groupie."

"Am I buggin or did you leave me?"

"Cause you never had the time!"

"This is my life!" Iverson roared as he stood up. "I spent every penny I had to make this label what it is. That's why I didn't have shit when we met. You said it yourself. The only reason you fucked with me in the beginning was because you saw me as a way to get to your singing career. Did you forget about that? I treated you like a Queen. When the label took off, I took you around the world. I bought you the finer things. Did you forget about that? Gucci, Prada, Chanel...you weren't complaining while I was spendin' all my money on you!"

"I never wanted that! I wanted you to love me!" Silence filled the room. Iverson and Cee Cee were locked in an epic stare off. They were both breathing heavily. Mascara tinted tears flowed from Cee Cee's eyes as she looked the man she once loved in his eyes.

"I don't know what made me think that things would be different this time around.

This label has turned you into someone else. I don't even know who you are anymore. You're not the Iverson I fell in love with a long time ago."

Cee Cee placed the note pad, which was now crumpled from her clutching it as she screamed, into her purse. She pulled a tissue from the same purse and wiped her eyes.

"It's cool though. You don't have to worry about me anymore. You and Natalie finally get what you want. I'm out of your life for good. Just remember one thing…"

Cee Cee walked to the door and paused. She straightened her clothes and fixed her hair.

"Karma is a bitch, Iverson Davenport."

Candace slammed the door so hard behind her that the windows rattled. Iverson flopped down onto the couch and covered his face with his arm. TyQuan poked his head in the door.

"You alright?" TyQuan inquired.
"I'm good. I just need a minute."
"I'll be down in the studio if you need me."
"Bet."

It is funny how things seem to work themselves out. Iverson and Natalie wanted

Candace out of the group and Candace wanted out of the group. Mixing business with pleasure can often be a dangerous game. The backlash can be very stressful. Even though Cee Cee's words came in the heat of the moment they were true. Iverson couldn't have expected this venture to be easy. The thing that made the situation difficult was when Cee Cee's started releasing those feelings that she'd had bottled up inside her for two years. It can really pluck the heart's strings.

A month went by. Cee Cee was no longer a member of Purrfection. Nobody had seen or heard from her since that day in Iverson's office. Kitty and Rolanda had mixed feelings about her departure but in the end were satisfied with the results. With Cee Cee gone, Iverson and Natalie were able to mend their relationship. Their bond became stronger than ever before. Black Reign network loved the idea of the reality show to find the next member of Purrfection and began putting it in motion. Things were back to normal at Future Records.

"What time is it?" Ivy asked looking up from a stack of papers.

"11:45," TyQuan answered. "I'm about to call it a night."

"I'm about to do the same thing. As soon as Natalie gets here, I'm leaving."

"That's what's up. You want me to lock the door on my way out."

"Leave it open so she can come on in."

"That's what's up." The conversation was interrupted by TyQuan's cell phone.

"I'm on my way, baby." After he hung up, he placed it on the table and gathered his things.

"Be easy, bruh. Tell Alexa I said what's up."

"No doubt. I'll holla at you tomorrow."

"Peace."

TyQuan hoisted his laptop bag over his shoulder and walked out of the conference room. Ivy organized the pile of songs he was sifting through. Once he had them all together, he stood up to walk back to his office. The digital tone of *Can We Be Tight* by Jagged Edge, came from TyQuan's phone that he'd left on the table. Ivy picked it up and answered.

"What's up, Alexa."

"Hey, Ivy. Where's T?"

"He just left about less than five minutes ago. He left his phone."

"That boy would lose his head if it weren't attached to his body."

"I know," Ivy laughed. "Tell him I'll put it on his desk."

"Okay. We still on for dinner tomorrow night?"

"Yeah. Its going to be a special night."

"Why?"

"You just have to be there to find out."

"That is so foul. You can't just leave a sister hangin like that. That's okay. I'll find out when T gets here."

"That won't work cuz I didn't tell him either. I know he can't hold water."

"That is true. Oh well, I guess I'll see you and Natalie tomorrow night."

"Okay. Talk to you later."

Just as Ivy hung up with Alexa, he felt something cold touch the side of his neck.

"Don't move or I will blow your fuckin' head off," a familiar voice commanded. "Give me the phone." Iverson handed the phone over his shoulder. "Good. Now walk into your office."

"Whatever you want you can have it."

The mysterious, gun wielding figure removed the gun from Ivy's neck and poked it into his back as they walked to his office.

"Now sit down behind your desk." Ivy walked behind his desk. As he turned to sit down, he got the shock of his life.

"Candace?"

"You can just call me Karma," Cee Cee grinned.

"What are you doing?"

"Shut up! You thought I was just going to go away forever and never be seen or heard from again didn't you."

As Ivy examined Cee Cee, he saw that her clothes were worn out, her hair was a mess. Her eyes told the story. She was high as a kite.

"Cee Cee…whatever it is, it can be worked out."

"No it can't!" she screamed. "You threw me out like yesterdays trash after I made you a few million. That's right. It was me. Without me there would have been no Purrfection. Purrfection…what kinda dumb ass name is that? Every time I hear it I get sick to my stomach."

"This is not the answer."

"Yes it is. I figured I'd come in here and hurt you just as much as you've hurt me. I think it's only fair." The text message tone from Iverson's phone went off. Candace walked over and snatched the phone from Iverson. A huge smile spread across her face when she saw that it was Natalie. The message read: I'm outside. Candace sent her a message back: I'm in my office. I'm not quite ready yet. Come on up.

"This has nothing to do with her. This is between me and you."

"This has everything to do with her. The way I see it; it's because of her that I couldn't get my man back. Maybe I need to let her feel a little bit of pain too." Candace sat down on the couch and tucked the gun by her side.

"Just chill. One wrong move and I will blow her into next week." Candace continued to smirk as they waited for Natalie's arrival. Three minutes later Natalie walked into the office. She didn't notice Candace sitting on the couch.

"Hey baby. You almost ready to go?"

"Yeah," Cee Cee answered. "He's almost ready."

"Cee Cee...what are you doing here?"

"I was gettin' ready to ask you the same thing." Candace pulled the gun from her side and stood up. "Now sit ya ass down and be a good little girl and maybe I won't kill you first."

"Ivy, what is going on?" Natalie asked nervously.

"Just do what she says." Natalie sat down in the chair that was closest to the wall and in front of Ivy's desk. Candace stood with her back to the door.

"Well, well well...now we're just one big, happy family."

"Are you high?"

"Shut up! I do not want to hear your voice!"

"Cee Cee..." Natalie began. Candace fired a shot past Natalie and into the filing cabinet.

"Say another word and I promise you the next one is going to be in you."

"Baby please," Iverson pleaded with Natalie. "Just relax."

"Baby? I thought I was your baby? That's what you told me. Remember? At least that's what you were calling me the night we came off tour. Let's show her how we did it." Cee Cee walked over to Iverson and turned him around to face her. She pointed the revolver directly at his forehead then propped her foot on the chair between his legs. With her free hand she pulled her skirt up her thigh.

"Show her how you rubbed my thighs that night." Ivy hesitated. "Do it! Now!"

"Baby, just do what she says." Cee Cee fired another shot into the filing cabinet as Natalie screamed.

"I thought I told you to shut the fuck up!" She turned her attention back to Ivy. "Now do it like you did that night. Start at my ankle and rub your hands all the way up to my thigh."Iverson wrapped his hands around Cee Cee's ankle and ran them up her leg and to her thigh.

"Mmmmm! Just like that Daddy. You're making Mommy so wet. Now show her how you squeezed my breasts that night." Iverson let out a huge breath then placed his hands on her breasts.

"Not like that. You gotta go under the shirt. Do it like you mean it." Ivy removed his hands and slid them under her shirt and onto her breasts."Now squeeze'em like I like it. Yes Daddy…just like that. Now stand up." Candace unbuckled Iverson's belt and unbuttoned his jeans. She slid her hand in his pants and grabbed his manhood.

"Looks like somebody doesn't wanna come out to play."

"Why are you doing this? What is this going to solve or prove?" She squeezed the package that was in her hand.

"Did I ask you to speak? Did I?"

"No," Ivy grunted. Natalie sat and helplessly watched Cee Cee seduce her man. The further it went, the more furious Natalie became.

"You know what? Fuck this." Candace removed her hand from Iverson's pants and pushed him back into the chair. She walked from behind the desk and over to where Natalie was sitting.

"Leave her alone, Candace. This is between me and you."

"No it's not. This is between all of us. She made that decision when she decided to set out on the journey to become Mrs. Davenport. Now you're in this together. Until death do you part. That has a nice ring to it." As Cee Cee taunted Natalie, Iverson slowly slid open the bottom drawer to his desk with his leg.

"Ms. WNBA superstar…let me ask you a question because I already know how Iverson feels. Did you want me out of the group too?" Natalie didn't say anything. Cee Cee fired another shot into the filing cabinet. Iverson was keeping count of how many times she fired the revolver. "Answer me!"

Through clinched teeth Natalie answered, "Yes."

"Was it business or was it personal?"

"Personal."

"Why? Were you scared that I was going to take your man? Were you worried that if he spent time around me old feelings would resurface? You were threatened by me. That is so cute. A real woman knows that if you are handling business like a real woman should, you wouldn't have to worry about what the next bitch is doing. I guess you're not a real woman."

"Put that gun down and let me show you what a real woman can do."

"Excuse me?" Cee Cee rushed over to Natalie. She pressed the barrel of the gun into her left thigh and grabbed her face. "It'll be real hard for you to run up and down the court with holes in your legs. I suggest you change your attitude, Missy." As Candace was in Natalie's face, she had her back to Iverson. He managed to pull his gun from the drawer and put it beside him in the chair.

"Let her go, Candace!" Ivy demanded.

"You are not in the position to be makin' commands. This is my show. I suggest you shut the fuck up before you become a widow before you get married." Candace stood up and backed away from Natalie. She was positioned with her back to the door.

"You two were so quick to want to get rid of me. I made Purrfection! It was me. Not Kitty or that bitch Rolanda. Well you two don't have to worry about Unique no more. I'll be alright. You just better watch your back. You never know when I might pop up again. I could kill you both right now and nobody would ever know who did it."

At that moment, TyQuan opened the office door. When the door swung open it banged into Cee Cee knocking her off balance. When T noticed that she had a gun in her hand he dove to the floor right outside the office. Cee Cee fired two more shots through the windows of Iverson's office. When she turned to the door to see if she hit TyQuan, Iverson grabbed his pistol and squeezed two slugs into the back of her legs. When the bullets hit her she turned and fired one more shot into the office. That bullet missed Iverson and lodged into the wall.

Iverson got up and walked over to where Cee Cee was laying on the floor clutching her legs as blood poured from the holes.

"Wait!" Natalie yelled. "She still has the gun in her hand."

"That's a revolver. She's out of bullets. Call 911." Iverson stepped over Candace to make sure that TyQuan was okay. "You good?"

Checking his body, "Yeah...I'm good. You got my phone?"

"Nigga, I was just held at gun point by this psycho and you're asking me about a phone."

"Is that a yes or a no?"

"It's on the desk."

"Cool. Now what the hell is going on?"

"It's a long story. I fill you in later."

"No you will not fill me in later. You will fill me in right now. You will tell me how you and your girl were being held at gun point by your ex girl."

"I said later. Go get some towels."

"Towels? Let this bitch bleed to death."

"Yeah!" Natalie agreed from inside the office. "Let that bitch bleed to death. As a matter of fact..." Natalie ran out of the office and dove on Cee Cee. Iverson quickly pulled her off. "The next time you pull a gun on somebody you better use it!"

"It's over, Baby. Calm down." The police and the ambulance arrived. Cee Cee was hauled off in the ambulance. Because Iverson had caused the wounds, he was taken downtown for questioning. In a matter of hours he was released. Once Candace was patched up, she was taken to the DeKalb Inn aka DeKalb County Jail. People check in but don't check out for awhile. In the wake of Cee Cee's psychotic rampage, nobody got hurt— except for Cee Cee.

As much as Candace said that she was over Iverson, she knew that she wasn't. The heart can be a dangerous tool. It has the power to control one's mind thus controlling their actions. Things really get twisted when you add in drugs. After she resigned from the group and Iverson told her that he wasn't going to do her solo album, something inside of her snapped. For a month straight she went on a drug binge. Rick James said it best when he said that Cocaine was a hellavah drug. Nevertheless, Natalie and Iverson survived all of her antics.

Chapter 30

The following night, as planned, Iverson and Natalie, Alicia, André, TyQuan and Alexa assembled for dinner at Iverson's estate in Buckhead. They all sat at the dining room table talking over drinks as they waited for the salads to be served. The previous night's event was the topic of discussion.

"Ivy," TyQuan began as he pulled his glass from his lips. "You gotta tell me...were you scared?"

"Scared? I was terrified. Can you imagine being alone in a room and all of a sudden someone puts a gun to your neck?"

"I probably woulda pissed all over myself," André laughed.

"I think one drop of pee came out."

"What do you think made her snap like that?" Alicia asked.

"It was probably the drugs. She was high out of her mind. I knew she bumped a little cuz she used to do it when we were together but I'd never seen her like she was last night. It was like someone else was controlling her."

"I'm just glad everybody is okay," Alexa added. "I don't know what I woulda done if something woulda happened to my T Bear." Alexa stroked the back of TyQuan's head and laid her head on his shoulder.

"T Bear?" everyone said simultaneously.

"Mind ya business," T laughed. "Don't get me started on Dymond and Futurama."

"You right," Iverson chuckled.

"Futurama?" André inquired. "Wow!"

"You have no room to talk," Alicia interjected. "Ginuwine. That was his online name back in the day."

"Now why you gotta put my business in the streets like that in front of company?"

"I'm telling you," Iverson paused and took a sip of his drink. "The internet is a crazy place. If I woulda known then what I know now, I woulda never started internet dating."

"I feel you on that," André responded. "I met some cool people but I did meet some crazy ones."

"Like the girl in New Orleans?" Natalie asked.

"That's exactly who I'm talking about."

"You never told me that story."

André went into details about the story as their salads were served. The all laughed as André and Iverson exchanged internet dating war stories up until the main course was served. The six feasted on Filet Mignon and Rock Lobster tails served with Fettuccini with Alfredo sauce, candied baby carrots and asparagus.

"I hate to bring this up," TyQuan started as he wiped his mouth. "But we look like some straight uppity Negros. We know we all grew up on fried chicken, collard greens and cornbread. Now that we've made a lil' piece of change, we sittin her eatin' baby carrots, asparagus and Fettuccini like white people."

"You a fool for that one," Iverson commented.

"What are collard greens?" Alexa asked.

"You're kidding me, right?" TyQuan inquired dropping his fork onto his plate.

"I'm serious. I'm from Cali. I've heard people talk about them but I've never had them."

"You gotta come to the crib next Sunday for some Soul Food," André invited.

"You are the first black person I've met that has never had collard greens," TyQuan joshed.

"When you meet my parents, you'll see why. My dad is darker than you but he is the whitest man on earth. He's from Colorado. I think my mom is blacker that my dad and she's white."

"I knew it!" T interrupted. "I was wondering why your nose was pointed like that."

"Shut up!" Alexa laughed as she playfully punched T in the arm.

"You guys have been together how long?" Alicia questioned.

"T and I have been kickin it since Luda's birthday party?"

"And T didn't know that you were mixed."

"I don't talk about my parents much. We don't really get along. My dad wanted me to go to Stanford but I wanted to come out here and go to Clark-Atlanta."

"That was the same thing that happened with my daughter's mother," André added. "Her Dad wanted her to go Cornell but she wanted to go Spelmen."

"Did she make it?"

"She wound up graduating from Clark."

"When?"

"I think Karen graduated in '97."

"You're not talking about Karen Union are you?"

"How do you know Karen?"

"She used to be best friends with my cousin."

"Charlene?"

"Yes."

"Wooow. This is a small world."

"I wonder what she's up to these days."

"Karen passed away a couple years ago."

"Really?"

"She had some complications while she was giving birth to our daughter. She slipped into a coma and never made it out. I'm surprised Charlene didn't mention it."

"Me and Charlene fell out because of her. I hadn't talked to her in about three years."

They continued to engage in small talk until the main course was finished. The catering staff cleared the table and prepared to serve dessert and coffee. The desserts were served on silver trays with the dome lids covering them. When the servers removed the lids, a slice of cheesecake drizzled with raspberry sauce sat in front of everyone except for Natalie. Under Natalie's dome lid was a black velvet box. Her mouth dropped open and her eyes widened. Iverson stood up and placed his napkin on the table. He grabbed Natalie by the hands and stood her up.

"I know we haven't been together for a long time but someone once told me that when you find the right one, you'll know. Since we've been together, my life has changed. I finally feel complete. In the beginning, the most fragile part of a relationship, we were tested. We put our relationship on the line and prayed that love would see us through. In the aftermath of everything, we're still together and our bond is stronger than ever. Two weeks ago I went home to visit my grandmother. While I was there I stopped by your parent's house and took them out to dinner. During that dinner, I asked your father for his blessings and your hand in marriage."

Iverson grabbed the black box from the tray. He dropped down on one knee. The tears that Natalie had been trying to hold back finally fell from her eyes and ran down her flushed cheeks.

"I'm getting ready to cry," Alicia sniffled.

"Me too," added Alexa. Iverson opened the box to reveal a ten carat, princess-cut, diamond solitaire. The stone was set in a platinum band that was encrusted with another five carats of diamonds. He grabbed Natalie by the hand.

"Baby, I love you more than life itself. Natalie Nicole Simms, will you make me the happiest man in the world and marry me?"

"Yes! A thousand times, yes!" Iverson stood up to a round of applause and embraced his fiancé.

"I love you, Dymond."

"I love you too, Futurama." The other two couples stood up and to hug and congratulate Natalie and Iverson on their engagement. The girls admired Natalie's ring as André joked about the fact that she was going to need a bodyguard.

"I'm going to take this moment and ask my President and best friend if he would do me the honor and stand beside me as my best man?"

"You didn't even have to ask, homeboy."

"And I want to ask my best friend if she will me by Matron of Honor?"

"I wouldn't miss it for the world."

"I would also like to ask my man, Dré, to stand beside me as well."

"It will be an honor."

"How about you Alexa? You down to be a bridesmaid?"

"Of course!"

"Alright girls…we have a wedding to plan!" The girls squealed with excitement as the server brought in the champagne. After the glasses were filled, they all stood in a circle.

"Do you mind if I do the toast?" TyQuan asked.

"You might as well get some practice in, Mr. Best Man. It's all you, bruh."

"The first time I met Iverson we got into an altercation. The next week he came back and we cleared the air. From that moment, I knew me and this man would be tight for a long time. Aside from the up's and downs of the label, I've stood as his right-hand man through thick and thin, good times and bad times. Every time he got excited about a female, I was excited, just as excited as he was. Every time a female broke his heart; I hurt just as much as he did.

Natalie, I just want to tell you that you got a good one on your hands. I can vouch for this man. When he first met you, I could tell that you were different from anybody he'd ever met. Every time he said your name, he smiled. He had a different look in his eyes. After rushing into relationship after relationship, he wanted to take his time with you. It paid off. Usually when a man's best friend get's married he feels like he's losing his brother but not me. I feel like I'm gaining a sister. I'd like to say to the both of you; from the bottom of my heart, I wish you nothing but happiness and prosperity. Glasses up…To Iverson and Natalie."

"To Iverson and Natalie!" Once the evening came to a close and the staff was gone, Natalie took the rest of the champagne upstairs into the bedroom. Iverson walked into the bathroom. When he came back out, Natalie was sitting Indian-style in the middle of his bed looking at her ring.

"You like it?" Iverson asked kissing her on her cheek.

"I love it."

"Its not too much is it?"

"It's perfect." Natalie sat in silence for about five minutes looking at it. "Tonite was truly a surprise. I had no idea."

"It was supposed to be a surprise."

"What did my dad say when you talked to him."

"He was actually cool. You know how fathers are. No man is good enough for his baby girl. He told me that he really liked the fact that I had enough respect to come to him and ask him for his blessings. I told him I couldn't see doing it any other way."

"You're gonna make a good son-in-law."

"You think so?"

"I know so. You love the three things that my Dad loves the most…music, basketball and me."

"Have you said it yet?"

"What?"

"You know what I'm talking about."

"No I don't. What are you talking about?"

"Have you said your name with my last name?"

"I'm not changing my name." Iverson sat up in the bed.

"Excuse me?"

"I'm not changing my name."

"You're kidding me, right?"

"Yup," Natalie laughed.

"I was getting' ready to say…"

"I love the way my name sounds with yours. Natalie Nicole Davenport."

"That sounds like music to my ears."

Iverson picked up the remote and turned on some music. From the same remote, he dimmed the lights. Iverson positioned himself in front of Natalie. At the drop of the first note of D'Angelo's classic ballad, *Send it On*, Iverson pressed his lips to the softness of Natalie's lips. He could feel her body begin to tremble.

"Are you okay?" Iverson asked as he paused from the kiss.

"I'm good," Natalie replied pulling Iverson back to her.

As he kissed her, he moved his body forward to lay her back on the bed. Passion danced on every note of the song escalating the mood further toward the ecstasy that was to come. Iverson stood up for a moment and pulled his shirt over his head. While still on the bed, Iverson unbuttoned the silk blouse that was the chosen top of Natalie's evening ensemble. When he opened it, he kissed her from her neck to her navel. In the midst of Iverson kissing her stomach, Natalie reached between her breasts and unfastened her bra to unleash the perfect breasts and nipples that Ivy loved so much.

Natalie reached up and pulled the rubber band that held Iverson's locs in place off and tossed it to the side. Iverson lick the underside of her left breast while squeezing the right one and stimulating her nipple with his fingers. In a circular motion he ran his tongue around the areola of the breast then sucked the nipple. Natalie released a soft moan and clutched the back of his head.

After D'Angelo went off, the intro to *Tender Love* by The Force MD's floated through the speakers that were in the ceiling. Natalie rolled Iverson onto his back and removed his pants and boxers. She stroked his soldier as she kissed him deeply. Once he was at attention, she removed her skirt and panties then laid beside him on the bed. Iverson reached into his nightstand and pulled out a condom.

"We don't need that."

"Are you sure?"

"I know that I'm the only woman you've been with. Besides, I'm on birth control. When we're ready to start our family, I'll stop. Put it back." Iverson tossed the condom onto the nightstand. "Now make love to the future Mrs. Iverson Davenport."

Iverson repositioned himself between Natalie's legs. Before he made his way inside of her, Iverson rubbed her love box with his fingers. Natalie was soaking wet. Even though she was wet as she was, she was still tight. Iverson slowly slide inside of her, inch by inch. Natalie arched her back upon insertion and let out a stuttered breath. He'd been inside of Natalie without a condom before but that night, it felt better than it had ever felt before. It was like he was making love to her for the very first time.

In and out he moved inside of his Diamond with slow and deep strokes. When in this position, Natalie loved to wrap her arms and legs around her CEO. What started of as a slow walk in the park, went from a stroll to a slow jog on to a full blown 100 meter dash. The curve of Iverson's manhood hit Natalie's G-spot with every inward stroke.

"Yes baby!" Natalie moaned. "Just like that! That's my spot." Ivy continued to make her body feel good in that position. When she unwrapped her arms and legs from around his body, Iverson grabbed her right leg and put it over his shoulder and pushed it toward her shoulder. This position opened her up and allowed him to journey deeper into her depths. After awhile, he did the same with the other leg. With both legs over his shoulders, Iverson rose to his knees, still inside of her, pulling her off of the bed. This position drove Natalie crazy. Ivy could feel her juices running down his legs.

"Don't stop baby! I'm coming! I'm coming!"

"Me too!"Natalie's body tensed up as she grabbed two hands full of Ivy's hair.

"Oooooooh! Iversoooooon!"

In unison, Ivy and Natalie reached an orgasm so powerful that she fought her way out of his clutches and crawled to the top of the bed. Iverson collapsed onto the bed. Their heavy breaths were in sync. Iverson drug himself to where Natalie was and laid his head on her sweaty stomach. The moment was so intense that he could hear her heartbeat from where he was. He listened to the rhythm of her heartbeat then put his hand on his own chest.

"Put your hand right here," Iverson said as he put her hand on his chest. "Now put your hand on your chest. Do you feel it?"

"They're beating at the same time."

"That means we've become one. That is what every couple should strive for."

"Becoming one?"

"Two minds yet one thought; two hearts yet one pulse."

It is amazing how things come together with effort and the willingness to overcome the trials and tests that life throws at you. Iverson and Natalie are a prime example of what a couple can achieve if you are down for each other. There is a belief that there is somebody for everybody and when you find your soul mate, you will know. A relationship is never going to be easy. It is up to the individuals to stand beside each other every step of the way.

Many people frown on internet dating because there is a belief that they're nothing but psychos, stalkers, and predators lurking in the shadows of online communities. A huge part of that belief is true but if you take time to sift through the coal, you might just find a diamond—Iverson did. There is no rule that specifies where one can find love. Love can be found anywhere. You just have to let it find you. After the stretch of bad luck that Iverson had with meeting women on the internet, the average man would have given up. The chance that Iverson took when he met Natalie was like a person in Vegas that is down to his last dollar. He puts it in that slot machine, pulls the handle and the next thing he knows, he has hit the jackpot.

Natalie, on the other hand, tried to find love the traditional way. Sometimes the ways that you continue to try don't work so you have to try a new method. She may have started out the wrong way by not being truthful about who she was but that's a true way to find out where a person's heart is. It was merely for protection. It wouldn't have been a good idea for a star basketball player to parade around on the internet — especially a female. That would have attracted every sorry man in the world trying to come up on a free ride.

The way that Iverson and Natalie began their relationship was the best. They did it how it was supposed to be done — they became friends first. As simple as it sounds, a lot of people fail to do that and wonder why it doesn't work. You have to take the time to get to know a person. That's just common sense. There is no way possible that two strangers can enter into a relationship and expect it to be successful. It just doesn't happen. There was something that drew Natalie and Iverson to each other. When Iverson was dating Shelby, Natalie did the right things as a friend by staying down for him despite her desire to see where it could possibly go between them. Often times, patience is the key to unlocking life's greatest treasures.

Six months passed and spring was in full bloom. Winter was gone and new life had begun. On the beautiful island of Jamaica, several close friends and family members joined for a joyous occasion. The crashing of the ocean's waves set a beautiful backdrop for such a lovely scene. An audience of thirty people sat in folding chairs on the beach. White Roses and Easter Lilies were the chosen flowers to give the event certain elegance. It was a beautiful site. Even the birds of the island flew overhead to catch a glimpse of what was going on.

Under an arc intertwined with Roses, Lilies, Baby's Breath and assorted greenery, the minister stood with bible in hand awaiting the one whose day it was. To his right, four gorgeous young ladies stood barefoot in the sand. The dresses they wore fell to just above their knees and were strapless. The brides chosen color for her bridesmaids was a beautiful shade of Tiffany blue. On the minister's left was the groom. Beside him were four handsome young men. They stood in white linen shorts and matching shirts. The groom wore white linen pants and the matching short sleeve shirt.

The moment of truth had arrived. When the bride came into sight, everyone rose to their feet. Future Record's R&B sensation, Legacy began to sing as the bride made her way to meet her groom. Her gown was pure white with diamond-like crystals elegantly imbedded in the front of the dress. Her shoulders were bare. Two young island girls carried her long train as she walked. When she arrived to the arc, her father kissed her on her cheek and the groom took her hand. Face to face, Teddy and Choco Latte stood in front of the minister as Legacy brought her song to an end.

"Dearly beloved," The minister began. "We are gathered here today to join this man and this woman…in holy matrimony. If there is anyone that has reason why this man and this woman should not be wed, let him speak now or forever hold his peace." There was a brief pause as the onlookers looked over the crowd for any objections. After the pause, the minister opened with a prayer which was followed by a scripture reading.

"The couple has elected to exchange their own vows."

"The first moment I laid eyes on you," Teddy began. "I knew that there was something special about you. As I got to know you over these past years, I learned the things that made you happy. I learned the things that upset you. I learned the things that you would and would not tolerate. Most of all, I learned what made you smile. The first time I saw that smile face to face, I knew that I wanted to see that smile for the rest of my life. I promise you that I will always strive to be the best man that

I can be for you. I promise to protect you, provide for you and to always be open and honest with you. I love you with my heart, I love you with my mind and most of all...I love you with my soul."

Natalie wiped tears from her eyes as she stood as Choco's Maid of Honor. Iverson smiled at her from the Best Man's position.

"When I first met you," Choco started. "If someone would have told me that you were going to be the man that I spend the rest of my life with, I might've wanted to fight them. When I decided to move my life from California to North Carolina, I had no idea what to expect. From the first day I set foot in Fayetteville, you've treated me like a queen. You backed up everything that you said you would do and for that I love you. Not only do I call you my lover and my best friend, I also call you my hero. I was lost in a life of confusion trying to figure out where I wanted to go with my life. You saved me from a dead end job and most of all, a dead end relationship. As I stand here on this day, in front our parents, family and friends, I can truly say that my life is complete. I promise to be the best wife I can be. I will always respect you, honor you, and obey you as head of our household. I loved you yesterday, I love you even more today and I will love you for the rest of my life."

Following their vows, they exchanged rings.

"By the power vested in me, I now pronounce you husband and wife. You may kiss your bride."

To thunderous applause, cheers and whistles, Teddy and Choco engaged in a passionate kiss that sealed their vows and made them one. After they kissed, they jumped the traditional broom and the wedding procession began. The guests moved from the ceremony area to the reception area as the wedding party took pictures. Once the pictures were over, the wedding party joined the guests and the reception began. Midway into the meal, it was time for the best man to give his toast. Iverson tapped his fork to his champagne flute, stood up and took the microphone.

"When Teddy asked me to be his best man, I was honored. I was sure that there was someone that was closer to him than I was. I've only known Nikky and Teddy for about four years but it feels like a lifetime. Teddy has always been a true friend. If I was wrong, he would tell me I'm wrong but he would still back me up. If I was right, he let the world know it. I've been apart of this union from day one. I remember when Nikky couldn't stand Teddy but look at them now. They look so beautiful together. I hope that when our day comes in a couple of months, my fiancé and I will look just as beautiful together as you two. I'm sure I speak for everyone here when I say that I wish you two a long and prosperous life together. To you Nikky, if he gets out of line, you know how to get in touch with me. I love you both like a brother and a sister. Cheers!"

"Cheers!" The crowd rumbled.

The reception ended as the sun was setting. Iverson and Natalie sat on a blanket on the beach. They were still wearing their clothes from the wedding. They sipped champagne and fed each other strawberries as they listen to the ocean's evening song.

"Teddy and Choco really looked happy together," Natalie said to Iverson as she brushed her hair out of her face.

"Yes they did."

"I can't wait for our day."

"Neither can I."

"Are we still gonna kick it on Just4kickz from time to time."

"Probably not. We may make an appearance every now and then. I know how to get in touch with the people that I really wanna keep in touch with."

"Yeah...the site is cool but I don't think its no place for a married couple to be hangin out."

"You're right about that. I don't need it any more I've found my Computer Love." Iverson wrapped his arms around Natalie and pulled her close to him. "I'm happy that you're a part of my life. After everything that I've been through, you are my breath of fresh air."

"I feel that same way, baby. Besides, Relationships Byte when they're just4kicks."

Thank you for reading Relationships Byte by PRINTHOUSE BOOKS; Author; Lorenzo 'El Gee' Gladden. Please check out more titles from Lorenzo and more at Printhousebooks.com and please leave a review; we would love to know what you think.

As always, the first honor goes to God. Without him, I'm nothing. To the Johnson-Cortez, Henry, Gladden, Aikens, Jenkins, Fanning and Rainey families, Thank you for all your continued support. When no one was there, my family was. To my one and only daughter Camille A'reon, Daddy loves you. You are my muse.

This next shout out goes to a special group of friends that inspired this book. You all became my cyber family. I enjoyed sitting up many nights talking, laughing and carrying on with you! This one is for Curt Curt, Stunna, Taught Well, Skittlez, Barbie, Krystal, Prymetime, Harmony, Danger, Mocha, Phatty, RusSIanN, Chocolate Thai, SoCal, MoJuci, Curve, 1uluv2hate, Chocomel, OhSoReal(your other name was too explicit..LOL!) Many came and went but this core group, were always there! I'll never forget you!

So many people have touched my life and have been an inspiration to me. To name them all would be a book in itself. Every city I move to I gain new friends. I would like to send a shout out to my people here in the Queen City, Charlotte, NC...My Ace...Erwin "Bam Bam" Evans, All of my coworkers @ Club Longhorn, Will Jacobs, James Dugan, Andy Perez, Chris Corrado, Brian Briscoe and the rest of the Charlotte Comedy Crew...Keep doing what you do!

To those that I may have missed in trying to keep this short, remember this: There is so much ink in my mental pen. This won't be the last book. Thank you all for your love and support!

Lorenzo "El Gee" Gladden

PRINTHOUSE BOOKS

Read it, Enjoy it, Tell a Friend!

Atlanta, Ga.

www.ingramcontent.com/pod-product-compliance
Lightning Source LLC
Chambersburg PA
CBHW021926110726
47901CB00003B/735